ARCADIA
BURNS

ARCADIA

BURNS

KAI MEYER

Translated from the German by

ANTHEA BELL

BALZER + BRAY
An Imprint of HarperCollins*Publishers*

Balzer + Bray is an imprint of HarperCollins Publishers.

Library of Congress Cataloging-in-Publication Data
Meyer, Kai.
    [Arkadien brennt. English.]
    Arcadia burns / Kai Meyer ; translated from the German by
Anthea Bell. — 1st U.S. ed.
        p.   cm.
    Summary: "When Rosa Alcantara becomes the head of a Sicil-
ian Mafia family, she must contend with her family's sordid past and
the secrets that keep haunting the present"— Provided by publisher.
    ISBN 978-0-06-200608-0 (hardback)
    [1.   Organized   crime—Fiction.   2.   Vendetta—Fiction.
3. Shape-shifting—Fiction.   4. Sicily (Italy)—Fiction.   5. Italy—
Fiction.]   I. Title.
PZ7.M57171113Ard   2013   2012019041
[Fic]—dc23   CIP
                                                  AC

Typography by Sarah Hoy
13   14   15   16   17   OV/RRDH   10 9 8 7 6 5 4 3 2 1
❖
First U.S. Edition, 2013
Originally published in Germany in 2010 by Carlsen Verlag.

CONTENTS

THE FIRST CHAPTER

"DADDY?" SHE TUGGED AT his sleeve. "There's a dead cat outside the door."

"Good. One less in the world."

"When I'm grown up I want a cat of my own. Just for me."

"Cats can't be tamed."

"I'll tame mine."

"It will hurt you."

"No, it won't. Never."

Silence.

"Never. Never."

FLIGHT

OUT ON THE RUNWAY, a plane began its ascent into the sky, and the world around Rosa fell silent.

No sign of Alessandro anywhere.

As she walked through the departures hall and past the panoramic window, she blocked out the voices of her six-man escort. For an endless moment she saw only, in slow motion, the aircraft taking off, the midday sun sparkling on its white fuselage, and behind it the majestic cliffs of the Bay of Palermo.

Where is he?

She knew the six men weren't going to take their eyes off her. They were trying to force her to listen to their advice and questions and warnings. Rosa heard nothing but the beating of her own heart, the blood pulsing in her temples.

Hair flying behind her, she raced ahead while her advisers followed close behind, talking, gesticulating, pestering her. Ticks in the thick protective coat she'd wrapped around herself these last few months.

Half a dozen men in expensive suits, handmade shoes, and silk ties, with their hair well cut and their hands manicured—conventional businessmen, and cleaner than clean to any stranger who happened to set eyes on them. But in reality just six of the countless criminals who looked after the fortune of the Alcantara clan.

Rosa's fortune.

She should have taken an interest in it. Instead she met her advisers' questions and demands with indifference—as if she had nothing to do with her own money. Anyway, what the six of them cared about most was their own share. For reasons that irked them, they were now, for better or worse, at the mercy of an eighteen-year-old girl's whims.

At least Rosa knew what to make of *that*. Refusing to talk was a little like stealing from them. She knew about stealing things—it was difficult to break a habit you'd come to enjoy. Silence equals stealing equals an adrenaline fix. That was about as much math as she could cope with in an over-crowded airport.

Her blond hair cascaded in wild confusion over her slender shoulders. It resisted brushing the same way her pale complexion resisted tanning. Nothing would take away the shadows around her eyes, and they'd become even darker in the last year. Some people thought it was makeup, kohl for a moderate Goth look, but Rosa had been born with them. They were part of her, like so many other things that she couldn't shake off. From her nail biting to her neuroses. And her origins, along with the addictions that came with them.

Where the hell was Alessandro? He should have been here. *I'll come see you off,* he'd said.

One of the men caught up and tried to block her way. Block him out; act deaf. His efforts to attract her attention made him seem like a ridiculous mime. She dodged him and hurried on.

Damn you, Alessandro!

It was four months ago, last fall, that she'd come to Sicily to escape the past. And now, in mid-February, she was taking off again. This time to escape from the present, from this island.

By all appearances, she was the heiress to an empire of companies. Since her eighteenth birthday two weeks ago, she had also become legally responsible for what her business managers did. It made Rosa's head spin to think what it meant to be head of a Cosa Nostra clan.

Security was coming up ahead of her. No Alessandro anywhere in sight. The bastard.

She quickened her pace, ignoring the piece of paper that one of the six men was holding in front of her. At the last moment she murmured something like "Back in a few days," and breathed a sigh of relief when she had left the six men behind on the other side of the security gate.

Rosa looked around her. The six of them were retreating toward the exit, swearing. She was searching for one person in particular among the crowd in departures. A face that she had come to know better than her own.

Had she passed him and missed seeing him in her haste? Surely not. Had he hung back when he saw her escort? That was more likely. A Carnevare in a relationship with an Alcantara—many of the other clans still regarded that as a declaration of war. Rosa and Alessandro knew that plenty of members of their own families were saying, off the record, that both their corpses should be sunk in the sea. For Rosa, this could have been an exciting game—exactly the element of risk that she needed for an adrenaline fix—if she hadn't been keenly aware that, as the two of them walked their tightrope, they could fall to the depths below. In the end either they would have to break up, or she would have to risk everything for love.

The six men beyond the barrier put up with Rosa's disinterest in them because they knew that, in the long run, they would derive greater authority from it. But her relationship with a Carnevare was a black mark against her. The Alcantaras and the Carnevares had been enemies forever, and only a mysterious pact between them, dating from ancient times, had kept them from wiping out each other's families long ago. Out of necessity, the two clans managed to coexist. But most of them would never tolerate an alliance made by two teenagers in bed.

How long are the others going to stand by watching? Rosa had once asked.

Until we can force them to close their eyes to it, Alessandro had replied. *And then hope they never open them again.*

It was Alessandro who really understood what it meant to be *capo* of a Mafia clan. Rosa had become head of her family against her will. Alessandro, however, had fought for his position. He had killed his parents' murderers, and over the past few weeks other enemies had fallen silent one way or another. He was keeping his options open through self-protection. While Rosa was on the run from responsibility, Alessandro faced hostility, warnings, and threats with determination.

Shit. He really wasn't here. She fought off her disappointment with a mixture of anger and anxiety. It made her stomach ache.

Calm down. It's not like you're addicted to him.

She adjusted the strap of her shoulder bag. As she did so, her black turtleneck stretched taut over her breasts—which, goodness knew, wasn't an everyday event. *They'll get bigger*, her sister, Zoe, had said once, and Rosa used to pray that they would. Now Zoe was in her grave, and Rosa's chest was still nothing to brag about.

Whenever Alessandro was late, or didn't call to say he'd be late, she feared for him. What they were doing was crazy. They had discussed going away together, leaving Sicily and everything else behind them. But Rosa didn't want him to give up anything for her sake. She would never make demands. If she really did want to go someday, she certainly wouldn't make him go with her. That wasn't her way. She'd rather be miserably unhappy without him than see him regretful. There were some risks even she wasn't willing to take.

There was still a good hour left before her flight. She showed her ticket and went into the business-class lounge. It had armchairs and sofas arranged in groups, a lavish buffet with options for vegetarians like Rosa herself, and rows of computer terminals with online access. Loudspeakers in the ceiling played classical music. And there was coffee, of course.

Several businessmen sized her up. Her turtleneck came down to her thighs, and she wore it with black jeans. She must look as if she'd rattle if anyone shook her, she thought, with her hip bones sticking out and her legs so thin—far too thin. But obviously some of the management guys in the armchairs didn't share her opinion. Rosa's lips formed a heartfelt, silent *Pedophile!* and then gave a sweet smile.

A young man's head appeared above one of the partitions dividing the groups of seating. It turned in another direction, disappeared, came up again. He was looking straight into her eyes. His own were green and bright. If she hadn't known him already, she could have invented a whole life for him at the sight of those eyes.

His dimples deepened, his wide smile as infectious as the day they first met. His face made the world a better place.

"I don't believe it!" She flung her arms around his neck; her bag jammed between them, so she wrenched it free and pressed close to him again. In fact, a little closer than before. Might as well give the others in the lounge something worth seeing.

He kissed her, looked at her, beaming, and kissed her again. He often did that. A short kiss, a smile, a long kiss. Like a secret Morse code.

"What are you doing here?" She sounded more breathless than she would have liked.

He waved a ticket in the air. "I bought this."

"But you said you weren't coming with me!"

"I'm not. But I wanted to see you. Without those hangers-on out there."

She stared at him. "You mean you paid *four thousand*

euros for a ticket just so they'd let you into the business-class lounge?"

"My father paid three times that for a set of golf clubs. This is a brilliant investment by comparison."

She pressed her lips to his and felt for his tongue until they were both out of breath. A woman on the sofa near them got up and made her husband move to a seat farther away.

Rosa felt a cool tingling inside her, glanced at her hand, and saw reptilian scales forming on her fingers. Her skin looked translucent as the transformation began under it. Startled, she pulled back, saw concern in his gaze, and knew what he had just seen in her blue eyes. Her pupils would have narrowed to slits.

Not now, she thought in alarm.

Damn hormones.

WITHOUT YOU

"HEY," WHISPERED ALESSANDRO SOOTHINGLY, pulling Rosa down on the sofa. The partitions between the groups of seats more or less shielded them from view.

She rubbed her palms on her jeans, as if she could wipe away the metamorphosis that was just beginning. She forced herself to take a couple of deep breaths. Gradually the chill shrank to a tiny point in her heart.

His hair wasn't dark brown anymore, but black. She was sure that if she put her hands under his shirt she could have stroked the fine down of the panther fur as it grew on his back.

"Not a good place," she said, suppressing a nervous laugh.

His eyes flashed with mockery. "For the price we've paid, we ought to get more than a sandwich from the cooler."

She took his hand and gently massaged it between her fingers. When he tried to lean forward to kiss her again, she smiled and fended him off. "You see what happens. Until we can control it—"

"Until then, no sex," he promised, grinning.

Their attempts to sleep together would have looked odd to other people. They generally ended in chaotic transformations, sometimes funny, sometimes annoying, usually just embarrassing. The worst of it was that they seldom reacted in the same way to them. When it made him laugh, she felt like dying on the spot. As soon as she teased him about his panther coat, he began to sulk.

Strong emotions brought out something in both of them that would have inspired more than just indignation in the other passengers in the lounge. Rosa felt that she was under close observation, watched by informers from other clans and undercover police officers, and by the eyes of predators lurking beneath the mask of normality. There must certainly be other Arcadians in this room.

"Change the subject?" she suggested—it was one alternative to a cold shower.

"State of the financial markets? The weather?"

"Responsibility." In her mouth, it sounded foreign.

His hair went back to brown at once.

"You saw those six guys back there," she said. "They were waiting outside the airport to hand me a whole bunch of papers to sign. Construction contracts for new wind turbines. Stock options. Applications for subsidies." Who said she couldn't be romantic when she wanted to?

"Maybe you should go see them in the city now and then. Or ask them to come to the palazzo."

"I'm signing *something* every day," she said ruefully. "I spend hours on the phone in the mornings with obscure second and third female cousins in Milan and Rome, just because they manage companies that happen to belong to me. I don't even know them. I'm lucky if I can remember their names."

"Just as long as you realize that they're lying with every word they say to you."

In October, the body of her aunt Florinda Alcantara had been fished out of the Tyrrhenian Sea. What had upset Rosa more than the bullet wound in Florinda's skull was the fact that she herself was next in line to be head of the clan. None of its members had wanted her, and no one had seriously expected her to accept the challenge. That was probably why she did. When the first of the new "good friends and confidential advisers," who now came thronging to the Palazzo Alcantara, suggested that she might voluntarily decline her inheritance, she made her decision. They'd just have to learn how to get along with her.

"I'm doing my best to remember they're lying"—it was one way of describing her lack of interest in them—"but I'm not Florinda. Or Zoe. I feel like a pilot who takes a plane thousands of feet up in the sky and then realizes he's scared out of his wits."

"Kind of limits your career options."

"But I don't want this career. I never asked to inherit everything. It's not the same for me as it is for you."

That was the difference between them. Alessandro had achieved what he'd always wanted. But she had never wanted anything, least of all this. Only him. Very, very, very much.

For all their disagreement on that one point, however, something else bound them together. Neither wanted to change the other. Perhaps that was the very reason she felt so at ease with him.

There was a thoughtful expression on his face. Difficult subject number one, business. Difficult subject number two, his family. Their discussions suffered from the same kind of ups and downs as their sex life—except that their conversations at least actually happened, while their sex life wasn't much more than speculation. They both had their ideas of what it would feel like—if and when it came to anything. Not having snake scales or panther hairs in your mouth would be a plus.

"I've begun cleaning up," he said quietly. "Clearing away some of the mess left by Cesare and my father." For decades, the Carnevares had dealt with the bodies of other clans' victims for them, burying them under the asphalt of highways or embedding them in the concrete of ruinous gray buildings. It was a profitable business. Alessandro was no saint, but he wanted nothing to do with the money his clan earned that way. Not all the other members of the family and its *capodecini* agreed.

She took his hand again, hesitated for a moment, and dropped a quick kiss on his cheek. "I guess that hasn't made you any friends, huh?"

"It's getting worse. Even the few who did accept me as *capo* are beginning to turn away. Not openly, but most of them are too stupid to be subtle about it." He seldom complained, and even now his eyes were clear as glass and his voice determined. "Sometimes I don't know if this is really what I wanted."

Rosa often wondered whether his wish to succeed his father as *capo* might just have been because he needed to avenge his mother. Now that his father's cousin Cesare was dead, Alessandro wasn't really sure what to do with the Carnevare inheritance. He had known he wanted it, but now that he had it, it was much larger and more complicated than he had expected.

"Cesare got what he deserved," she said.

"Yes, but did *we* get what we deserve?" He raised one hand and caressed her cheek. "Maybe I ought to come with you. Just to be somewhere else for a few days, and maybe after that—"

"Go away forever?" Smiling, she shook her head. "I know you better than that."

"At this moment, the idea that you'll be on the other side of the world while I'm still here is driving me crazy."

She put her finger to his lips and moved it gently down to his chin. "How many times a week do we see each other? Three? And not always even that much. I'll only be gone a few days. You won't even notice it."

"That's not fair."

Of course it wasn't fair. But much as she, too, longed to be near him when he wasn't in the same room—and even more so when he *was*—she didn't want him on this flight with her today. Not on her way to New York. On her way to see her mother.

"I could cancel a few meetings," he added. "I'm still their *capo*, whether they like it or not."

"That's nonsense; you know it is. They'd like to be rid of you yesterday." Rosa held his glance, marveling at the intense, bright green of his eyes. "What would they say if you flew off on vacation with an Alcantara, with things here the way they are?"

When Zoe was dying in her sister's arms, she had made Rosa promise something: to find out what linked their dead father to TABULA, the mysterious organization secretly at war with the

Arcadian dynasties. It was Rosa's bad luck that she could think of only one place to begin, only one person who could tell her more about their father, and that was their mother.

There was no one in the world Rosa wanted to see less. Not after all that had happened. Not after Gemma had refused to come to Sicily even for Zoe's funeral. Bitch.

Alessandro sighed. "I wanted to be in charge of my family, and now it's in charge of me."

"Well," she said with a glance of wide-eyed innocence—she'd worked hard on perfecting that—"you should have thought of that before, right?"

A voice over a loudspeaker announced that her flight was now boarding.

"I'll probably dream of you every night," he said. "And when I wake up, I'll know that the best part of the day is already over."

"You read that somewhere."

"Did not."

She kissed him again, a long kiss, and very tender. He still tasted of another world. The snake began to stir once more as he put his arms around her.

"Hey!" she said, laughing. "My flight. The gate. I have to—"

"What we have won't ever end," he whispered.

She ran her fingers through his unruly hair. "Never."

Then she freed herself from his embrace, picked up her bag, and hurried to the exit.

NEW YORK

WHAT ROSA FOUND THAT evening was not her own New York, but the New York of tourists and theatergoers, the glittering madhouse of Broadway.

It was almost thirty degrees colder than in Sicily. Her jacket was too thin, her nose was running, and she'd packed only one of a pair of gloves in her suitcase. Home, sweet home.

Wearily, she left the lobby of the Millennium Broadway Hotel, trudged through the snow around the candy-colored corner facade of Toys "R" Us, and was in Times Square surrounded by milling crowds of people, bright billboards, and walls of video ads.

She had spent almost her whole life in New York, although admittedly on the other side of the East River. She knew what went on between Wall Street and the Bronx more from TV than from her own experience.

Rosa had grown up in Brooklyn, in one of those down-at-the-heel neighborhoods that didn't have views of the Manhattan skyline. Home had been a dump of a building with too many tenants in apartments too cramped for them. With graffiti in the stairwell, busted central heating, drafty windows, clattering fire escapes that drove you crazy with the noise they made during storms. Cats had their kittens next to dead rats on the ledges outside the basement windows, and Rosa could remember more than one cockroach plague of biblical proportions.

All around there were endless rows of apartment buildings like hers, basketball courts surrounded by high fences, grubby playgrounds where young mothers stared vacantly at sandboxes during the day and speakers played at full volume in the evenings. Traffic lights dangled from cables above the streets. Photocopied faces of missing children, dogs, and cats looked out from tree trunks. Faded American flags hung under windowsills. And sometimes, at night, an empty baby carriage rolled across an intersection, on fire, a declaration of war by a gang fighting off boredom.

That had been Rosa's New York. Today, only a few months after leaving it all behind, she was staying in a luxury hotel booked by her secretary in Piazza Armerina. She was paying with a platinum credit card, and the doorman addressed her as Ms. Alcantara. Six months ago he'd have thrown her out on her ear. She didn't just feel like a stranger in this city; she felt like a stranger in her own body. Taking over some other girl's identity.

She walked around for almost an hour, let herself drift with the flow of the crowd, and finally decided that what she needed was a grubby backyard, a snow-covered blind alley, some kind of still eye in the hurricane of the metropolis. She found an alley wider than she had hoped for, but dilapidated enough to remind her of the New York she knew. She felt the worn asphalt through the snow, listened to the roar of traffic in the streets, smelled the stale air coming up through a subway grate.

Why did her longing for him have to hit her here, right at this very moment? Well, nothing she could do about it. One moment she was thinking, So here I am again, and the next, It would be better if *he* were here. If she wasn't careful, she'd soon be dreaming of ironing his shirts.

Almost reluctantly, she started rummaging around for her iPhone, began to think someone must have stolen it in the crush of people, but finally she felt it among the other stuff in her bag: paper tissues, eyedrops, a notebook. She wasn't sure why she even carted the notebook around with her.

But what she'd thought was her cell phone turned out to be another book. Smaller, fatter, in a disintegrating binding. The leather on the spine bore the words *Aesop's Fables* in tiny lettering. She held it under her nose and breathed in deeply. The smell took her straight back to a sun-drenched graveyard deep in the Sicilian countryside.

Silly. Totally childish. She quickly put the book away, found her phone, and discovered that it had been on during the entire flight. Obviously God wanted her to live and suffer.

No text message. No email. Out of sight, out of mind.

She tapped in: *arrived. new york in the snow. v. romantic.* Then she hesitated, and added: *getting a bladder infection. bad climate for snakes. stupid weather. stupid city.*

SEND. And her sensitive love letter was winging its way to the other side of the Atlantic. Where it would be two in the morning. She bit her lower lip, feeling guilty. Alessandro's cell phone always lay beside his pillow, switched on.

It was only a minute before the answer came back.

can't sleep. thinking of you too much.

Her heart beating faster, she typed: *did you shift shape?*

deprivation = no transformation, he replied.

This must be International Bad Equations Week.

new york minus alessandro = even colder, she wrote back.

He replied: *cold + rosa = snake (better not).*

only when cold + sex.

sex + city, like on TV?

must buy manolos. hope you sleep better now.

His reaction was a little while coming. *rosa?*

alessandro?

steer clear of the new york carnevares. meant to say so at the airport, but your tongue got in the way.

idiot.

i mean it. my ny relations don't like the alcantaras.

OK.

I really do mean it.

I get the idea.

have fun buying shoes.

That's not likely, she thought. *will be in touch soon.*

wow, HAIR everywhere . . . ewww!

She was grinning at the screen like a lunatic. She waited a moment to see if there'd be anything else, then put the cell phone back in her bag.

She stood there in the alley, undecided, rubbing her hands

to warm them and staring at the snow around her shoes.

Well, why not?

The next morning she took a taxi to Gothic Renaissance on Fourth Avenue and bought black steel-toed boots with a diagonal seam and eight lace-up holes, the only winter-weight tights in the store, and a heavy-duty stapler at a shop around the corner.

Now she had really arrived.

The stapler felt good in her hand and contained a hundred steel staples that could be driven into practically anything by compressed air at intervals of a second. After the rape she'd made it a habit to have a stapler like that always ready. Why make do with pepper spray when you could buy one of these in any hardware store?

Of course she had enough money now to hire bodyguards to protect her full-time, but the mere thought of it made her feel unlike herself. She hadn't come to New York to ask for trouble; she'd come to talk to her mother. But the weight of the stapler in her hand made her feel safer.

It was sixteen months since she'd been drugged at a party and then raped by a stranger or strangers. Afterward, they'd left Rosa unconscious in the street. To this day she knew nothing more about what had happened that night, and after endless sessions of counseling and therapy she had come to the conclusion that she didn't really want to remember. She had given up searching for suppressed images and scraps of thoughts, emotions blocked out by her unconscious mind. If there was one thing to be grateful for, it was the blackout that kept her from knowing the details, the memory of faces or voices. Not even physical pain remained. Only her fears. Her neuroses. Her bitten fingernails, her kleptomania, and for a long time the feeling that she couldn't trust anyone—until she met Alessandro. Sometimes you had to see through another person's eyes to understand yourself better.

But the rape had left other traces behind. Nathaniel. The baby she'd aborted. She knew it would have been a son; she just sensed it. She had waited a long time, until the third month, before caving to pressure from her mother and the advice of all the doctors. The operation had been under total anesthesia—just routine, the doctor had said. Routine for the doctor, maybe.

Slush sprayed up on the sidewalk. There was a white bicycle chained to a lamppost on the other side of the street, one of many ghost bikes in New York, placed around in memory of cyclists who had been run over. Rosa stood outside the hardware store, weak at the knees now, staring at her stapler as if it held the answers she'd been avoiding for months. Maybe it had been a bad idea to come back; she hadn't put enough distance between herself and the rape yet. Confronting her mother wasn't going to make matters any better. A conversation to *clear everything up.* As if there were still anything to be cleared up.

She walked to the Union Square subway station at Fourteenth Street, hesitated at the stairs, and then continued to the next entrance, at a traffic island on Astor Place. Here again she couldn't bring herself to go down to the platform, and instead went on to Broadway-Lafayette, where she'd have changed trains anyway.

On the way, however, she decided it was ridiculous to put off the meeting any longer. After walking through the cold, it occurred to her that she didn't have to watch every dollar anymore, and she took a taxi over the Brooklyn Bridge in the direction of Crown Heights.

She got out of the cab outside the building where she had grown up, searching her mind for any sense of coming home, or at least of familiarity. Nothing. She had felt a void like this before, when she'd arrived in Sicily last October. Now she wondered where her home really was. Her hand went into her bag and touched *Aesop's Fables*.

Slush spurted up from the tires of the taxi as it drove away. Rosa stood on the sidewalk staring at the eight steps up to the front door. The building had only three floors above ground level, and there was a faded burn mark below the flat roof, left by the riots during the 1977 blackout. In all the decades since, the owner hadn't thought it necessary to invest a few dollars in painting the facade.

The curtains of her mother's apartment were open, all the windowpanes clean and shiny. A bunch of fresh flowers stood at one window. Gemma must have chosen the place because it got the most sunlight. The Petersons' station wagon was parked right outside the door to the basement apartment, as always. If Mr. Piccirilli hadn't drunk himself to death on cheap bourbon yet, there'd be the usual trouble.

And if she went on staring at the building like this, she was going to burst into tears of sentimental nostalgia.

It was only a few steps to the front door and the apartment buzzers beside it. She hadn't taken a key with her when she left for Italy. Now it felt as if she'd been away not four months but forty years. That, more than anything else, made her realize how definitively she had broken with everything here.

The idea of climbing those steps made her feel terrible. Her mother probably wouldn't be home anyway. She must still have that job at Bristen's Eatery, and the second job at the Laundromat. At night she sometimes cooked glass noodles in a Chinese restaurant two blocks away, and then took the next day off. So she might be home after all. Which only made it worse that Rosa was standing there on the sidewalk as if frozen to it, easily visible.

What would she have chosen if her mother had advised her to keep the baby? Would she have brought Nathaniel into the world? And then what? She'd still be living here, hearing Mr. Piccirilli's snores through the floorboards at night, feeding a howling infant, trying to get by somehow or other.

She had to get away from here. Right away.

Hadn't Gemma been right to say Rosa would be doing herself no favors by having a baby at seventeen? Didn't she have enough trouble with herself already? But they didn't have to talk about that. She only wanted to find out something about her father and TABULA.

It was pathetic, just standing here doing nothing. Not going in, but not going away, either. Indecision of that kind had killed Nathaniel.

The lace curtain beside the bunch of flowers moved. A draft of air?

Why didn't the snowplow come along and run her down? That would make it all so much simpler.

Her hand, she noticed almost to her own surprise, was still clutching *Aesop's Fables* inside her bag. She let go of the little book and took out her cell phone instead. She tapped in the number and stopped with her finger hovering above the CALL key.

The curtain moved again. Yes, just the wind. The windows had hardly any insulation. Rosa took a deep breath and pressed CALL.

Was tempted to hang up.

She saw a silhouette behind the lace, someone going from the bedroom into the kitchen.

"Hello?" Her mother sounded tired. So she had indeed been working the night shift. "Hel-lo?" More awake now, and annoyed.

Rosa's eyes were burning. She heard Gemma breathing. A small dog appeared at the entrance to the building and barked. Her mother must be able to hear it too. Twice, like an echo—through the window and over the phone.

Rosa quickly hung up and walked away.

The dog, yapping, followed her a little way down the street and then left her alone, pleased with itself for chasing off an enemy.

HIS FACE

SHE DISCOVERED THE BRONZE panther by pure chance.

He was crouching on a hill in Central Park, his black eyes looking down on East Drive, one of the two streets running north to south through the park. From up there his view over the treetops must reach as far as the skyline of high-rise buildings on Fifth Avenue. Up there on his rock, surrounded by leafless tendrils of Virginia creeper, he seemed about to pounce.

Rosa sat down on a bench and examined the statue from a distance. Joggers and walkers passed by, and now and then one of the horse-drawn carriages driving tourists and amorous couples around the park. Icicles hung from the big cat's jaws as if he were baring his teeth. But she could see only sadness in his dark eyes, nothing threatening.

She had grabbed her laptop from the hotel before coming here. She brushed the snow from the bench, but a chill still seeped through her jeans and tights.

The bronze panther looked as if he were watching her. She knew how that effect was achieved from the oil paintings in the Palazzo Alcantara. If she got up and walked a little ways away, the statue's eyes would seem to follow her.

The laptop lay closed on her knees as she tapped Alessandro's number into her phone. It would be just after nine in the evening in Italy now. She had once asked him what he did during the evenings they didn't spend together. "Nothing," he had said. "I sit there doing nothing."

"You mean reading? Or watching TV?" Even as she said it, it struck her as such a boring question that she could have screamed at herself.

Alessandro shook his head. "If it's hot, I go up on the battlements and look across the plain to the south. Over the hills on the horizon. When the sirocco blows, you can smell Africa."

"Is that a panther thing?" She gestured clumsily. "I mean . . . like panthers. Jungles. Africa."

"That's where we come from. Originally, anyway."

"I thought it was Arcadia."

"The human part of us. But the origin of the other part, the roots of the Panthera, they're somewhere in Africa."

"How about snakes?"

"Same for snakes, I guess."

"Will you show me? How to smell Africa up there on your battlements?"

"Sure."

The panther on the rock looked as if he, too, were dreaming of somewhere far away.

The ringing of the phone brought her back out of her thoughts, and the next moment Alessandro's voice mail kicked in. Rosa hesitated for a second, cleared her throat, smiled, and said, "I was just thinking of you. What you said about Africa. There's a panther here with me. He's made of metal, but I'd love to climb up and put my arms around him."

Good God. That was easily the most ridiculous thing she'd ever said. In panic, she broke the connection, and realized at the same moment that it was too late. She couldn't unsay what she'd said. *Climb up and put my arms around him.* She felt like crawling under the park bench.

But the panther kept looking down at her, and now his icicle teeth flashed in a sunbeam as if he were grinning at her, saying, *Come on up here, then.*

She let the cell phone drop to her lap, picked it up again, and buried it deep in her bag. Maybe he'd forget to listen to his messages. For about the next fifty years.

Almost automatically, she turned to her laptop. The casing felt icy. She desperately needed gloves and was annoyed with herself for not having bought a pair at Gothic Renaissance. Although black lace probably wouldn't have been the best choice for this cold weather.

Her new emails wouldn't all fit on a single screen. A handful were addressed directly to her—mostly from the men who had escorted her to the airport—but the majority she was only cc'd on. Correspondence between the managers of her companies, meaningless stuff to give the police surveillance experts something to do. Some of it seemed to be in a bewildering code, but really it was only randomly picked sequences of letters and numbers. Every minute that the anti-Mafia commission wasted trying to decipher the code was taking police attention away from other work.

The remaining messages were confined to the legal activities of the Alcantara companies, particularly the building of wind turbines all over Sicily and the delivering of wool blankets and food supplies to the refugee camp on Lampedusa.

One of the last emails, however, made her frown. It came from the Studio Legale Avv. Giuseppe L. Trevini. An attorney, Trevini had worked exclusively for the Alcantaras for many years, ever since Rosa's grandmother had been head of the clan. Rosa had visited him three times in the last few months and realized that he knew every last detail of all the family's dealings—legal and illegal. Whenever she had questions, he had told her, she could turn to him. Trevini was old-fashioned, cranky, but also crafty, and he was a technophobe. He had never sent her an email before. What he didn't want to keep in the archives on paper, for reasons of security, he stored in his personal memory. She had never met anyone with such total recall. In spite of his close connection with the Alcantaras, she didn't trust him. In the days just before she left, he had asked her no less than four times to visit him. But that would have meant going to Taormina. Trevini was in a wheelchair and refused to leave the grand hotel looking out on the bay where he had been living for decades.

So it was unusual for the attorney to send her an email. Even more startling, however, was the subject line: *Alessandro Carnevare—important!*

Avvocato Trevini had made no secret of his extreme disapproval of any relationship between an Alcantara woman and a Carnevare man. That was another reason why she felt uneasy as she opened the message.

Dear Signorina Alcantara, he wrote. *As your family's legal adviser for many years, I would like you to look at the attached video data file. In addition, I ask you again for a personal conversation. I am sure you will agree that the attachment and further material in my possession call for urgent consultation. On that occasion, I would like to introduce you to my new colleague, Contessa Avvocato Cristina di Santis. I remain, with the deepest respect for your family and in the hope of meeting you in the near future, yours sincerely, Avv. Giuseppe L. Trevini.*

Rosa moved the cursor over the attachment icon and then stopped. She read that last sentence of his email again, annoyed. *Deepest respect for your family.* By which, of course, he meant *Don't forget where you belong, you stupid child.*

With a snort of indignation, she clicked on the attachment and waited impatiently for the video to come up. The picture was no larger than the size of a pack of cigarettes, pixelated and much too dark. Metallic rushing sounds and distorted voices came from the speaker.

She was seeing a party, evidently filmed on a cell phone, with wobbly, indistinct images of laughing faces. The video panned across a large room. Scraps of conversation were barely audible; the sound was a blurred mixture of words, clinking glasses, and background music.

Now the camera was turned on a single person, and stayed there. Rosa was looking at her own face, shiny in the heat of the room. She was wearing makeup. In one hand she held a cocktail glass and a cigarette. She hadn't smoked or drunk for almost a year and a half now. Not a drop of alcohol since that night.

A girl's high-spirited voice asked how she was. The Rosa in the video grinned and shaped a word with her lips.

"What?" called the voice.

"B-A-T-H-R-O-O-M," Rosa spelled out. "The bathroom. Coming with me?"

The answer couldn't be heard, but the picture wobbled. A head was shaken. Rosa shrugged her shoulders, put her glass down on a buffet table, and walked out of the frame, listing heavily. She'd drunk a lot that evening.

The picture changed again. The camera panned over faces, lingering on them when it found a good-looking man. Now and then someone grinned into it; several greetings were called out to the girl holding the cell phone. "Hi, Valerie!"— "How's it going?"—"Hey there, Val!"

Valerie Paige. Rosa hadn't thought of her in months. How did Trevini come by a video made by Val of that party? He must have found out what had happened there. That was all she needed.

Valerie stopped again. She zoomed in and out a few times—more faces, most of them pixelated beyond all recognition. Then she concentrated on a group of young men in one corner of the room.

Five or six of them talking, three with their backs to the camera. One of them waved to Valerie and gave her an appreciative wolf whistle. Rosa had never seen him before. Val zoomed in again. Off camera she called, "Hey, Mark!" The others turned to her as well. One of them was looking straight into the camera, smiling.

The picture froze. The sound broke off.

The status bar showed that the file wasn't finished yet, but the rest of it was occupied by the still of that one face. With that silent, frozen smile.

Trembling, Rosa enlarged the window until the young man's features consisted of brownish rectangles. Then she minimized it right down again.

She could have spared herself the trouble. She'd recognized Alessandro even before he'd turned around. From the way he moved. From his unruly hair.

Muttering curses, she leaned against the back of the park bench. Above the lid of the laptop, the bronze panther, unmoving, was still staring at her, up on his rock framed by a background of bony branches.

Alessandro had been there. On the night it happened. In that apartment in the Village where Rosa had never been before, and would never be again.

His hair was shorter than today—a boarding-school haircut, he had once called it. The others with him had similar hairstyles.

Damn it, *he had been there.*

And had never said a single word about it.

VALERIE

IT WAS A TRICK. A lie. Some perverse ruse to make her feel insecure, distract her attention, keep her from messing up any of the Alcantara deals from which Trevini earned his money.

It wasn't hard to see through his ploy. He wanted to unsettle her so that she'd be easier to manipulate. Most people thought the Mafia shot down anyone who stood in its path with a machine gun. That was nonsense; there were many other ways to get rid of them, and Avvocato Trevini knew them all. A man who had been working for the Cosa Nostra for decades, defending murderers, springing criminals from prison, discrediting public prosecutors—a man who had survived all the changes of leadership intact, and even the bloody street warfare of earlier years, knew what he was doing.

A video clip could be faked. How hard was it to replace one face with another? Trevini must know that she didn't trust him. That, naturally, she would sooner believe Alessandro. All she had to do was call Alessandro, ask him, and the whole hoax would be exposed.

And yet Trevini had sent her the video.

She took her cell phone out of her bag and dialed Alessandro's number for the second time that afternoon. The ring seemed louder and shriller this time. Voice mail again.

His smile was still caught on the monitor of the laptop, blurred like a half-forgotten memory. Had she seen him that evening? When Valerie thought a man looked sexy, it was her habit to point him out. Had she pointed him out to Rosa at the party? And more important, had *he* seen Rosa and failed to tell her later that he recognized her? Why had he kept quiet about it?

He hadn't been straightforward with her once before: when he'd taken her to Isola Luna so that her presence would interfere with Tano's plans to murder him. They hadn't been a couple yet at the time. Did that make a difference?

She decided to send Trevini an email.

You're fired, she typed. *Get out of my life.*

She deleted that, and instead wrote: *You'll be hearing from my contract killers. Shitty attorney. Shitty cripple. I hope you miss seeing a shitty staircase in your shitty hotel.*

It was almost poetry.

After a moment's thought, she deleted that, too. *Dear Signore Trevini, I am not at home right now. I will be in touch about a date for a discussion in the next few days. Where did you get that video? And you mentioned other material; what kind of material is that? Sincerely, Rosa Alcantara.*

PS: I HOPE YOU CHOKE ON YOUR SHITTY LEGAL LIES IN YOUR SHITTY WHEELCHAIR, YOU MISERABLE BASTARD.

She stared at the postscript, then deleted it letter by letter, very slowly. Finally she hit SEND and closed the laptop.

Her cell phone rang at the same moment. She saw

Alessandro's name on the display, waited a few seconds, and then answered.

"Hey, it's me."

"Hi."

"What are you doing there with that panther?"

Puzzled, she looked around her, and then remembered the voice mail.

"Where've you been?" she asked.

He hesitated briefly. "Discussions?" It sounded like a question, as if he couldn't believe that she'd forgotten that. "Good to hear your voice."

She hated herself a little for being unable to pretend better. For not managing to sound, at least for one or two minutes, as if everything were all right. Instead she said, "You were there."

Another pause. "Where? What do you mean?"

"At that party. A year and a half ago in the Village. You were there."

"What are you talking about?"

Relieved, she thought: Good. So it *was* a trick. All lies. He had no idea what she was asking him.

Only she didn't say that. "I saw you. On a video. You were at the same party as me, on the same damn night."

His reaction was calm. "When exactly was this?"

"October thirty-first. A Halloween party, but no costumes. Anyone who did come in costume had to strip down to their underwear and run right through the apartment."

She heard him draw his breath in sharply. "*That* was the

party. Where they . . . It happened *there*?"

Suppose he was lying so as not to hurt her? Would she rather it was that way? She wanted to know the truth, never mind how bad or bewildering it was.

"Yes," she said dully.

"I didn't know. You never mentioned it."

"Did you see me there?"

"No." He almost sounded distressed, something she'd never heard in his voice before. She didn't like it, and it only confused her even more. "No," he repeated more firmly. "Of course not."

"Are you sure?"

"Shit, Rosa . . . I had no idea! There were so many people around, and we went out to parties like that all the time. I went with friends from boarding school; we used to drive into different parts of the city. Including the Village. Someone always knew someone else, and there was always a party somewhere."

That sounded plausible. And there was no reason at all to distrust him. She did love him.

Only there was an undertone, a slight hesitation in his voice that made her wonder. *Someone always knew someone else.*

"Did you know them?" she asked quietly. "The guys who did it?"

Now he understood. "You think I knew about it and never said anything? Never said anything all this time?"

"I don't know what I think." She couldn't even feel her fingers on the cell phone now. The sun was shining over Central

Park, but a freezing wind was chasing down East Drive, making ice crystals swirl up in the air and getting under her clothes. "I don't know anything anymore."

"You don't seriously think I'd cover up for someone like that, do you?" He sounded hurt, and she was sorry. "If I knew who the bastard was, I'd personally put a bullet between his eyes."

She passed her free hand over her face. She still couldn't think straight. "When I saw you on that video . . . well, I hadn't expected that."

"I wish I was there with you."

"Not a good idea talking about something like this on the phone. I know."

"No. I . . . I'm so sorry, Rosa. What can I say? I didn't know."

"You can't help that."

"I'll get on a flight for New York. Tomorrow morning."

"No, don't be silly; I'll cope. You can't help me anyway. I'm too much of a coward even to speak to my mother. And now this . . ." She rubbed her knees together to warm them. "I just have to get over it and then everything will be okay."

"No, it won't," he said firmly. "You don't *sound* okay."

"Let's just call each other again later."

"Don't hang up now. Or I'll fly out tonight." With the Carnevares' private jet on call, that wasn't such an outlandish idea.

"Oh, really, Alessandro . . . don't do that." She had to pull herself together. It was a bad sign if the video could knock her off balance like this. It meant that Trevini was right about her. "I'll manage here on my own. Maybe I ought to just drop that business about my father and TABULA." They both knew she wouldn't. Not after her promise to Zoe when her sister was dying. "It's odd to be back here. New York is . . . kind of different."

"Of course it's odd. You're different now yourself."

"Once I wouldn't have lost control like this."

"You haven't lost control. You're annoyed. Of course." He cleared his throat, and she imagined him rubbing his nose as he sometimes did when he was thinking. "Who sent you this video?"

"Trevini."

"The bastard."

"He says—" she began, but she swallowed the rest of the sentence: *He says he has further material in his possession.* More evidence? Of what? "He didn't tell me where he got it. But you can bet he will."

"He's the same as the others. They all hate that we—"

"I can ignore the others. But not Trevini. He's the only one who knows absolutely everything about the way the Alcantaras earn their money."

"He doesn't like an eighteen-year-old girl having the authority to give him orders."

"You can't really blame him."

"Did he say anything else?"

"He wants me to go and see him."

"Maybe you'd better not."

"He can't do anything to me. It would be stupid of him to. My managers don't trust him—none of them like him knowing so much. If he tried murdering me, he wouldn't survive very long himself. The rest of them think I'm naive and out of my depth, but they believe that sooner or later they'll be able to guide me in a direction that suits them. Trevini could never be *capo*; no one would accept him. Thirty or forty years of working for the Alcantaras still doesn't make him one of us."

"All the same, don't go to see him. He's planning something. Why else would he have sent you the video?"

She was beginning to calm down. "Does the name Cristina di Santis mean anything to you? Contessa di Santis?"

"Who's she?"

"Trevini's new colleague, he says. He wants me to meet her. It may not be important."

"With the jet, I could be with you in ten hours."

"No, you have to make sure your own people aren't about to stab you in the back. I can deal with Trevini. And my mother, too."

His long silence showed that he wasn't convinced. "Who filmed this video?"

"A friend of mine . . . at least, she was at the time. Valerie Paige. She was the one who dragged me to the party." She sensed that he was about to say something, but she kept talking. "It wasn't the first time. She waited tables in a club; she was always getting invited somewhere, and sometimes I went with her."

"And she filmed me?"

"Not just you. A whole crowd of people who were there. Later on someone froze the picture on your face. I assume that was Trevini's doing."

"How does a lawyer stuck in a wheelchair in Sicily come by a cell phone belonging to a New York waitress?"

"FedEx?"

"I mean it, Rosa."

"I have no idea. And I don't care. But it's helped to talk to you about it . . . and Alessandro? I'm sorry that I . . . you know what I mean, right?"

"I care about you a lot," he said gently.

"I care about you too. And I can't wait to see you again. But not here in New York. I'll be home in a few days. This is something I have to do on my own." She hesitated for a moment. "And don't get any ideas about speaking to Trevini yourself. This is my business. Okay?"

"But it's just as much—"

"Please, Alessandro. They'll never take me seriously if as soon as things get tricky I send a Carnevare, of all people, ahead of me. Anyway, you have enough trouble of your own."

He didn't contradict her. She wished she could kiss him for that.

"Call me every day, okay?"

"I will."

They said good-bye. Rosa put her cell phone away and listened to the pleasant echo of his voice in her head. Her conversation with him, and the fact that they were so far apart, drained her even more than her failure to get in touch with her mother. She longed for him, but when she was with him she couldn't express her feelings the way she wanted. And it didn't help that he certainly knew how she felt anyway. Yet she was surprised by her own desire to let him see her feelings; that wasn't like her. So why this sudden need for communication? It was embarrassing. Or at least unusual.

Finally his voice in her head died away. She had silence back, in the middle of the noisiest city in the world. She was briefly tempted to watch the video again. But not here in the park, not in this cold, where she wouldn't feel it if the *other* kind of cold began rising in her.

The bronze panther bared his icicle fangs. She didn't think he looked like Alessandro anymore. As she set off, his moody gaze followed her.

If she wanted to find out how Trevini had come by that video, there was only one person she could ask.

FREAKS

Rosa and Valerie had first met online in a community called the Suicide Queens; none of them were personally acquainted with any of the others. All they knew about one another was how they looked in various states ranging from wide awake, to out of it, to near death. The webcams were unforgiving when it came to recording their dying moments, which would be posted on the site.

All the members were girls and young women, although opinion was divided on the question of whether a woman named Lucille Seville had once been a man. At the very least, she wore a wig, which they knew because the paramedics accidentally knocked it off when they were taking her away.

The rules of the Suicide Queens were extremely simple. They took turns, one of them every evening. A greeting on camera to everyone who was logged in, then the presentation of the pills. Usually this introduction occurred in front of the bed or the sofa on which the rest of the drama was to unfold. The first points awarded by the other Queens were for the number of tablets. More points could be scored for powers of persuasion, which were on display during the emergency phone call. Some members of the club screamed and cried hysterically. Others kept perfectly calm and said only, "I'm going to die very soon. Come and get me if you can."

Valerie was one of the latter sort. She swallowed more sleeping pills than anyone else, and somehow or other she got hold of the really hard stuff. Her next step could only be rat poison. She washed the medication down with alcohol and kept her emergency call short. After that she lay on the bed, in full view of the community at home in front of their monitors, waiting for sleep to come. And for the paramedics. Sometimes they took only a few minutes, sometimes half an hour. Valerie claimed to have seen the light at the end of the tunnel a number of times already. She knew the movie of her life by heart, she said, because she'd seen it flash before her eyes so often.

No one could compare to Val. She took the most pills, stayed conscious longest, and at least once she hadn't given the emergency services switchboard the number of her apartment. The paramedics had to go halfway around the block asking questions before they found it. Valerie almost died that night. But a week later she was sitting in front of her webcam again, back in the running—with the highest score since the founding of the Queens. Her smug demeanor told everyone that she thought the point of life was in the expectation of death.

Rosa had competed actively only once. She had spent days on Google, reading everything she could find out about committing suicide by taking sleeping pills, pages upon pages upon pages, until the idea almost took on its own kind of morbid romance.

She hadn't even fallen asleep yet when the ambulance pulled up outside the door of her building. The only club member with fewer points to her name was a punk from Jersey who claimed that aspirin had the same effect as zopiclone and tried to convince them that she had fallen into a coma after the fifth tablet. Rosa had not taken part again.

A week later she met Valerie at Club Exit on Greenpoint Avenue. Valerie spoke to her as easily and cheerfully as if they had met out shopping. Val was wearing a T-shirt that said *Your hardcore is my mainstream*. Rosa would never have recognized her on her own. The distorted perspective of the webcam, the pixels, the poor lighting had given her a ghostly look that did justice to the name of the Suicide Queens. In real life, however, Valerie was a pale teenager like Rosa herself, with a black bob that gave her the look of a 1920s silent movie star. Like Rosa, she was thin and heavily made up, and at their second outing, at the Three Kings, it was obvious that she also thought much like Rosa. After half a dozen meetings, some by chance, some planned, she admitted that her appearances on the Suicide Queens site were all a hoax. The pills were magnesium tablets, the bourbon was apple juice, the paramedics were friends from the apartment on the floor above hers.

Rosa was both fascinated and disappointed. "How about the Queens and their code of honor?"

Valerie stared at her, astonished. "But they're *freaks*!" she blurted out, and that was that.

In the end, Rosa's admiration for the way Valerie coolly fooled a bunch of idiots who were tired of life—including Rosa herself—won out. During the online chats, the others were all eating out of Val's hand and never thought of criticizing any of her absurd theories about life after death.

For Valerie it was all a big joke. Offline she laughed unkindly at the other Queens, and Rosa felt flattered because this strange girl trusted her. Of course she would never mention it to anyone; she'd had to promise that just once and never again. She had entered Valerie's close circle—a circle that consisted of Valerie and Rosa. For the first time since Zoe had left for Sicily, she felt there was someone who took her seriously and accepted her. In spite of the differences between them, her sister had left a vacuum behind, and Valerie filled it with her bizarre charm and charisma.

After that, they danced together through the clubs, from Bushwick to Brighton Beach, they smoked pot under the Brooklyn Bridge, and they tried to think up ways of outdoing Valerie's triumph over the Suicide Queens. Twice a week Valerie waited tables at a club in Manhattan's Meatpacking District, but she wouldn't take Rosa with her. It was work for her, not play. Rosa respected that.

Valerie had an eye for cute boys, but all she ever did with them was drink and smoke. For Valerie, her attitude was nothing but a show, an illusion—an act she put on for the Suicide Queens as well as men. Even Rosa wasn't quite sure whether she had ever met the real Valerie, or only the mask she wore for show.

The Halloween party in the Village had been one of thousands of parties thrown in New York that weekend, and what happened to Rosa could have happened to any girl. The drugs in Rosa's cocktail, the strangers who raped her—it was pure chance that it was her. There were probably several dozen such cases on the same night. She was nothing out of the ordinary; the police had no doubt of that. She'd been drinking; she was wearing a miniskirt. That was enough to make the rape an everyday event with an eleven-digit reference number in the files.

The party had been Valerie's suggestion. Someone had given her the address while she was waitressing. She and Rosa took a taxi because the subway on Halloween would be hellish, and they began drinking in the back of the cab. All Rosa knew was that they were going to the Village, but she didn't know the house, and she had no memory of the building where they got out. A typical brownstone: an old building with several floors. The police spoke to Valerie later, but she too said she couldn't remember the address. Maybe that was the truth, maybe just another lie so she didn't get a reputation for hanging out with the cops.

Not that it ultimately made any difference. After that evening Rosa didn't want to see Valerie again, and for reasons that Rosa first put down to a guilty conscience, and later to indifference, Val herself never tried to get in touch. What had looked like a close friendship for a couple of months had really just been a kind of useful link between them based on Valerie's idea of a good time, and the rape had put an end to any fun for one of them. In Valerie's world of trendy clubs in Brooklyn and downtown Manhattan, there was no place for regret or for Rosa.

Sixteen months later Rosa didn't know Valerie's number by heart anymore, and the cell phone where it had been stored no longer existed. They had never met at home. There was no Valerie Paige listed, and the last name was far too common to be used as a starting point for inquiries.

In retrospect, it seemed odd that Valerie had disappeared from her life without a trace. Even the Suicide Queens weren't to be found on the internet anymore, after one of the girls had taken the game too far. For her, there'd been no going back. Rosa did find hints in one forum that the community still existed on another server, under a new name, but there were no direct links, and no other clues to the new online identities of its members. Anyway, she doubted she would have found Valerie there; she had probably gotten tired of playing around with placebos and apple juice long ago, and was looking for her fun elsewhere.

When Trevini still hadn't called by late that evening, Rosa took a cab to the Meatpacking District. She had never seen the club where Valerie waited tables, but she remembered its name: the Dream Room. She had found the address on the internet and was almost surprised to see that not everything connected with Valerie had vanished into thin air, leaving no trace.

She got out of the taxi just before midnight and joined the line waiting outside the club. It was on a side street and, like so many other buildings in this neighborhood, had once been a slaughterhouse, as an antiquated inscription on the dark brick masonry of the second floor boasted. The neon sign of the Dream Room, however, looked almost modest. A few dozen people were waiting outside its steel door. Two burly doormen were checking the guests' IDs. Rosa, in her short dress, black tights, and steel-capped boots, was let in easily enough. She hadn't gone to much trouble with her outfit, but because her wild blond hair wouldn't be tamed, and was in such contrast to her black clothes, she looked dressed up enough for Manhattan's chic club scene. At least an Asian girl with pink hair extensions, on her way down the concrete steps, cast an envious glance at Rosa's blond mane.

The interior designers of the Dream Room had removed the floor of the second story to make an enormously high-ceilinged chamber. From the stairs, all you saw was a wide, wavering surface—cloud cover made of dry ice concealed the view of the dance floor from above. Here and there the swathes of mist parted to reveal a milling throng of bodies. A continuous salvo of beats, somewhere between industrial and jungle music, boomed from unseen speakers.

Now Rosa could see how the Dream Room got its name. Thousands of dream catchers hung from the ceiling, high above the sea of dry ice. Someone must have bought up the entire stock of the souvenir shops on Indian reservations to get so many. The dream catchers dangled up there like mobiles made of wickerwork and feathers, strings of beads and horse-hair, some right beneath the ceiling, others deep in the mist. There were dream catchers large and small, plain and extravagant, and they all shook, swinging and turning, from the booming music from the loudspeakers.

Only now did she realize that she had stopped halfway down the stairs. Guests impatient to get in pushed past her, but a few others also stood there taking in the sight.

She tore herself away, walked down the remaining steps, and broke through the layer of dry ice. The scene below was equally eccentric. The floor was crisscrossed by a labyrinth of corridors, like trenches on a battlefield overhung by mist. They linked half a dozen dance floors together. Guests dressed to the nines pushed along the narrow aisles; physical contact was desirable and couldn't be avoided anyway. Spotlights flickered above their heads. In the trenches themselves, diffuse strip lighting showed the way, and there were other dim lamps here and there, illuminating the corridors for only a few feet ahead. Most clubs tried to present their guests with a world of their own, but Rosa had never seen one that did it so effectively, and by such simple means, as the Dream Room.

Soon she too was making her way along the aisles, looking hard at the waitresses, but she didn't see anyone at all like Valerie. She hadn't really expected her to still be here, but maybe someone remembered her and would know where to find her. Trevini would certainly have some explanation ready of how he had come by Valerie's video, but she doubted it would be the truth. It couldn't hurt to find out as much about Valerie as possible on her own.

On the edge of one of the dance floors, she leaned over the bar and asked the bartender if he knew a girl called Valerie Paige. He shook his head. The same with her second and third attempts. She was about to plunge back into the turmoil of the trenches when she stopped to watch a remarkable entrance.

The crowd gave way before a group of black-clad body-guards. The men towered above most of the guests by a head, and beside the wraith-like emo girls and the heavily made-up Goths they looked like trolls. In their midst swooped a fig-ure from another age. A young woman in her midtwenties, with raven-black hair, high cheekbones, and strikingly large eyes, came gliding out of the mist of dry ice onto the dance floor and immediately took possession of it. She was wearing a wide, black hoop skirt, floor-length and trimmed all around with lace at the hem. Entirely absorbed in herself, she swayed her slender torso above the huge skirt in fluid, circling move-ments. Her bodyguards shooed away any guests who came too close to her, but she seemed not to notice. If she was aware of the presence of other people, she didn't let on in any way. Countless pairs of eyes were watching her, and hardly any of them showed less than awe and respect.

"Who's that?" Rosa asked one of the waitresses, who looked at her with as much scorn as if she had been in St. Peter's, in Rome, inquiring about the identity of the old man at the altar.

"Her name is Danai Thanassis," said a male voice beside her. A slender young man, a little older than Rosa herself, leaned toward her. His girlfriend couldn't take her eyes off the graceful dancer. "She's from Europe. Former Yugoslavia or Greece, I think. Whenever she puts in an appearance, the world stops turning." He sounded slightly injured, as if his companion had dragged him here just so she could see the dancer make her entrance.

"So what is she? A pop star or something?"

He shook his head. "A millionaire's rich daughter, they say. *Very* rich. And very strange."

The circles made by the woman as she moved around the floor grew larger, forcing bystanders closer and closer to the walls. Some of them tried to retreat into nearby corridors but met a solid rampart of guests pushing forward to see Danai Thanassis and her fascinating dance.

Rosa noticed a man, accompanied by one of the doormen, making his way out of the crowd behind the bar. He looked Italian, or at least of Italian descent. He was talking to the staff, who gathered obsequiously around him. The owner of the club, or at least someone with a say in running it.

As Danai Thanassis went on with her captivating solo performance, Rosa wove her way toward him, moving against the current with such determination that she caught the doorman's attention.

The music rose to a frenetic roar of bass and heavy beats as Rosa reached the end of the bar, and went up to him, a colossus, with her chin raised. "I want to speak to your boss."

The corners of the man's mouth turned down in a pitying smile. Behind him, his boss was still talking to the staff and taking no notice of Rosa.

"I can wait until he's through with those people," she said, assuming an innocent expression. "That's no problem."

"Why do you want to speak to Mr. Carnevare?"

She was surprised, but not very. Every pile of shit along her way just seemed to be waiting for her to step in it. All a question of habit. Alessandro had warned her about his New York relations—and guess what?

"I'm his cousin," she said, without batting an eyelash. "From Palermo." When the colossus wrinkled his brow, she added in pretend desperation, "Sicily? Italy? There's land on the other side of the ocean, you know."

The bouncer's eyes darkened menacingly. She was afraid she'd turned the screw too far. Did he hit women as well as men? She hardly needed to ask.

"Say hi to him from me," she said, before he could get any stupid ideas, "and tell him I'm here." She glanced back over her shoulder at "Mr. Carnevare" and saw that he wasn't bad-looking up close. Not at all bad-looking.

"His cousin?" repeated the doorman, like a robot.

"Second cousin."

"From Paris?"

"Palermo." She dismissed the point and gave him a smile. "Oh, let's just say Europe."

Once again he looked her up and down suspiciously, probably wondering whether she had already given him a good enough reason to throw her out of the club. But then he turned and went over to his boss.

Rosa used the moment to glance at the dance floor. Danai was now standing motionless in the middle of a gap in the crowd; her bodyguards were keeping it open for her. Her eyes were closed, her head tilted to one side, as if she were a mechanical doll whose clockwork had run down. Suddenly she moved again, seeming to hover gracefully above the lace hem of her skirt as she went toward the nearest passage. Her bodyguards hurried to forge a path through the throng for her. Although they were none too gentle about it, there was surprisingly little muttering or resistance from the bystanders. They were all under the dancer's spell.

While Danai Thanassis glided closer to the exit, and the crowd slowly shook off the magic of her presence, someone behind Rosa placed a hand on her shoulder.

BLOOD RELATIONS

"LILIA," SAID ROSA, LOUD enough to be heard above the music. "Lilia Carnevare."

The club owner leaned forward as if to smell her breath. She felt beads of perspiration break out on her forehead, but down here in the club everyone was sweating.

"Lilia," he repeated. "Forgive me, but have we met before?"

She tried a random shot, knowing how horribly wide of the target it might go. "At a birthday party for the baron . . . Uncle Massimo. I was very young then. Seven or eight."

"Then you must forgive me for failing to remember you." He even succeeded in sounding like a gentleman as he said that.

"I wasn't very . . . well developed at the time." That got a smile out of the doorman but left his boss cold. She had to pull herself together. Under no circumstances should she underestimate this man.

He was taller than Alessandro and looked equally athletic, but he was attractive more in the way she remembered of Tano and Cesare. His shirtsleeves were pushed to his elbows, not rolled up, and his muscular forearms were hairy. He seemed used to having his orders followed. When he smiled, his lips revealed two perfect rows of snow-white teeth. His sparkling brown eyes unsettled her. She could imagine how many women must have fallen for the promise in his gaze, but she had no doubt that the passion in it was mainly for his own well-being. All the same, she had to admit that she liked his voice.

She could have left and called Alessandro, asked him to have a word with his relative for her. But that was exactly what she didn't want to do. She'd had to cope with her problems on her own for years. Alessandro would certainly have backed her up in this case, but she didn't want to rely on him too much or have him try to stop her.

"Sorry to turn up like this. I'm au pairing in Millbrook. They gave me three days off, and I thought I'd—"

"Visit your family in this city."

She smiled. "I really wanted to buy some shoes."

He looked down at her steel-toed boots.

"Oh, not these!" she added in pretended indignation. "My new ones are at my hotel."

"Where are you staying?"

"The Parker Meridien." She knew the place because the best burgers in town were sold in the restaurant in the lobby.

"Good address. Not cheap."

"The family's paying for everything."

"Who's your father?"

"Corrado Carnevare." A name that Alessandro had once mentioned.

"Never met him."

"Cesare's cousin." She batted her eyelashes in the direction of the doorman. "I thought we were a little more closely related than it seems we are. Sorry about that."

He was still inspecting her, but she had an uncomfortable feeling that he trusted his instinct more than what he saw before him: a pale girl with glacier-blue eyes, a mane of blond hair, and the gleam of nervous sweat on her forehead.

"So how can I help you?" he inquired. *Help her.* If that was his idea of her, okay. "You didn't come here just to say hello."

She looked around as if to locate the source of the noise in the club. "It's so loud in here," she shouted against the beat.

"Michele," said the bouncer, turning the microphone of his headset aside to speak to his boss, "we'll have to leave in half an hour. The others are there. Everything's almost ready." He listened to a voice in his earphone again, then whispered something to Michele. Michele's expression didn't change; he simply nodded.

Rosa waited until he turned to her again and then said, "Can you give me five minutes?"

Michele Carnevare smiled. "Come with me."

She followed him behind the bar and down a narrow staff corridor. At the end of it, a flight of steps led up to a gallery of wrought-iron latticework just under the layer of mist. It was closed to the public. Apart from the two of them, there were only a few security guards up here, black-clad and also wearing headsets. They were watching what went on down below.

Rosa's glance fell on Danai Thanassis moving toward the exit on the other side of the hall under the protection of her bodyguard. "She's beautiful," she said, impressed.

"So everyone here thinks." He didn't say whether that included him. "She lives on a cruise ship belonging to her father. Whenever the *Stabat Mater* docks in New York, she comes here. Every evening for a week or so, then she's gone again for a few months."

"The *Stabat Mater*?"

He shrugged his shoulders and changed the subject. "Well then, Lilia Carnevare. What exactly can I do for you?"

"I'm looking for a girlfriend," she said. "More of an online friendship, really. She told me to visit when I was in Manhattan, said that we'd, well, go out together."

He nodded as gravely as if she had just been explaining his taxes to him.

"And now she doesn't answer when I call her." Rosa hoped she wasn't laying the naiveté on too thick.

"So?"

"I think it's mean of her."

"And what's that to do with me?" His tone of voice was still calm.

"She and I are friends. Or I thought so, anyway. And now she's just disappeared on me. There I am in my stupid expensive hotel, going on tours around the city instead of hanging out with her."

He sighed quietly. "Look, you're cute and all that, but I'm in a hurry. A club like this doesn't run itself. If I can help you, then—"

"She works here, she said. But that was quite a while ago."

"If she works here, then she has her hands full right now."

"I just want a quick word with her. I won't take her away from her job."

He was still looking at her intently, not offensively, as she had half expected, but with curiosity. As if the way she was taking up his time with trivialities intrigued him.

"What's her name?"

"Valerie."

"And what else?"

"Valerie Paige."

If this was a name that he linked with anything more than a paycheck, he didn't show it. "Yes, she worked here two or three years ago. Not since then."

"Fuck."

"I'm afraid I can't help you any further."

She looked at her shoes. "Sorry. You're in a hurry, and I've been wasting your time with this garbage."

He touched the tip of her nose with his finger and smiled. He was alarmingly attractive, and for the first time she really did see a resemblance to Alessandro. "But after all, we're blood relations, right?"

She cleared her throat and tore her eyes away from his face. The layer of mist hovered just above their heads. Here and there dream catchers hung down through the swathes of vapor.

"What do those do?" she asked.

"They catch the dreams of everyone dancing down there and then throw them back down, arranged and sorted. Better than any drug."

Now she did turn back to him, to see whether he was making fun of her. But his smile and his nut-brown eyes still seemed perfectly honest.

Naively she asked, "What, right now?"

Michele leaned on the balustrade of the gallery. Even his damn hands looked good. "Anyone who comes to the Dream Room sees things you don't see anywhere else. Or that are invisible anywhere else."

"You should put that in your ads."

"We do."

"Oops." She smiled. "Looks like you know how to run your business."

It was the dimples. They were just like Alessandro's. They were there even when he wasn't smiling. Blood relations, yes—only the relationship wasn't with her.

She leaned over and dropped a light kiss on his cheek. "Thanks," she said. "And again, I'm sorry to have been a nuisance." He smelled of aftershave.

"How old are you?" he asked.

"Eighteen."

"You look younger."

"A lot of people say that."

"I'm sure those guys at the entrance asked to see your ID." Now he sounded almost sorry about something. But the dimples were still there. "If not, I'll have to fire them."

She was boiling hot all of a sudden. "Oh," she said quietly.

"Don't let it bother you. You couldn't have known who owned this place."

"They saw my name."

"They recognized it. And they have their instructions. Some names mean trouble for us here. Obama. Bin Laden." He shrugged his shoulders. "Alcantara."

She didn't have to look around to know that she wasn't going to get back down from this gallery. He was standing in her way, and here came his security men. She heard footsteps on the iron latticework. Very close.

"That was a lie," she whispered. "You're not in any hurry."

"Oh, but I am."

"Then why didn't you say right away that—"

"I wanted to find out what it is that Alessandro likes about you." That charming smile again. "Apart from the obvious."

She tried to spin around, but a powerful arm grabbed her from behind and held her. She heard distorted voices from a headset very close to her ear.

The worst of it was that she couldn't avoid his eyes anymore.

"Shit," she murmured.

With his fingertip, he touched his cheek where her lips had touched it. "I know what you did."

RETRIBUTION

THEY GAGGED ROSA, BOUND her hands and feet, and threw her into the back of a delivery van. When the metal door was bolted behind her, she lay there alone in the dark, doing her best to rouse the reptile within her.

It didn't work.

She tried to do it by concentrating hard, but that was hopeless in her present situation. Then by dwelling on her fury with Michele. No chance.

The van began to move uphill. Rosa rolled over the floor, groaning, and collided with the rear door. The noise of the nighttime streets grew louder. They were climbing the ramp of an underground garage, and now they joined the traffic. She heard the muffled voices of two men in the front seat but couldn't make out the words.

Now she was lying on her side, with her knees drawn up, her tights torn, her hands tied behind her back, and her feet painfully lashed together. The cables cut into her skin and wouldn't work looser by even a fraction of an inch. There was a rubber ball in her mouth, held there by a strap buckled tightly behind her head. With the tip of her tongue, she could feel someone else's tooth marks in it. She wasn't the first to go through this ordeal.

The floor of the van was sandy. God knows what they usually carried around in it. When the tires bumped over manhole covers and potholes, she was tossed around, grazing her skin. Once, the back of her head hit the side wall of the van, and for a moment she saw swirling lights in the darkness.

The more desperately she tried to force herself to shift shape, the more impossible it seemed. She felt not a rising chill but waves of heat as her fear got the upper hand. Her clothes were drenched in sweat; her hair stuck to her forehead.

They hadn't even given her an injection, like Cesare had that time when he'd wanted to make sure she didn't get away from him in her snake form. Michele Carnevare didn't need second sight to guess at her lack of experience. She had known for only four months what she was, and what she had inherited. An Arcadian first shifted shape on the verge of adulthood, seldom before the age of seventeen. Merely by counting on his fingers, Michele could tell that the hormonal turmoil of adolescence had only recently given way to something much worse.

All the same—it ought to be possible. Several times, she'd seen Alessandro change into a panther at will. Yet something or other kept her from doing it. No self-control, probably.

And then she knew what it was. She literally couldn't change her spots, like the proverbial leopard. While Alessandro was able to put his own interests to the back of his mind when he had to do something he didn't like, to achieve his one great aim, she couldn't do the same. For her, changing shape at will was about as realistic an idea as jumping across the

East River. She was always herself, and anyone could see what she was thinking from a mile away. The whole show she put on of being head of her clan was a farce. She didn't want it; she wasn't able to do it.

It was the same with changing into the snake. The harder she tried to force the transformation, the more useless it was. Her body wasn't interested in the least—it just wanted to crouch there in a heap and wait for the danger to pass.

When Salvatore Pantaleone, the former *capo dei capi*, had attacked her at the top of the Sicilian ravine, she had turned into a snake within seconds. Maybe if Michele or one of the others went for her . . . but could she wait that long? And wouldn't Michele foresee that very thing? He was no fool—he might even be counting on her transformation.

He had something planned for her, and it seemed to be only part of a larger scheme. That was why they were in such a hurry. Everything was almost ready, the security man had said. Ready for what? They hadn't been expecting Rosa, but there was obviously room for her, too, in whatever net they had cast.

Bitter gall rose in her throat. In disgust, she swallowed it down. With the rubber ball in her mouth, she'd choke on her own vomit.

She had shifted shape twice when the lives of others were at stake. The first time out of love for Alessandro, in a cellar near the Gibellina monument while Cesare's henchmen were coming to kill him. And the second time beside her dying sister, when her hatred for Pantaleone blotted out everything else.

But how about her own life? Would the snake show up to save itself?

She had to lie there and wait. The men in the front seat were laughing. The sound of the honking horn and the engine noise came in through the vents of the van, and once there was music, like a gigantic carnival. Maybe they were in Times Square.

Now and then, when they stopped, Rosa kicked both feet against the side wall of the van with all her might. Again and again, until her tights were hanging around her calves in scraps and the skin underneath wasn't in much better shape. But nothing she did in here would attract any attention outside. This was Manhattan. No one was going to notice a clattering sound in a delivery van driving by.

In her helplessness, she bit on the rubber ball until her jaws ached. Her pulse was racing, but the Lamia in her was not impressed. It might have been putting Rosa to the test.

Her ability to change shape could have been a gift. Instead it just confirmed what Rosa already knew. She was different. Not like ordinary people, not like the other Arcadians. Her head was simply too messed up.

She stretched out full length on her back, swallowed sour saliva, breathed more slowly, and waited to see what would happen.

At last the van stopped, and this time she heard the doors of the driver's cab being opened. More voices joined those of the first two men. They were expected.

It was bitterly cold in the back of the van.

Footsteps crunched in the snow outside. The street noises had died down a good deal. They weren't in the middle of city traffic anymore. Maybe this was someone's yard.

When the rear door was opened, she saw the men's outlines, with gnarled branches behind them. Leafless trees, made visible in the darkness by the red back lights of the van. A park. Maybe *the* park.

One of the men climbed into the back while another leveled a shotgun at her. They knew about it. They were making doubly sure.

"Same as before," said the man in the van. "Only a girl."

Her stapler was in her jacket back in the club, and they had taken her cell phone away from her.

She heard Michele's voice outside. "Then give her the injection now."

She screamed in spite of the rubber ball when the man rolled her roughly over on her stomach, raised her skirt, and dug a needle into one buttock. Then they were holding her. The hands of strange men on her skin. She had no memory of the events of sixteen months ago, but her body recognized the situation at once. She began kicking and struggling, hit the man on the chin with her elbow, defended herself as best she could.

It made no difference. He hauled her out into the open air and set her on her feet in the snow. Someone undid the strap at the back of her head and took the ball out of her mouth.

"Assholes!" she spat.

There were four men, including Michele Carnevare and

the bouncer, obviously now promoted to bodyguard. Behind them in the snow stood a black jeep with mirrored windows. Both vehicles had stopped beside a wide pathway through the park, near empty benches and overflowing trash cans. There was light behind a nearby avenue of trees, as if searchlights had been set up there. Indistinct voices came from that direction; figures were moving around. Was there any point in screaming to draw attention to herself? But Michele would never have made her get out in this spot if the people over there hadn't been in his pay.

"What do you want with me?" she asked him, ignoring the other three.

"And what do you want with Valerie?" he replied. "I wasn't lying when I said she'd disappeared. I'd very much like to know where she is myself."

"So?"

"Did she have anything to do with the murders?"

"What murders?"

He gave her face a resounding slap. Her head flew to one side, her cheek burning. When she looked at him again, all she saw was his dimples. Alessandro's dimples.

"What murders?" she asked again.

This time it was the bouncer who moved to hit her. Michele held his arm back. "That'll do."

She laughed at the bald-headed man. "Go fuck yourself." She could taste blood in her mouth, but she held his angry gaze until Michele sent him back to the jeep. Only then did he turn to her again.

"The serum will keep you from shifting shape for the next quarter of an hour. You know how it works, I assume. It's very effective. Tano got the stuff—you knew *him* as well, right? One hears this and that. For instance, that you're to blame for his death."

Did he expect a reply to that? She said nothing.

"I wasn't expecting you," he went on. "Or any other Alcantara. This was to be just a party, a bit of fun in the snow for members of the family."

The lights beyond the trees. The shadowy movements. She began to guess what was going on here. She felt sick to her stomach, and everything about her hurt—her face, her bruised legs; even her butt felt as if the needle were still in her flesh.

"You're going to hunt human beings? Here in *Central Park*?" By now she had recognized the nocturnal skyline above the trees; in the distance to the left, she thought she saw the roof of the Dakota building. West Drive couldn't be far away. They were probably somewhere near Seventy-Fifth or Seventy-Sixth Street, maybe a little farther south.

"The murders," he repeated. "Don't tell me you haven't heard about them. Are you trying to say that you just happen to be here in New York by chance? Now, of all times? Does Alessandro know you're here?"

"Who's been murdered?" she asked. "Some of the Carnevares?"

Once again he took a menacing step toward her, and this time she saw that he could barely restrain himself. He had enviable powers of self-control, but below the surface he was seething.

"My brother Carmine is dead. Two of my cousins, Tony and Lucio, were gunned down in the street when they were taking their kids to school. A third cousin has a bullet in the back of his neck, and no one can say how much longer he'll live. His name is Gino." His eyes were focused intently on hers now, as if he were trying to read the truth there.

"I don't know anything about that," she said.

He took a deep breath, and only when he retreated again did she realize that he had picked up the scent of her sweating terror. He didn't believe a word of what she said, but obviously he was in no mood to interrogate her. She could sense the excitement that had hold of him now. Sheer bloodlust.

"Take her over to the others," he ordered. "And give her another injection before we begin."

ONE OF THEM

THEY CUT THE CABLES tying Rosa's ankles and pushed her forward through the trees. Blood streamed down the backs of her legs to her numb feet. It was a miracle that she could walk at all.

Soon they reached a snow-covered clearing surrounded by oak and beech trees. Two trucks with the inscription MOBILE LIGHTNING, INC. were parked along the edge, their headlights switched on.

Between them, where the two beams of light intersected, four teenagers lay in the snow, bound hand and foot and gagged with rubber balls. Each of them wore several layers of ragged, dirty clothing. The white light made their emaciated faces look even sicklier. Rosa would have assumed they were junkies if she hadn't felt sure that Michele was anxious to have healthy prey, and wouldn't want to infect himself by hunting anyone who might have HIV or hepatitis.

"You can't be serious about this," she managed to say. "Not right here in the middle of Manhattan."

Michele was staring pitilessly at the four captives on the ground. "No one's going to miss them. And no one will disturb us."

"But the park is under surveillance! There are park rangers, police, helicopters . . ." She saw the corners of his mouth twist in a smile as his dimples deepened. "How many people did you bribe to turn a blind eye to this?"

It was a rhetorical question, and she didn't expect any answer. All the same, he said, "It's all official. As far as the park administrators know, a movie's being filmed here. There's a special police department responsible for closing film sets to the public. That's in force for this terrain and a long way around it. Doesn't come cheap, but the budget will cover the expense." He was grinning even more broadly now. "For the next few hours, no one will even blink at the occasional scream or so—it's all in the screenplay we handed in."

"It's not the first time you've done this."

"Do you have any idea how many movies are made in New York? A few hundred film crews are at work in the city every day. All we have to do is persuade one or two people in the film office to eat out somewhere classy tonight instead of hanging around here."

As he talked, she couldn't tear her eyes away from the young people. She knew kids like these; there were thousands upon thousands of them in the city. They slept in the entrances to buildings, in backyards, among cartons and containers. If the cops picked them up, they got hot meals for a day or so, and sometimes—not nearly often enough—a bed in a shelter. After a week, at the most, they were out on the street again. Michele was right. No one was going to miss them.

There were two boys and two girls, terrified and frozen. They couldn't lie there in the snow much longer. They'd probably been brought in one of the trucks.

Other vehicles were standing outside the illuminated area. Most were parked among the trees with their lights off and their engines running. She could make out the vague outlines of figures inside them, two or three to each car. Here and there cigarettes glowed in the dark.

The doorman who had been going to hit Rosa had followed them to the clearing. Michele signaled to him. She saw him approach her with a syringe in his hand, and this time she didn't resist. He sank the short needle into the back of her neck. Her skin was so cold that she hardly felt it prick her.

Car doors were opened. Men and women climbed out of their vehicles. Most of them wore only bathrobes, in spite of the icy cold. The first Arcadian to step into the light could hardly control himself. His eyes were glowing like a big cat's, and his lips were thrust forward because fangs were already forming in his jaws. Others were shifting rhythmically from foot to foot in their excitement, as they tried to suppress the transformation until they heard the signal for the hunt to begin.

Michele looked at the other Panthera with mingled arrogance and satisfaction. He must have sensed that Rosa was watching him, because he turned to look at her and asked impatiently, "Anything else you want to say to me?"

She held his gaze. "Can you still remember it?"

"Remember what?"

"The reason for the war between the Carnevares and the Alcantaras. And for the concordat."

"The concordat!" He laughed softly. "The tribunal of the

dynasties, the myths of Arcadia, the Hungry Man—all that and its rules and regulations may still strike terror into you back in Europe, but for us it's about as real as all that stupid talk of our Sicilian homeland and the good old days. Look around you! This is the United States! Everything is more colorful here, louder, and now we even get it in 3-D." Michele shook his head. "I'm not interested in the concordat, and as for the long arm of the tribunal . . . well, we'll see whose muscles are bigger. If it ever comes to that."

"You didn't answer my question. Do you remember the reason?"

Michele's head shot forward as if he and not she were the snake. "No, and right now it makes no difference. Someone in this city is systematically killing Carnevares, at a time when there are no local clan feuds, no open hostility between the New York families. And then you of all people turn up, and that suddenly explains a lot. How many reasons do *you* think I need to throw you to the lions?"

Even in this situation, in view of all the Panthera in the dark among the trees, she realized that there was something she didn't know. A missing link in his line of argument, something that he wasn't withholding from her deliberately; he simply assumed that she'd known it all this time.

"Listen, Michele—"

He waved that aside. "Save your energy for running. Maybe you'll make it as far as one of the barriers." His smile seemed to turn time back to their meeting in the club. "Not that I'd bet on it."

While he was talking, the cables tying the hands and feet of the street kids had been cut. Two of them had managed to get up on all fours, but the other couple were still lying in the churned-up snow. They had been tied up too long to be able to get to their feet.

Rosa cast Michele a withering glance and then hurried over to them. She took one of the girls under the armpits and helped her up. "What's your name?"

"Jessie." There was naked terror in her stare. Living on the streets had left its mark on her face, but she couldn't be any older than fifteen. Suddenly she seemed to realize that Rosa had just been standing beside the kidnappers. Her eyes flashed with rage and defiance. "Don't you touch me!" She tore herself away, stumbled two steps back, and almost fell over one of the boys.

"I'm not like them," whispered Rosa, as if trying to convince herself. Louder, she said, "It can't be too far to Central Park West." The street running along the outer side of the park.

"What are they planning to do with us?" asked one of the boys.

"They trade in human organs," said the other with conviction.

It was on the tip of Rosa's tongue to say, *There's not going to be much left of your organs to trade*. Instead she said, "Run as fast as you can. Keep going straight ahead. Don't even think of doubling back—that won't stop them. They can pick up your scent, so don't hide. Running is all that may save you." *Us*, she should have said.

The whole situation still felt totally unreal. The one thing that did seem real to her was the cold. And now that she had noticed it, it got worse. She was wearing nothing but her short dress and her torn black tights. Her jacket was still in the coatroom at the club. If she didn't turn into the snake very soon, suiting her body temperature to her surroundings, she could forget about running at all.

Suddenly Michele was beside her. "You've explained what it's all about to them much better than I could have done. Anyone might think you'd had experience with it."

Jessie spat in front of Rosa's feet. "I hope you die a horrible death with the rest of them."

Michele smiled, impressed by the child's courage. Rosa had a nasty feeling that he had just picked his personal prey—for before or after he had finished with Rosa herself.

"And whatever you do, don't stay together," she told the four kids. "Run different ways."

"Don't listen to her," one of the boys objected. "If we stick together, maybe we can make it."

"No!" Rosa snapped at him. "You have to split up."

Michele was beaming with satisfaction as he watched this scene. "Remember, she's one of us."

The second girl began begging for her life, but no one took any notice of her.

"They'll kill you all if you stay in a group," said Rosa. But the four weren't paying any attention.

"We'll kill you whatever you do," said Michele complacently.

Rosa spun around, and before he could avoid her, she struck him full in the face with her clenched fist.

Michele staggered back with a groan, and at that moment one of the boys thought he saw a chance. "Come on! Run!" he shouted to the others, and they stumbled off, four weak, emaciated, helpless young people who would have all the Panthera on their heels in a few moments. They reached the trees and disappeared from Rosa's field of vision. The girl was still in tears, and her sobs gave away their whereabouts.

As Michele straightened up again, the first Carnevares were throwing off their robes in the background. Outside the headlights on the trucks, human silhouettes changed and distorted. Snarling, growling sounds came from all directions. There were women among them. Unlike the Lamias, Panthera of both sexes could change shape. Rosa saw one of the women fall to her hands and feet—in the next moment she had four paws.

With an angry gesture, Michele shooed away two of his henchmen, who were about to fall on Rosa. "I'll have a part of you sent to Alessandro," he said. "Deep-frozen. Which do you think he'd like?"

"He'll kill you for this, Michele." She had simply said that without thinking, but as she spoke the words, she knew it was the truth. She had seen how vengeful Alessandro could be. He wouldn't rest until he'd killed her murderer.

Not that that was any help to her right now.

The boss of the New York Carnevares wiped a drop of blood off his split lip, looked at it on the back of his hand, and licked it off—with a tongue that wasn't human anymore, but supple and rough. His hair also changed color, growing lighter. He didn't go to the trouble of taking off his clothes.

"Run, Rosa Alcantara," he spat at her, as more and more of the others sank to the ground on four paws. "Run, and keep your meat warm until I catch up with you again."

Then she raced away, out of the bright light to the other side of the clearing, through the ranks of the snapping, growling, howling predators who could hardly keep their greed under control.

She ran westward in the shadow of the trees, over virgin snow.

THE PACK

Soon she was stumbling down a slope, at the bottom of which was a narrow path. Ahead of her in the darkness rose a mighty arch made of rough-hewn stone blocks. She knew this part of the park; she had been here before, years ago.

It was the Ramble, an artificially laid-out wilderness with dense woodland, winding paths, and steep rock formations. Streams and pools of water looked idyllic in daylight, but on a winter night the open, unprotected, icy surfaces became insurmountable barriers.

Somewhere in all these thickets there was a man-made grotto that had been closed to visitors for years, as well as countless other nooks and crannies that might provide a hiding place. Michele certainly assumed that his prey would look for cover somewhere, hoping that the Panthera wouldn't find them. But Rosa knew what a keen sense of smell the big cats had and didn't make the mistake of underestimating it. She had seen Alessandro and other Carnevares in their animal form, and it was obvious that there was nowhere to hide from them. Sooner or later they would track down anyone who crept into one of those places for shelter.

Run straight ahead, she had told the others. But you couldn't do that in the Ramble. The network of paths wound this way and that, there was no way to see straight in front of you, and steep slopes and precipices rose on either side. Michele had chosen the best imaginable playground, for the same reasons that Cesare had once chosen the Gibellina monument. There was no escape from the narrow aisles between the rocks and the rampant undergrowth.

Rosa ran through the crusted snow and tried to control her racing breath. The soles of her heavy shoes kept her from slipping, but she was still too slow. She wanted to go west, to the edge of the park, but whenever she caught a glimpse through the trees, she saw only darkness, no skyline. Maybe she was running the wrong way, farther and farther into the park. She didn't dare turn around. The Panthera had to be on her trail already.

She heard the first scream when she was ducking low as she crossed a small bridge. One of the boys, probably, but it was hard to tell for certain—the voice was shrill and high, a shriek of mortal terror.

Rosa ran on. No time for pity, not now. She felt sick. She just made it to the handrail of the bridge and threw up on the frozen surface of the water.

When she looked up, she saw movement in the bushes, the outline of something gliding along the bank in the darkness. She flung herself around and ran on. She would have liked to listen to the sounds made by her pursuer, but could only hear the crunch of her own footsteps in the snow and her own breathing, both of them too loud.

The second scream came from one of the girls, and was

from a different direction. So the four of them had separated after all. Not that it had done them any good. The Panthera had taken their second victim. Rosa wondered if they killed their prey at once or just injured it, let it get away, gave it a head start, and then followed the scent of hot blood.

Once again something moved among the trees, beside her now. Keeping low and close to the ground, as if the black silhouettes of the trunks were forming growths that moved from tree to tree and merged. Whatever it was scurried through the brushwood parallel to the path. But she immediately lost sight of it again when, after a few steps, the next high slope cut off her view.

How long had she been running now? Less than five minutes. It was going to seem forever before the effect of the serum wore off and she, too, had a chance to change shape. Would Michele wait that long before attacking? Did he want a fight with an opponent who could defend herself? Rosa remembered the duel between Zoe and Tano that she had seen in the woods on the Alcantara property, snake and tiger locked in combat. She doubted whether she could fight back as well as her sister.

Another scream, and this time it seemed endless. The snarling of the big cats echoed through the night. Several Panthera scuffling with one another for possession of the prey. Then came the mighty roar of a lion, and after that, silence. The argument had been settled.

She reached a crossroads in the path and turned right. Another bridge under branches hanging low. Ahead of her yawned the mouth of a pedestrian underpass. She could see the other end of it, not thirty feet away, a vague gray patch in the black of the darkness.

She stopped, listened, heard her heartbeat thudding. Alessandro's face appeared before her mind's eye, but that was the last thing she needed right now. She was waiting for the snake, for the ice-cold reptile in her. She didn't want to think of Alessandro at this moment. But the more she fought against it, the more her feelings rose to the surface. She couldn't let them distract her from what lay ahead.

From the black mouth of the tunnel.

From the muzzle of the black panther suddenly barring her way.

They stared at each other, and for a crazy moment she felt sure that the panther was Alessandro.

She hadn't yet seen many Panthera after their transformation into big cats, but she knew that their human features could still be recognized in animal form. Only in small details. There was a certain sparkle in Alessandro's eyes. Not in this panther's.

She took a step backward.

Behind her, the snarling of the pack could be heard again, and then branches breaking and snapping. They were coming through the frozen winter woodland of the Ramble now, ignoring the paths, racing through the undergrowth.

The panther in front of her didn't move, just imperceptibly raised his nose and waited. Then she realized that he was picking up the scent of the others as they charged this way through the night. Presumably working out how much time he still had to claim her just for himself.

Quickly, Rosa began climbing the steep slope to the left of the path. The panther wasn't twelve feet away, with the tunnel opening directly behind him. Somehow or other she had to get to the top, crossing the frozen snowdrifts caught in the tangled tendrils and roots. Broad tree trunks rose above the slope. Something was moving behind them.

The panther let out a snarl, but she didn't turn around.

Then the sounds coming from his muzzle changed.

"Not that way."

She looked down on the path. A naked man was crouching in front of the tunnel, at first glance not much older than Rosa herself. As she stared at him, he stood up, swaying, dazed by the speed of his shift back to human form. Strands of panther fur scurried over his muscular body, branched out, and disappeared. But his eyes were still glowing; his hair was still raven black.

"I'll help you," he managed to say hoarsely, as his interior organs went on changing and his vocal cords became human again. He looked pale and defenseless in front of the deep, black mouth of the tunnel.

"Come with me." He stretched out a shaking hand.

She went on climbing. Up to the trees. To the figures moving among them.

Swaying, she straightened up, and now she could see just over the top of the slope.

Two lions were prowling through the undergrowth. Then

she saw the girl. Jessie was cowering behind a tree over to the right, trembling with the freezing cold as she hid from the beasts. When Rosa looked left again, there were more Panthera there. A leopard. Two tigers. A graceful lioness with huge eyes, her beautiful feline face seeming almost innocent.

The beasts were approaching Jessie's hiding place. The girl couldn't see them, but she probably smelled them, heard the crunch of frozen foliage and twigs under their paws. But Jessie stood there, frozen to the spot, behind the trunk of the oak tree, not daring to move.

Only her eyes were turned toward Rosa, over a distance of some twenty-five feet, pale pearls shining in the darkness. A pleading, terrified glance.

A hand was placed over Rosa's mouth from behind and forced her down, into the shelter of the edge of the slope. A whisper in her ear, almost inaudible: "There's nothing you can do for her."

As if she had no will of her own left, she let him lead her down the hill. She knew he was right. But she had just turned her back on a stranger who, in those few seconds, had begged Rosa for her life.

Down at the foot of the slope she tore herself away from the man, ready to scale it again and intervene after all, shout at the Panthera that she was the only one they really wanted, the Lamia they hated so much.

Except that that wouldn't change anything.

Up in the darkness, Jessie began to scream.

The man leaped after Rosa and hauled her down again. "If

you don't come with me, you'll die," he hissed at her, still with that dangerous feline growl in his voice. She thought it attractive in Alessandro, merely menacing in this man.

She wanted to resist, contradict him, run to help the girl.

But she did none of those things. She just stared at him, feeling something die inside her, maybe her pity, maybe only her brief moment of desperate courage, and then she nodded.

"This way," he whispered, and ran into the tunnel ahead of her. "Come on."

She followed him, hoping that Jessie's screeching and howling would lessen down there, but instead it was amplified. Many growls and much feline mewling mingled with it as the Panthera quarreled over their prey again, and then, as before, an animal roar silenced them. It did not sound as fierce and barbaric; more domineering. A short command in the language of the Panthera, and immediately there was quiet apart from Jessie's weeping and pleading.

The sounds that finally silenced the girl almost brought Rosa to her knees. The noise of snapping and tearing echoed through the tunnel, as if the Panthera were feasting down here in the shadows, right beside Rosa.

The man seized her again and pulled her along. "They'll kill us both if they catch up with us."

"You're one of them."

He didn't deny it.

"Why are you helping me?"

She might have expected anything, or nothing. An ally of Alessandro, one of his informers in the New York branch of his clan. Or one of the Panthera wanting her all to himself.

But not this.

"Because of Valerie," he said quietly.

She asked no more questions, but only ran faster now, away from the sound of the angry jaws snapping behind her.

They reached the other end of the tunnel, turned down a path branching off, and ran along the bank of a small lake. Then the man pulled her after him, by the arm, into the undergrowth. It didn't grow so luxuriantly here. They were near the edge of the Ramble, approaching the well-tended, neat, and tidy part of the park.

In the cover of a line of trees, the outskirts of a little wood, he stopped and looked out at the open terrain beyond. He was still naked, and by the light of a nearby lantern she saw that he was trembling. Now that he had no panther coat to protect him, he was freezing like any ordinary human being. Neither of them would last much longer.

"Is that East Drive?" she whispered. Ahead of them, beyond a narrow snowfield, lay a paved road, entirely empty.

He nodded. His lips were blue.

"But you're heading for somewhere, right?" she asked doubtfully.

"Not far now." He looked right and left, then back over his shoulder. "Run!"

They left the protection of the shadows under the trees. Rosa's steel-toed boots left deep prints in the frozen snow, while he ran across it barefoot as if part of him were still a cat.

"Are they following us?" she asked.

"They won't stop to eat their fill until they have you all. Then they take all the prey to a place where they divvy it up."

They crossed the street, and Rosa thought of following it south. He saw the way she was looking, and shook his head. "There's a barrier where this road meets Terrace Drive. You wouldn't get far. Not in human form."

"What's your name?" she asked, as they reached the trees on the other side of the road. The trunks were much farther apart here, and there were few bushes.

"Mattia."

"Carnevare?"

He nodded again. "You're Rosa."

She was going to ask how he knew, but he got in first. "Valerie," he said. "She sometimes talked about you."

Behind them she heard a triumphant roar as the pack streamed out onto the snowy field.

THE BOATHOUSE

THE SWEAT ON ROSA'S forehead was icy cold. Her face felt numb. She was running eastward with Mattia through the trees, while the Panthera chased after them.

How much longer before the effect of the serum wore off? Five minutes? Seven? There were no general rules; every Arcadian reacted to it differently. She could be bound to her human form for another ten minutes or more.

And who knew whether she'd be able to force herself to change shape? She just had to hope that the transformation would set in when danger threatened.

Out of breath, they passed the statue of a man sitting on a bench with an open book on his lap, a bronze duck looking up at him from the ground. Ahead, a paved promenade stretched around the perimeter of a pond. A silvery shimmer came from the ice on the water. In the light from the opposite bank, Rosa saw a single-story building with a pale green roof that reminded her of a circus tent. It had a tall spire like that of a church on top of it.

"Conservatory Water," said Mattia breathlessly. "If we can make it over to the other side . . ."

He didn't say what exactly would happen then, but she assumed that he meant they'd reach the high-rises on Fifth

Avenue whose lighted windows stood out against the night sky, beyond the building with the green roof and a row of bare treetops.

"If we go around it, we'll never get there," she managed to say, with a groan. The cold was beginning to hurt, and as soon as she saw his bare skin, it got even worse. Why was he doing this?

Rosa wanted to run over the promenade and cross the ice, but Mattia held her back.

"No, don't! The pond is thawed out in the day so that sailboats can go on it. The layer of ice is far too thin to support us."

Sailboats? On this tiny pond? But she wasn't stopping to argue. She tore herself away from him again and ran northward along the perimeter. When she looked over her shoulder, she saw dark shapes on the snow-covered space between the trees, at least a dozen of them, maybe more. Several were carrying something in their mouths, and that held them back, but the rest of the pack adjusted their speed to the others, as if they didn't trust them enough to let them lag behind with the prey. Four human bodies, to be divided among too many big cats.

Rosa was running so hard now that she could hardly breathe. Frost was getting into her lungs, and her throat felt as if she had swallowed splinters of glass.

Another set of bronze statues at the far end of the lake: Alice in Wonderland, the Mad Hatter, and the White Rabbit.

Mattia, too, was slowing down. The cold was beginning to numb him.

"Change shape!" Rosa called to him. Even her voice sounded like crushed ice.

"They can see us," he replied, shaking his head. "They can't know that I'm one of them."

"You're naked!" she snapped at him. "What do you expect them to think? That I picked up some kind of pervert on my way through the park?"

He swore—and turned into the panther. The change happened so fast that Rosa's eyes could hardly follow it. His torso and limbs morphed at high speed; fur flowed over his skin like black oil. Then he was running ahead of her on all fours. For a moment she was almost overcome by envy. He was at most three years older than her, yet he had mastered the transformation perfectly. For him it was a gift. For Rosa, so far, it was a curse.

With the last of her strength she followed him to a terrace leading down to the pond, in front of the brick building with the green roof. She had expected them to run past the house and under the trees behind it. Fifth Avenue was so close; she could hear the nocturnal traffic as clearly as if she were standing on the sidewalk. A police siren howled as it went by, going south, and merged with the noises of the Upper East Side.

But the big cat was heading for the entrance of the building, and she realized that he intended to go in. She looked back once more. The Panthera were less than forty yards behind them. A gigantic leopard in the middle of the pack was carrying a human body in his jaws as if it weighed no more than a rabbit.

Jessie's thin legs brushed the ground on one side of his muzzle, her hair on the other. Her arms swayed up and down at every step the big cat took. His head held high, the leopard was carrying her as the trophy of his victory. Full of pride, full of scorn.

"Michele," whispered Rosa, her voice full of hatred.

When she turned to the single-story building again, Mattia was standing at the entrance in human form, beckoning to her with an exhausted gesture—and opening the gray metal door with his other hand. It swung inward. There was a key in the lock.

"I work here," he managed to say, with a groan. "That's why."

The Panthera reached the terrace. Some of them, those who had killed no prey yet, couldn't control their greed any longer and sped up. Rosa ran past Mattia, dragging him with her, and the two of them flung themselves against the heavy door from the inside. It latched. With trembling fingers, Mattia turned the key in the lock. Outside, several of the big cats uttered howls of fury as their claws scraped over the metal. The noise was deafening.

"The windows have grates over them," Mattia whispered to her. "They won't get in here even in human form." His cat-like eyes were glowing as brightly as the single emergency light above the entrance. While she saw him only as a vague outline, he must have as clear a view of her as if it were daylight. She put out one hand, her fingers so cold that she was afraid they might break off if they met the slightest resistance.

Hesitantly, she touched his shoulder. It could have been made of ice.

Only now did she realized that it was improbably warm in this building. The heat was on full blast.

"You planned to bring me here," she said.

He nodded, faintly. "The key was on the outside of the door, and I turned the heat up hours ago. I knew what state we'd be in when we got here."

He moved away from the entrance and opened a small switch box on the wall. A red light showed. Mattia pressed it.

"The alarm system," he said, loud enough for those outside the door to hear it. "It's switched on now."

The scraping of claws stopped. Something dropped on the snow—Jessie's body?—and now they heard Michele speak. He was back in human form.

"How long are you going to hide in there? Until morning?" He uttered a sound that was possibly meant to be a laugh, but wasn't. It was more of an animal screech. "There's already someone on the way to fetch men with tools."

Mattia lowered his voice. "If the alarm goes off, this place will soon be teeming with security guards. They won't risk that until they've hauled some park official out of bed and bribed him. That'll take at least an hour, and by then the effect of the serum will have worn off."

As if that guaranteed her survival. "Let's set off the alarm ourselves," she said.

"I have to talk to you before all hell breaks loose," he said. "What's more, then they'd find us both here, me naked and you . . . well, with not much more on."

She followed his glance to her legs, which were blue with cold. There was hardly anything left of her tights.

"Better to appear in court on immorality charges than dead," she said, going to the window and peering out. The Panthera had retreated to the edge of the terrace. Only Jessie's body lay in the snow, distorted, looking like a dirty garment and easily visible from the window. A promise.

Rosa abruptly turned away. She stepped aside, leaning against the brick wall. "They're waiting."

"Good. That gives us time."

Long tables dominated a gloomy room that occupied the entire single story. Several dozen model boats stood there, none of them more than a foot long, with pointed sails, countless little pennants, and colored symbols. By one of the side walls stood a workbench with carpentry tools, stacks of paint and varnish cans, plastic canisters, and rolls of sailcloth. There were more tools hanging above it.

"Kids and tourists rent the boats and sail them on Conservatory Water," said Mattia, as if it were something she would need to know. "I repair them when they break down, which is quite often."

She looked at his glowing eyes. "What's the plan?"

"We have to talk. About Valerie."

"They're going to kill us, Mattia, whether or not the serum's still working." She fell back against the brick wall, which was so cold that she hardly noticed her backbone rubbing against the joins in the brickwork as she slowly slid down it. She sat on the floor with her knees drawn up. "Why Valerie? What does she have to do with any of this?"

"She and I," said Mattia hesitantly, as if it were something to be ashamed of, after he had been running around beside her stark naked all this time, "we were a couple. And she still loves me, I know she does."

She stared at him, unable to take this in. She didn't feel like laughing, but she laughed all the same. It sounded slightly crazy, but it felt good.

"Love?" she repeated. "So that's what this is all about?"

He shook his head as he crouched in front of her until their faces were level. Her eyes traveled down. "You thought of everything, but not a pair of *pants*?"

"Sorry." He stood up, glanced at the window, and went over to the workbench. A moment later he came back with a piece of cloth, spattered with varnish, knotted around his waist. "Better?"

She nodded.

"Valerie and I," he started again, "were inseparable for almost a year. Then I made the mistake of introducing her to my family. I took her to parties with me, to the Dream Room and a few of the other Carnevare clubs. That's how she met Michele."

Rosa tried to forget about the murdered girl out in the snow for a moment. To forget about her own fear. She began to guess where this story was going. "Michele took her away from you," she said, and only then did it finally sink in that they were talking about *her* Valerie. The Valerie who always steered clear of men. Who had never mentioned so much as a one-night stand, let alone a steady boyfriend.

"She fell for him." Mattia sounded as if it still hurt to talk about it. "She'd have done anything and everything for him. . . . She *did* do anything and everything for him," he corrected himself. He paused briefly, as if to choose his next words carefully. "She found out somehow or other. What he is, what we all are. I never told her; she must have watched him, or else she found something out by chance."

"Mattia," Rosa said imploringly, "why here and now? You could have asked me out for coffee to tell me this. Those people out there are going to kill us."

"Valerie disappeared," he said. "Sixteen months ago."

Rosa jumped to her feet as if electrified. Her chilly skin was tingling all over from the warmth in the room. The question slipped out. "When, exactly?"

He bowed his head slightly as he looked intently at her. "Just after Halloween."

She pressed her lips together and breathed out sharply through her nose.

Mattia went to the window again and watched the Panthera. As she waited impatiently for him to go on, she looked past him outside. All was still calm out there. Michele and the others were waiting for reinforcements to arrive with crowbars. Presumably a parks department official had already received a phone call to warn him, and to make sure that no security guards responded to an alarm from the boathouse.

"Well?" she asked.

"The last I heard, she was traveling in Europe." He was still looking at the scene outside, and without doing so herself Rosa knew that he was staring at the girl's corpse. "I don't know if that's the truth. It's possible that Michele—"

"Killed her?" She went over to him. "Why?"

"To keep her quiet. The concordat was still in force at the time, and there was something that no one could know." He turned his head and looked her in the eye. "I know what happened to you at that party. So does Michele."

Her face was numb. She bit her lower lip, but didn't feel it until she tasted blood.

"Michele?" she asked tonelessly.

Mattia nodded. "He was there," he said. "Michele was one of them."

THE TRANSFORMATION

Rosa was perfectly calm. Exhaustion that had nothing to do with her run came over her. Like the feeling when hysteria changes to dull indifference. She had passed the point of screaming and raging, and had reached a state when she felt nothing anymore.

"Who else?"

Mattia sighed. "The building where the party was held, Eighty-Five Charles Street . . . it's in the West Village. Does that address mean anything to you?"

Her fists were clenched so hard that her fingernails dug deep into the palms of her hands. "Tell me names. One or two of them, any names you know."

Something was happening outside. Mattia's glance moved nervously from Rosa to the terrace. He cursed under his breath. "There's a car coming, on the other side of the pond. Those are Michele's men."

"Mattia, damn it!" she shouted at him. Now, at last, she felt something again, and she welcomed that familiar but still strange sensation like a friend.

"One of the apartments in that building . . . it belonged to Gaettano. That's—"

"Tano?" She stumbled back and knocked into one of the

tables covered with model boats. "*That* Tano?"

"He was here a lot. He and Michele were good friends. Michele's younger brother was shot a few days ago, but that didn't hit him half as hard as Tano's death a couple of months back. His brother Carmine was a bastard, even Michele could see that, and a coked-up walking corpse, too. More people mourned him in Colombia than here in New York. But to Michele, when Tano died it was—"

"I was there."

He nodded. "Michele says you're responsible for his death."

"I wish I were." She ran her hands over her face. After so long, she suddenly felt dirty and humiliated again, as if the rape had been only yesterday.

Tano. And Michele.

Once again she had to lean against the wall for support. "Anyone else?"

"Those two are the only ones I know about." He was obviously uneasy, and not just because of the headlights approaching along the perimeter of the pond. "But there must have been others involved, probably two of three of the men waiting outside for us now."

She closed her eyes, felt her breath streaming into her lungs and out again. And every time she let air out, something else rose with it, slowly, as if it first had to dig its way out from deep within her up to the surface. A chill that had nothing to do with winter was spreading through her rib cage, rolling over the remains of the serum in her bloodstream like a wave of quicksilver.

"What do you want from me?" she asked Mattia.

"If Valerie really is in Europe, then she'll turn up at your place there sooner or later."

"She dragged me along to that party with her, Mattia. If she knows what happened there, and that Michele was involved—"

"She was the one who told me about it, the very next day. That was the last time I saw her."

Scales were forming on the backs of her hands. They felt like tiny hairs standing erect in an icy draft of air. "If I see her, I'll kill her."

"But she couldn't help it! She swore that to me. She didn't find out until later that night, when Michele told her. Michele was doped up to the eyeballs at the time. It knocked her sideways, and she came to me to—"

"Oh, sure," she interrupted icily. "I bet she felt truly terrible. Because *I* had been raped. By *her* boyfriend."

The sound of the car engine laboring as it made its way through the snow was getting louder. But Mattia was so desperately trying to justify Valerie that he took no notice of it.

"It wasn't her fault," he said. "She said she wanted to talk to you. She was going to ask you to forgive her."

Forgive her. Rosa felt like laughing at him for his stupid, blind love for a girl like that, but then she remembered how she herself had fallen under her spell. Valerie had charisma that made it easy for her to bewitch other people.

"What do you expect me to do?" she asked. "Act as if nothing happened?"

"When you see her, tell her I'm waiting for her," he said. "Tell her she can always come back to me, never mind what she's done. You're the only hope I have left. If Valerie's alive, she'll go to you to ask your forgiveness. That's what she said then."

Rosa thought of the video, and she wondered whether Valerie hadn't, in fact, tried to get in touch with her long before this. She just didn't understand how Trevini had come to be involved.

The car stopped by the terrace. Its headlights shone through the window, casting the shadows of the sailboats on the back wall of the room. They looked like rows of black teeth.

Rosa's skin was moving beneath her clothes. Scales caught on fibers of fabric, rubbing against each other like the surfaces of Velcro fasteners. Her tongue split into two in her mouth, but it happened so naturally that she noticed only when she tried to speak.

For a second she wondered whether he had told her all this intentionally, to set off exactly this reaction—the one moment when she lost all control over her body.

Metal clinked as tools were unloaded from the car. Footsteps stamped through the snow, and then she heard voices outside the door.

Rosa realized that she wasn't in human form anymore only when she sank to the floor in the middle of her clothing. It didn't hurt; it never did. It was almost pleasant, as if in leaving her human body she also left behind some of her fears. She perceived everything now with a cold, precise, reptilian mind.

Outside, orders were given, and then there was a long-drawn-out mechanical hissing sound. Mattia swore. "They've brought an oxy-acetylene cutter with them. They'll be through the door in a couple of minutes with that."

Rosa looked up at him from the floor, trying to get her bearings in her new shape. She wanted to say something to him, but found that only a hiss would come from her throat. Anger took possession of her, and she couldn't direct her feelings in any particular way or against any individual. Valerie, Michele, even the dead Tano—they had all merged into a faceless phantom that aroused nothing but rage in her. Rage that banished her human thinking and dominated the mind of the snake.

An acrid smell wafted under the door. She felt vibrations that she couldn't have perceived in human form. But the noise was suddenly more diffuse. She knew that she had to rely more on her sense of smell than on her hearing. Her field of vision was more restricted, too, and she didn't see as clearly, although she saw differences of temperature optically, almost as an infrared camera would show them. That may have been why she saw the glowing patches on the door way before Mattia. The men were moving the oxy-acetylene cutter in a semicircle around the handle and lock. If the door had nothing else securing it at the top and the bottom, it would swing open as soon as the locking mechanism was cut away.

Mattia called to her to get to the back of the room and escape through one of the windows while he distracted the Panthera. She heard him, but it was a moment before she could connect the sound of his words with their meaning. Then she slid nimbly under the tables of model boats and deeper into the shadows.

Mattia was still in human form when he ran over to the

workbench and pulled a plastic canister out from among the cans of paint and varnish. Rosa waited a moment to see what he was doing. With frantic movements, he opened it and held it upside down over a plastic bucket. The caustic smell immediately threatened to cloud her heightened senses; as a snake, she felt as if someone were dripping acid into her nose. Rosa hurried away, but the odor of the solvent followed her through the boathouse.

The gurgling as the canister was emptied into the bucket was dull to her snake's ears. The hissing of the oxy-acetylene cutter was more aggressive. When she looked back, the tops of the tables got in the way of her view of the door. Between two of the tables, she raised the front half of her serpentine body almost five feet up in the air, saw a window in front of her, and glanced back once more.

Mattia threw the empty canister aside, picked up the bucket, and ran to the door. He took up a position two steps away from it. The cutter had left a glowing track in the iron, a white half-moon shape around the lock. Sparks were flying into the room. Outside, two men called something to each other, but to Rosa it only sounded muffled, strange, incomprehensible.

But she felt new vibrations, much stronger now, as someone kicked the door from the outside. She knew from experience that her hypersensitivity would wear off soon, as soon as her mind was used to the new body. At this point, however, it was still almost unbearable. The air itself seemed to throb with every blow to the door.

She went down between the tables again, heading for the

window in the back. Only when she had reached the wall did she raise her snake's head again and look out through the glass. Leafless bushes stood outside the window; she could see the lights of Fifth Avenue through their branches. It wasn't far, but at this moment the street might as well have been on the moon.

The damn mesh over the glass was too narrow.

Her amber-colored snake's body was the size of a human thigh at its widest point. She would never be able to force it through the fine steel screen, even if she succeeded in pushing out the glass without beheading herself.

Her head swung around when there was a metallic grinding sound from the entrance. The point of light showing the cutter's path blazed with painful intensity while it moved once more along the glowing track. Mattia stood motionless in the dim light, holding the bucket of acrid solvent in his hand.

He glanced at her. "The other window! Quick!"

While the bright tip of the cutter in the iron traveled the last half inch, Rosa slid over to the next window. The pane stood ajar; she could easily open it with her head. It swung open without a sound, and cold night air immediately blew in. Mattia had planned ahead here, too. The steel mesh itself was as narrow as in the other pane, but now she saw that the long screws holding it in place had been removed. It was loose in the frame, and a firm push from inside would be enough to—

Something was making its way through the bushes. Twigs cracked under mighty paws. A muscular body with tiger stripes.

The big cat was patrolling the back of the boathouse. Even

as Rosa stared, the tiger raised his head and looked straight at her. Their eyes met. He opened his mouth and let out a savage roar.

Rosa heard the sound of feet kicking the iron door behind her again. This time, the glowing edge of the hole traced by the cutter gave way. As she swiveled around, Rosa saw the door swing in and the shapes of two men appear. One with the oxy-acetylene cutter, its blade of flame blazing in the darkness as if through a half-closed eye, the other with a shotgun raised.

Mattia flung the contents of the bucket at them. As it flew through the air, the flame set the solvent on fire. The explosion enveloped the men, turning them into living torches. Screaming, they stumbled apart. The gun fell to the floor; the flame of the cutter went out. The burning fluid was blazing in the doorway and in front of the entrance.

Rosa was briefly dazzled. For a few seconds all she saw was brightness. She was almost stunned by the stench of the chemicals and could hear hardly anything except the men's screams. Within a moment Mattia took on his panther shape and, with one great leap, sprang through the flames. Here and there sparks caught on his fur, leaving little tracks of light.

Now Rosa was alone in the boathouse. She turned to the window again, hoping that the tiger had been driven away by the noise and heat, but instead he had come closer and was looking straight in at her. He stood up on his hind legs, propping his forepaws on the windowsill. The light of the fire danced in his eyes; glittering saliva dripped from his fangs.

Rosa ought to have known better than to count on his mind being a tiger's; this was a man in the shape of a big cat, and he had worked out long ago what she planned to do. Soon he would notice that the mesh was loose in the window frame, he would pull at it from outside, and with one leap he would be in the room with her.

She abruptly dropped to the floor and slid under the tables in the direction of the door. The heat was fiercer here. The glow and the wavering heat haze blurred Rosa's vision more and more. The noise could no longer be unraveled into voices: It was a chaotic mixture of human screams, the sound of the flames, and the roaring of the Panthera. Had they caught Mattia? Were they waiting for Rosa to find a way out into the open air? Or had they started to retreat, well aware that no bribe, however large, could keep the firefighters away from this?

Rosa realized that the place was also burning overhead when scraps of sailcloth sank to the floor around her in flames. Splashes of solvent must have carried the fire to the front tables. Several model boats had caught at the same time, and now the flames were leaping from table to table, fanned by the draft between the entrance and the open window.

The only way out was through the door. Large areas of the floor were burning on both sides of it. One of the men lay twitching in the middle of the puddle of bubbling solvent; the other was nowhere to be seen.

The tiger roared at the window behind Rosa. With a furious blow of his paw, he tore the mesh out of the frame. It fell with a clatter.

Her chances of getting out of here alive were shrinking with every second that passed. In human form, she could have tried leaping across the sea of flames. As a snake, however, she could move only over the floor, through the middle of it.

She couldn't close her eyes because they had no lids. She could hardly breathe for the stench, and the heat was nearly intolerable. Even the concrete seemed to be burning where the solvent had seeped into its hairline cracks. The steel threshold of the doorway glowed like a red neon sign.

The glass of the window broke behind Rosa as the tiger leaped into the room, and the frame crashed against the wall. He raced toward Rosa under the tables where the burning boats stood. His jaws snapped shut just where one of her coils had been lying. His fangs scored furrows in her scaly skin, but missed her backbone. Fire rained down on the tiger's fur and made him shrink back, but not for long. The stench of burnt hair mingled with all the other fumes, choking her.

Rosa hissed. Quick as lightning, she drew up the back part of her body, giving herself enough of a forward thrust to shoot through the flames as fast as an arrow, straight into the boiling chemicals.

Blazing brightly, her scales scraped over the glowing floor. Fluid that didn't extinguish anything but was several hundred degrees drenched her skin. Her flesh hissed and bubbled; the tips of her split tongue drew far back into her jaws, like sizzling plastic.

Her snake body was almost nine feet long, but she managed

to catapult it forward with a single thrust of her muscles. The way out of the flames seemed endless, although it lasted only seconds. She passed swiftly under something, and realized only later that it had been the drawn-up legs of the burning corpse. She could hardly see anything, and her other senses were also failing her. It didn't seem to matter anymore that the Panthera were waiting.

Wrapped in flame, she shot out of the oily, seething puddle and onto the terrace. The ice had melted around the fire, but Rosa was in the snow again. She hardly felt the cold. Her pain was all around her. Her mind had withdrawn; all that was left were the motor functions of her reptilian body.

But then she did hear something: the howling and roaring of the Panthera everywhere around her. She barreled through them, enveloped in water vapor and the smoke that rose from her roasting, scaly skin. By the time the first Panthera had overcome his fear of the flames and taken up pursuit, she was already slithering over the side of the terrace and down to the frozen pond.

The layer of ice was no thicker than a finger's width. It couldn't support the heat and weight of a gigantic snake on fire.

Frigid water swallowed Rosa up immediately after she hit the ice. She vaguely heard some of the Panthera jump in after her, and then sink with roars of panic.

But she swam forward, on and out into the freezing, healing, trance-like darkness.

CALL IT A DREAM

SHE WAS RUNNING, IN human form, over the muddy bottom of the pond, running as fast as she could, although her feet sank into the silt with smacking noises every step she took. Sludge swirled around her in the water, blurring the green light in the depths.

Looking over her shoulder, she saw that she was being followed.

A yellow taxi, a typical New York cab, was racing after her over the muddy ground. Its tires kicked up even more dirt; brown ramparts of cloud drifted on both sides of the car. The windshield wipers washed waterweeds away, oscillating right and left, right and left. A rubber figurine of Simba from *The Lion King* dangled from the rearview mirror.

Rosa could hear much better than before. Not just her own footsteps on the bed of the pond and the engine of the car, but also the music coming out of its open windows. The song was "Memory," from *Cats*. Another good reason to run.

The metal frame of a burnt-out baby carriage appeared in the darkness ahead of her, bowling along through the sludge and the aquatic plants on wheels made of spokes without tires. It crossed Rosa's path. She could hear the axles squealing, a sound that grew louder and then softer again. As it moved away from her, she looked inside it and saw a bundle lying in the carriage, with arms and legs flailing in the air. The metallic squeals turned to the sound of a baby crying.

She changed direction and ran after it in the dim light. The headlights of the taxi followed her, and "Memory" turned into Scott Walker's cheerful "The Girls and the Dogs," its quick rhythm making her race with the carriage look ridiculous. Laughter sounded on the recording as she stumbled and grazed her knees. Clouds of blood swirled up, and the laughter swelled even louder.

Glancing over her shoulder, she saw who was at the wheel of the taxi. Tano waved at her and grinned. She recognized him in spite of his sunglasses and the gap left by the bullet wound that had blown away part of his forehead. Valerie bobbed excitedly up and down next to him in the passenger seat, wearing a T-shirt with the Suicide Queens' logo on it. Michele was in the back seat, waving a machine gun in the air. There was a rose stuck in the barrel of the gun.

She tried to run even faster to catch up with the baby carriage. The sharp ends of the spokes threw up dirt until the taxi was barely visible in the drifting swathes of brown water. But Rosa kept running, even when the distance between her and the carriage increased, while the spokes rotated in a hectic time-lapse effect. That's not fair, she thought indignantly. Tano turned up the volume of the music, and Scott Walker's voice vibrated through the lake.

Tano tooted his horn in time with the song, until Michele hit him over the head from behind with his gun. Valerie laughed hysterically. The taxi began weaving around, and Tano took one hand off the wheel, put it into the hole in his head, and adjusted something displaced by the blow. After that, the car drove more slowly again.

Rosa looked ahead—perhaps she'd been doing that the whole time, yet she knew what was going on behind her. All that mattered was reaching the carriage. Its front spokes suddenly collided with a rock, and the carriage fell apart into separate pieces. The screaming bundle was flung up, and then it bobbed through the turbulent water at a leisurely pace, so slowly that Rosa was able to catch it as she ran.

She clutched the child to her. He was wrapped in a cloth spattered with paint and varnish. A pretty little boy. "My name is Nathaniel," he said.

"I know."

A cat's paw shot out from under the cloth, and claws dug furrows in Rosa's face.

Nathaniel laughed in Tano's voice.

Tano in the taxi was yelling like a newborn baby.

Rosa let go of the child, and watched as a current carried him away. There was a haze of blood before her eyes. She heard the taxi behind her coming closer and stormed forward again, half blind in a cocoon of red.

Then, all of a sudden, she was moving upward. The ground rose more and more steeply. The tires of the taxi's wheels stuck in the mud; the engine howled, so did Tano, and Valerie laughed louder than ever.

Rosa's head came up through the surface of the water, through leafless branches. She slipped through railings much too narrow for her, yet they couldn't hold her back. Light surrounded her, yellow streetlamps, bright white cones from headlights.

A taxi pulled up in front of her. She flung the door open and slipped in. There was a child's hand dangling from the rearview mirror. Or perhaps it was only a twig.

She gave an address, and then her head fell to one side.

She dreamed, and everything was all right.

GEMMA

ROSA COULD FEEL EVERY pore in her body, every nerve, every single point of contact with the fibers of the sheets.

She opened her eyes, and looked at the past. She was in her old room, in the building with the burn marks on its facade. She recognized her closet, her dresser with photos and Post-its stuck all over the mirror, her bookshelf of paperbacks, her old stereo surrounded by stacks of CDs that she'd burnt herself, a few posters, and another photo, a larger, framed one—a picture of Zoe.

Her sister was dead now; she remembered that. Dead, like Tano Carnevare.

The bedroom door was open. She heard dishes clattering outside it.

Mattia's face flitted through her mind. Had he escaped?

A scream began to surface in her before she even realized why. Then she remembered it all: the boathouse, the flames, her scaly snake skin on fire.

With a great effort, she flung off the quilt and looked down at her body. She was naked except for a pair of brightly colored Simpsons shorts. She'd left them behind when she fled to Sicily, and she hadn't missed them.

She was intact apart from some bruises on her knees and

her shins. Her skin seemed to have an abnormal amount of blood flowing through it. It wasn't as pale as usual, much pinker, like that of a newborn baby. When she cautiously ran her fingers over her flat stomach, her prominent hip bones, her thighs, it felt as if lotion had only just been rubbed in, all smooth and silky.

That's not my skin, she thought. This is new.

"Oh, my God, Rosa!"

Someone rushed through the doorway, fell on her knees beside her, and hugged her hard. The woman's face was surrounded by fair, reddish hair drenched in the smells of cooking and cigarette smoke. Rosa knew that smell, and in spite of herself she found its familiarity comforting. Cautiously, she turned until she could put her own arms around her mother. It was just a reflex action, but at the moment it seemed right to her, if not perfectly honest.

Her mother was crying, and couldn't say a word. When she tried, it just came out as a sob.

"I'm okay," whispered Rosa. "Nothing—" She was going to say *happened*, but then she thought of Jessie and the ragged street kids. Michele's leopard eyes, and the angry roar of the tiger at the window. Mattia and Valerie.

Fire reducing her skin and muscles to black cinder.

The only thing that didn't come back to her was the pain. It was as if it had shrunk to a tiny dot, like a crumpled little ball of paper that would unfold again only slowly. Her mind couldn't possibly suppress what she had felt forever.

But hadn't she blotted everything out once already,

everything bad and painful?

Tano. Michele. And in a way Valerie, too.

A shiver ran through her body, and suddenly she felt frail and vulnerable in her mother's arms. Then she heard herself talking, but none of it made any sense, and Gemma replied without letting go of her: something about a cab driver who, complaining loudly, had dropped her off here stark naked, smelling of soot and smoke, saying she should count herself lucky he hadn't either taken her to the police or flung her out of his taxi.

Only in this city could things like that happen. Rosa's mind went to an old *I Love New York* T-shirt in her closet, and she thought she ought to wear it now and then, by way of saying sorry.

When a pause for breath started turning into a long silence, she asked, "You didn't call the cops, did you?"

Her mother gave her a long, considering look. "No," she said at last. No explanation. Just an unspoken question in her glance.

Rosa nodded. "Better not."

That's how it is in our family, she thought. My mother's eighteen-year-old daughter is delivered naked to her door in the middle of the night, and she doesn't call the police. Or even a doctor. And a part of Rosa wanted to ask: *Why not?* Wanted to revive her old resentments, because whenever she looked her mother in the eye, only one word occurred to her. *Why? Why? Why?*

Then she realized that she was the one who owed Gemma

an answer. Even if the question hadn't been asked.

"It wasn't . . . what it looked like," she said, avoiding Gemma's eyes. "Not like that other time."

Her mother put a hand to her mouth, and breathed in twice as if to keep herself from hyperventilating. She managed to stay calm. Her blue eyes blazed, but she stayed remarkably well under control. "They hurt you," she said. She had fresh scabs on little bite marks on her lower lip, and her hands shook. Her fingernails were cut very short, and slightly discolored from nicotine.

"I'm all right now," said Rosa. "Thanks for . . . for letting me come here."

"Did you ever doubt you could?" Gemma got up from the edge of the bed, moved a couple of steps away, and stood with her back to Rosa. "You still can't quite trust me, can you?"

Rosa sat up and drew her legs and the sheets closer to her body, put her arms around her knees, and laid her cheek on them. She watched her mother, the long pale hair with a touch of red in it, the slender body that not even constant night shifts, fast food, and too much wine could harm. Gemma would always be a good-looking woman, whatever fate had in store for her.

Rosa let her eyes wander over the walls, the furniture, the photographs on the mirror. Difficult to imagine that this had once been her life. Everything here was strange to her now.

"You never mentioned anything," she said. "About the family. The dynasties. But you knew all along."

Gemma spun around, her face flushed. "I didn't want

you to find out from Florinda, least of all from her," she said firmly. "But I couldn't . . ." She interrupted herself, searching for words. "I'd already lost Zoe to her, and I knew it was wrong to keep your origin and . . . and all the rest of it secret from you. But I couldn't help it. I tried to say something, and it was no good. Talking to you about it would have been like . . ."

"Like Dad was still here. As if he hadn't died."

Her mother stared at her. After a while, she asked quietly, "What do you think I should have told you? That one of these days you'd turn into a snake?"

"Well, for example, yes."

Gemma leaned back against the chest of drawers, supporting herself on it with both hands. "And you think that would have one of those cozy mother-daughter moments, like on the *Gilmore Girls*?"

"It would have been honest."

"I had to stand by helplessly for years, watching you get dragged off to a police station for questioning again and again. You were still a child! But they didn't leave you alone. Because you're an Alcantara. Because you inherited that damn name." She gesticulated energetically, but a moment later the strength went out of her. "Because someone thought a girl of thirteen or fourteen could tell them about the Mafia!" She laughed bitterly. "About crimes committed by people she'd never met, who lived on the other side of the world."

"I didn't choose my family, Mom. You did that."

"I chose your father, that's all."

"And then there were suddenly two daughters, and they were useless, too."

"*That's* not what I meant, and you know it."

"Yes, it went wrong. Obviously."

Gemma pushed herself away from the chest of drawers, took a couple of hesitant steps, and stopped in the middle of the room. "You were never an easy child, Rosa, but you didn't used to snipe at everything before you went to join them."

"Well, at least *they* aren't a problem to you anymore, right, Mom?" Rosa jumped up, then felt as if someone had hit her over the head, but she managed to stay on her feet, and went over to the closet, passing her mother. "Zoe and Florinda are both dead. Maybe you'd be able to remember them better if you'd turned up for their funeral."

Gemma flinched. "I'm never setting foot on that island again."

"So you said already. More than once."

When she'd changed back into human form, Rosa had shed the snake's burnt skin, but this new one didn't seem to hold her together just yet.

She rummaged around in the closet with both hands. Everything was just as she had left it four months ago. Her mother hadn't changed anything.

Gemma said quietly, "Would you have contacted me? I mean, being here in New York and all . . . no, you wouldn't even have called me, would you?"

Rosa was looking at some old jeans and sweaters. Most of them were black and had once belonged to Zoe. "I came especially because of you, Mom. Maybe that was a mistake."

"You expect me to believe that?"

"Believe whatever you want." She took out a pair of jeans, a T-shirt, and a heavy wool sweater. There was no underwear, so she had to keep the Simpsons shorts on. As she went to pull on her jeans, and was wobbling on one leg, she felt dizzy. She lost her balance and tipped over, just like that.

Her mother was beside her in a split second, and caught her.

Rosa cursed in Italian.

"That was quick," said Gemma.

Rosa tried to break away, but her mother wasn't letting go. Gemma forced her daughter to look her in the face. "I *couldn't* come to Zoe's funeral," she said forcefully. "I know you don't want to understand that. But I swore never to enter that house again."

"Swore to who?"

"Myself. And you can think that's ridiculous or pigheaded, whatever you want. But things happened there that . . . anyway, I'd rather die than go up that mountain again and set foot through the palazzo doorway."

"There's no one there now, Mom. No one but me." She could have mentioned Iole, but this was hardly the right time.

Gemma stared at her, and suddenly there were tears in her eyes. "I'm so afraid for you. I lie awake thinking what . . . what might become of you. That place, that island . . . they made Zoe into a different person. And the same thing will happen to you."

"I'll turn into a snake; that's the only difference. And it has nothing to do with Sicily or the Palazzo Alcantara. Or even with Florinda." She pushed Gemma's hands aside and pulled the jeans up. She felt weak at the knees, and not just because of her new skin. "What would it have been like if it had happened here? In school? Or on the subway? Fuck, Mom, you should have warned me!"

"I suppressed it. Not always, not at the start, but the more I made up my mind to talk to you about it, the less I found I could."

"Too bad for you, right?"

"Your father . . . Davide . . . he never said a word about it. Not after Costanza chased us out and we came here—"

"Grandmother threw you out?" She hadn't known that.

"Grandmother!" repeated Gemma scornfully. "Sounds as if you knew her. God, how I wish I'd never met that witch myself."

Rosa blinked at her, intrigued, and slowly shook her head. No one had ever told her anything about Costanza Alcantara, her father's mother. Not when she was a child, not in the months she had spent in Sicily. She was no more than a name. Two words on a granite slab in the family vault. A face in an oil painting that Florinda had taken down from the wall and pushed behind a cupboard years ago.

Gemma went to the door and leaned against the jamb with her arms crossed. She was even paler than usual. "You don't know anything about Costanza, do you?"

Rosa pulled the T-shirt and then the sweater over her head.

To her surprise, they both smelled as fresh as if they'd just come out of the washing machine. "This has nothing to do with her."

"It *always* has to do with her! No one ever mentioned her name in this house. She never called or sent news in any other way. But she was always around, all the same, every damn day."

Rosa was going to make a snide remark, but a glance at her mother's eyes kept her from doing so. Instead she said hesitantly, "So you didn't have a good relationship with your mother-in-law?"

Gemma snorted. "Costanza was the head of the Alcantara clan for several decades. She was one of the most powerful Mafia bosses in Italy. Do you really think a woman like that would have been satisfied with the usual mother-in-law role?"

"What happened?"

"Would it make any difference if I told you?"

"Look, this is exactly our problem! You always think you know what's good for me. And what I should know or not know. Would it have made any difference if I'd known about Arcadia? Yes, it would have. A lot of difference, actually. Would it have made any difference if I'd known what TABULA was? Maybe."

"TABULA?" Gemma looked at her, baffled.

"You've never heard of it, of course."

"I haven't the faintest idea what you're talking about. What is it? Something to do with the dynasties?"

"Dad never mentioned it?"

Her mother shook her head.

Rosa made a dismissive gesture and was immediately aware that she was acting just like her mother. In how many ways were they more alike than she wanted to think?

"Are you sure Dad never mentioned TABULA?" Now she had come to the real reason she had traveled to New York. Suddenly it didn't seem half as important as before.

"I promise you I never heard that name before today," said Gemma.

Rosa sighed and leaned against the windowsill. The pleasant smell of clean laundry reminded her of the past. "Tell me about Costanza first."

Gemma was still standing in the doorway, rubbing her upper arms. With a shiver, she said, "Davide was always special to her. Most male Alcantara offspring don't live very long; he was the great exception. And the men don't have the same . . . abilities as the Alcantara women. It must have surprised his mother that Davide grew up at all, *let alone* that he had all the qualities that would have made him a good *capo*. If she was able to feel anything like love, presumably she loved him. She always preferred him to Florinda and didn't bother to hide it. That was one of the reasons why your father and his sister never got along particularly well. When he turned up at the palazzo with me one day, Costanza didn't like it one bit. An American with Irish roots instead of a native Sicilian girl . . . Costanza did all she could to nip it in the bud. She tried to talk him out of it, she was involved in schemes all the time, but it made no difference. Only when Zoe and then you were born did she give up for a while—most of the time she wasn't at the palazzo anyway, but in Rome or Milan or Naples, or God knows where."

Gemma turned her head, so Rosa could see her only in profile. Zoe had looked remarkably like her. "Then, one day, she came to me and offered me money to go away. I was to leave you two with her—with her and Davide. First it was a few hundred thousand dollars, then a million, after a while two million. One million for you, another for Zoe. I told her I'd never in my life sell my daughters or my husband. It was the only time I ever saw her lose her self-control."

"She changed?"

All the color drained out of Gemma's face. "I saw it only that once with my own eyes. Davide couldn't shift shape. Like all the Alcantara men, he was just an ordinary human being. But Costanza . . . she turned into a gigantic black cobra. I think she'd have killed me if Davide hadn't shown up right then."

Rosa frowned, feeling the wintry cold seep into her back through the windowpane.

"A few hours later we were on a flight to New York. I never saw her again. And she ceased to exist for Davide, too. But to me, she was still there, like a smell that we'd brought back from Sicily. And even when we were talking about something entirely different, her presence still seemed to linger. Sounds silly, I know . . . but if you'd seen her that day, and heard what she said to get rid of me . . ." Furiously, Gemma rubbed her eyes. "She left us in peace for a while.

Until fourteen years ago, and that phone call."

"That's the year he died, isn't it?"

Gemma laughed—a bitter laugh that made Rosa feel colder than ever. "Obviously Costanza had been very sick for years, and finally she was bedridden. Florinda had been running the clan's business for a while already—circumstances more or less forced her to do it. I don't think Costanza had planned for that to happen, and it was something else she couldn't forgive your father for." She took a deep breath, as if gathering all her powers for the final stretch of her story. "Fourteen years ago Costanza died. Soon after her death, Davide got a phone call, I don't know from who. Probably Florinda or one of the *consiglieri*. He was a different man after that. He changed completely."

"I guess they were offering him the inheritance."

"That's what I thought. Even if Costanza's death had affected him so much . . . well, I could have understood that. I don't mean I could have *forgiven* it, but for God's sake, she was his mother." Gemma slowly shook her head. "But it wasn't any of that. For two or three hours after he put down the phone, he didn't say a word. He just stared out the window—and then he stood up and told me he was leaving us, you two girls and me. That he was going away and wouldn't be back. Just like that."

Rosa's hands pressed firmly down on the edge of the wooden windowsill. A splinter ran into one thumb, but she didn't feel it. "So he left you?"

"Us, Rosa. Not only me: all three of us." Gemma's tone

of voice demonstrated to Rosa, for the first time, the self-discipline it must have taken for her to keep that secret all these years. She and Zoe had always been told that Davide was dead; he had been traveling in Europe and died there of heart failure. His body had been laid to rest in the family vault in Sicily. Rosa had been four at the time, Zoe seven. Gemma had told them it was impossible to fly to Italy for the funeral. Rosa didn't remember what reason she had given—probably that they couldn't afford it.

But no one had ever told her that her father had left his family before he died. Oddly enough, she felt more shocked than upset. It was so long ago, and he hadn't been around anyway, for whatever reason. Yet it affected her in a way that surprised and shook her.

"Did Zoe know?" she asked quietly.

"Not from me. I never told either of you." Gemma raised her hands defensively. "And before you blame me for keeping quiet about that, too, put yourself in my position. I was deeply hurt when he told me he was leaving. We had our problems, sure, but who doesn't? With two small children, and no money, but the knowledge that there was so much wealth almost within reach, but only almost . . . he'd have had to take you girls and go back to Costanza to get the money. Instead he cut himself off from her, never said a word about her, and accepted all the deprivations of life in a shabby apartment in this run-down neighborhood. I'd be lying if I said we were always happy. And I'm sure he missed Sicily, the countryside, the loneliness of the hills, the Mediterranean . . . but I don't think any of that was the reason for his final decision. Long-ing, or discontent, or simply disappointment—I could have explained any of that to you. But when he said *nothing at all*, gave no reason . . . how could I make that clear to two little girls?" Gemma let herself drop to the floor in the doorway, drew up her knees, and stared at them. "So I thought I'd wait until I heard from him, until we could discuss it all again."

"Did you hope he'd come back?"

Gemma shook her head. "I looked him in the eye when he said he was leaving. And he seemed so determined . . . Perhaps it was also fear that—"

"Fear?"

"It was a look I'd never seen on his face before. Almost panic."

"What could have scared him so badly? Something he'd heard about Costanza?" She used the name deliberately this time, because Gemma was right about one thing: Rosa had never known the old woman, and the word *grandmother* sounded as if they'd had a close relationship, which they hadn't.

"He didn't tell me who had called or what it was about," her mother said. "And he hardly said a word himself during the phone conversation."

"Did you ever hear anything from him again once he left?"

"No, nothing. Soon after that, Florinda called and said he was dead. The doctors discovered that he'd had a weak heart—in fact it was a miracle that he lived as long as he did, they said. Maybe there's something to the story of the curse on the male Alcantara descendants after all."

"Nathaniel didn't die because of any curse. That would have been nice and neat, wouldn't it have? But it wasn't like that."

"You can't blame me for that all your life. I knew exactly how tough it is, bringing up children as a single mother, holding down several jobs—and *I* wasn't seventeen! How could you have—"

"You were just afraid of being saddled with another kid."

"And you blame me for that?" Both Gemma's hands had clenched into fists on the floor, but the gesture was helpless, not aggressive. "Take a look around! Is this what you'd want for your child? Crown Heights, a dump of an apartment?" Resigned, she leaned her head back against the door frame, took a deep breath, and said more quietly, "There's something else I didn't tell you."

Surprise, surprise, thought Rosa.

"A day after you called Zoe and told her you were pregnant, Florinda called me. She made me the same offer as Costanza all those years ago, if I'd send you to her with your child."

"She offered you money?"

"Florinda wasn't as obvious about it as her mother. She promised me that you and the baby would never want for anything. And that as soon as you were eighteen, you would also be free to provide for me." Her laugh was a little too shrill. "'Provide' for me. That's how she put it."

Rosa remembered Florinda's expression when she first arrived in Sicily, the smile on her aunt's face. Maybe it hadn't been friendliness. Only triumph, because she had won at last.

In fact Rosa had been used more often than she'd thought. By Tano and Michele; by Salvatore Pantaleone, the *capo dei capi*; by Florinda; even by Zoe, who had gone along with her aunt.

The only one who hadn't been using her was her mother. The person she'd blamed most for everything.

"Did it ever occur to you," she asked, "that Florinda might be responsible for Dad's death?"

Gemma laughed quietly. "I was sure of it for a long time. They never liked each other, and Florinda was in charge of the Alcantara businesses after Costanza got sick. In a way she earned her claim to the inheritance, and in the end she enjoyed managing things after all. Maybe she was afraid that Davide would come back after Costanza's death and take it all for himself, the way their mother had originally planned. Florinda would have had good reasons to get rid of him."

"But now you don't think she did?"

"No. Because I know Florinda . . . or knew her. And because she came to New York to see me a few months after Davide died."

That was news to Rosa, too.

"We talked for a long time, she and I, and she assured me that she had nothing to do with his death."

"She was a good liar," Rosa pointed out.

"But not a hypocrite. There wouldn't have been any need for her to show up here and pour out her heart to me. However, that's what she did. She told me how Costanza had made her suffer, even as a child. Part of that was because Costanza always preferred Davide. And Florinda made no secret of the fact that she was glad at first when Davide left Italy with me. Until she realized what it meant to be head of the clan with her mother breathing down her neck. If Florinda ever killed anyone, it was Costanza herself—I could have understood that. I don't know if she did, and I never asked. But she swore to me that she was in no way to blame for Davide's death. I mean, she was head of a Cosa Nostra family! Why would she bother to come and talk to me about it? Never in her wildest dreams could I have harmed her. And whatever can be said about her, I had the feeling back then that she was honest with me."

Rosa tried to reconcile all this with her own picture of her aunt. She had certainly hated Florinda's methods—but at the same time she had to admit that her aunt had been a woman who lived by principles of her own. If Florinda had done away with her brother, she wouldn't have made any secret of it. She had been cold as ice, and must have walked over corpses more than once to get where she wanted—but she would never have flown halfway around the world just to put on an act for the benefit of Davide's widow.

Rosa leaned against the cold glass of the window. "How did he die?"

"A heart attack. It was very quick. In business class, on a Boeing 737 as it took off. There was an autopsy, and Florinda had him laid to rest in the vault in the chapel of the palazzo."

"I've seen his slab on the tomb."

What connection had there been between her father and

TABULA? Had he really died a natural death? And if not, could it maybe have been the work not of a Mafioso or Arcadian, but of TABULA?

"Why are you telling me all this now?" Rosa asked.

"Because you blame me for keeping secrets from you and Zoe. And I want you to understand why. Should I have made everything even worse for you both after Davide's death by telling you the truth? That I didn't lose him because he died, but because it was his own decision to walk out that door and never come back? Exactly how would that have made anything better?" She shook her head. "Think whatever you like about me, Rosa—but I still believe I did the right thing. I wanted you and Zoe to have a chance to grow up as normal girls, and it was bad enough with all that Mafia garbage, all the times you were summoned by the police for interrogation." She looked tired now, drained by her memories. "And as for the transformations: I'm not an Arcadian, and Davide never had the ability to be anything but himself. I hoped that as the children of ordinary parents, you'd be like your father and me—not like Costanza. Just what should I have told you? That the two of you might turn into snakes someday when you grew up? Don't you think that I'd have lost you much earlier that way?"

Outside, an ambulance raced down the street, its siren howling. The little dog that Rosa had seen on her first visit ran around the building and barked at the noise.

"If you think I've let you down, then I can't change it now," said Gemma. "It's too late for so much—certainly too late for that."

"Maybe you did lose Zoe to Florinda," said Rosa. "But not me. I almost shot Florinda once."

Gemma smiled sadly. "Sounds like my girl."

"You can always come back to Sicily with me. They could show up here looking for me."

"Arcadians?"

"Carnevares."

"What about the concordat?"

"That was broken months ago, by both sides. I guess it's not valid anymore."

"I thought that was for the tribunal to decide."

"You still remember a lot about it."

"I lived with the Alcantaras long enough."

"Come back with me," Rosa said again.

Her mother shook her head. "That's nice of you. But no thanks."

"You're not safe here."

"I wouldn't be safe in Sicily either. No one who has anything to do with the dynasties is safe there."

Rosa's eyes wandered over to the photos on her mirror—and there he was, half covered by a picture from a magazine. "You really did love Dad, didn't you?"

"Very much."

"And he loved you?"

"I think so."

"But he left anyway."

"Yes."

This time she didn't ask why.

Her mother gave her the answer, anyway. Or *an* answer.

"I think he had no choice." Gemma stood up, but stayed there in the doorway. "You know, it's a lie when people say there's nothing as strong as love. It's one of the biggest, worst lies of all. Love isn't strong. It's incredibly vulnerable. And if we don't take care of it, it shatters like glass."

"But you still love him. Even now."

"Does that help me? Does it make me any stronger?" She shook her head. "It just hurts, that's all. It hurts like hell, every day and every night. And it's not true about time healing all wounds, either. It makes them worse. Time just makes everything even worse."

Outside the window, the little dog turned its head, saw Rosa on the other side of the windowpane, and howled as if it were howling at the moon.

SICILY

Rosa's connecting flight from Rome landed in Palermo late in the afternoon. A limousine met her at the airport. As the driver stowed her suitcase in the trunk, she was already dozing off in the backseat.

Somewhere along the way she woke up, freezing, and realized that ever since that night in Central Park, cold temperatures had new and unwelcome associations for her. She asked the driver to adjust the air conditioning, and soon after that the sense of being hunted and the heavy weight of winter started to drain away from her limbs.

Golden sunlight shone in through the tinted panes. Although it was mid-February, on the island it already looked almost like summer. Outside temperature fourteen degrees Celcius—around fifty-seven degrees Fahrenheit—Rosa read on the dashboard, and it rarely got any cooler during the day in Sicily. The difference from the biting cold in New York was so great that she was going to have a hard time adjusting to the climate change as well as jet lag over the next few hours.

The expressway passed across a wide, ocher plain with mountains rising steeply on either side. Abandoned farmhouses falling into ruin, the remains of feudal Sicily, lay on their yellowish-brown slopes. Now and then a billboard shot past beyond the guardrails, and then there was nothing but sunlit emptiness again. The rectangular white buildings of a mountain village dotted one of the peaks like a cap. Behind them small clouds drifted across the deep blue sky.

Rosa had never said much about the love she'd felt at first sight for this landscape, but now she felt it again—this was a place so close to the ancient history of the Mediterranean. After tightly packed New York, where everything aspired to height—buildings, expectations, egos—this was the exact opposite. The world went on and on, far beyond the horizon.

She couldn't wait to see Alessandro. There was a lot that she anticipated with distaste: meetings with her advisers, with the managers of her companies, many of them women, and—worst of all—with Avvocato Trevini. But looking forward to seeing Alessandro helped her feel better about the pressure and terrors of the last few days. She would have liked to ask the driver to take her straight to Castello Carnevare. However, Alessandro was in the conference room of one of his firms in Catania; she hadn't told him when her flight was landing, only that she was on her way home. What she had to discuss with him wasn't a subject for phone calls or crowded airports. And there was something new that they did have to talk about. An address: 85 Charles Street. An apartment that had belonged to Tano.

The memory of Mattia briefly surfaced in her mind. She saw his face before her, his last desperate leap through the flames in his panther form. Had the other Carnevares caught up with him? Michele would show no mercy to the man who had saved her life.

At the Mulinello exit they left the expressway and raced along Route 117, going south. After a while the domed church tower of Piazza Armerina and the rooftops of the town appeared behind the bare trees. Rosa had expected to feel uneasy on her return, but it was just the opposite. She was glad to be back.

A good six miles outside of the town, right after the road forked off for Caltagirone, a driveway on the left led into the wooded hills. When the two guards recognized the car and its driver, a heavy iron gate slid aside on a guide rail, clattering.

As they closed the gate behind the limousine again, Rosa glanced through the rear window. A silver BMW passed the entrance to the drive and continued south. It had been following them ever since they'd left the expressway. Judge Quattrini's anti-Mafia team had only a limited number of cars at its disposal, and Rosa knew most of them. This one had shadowed her a few weeks ago. She sent the judge a text message with a brief thanks for the welcome committee.

The driveway rose gently uphill for just over a mile. Gnarled olive and lemon trees covered a large part of the slope, and pines grew here and there. When the rooftops of the Palazzo Alcantara appeared above the crowns of the trees, she finally felt the uneasiness that she had been expecting ever since she landed. There was only one car parked in the courtyard of the palazzo: a decrepit red Toyota, none of the flashy roadsters that her business managers drove. Thank God. The old rust heap belonged to Signora Falchi, Iole's private tutor.

The fountain with the stone statues of fawns wasn't back

in working order yet, but the gardeners had stopped collecting birds' nests in it. One of Rosa's first acts had been to revoke Florinda's orders for the regular removal of all nests from the trees around the palazzo, to be burnt in the stone basin of the fountain. She'd decided to make sure that water flowed from the blackened jets again as soon as possible.

The palazzo had four wings, arranged in a square around an inner courtyard. Plaster was peeling off the pale brown facade in many places. And the tuff statues looking out of niches and down from the edge of the roof were also in urgent need of restoration. Wrought ironwork on the balconies nodded to the property's former magnificence. Today it was a sad, neglected sight.

The limousine rolled through the tunnel beyond the gate in front of the house. The flower bed in the center of the inner courtyard was still overgrown with weeds; the four facades around it were the color of terra-cotta that had been outdoors for too many winters.

The car stopped at the foot of the double flight of steps leading up to the main entrance on the second floor. Rosa got out before the driver could open the door for her. The smell of damp, crumbling stone was everywhere, even in high summer, and you certainly couldn't ignore it in February. Once again she wondered whether it would be a better idea to find somewhere else to live. Another decision that she kept putting off.

There was a sound of frantic barking as a black mongrel raced down the steps, leaped at Rosa, and planted his paws on her shoulders. He exuberantly licked her face, panting with excitement.

"Hey, Sarcasmo!" she managed to say, crouching down to hug the dog. Smiling, she ran her hand through his woolly coat, scratched him behind the ears, and buried her face in his neck. "I've missed you, boy. Wow, you still smell just as good as I remember." No wonder; Sarcasmo lounged about on the antique sofas and rugs in the palazzo all day long. At night he jumped up on Iole's bed and snored for all he was worth.

The driver carried Rosa's suitcase into the house, and almost collided at the door with a frail-looking woman who came hurrying out at the same moment. She wore wire-framed glasses and a white blouse, and her jeans had creases ironed into them.

"Signorina Alcantara," she cried, sounding as if she might suffer a stroke any minute. "Ah, *signorina*, it's high time you were back here!"

Rosa hugged Sarcasmo one last time, and stood up. The dog ran into the building ahead of her as Rosa climbed the steps, looking at the tutor through the unruly hair that fell over her eyes. Raffaela Falchi was in her midthirties but looked fifteen years older, and seemed to have given up fighting against her advancing age. She looked sober and a little matronly, and that was why Rosa had trusted her impressive references. It would never have crossed the mind of a woman like Signora Falchi to have her résumé produced in some Sicilian forger's workshop. She didn't seem likely to be an informer for the public prosecutor's office, either. Ultimately, though, Rosa had left the choice to her secretary in Piazza Armerina. Her own high-school days were barely a year behind her, and she felt totally unequipped to be the judge of a tutor's competence.

"Signorina Alcantara!" cried Raffaela Falchi for the third time. By now Rosa was wishing she was surrounded by the advisers she usually disliked, so that she could hide behind them.

"*Ciao*, Signora Falchi," she said unenthusiastically.

"Now then—about your cousin. I just don't know where to begin . . ."

Irritated, Rosa pulled her blond hair back from her face. They had said that Iole was her cousin in order to avoid unwelcome questions. "Didn't we agree that you'd decide all that for yourself?"

The tutor's feathers were obviously ruffled, and as she was still standing a few steps above Rosa, it made her look quite intimidating. "Iole won't discuss it with me, and it would be better if you didn't make the same mistake, Signorina Alcantara."

Rosa sighed. "What happened?"

"Iole doesn't turn up regularly for her lessons. She talks to herself. She scribbles in her exercise books. Sometimes she hums to herself, and not even in tune. She won't accept my authority." And so it went on, while Rosa mentally ticked off the complaints she'd already heard before she went away. "She does her makeup while I'm teaching her. And she goes 'la-la-la' when I ask her to listen to me."

"'La-la-la'?" Rosa raised an eyebrow.

"In a loud voice!"

"And then what?"

"Then nothing. She just does that." The tutor was wringing her hands. "Yesterday she belched like an uneducated peasant! The day before yesterday she insisted on wearing a hat with a veil. Heaven only knows where she found it. And then there are those dreadful scented candles."

"Scented candles?"

"She ordered them on the internet, she says. Do you know how many hours a day that child spends in front of the computer?"

"That *child* will soon be sixteen."

"But we both know that she hasn't reached the intellectual level of a sixteen-year-old."

"Iole isn't mentally challenged, Signora Falchi," said Rosa firmly.

"I know that. And I'm well aware of what she's been through. Six years in the hands of criminals . . . but that doesn't change the fact that she has to adhere to certain rules if I'm to help her catch up on those six years. I'm not a therapist, but as a teacher I know what I have to do. And what's necessary to make Iole an educated young woman. But to do that she'll have to take my advice to heart whether she likes it or not."

Rosa took a deep breath, then nodded. "I'll talk to her." She continued climbing, and reached the tutor's side on the wide step in front of the entrance. "But I'm not Iole's mother. Or even her big sister. Maybe she'll listen to me, maybe not. Where is she, anyway?"

Signora Falchi straightened her glasses, puffed out her cheeks, and then let the air escape with a plopping sound. "In the *cellar*!" she uttered.

"What on earth is she doing in the cellar?"

"How *on earth* would I know?"

There it was again. Responsibility. For the business affairs of the Alcantara clan, for her relationship with Alessandro, for herself—and for Iole as well. She felt a sudden urge to get into one of the sports cars in the garage and race off toward the coast at high speed. Or through the mountains. Anywhere so long as she was alone.

"Talk to her," said the tutor, adding, surprisingly gently, "and if you need my help or advice, I'm here for you. For both of you, Signorina Alcantara." It was one of the few moments when she showed that she knew very well that her employer wasn't much older than her pupil.

"Okay," said Rosa. "Thanks. I'll see to it."

The indignation disappeared from Signora Falchi's features, and suddenly there was understanding and sympathy in her face. She *was* a good teacher, and although she could also be a terrible battle-ax, so far Rosa hadn't seriously regretted hiring her.

"Iole is a clever girl," said the tutor. "She just has to give herself—and me—a chance."

Rosa nodded, and headed down to the vaulted cellar.

"They smell of vanilla! And mango! And amber! And snow-flakes!"

"So what do snowflakes smell like?"

"I've never smelled one. I've never seen a real snowflake. Only on TV."

"Amber, then?"

"Like honey. Honey with *raspberries*!" Iole laughed happily, took Rosa's hands, and, doing a silly dance, swung her around in a circle. "They smell *so* good! And there are so many different kinds! And if you order five hundred they cost hardly anything!"

"You ordered five hundred scented candles?"

"Only in that one shop." Iole let go of Rosa but kept dancing in a circle by herself. She had often done that for hours, all alone and chained at the ankle, when she was the Carnevares' hostage.

Rosa groaned. "How many stores did you order from?"

"All of the ones that had great offers!" she gushed, and looked at Rosa out of her pretty eyes as if she couldn't imagine that her friend wouldn't understand. "That's why they have them on sale, see? So that everyone can buy them cheap. Even people who don't earn much money. It's so, *so* great!"

"And what exactly do you do with all those candles?"

"I light a different one every hour. Signora Falchi likes the place to smell good, too."

"That's not true."

But Iole was already changing the subject, as she turned a final pirouette and came to a halt, swaying slightly. "Alessandro called."

Rosa chewed a fingernail. "So?"

"Don't you want to know what he wanted?"

"You're about to tell me anyway."

Iole lowered her voice conspiratorially. "He asked me how I was."

"That's nice of him."

"I think he still worries about me."

"Alessandro worries about a lot of things."

"But he likes me."

Rosa smiled, took Iole by the shoulders, and held her close. "Of course he does. Everyone likes you. Including Signora Falchi. Or she would if she saw more of you."

The dank smell of the cellar clung to Iole's short black hair. She must have been down here for some time.

"But he likes you best of all," said Iole.

"Maybe."

"You know he does!"

"Can we talk about something else?"

"He's had Fundling moved. To a hospital near the sea."

Rosa felt guilty for not having asked about Fundling herself. He'd been in a coma ever since the exchange of gunfire at the Gibellina monument. The doctors had removed the bullet from his head, but four months later he still hadn't regained consciousness. Alessandro paid all his bills, and he had made the decision, some weeks ago, to have Fundling taken from the public hospital to an expensive private sanatorium. Rosa still wasn't sure why. Alessandro said very little about it, but she sensed that he felt responsible for Fundling, maybe because of the crucial role Fundling had played in opposing Cesare

Carnevare, the murderer of Alessandro's parents.

Iole picked up a lock of Rosa's hair and smelled it, as if that were the most natural thing in the world to do. "Have you asked the judge yet?"

"I'll talk to her when . . . as soon as I see her."

"She *must* let me go! I'd love to see Uncle Augusto again."

Augusto Dallamano was Iole's last living relation. Six and a half years before, the rest of her family had been murdered by the Carnevares. Iole herself had been held hostage—until Rosa and Alessandro had freed her. She'd been pestering Rosa for weeks to be allowed to visit her uncle. But that was far from easy to arrange.

"Uncle Augusto taught me how to shoot," announced Iole.

"Terrific."

"With an automatic pistol. And a shotgun, too."

"How old were you then?"

Iole frowned, and counted silently. "Eight?"

Rosa groaned.

Dallamano was living, with a new identity, under the witness protection program of the state prosecutor's office. Rosa had met him once, in Sintra, near Lisbon, and in the park of the Quinta da Regaleira he had answered some of her questions about the mysterious find made by the Dallamanos on their diving expeditions in the Strait of Messina.

"The judge isn't very happy with me right now, did you know that?" Rosa guessed that her explanations would simply bounce off Iole. She had missed six years with other human beings, six years of contact with the outside world. It was easy to like her, but sometimes she could rile you, without knowing what she had done wrong. She had quit therapy after the first session, and Rosa could understand that. Her own experience with psychotherapy had not been a good one.

"Judge Quattrini never gives you anything for free," added Rosa. "If there's nothing in it for her, she isn't interested."

"Then we'll have to give her something."

"Like scented candles?"

"She could have the pine-scented ones. I don't like those so much."

"I kind of think that won't be enough."

"How about some sort of Mafia information?"

Now and then Iole said something so disarmingly naive that Rosa wondered whether there wasn't an element of calculation in it after all. But the girl's mind had already moved on to another thought. "There's something I have to tell you."

"What else did you buy?"

Iole leaned forward conspiratorially, as if someone might be eavesdropping on them. "I explored the cellar."

Rosa looked past her and down the long corridor. She'd been down here only once since the deaths of Florinda and Zoe. The light came from yellow lamps held in latticework grilles at wide intervals on the ceiling. In between the circles of light they cast, strips of shadow moved over the masonry. Like striped tiger fur.

"There's an iron door right at the back, under the north wing," said Iole, with an air of mystery. "And something mechanical humming behind it. An engine, I think."

"It's the old freezer. It still works, but it's not in use. No one can get in there to turn the thing off."

"They can now."

"The door has a lock with a number code."

Iole nodded, and the corners of her mouth turned up in a grin of pride.

Rosa looked at her doubtfully. "You cracked the code?"

"Maybe."

"How did you do it?"

"I tried everything."

The code consisted of four or five digits. Millions of possible combinations. Rosa shook her head, unable to take it in. "Nonsense," she said.

"Well, I had luck. And five days without Signora Come-Do-Your-Lessons-This-Minute."

"Did you write it down?"

"Memorized it."

Shaking her head, Rosa took Iole's hand and said what she assumed she *should* say. "I don't want you running around down here on your own."

"There's nobody else around."

"But it's . . . dark." God, she thought, she was worse than her own mother.

"So?" Iole laughed. "I'm not scared of the dark. It was dark in those places where they shut me up. The huts up in the mountains. The empty farmhouses. Even in the villa on Isola Luna."

Rosa felt that the role of big sister was beyond her. Zoe

hadn't been much good at it, and she wasn't doing any better herself. "Okay," she said, resigned. "I guess there's no real reason why you should stay away from the cellar. Do what you want, but don't come to me later and . . . and complain." Good god.

Iole looked at her triumphantly. "Don't you want to see?"

"See what?"

"The freezer. What's behind the door."

"Is it important?

"Well, important . . ." Iole shrugged her shoulders.

"Then it can wait until tomorrow, okay? I'm worn out." She glanced along the dimly lit cellar corridor again. Dust hovered in the yellow, tiger-striped light. She suppressed a shudder. "Anyway, *I'm* scared of the dark!" She said that with a twinkle in her eye, but at the moment it was closer to the truth than she liked.

Iole poked a finger into her stomach. "You are not!"

Rosa sighed. "Today I am."

A REUNION

ROSA SLEPT LIKE THE dead until morning. Once awake, though, she remembered her date with Alessandro, and got up in frantic haste, showering and eating breakfast in record time.

The helicopter was waiting on the landing pad near the palazzo. In jeans, black sweater, and sneakers she climbed aboard and buckled her seat belt. As usual, the pilot complained about everything that was wrong with the old chopper, but she trusted him when he told her, with a gloomy expression, that they were likely to arrive safe and sound just this once.

Soon the gray volcanic cone of Mount Etna rose ahead of them. To avoid the treacherous winds blowing up its slopes, and to keep out of the monitored airspace of Catania, the pilot took the helicopter farther south over the open sea. Keeping their distance from the coast, they followed its course northeast and then, flying low over the water, raced toward the Strait of Messina between Sicily and the toe of the Italian boot.

Below them, the steely blue Mediterranean rushed past, the crests of the waves throwing the helicopter's shadow back and forth like an oil slick. Apart from a few sailboats, the sea could have been swept clean.

Only some time later did two dots appear on the horizon.

"There they are," said the pilot's voice in Rosa's headset. She was sitting beside him in the cockpit, but the helicopter made too much noise for her to go without ear protectors. Soon after that the headset began to crackle. They were entering the area where Alessandro's people scrambled radio traffic.

The *Gaia*, the Carnevares' 130-foot yacht, lay dazzling white on the water. From above, Rosa saw that the whirlpool on the sundeck had been covered with an awning. No one was using the luxury seating either.

The second boat, rocking on the waves not far from the yacht, was not as impressive at first sight, although Rosa was sure it couldn't be worth much less than the *Gaia*. Belowdecks the modest-looking vessel had hundreds of cubic feet filled with high-tech equipment. She knew what vast sums the *Colony*'s day-to-day operations—not to mention the use of the unmanned drone diver—required.

The helicopter came down squarely on the *Gaia*'s landing pad.

Alessandro, ducking low, hurried toward her as she jumped down from the cockpit. He hugged her while they were still below the circling rotors, and then they walked hand in hand to the railing, as the chopper rose in the air again behind them. The pilot waved a hand in farewell, turned west in a tight curve, and flew back toward the coast.

She gave Alessandro a long kiss as the noise of the helicopter died away in the distance. He held her tight as if the wind might carry her off with it across the sea. A hot, tingling sensation ran over her from head to foot, so unexpected and exciting that it took her a moment to work out what it was—her new skin reacting to his touch. Its tinge of pink had faded by now, but her nerves were in turmoil as she felt Alessandro near again. She had expected a chill, the sign of the snake stirring inside her, but instead a comfortable warmth took possession of her. She nestled closer in his arms.

When they finally moved apart, she realized that so far she had felt him but hadn't looked at him. She looked now—and it was a shock.

He was pale and seemed exhausted, with dark rings under his eyes. His brown hair was even messier than usual, and the dimples that were always there couldn't disguise the fact that he clearly hadn't had much to smile about in the past few days. Even in his weary state he was still outrageously good-looking, and his green eyes easily outshone his pallor, but she could tell that something was wrong. All at once her own exhaustion disappeared.

"You look terrible," she said.

"I haven't been sleeping much. And when I did, I had bad dreams."

She'd had those, too, but she had already decided to keep the reason for them to herself for the time being. Not just out of consideration for him, but also out of sheer self-interest. She wasn't going to let Tano's ghost cast a shadow over their reunion. She had that much power over it. Tano might have taken possession of her body, but with a little effort she could wipe him from her memory.

"If I'd known you were coming here, I'd have—"

She put her hand on the back of his neck and silenced him gently with another kiss. Only then did she ask, "What's wrong?"

"Well, my own people would like to be rid of me, and sooner or later someone will try to do something about it, but that's nothing new." He smiled with the mixture of melancholy and determination that no one had mastered as well as Alessandro. "How about you?" he asked. "You stopped calling."

"Later, okay?"

He looked her in the eye. "You've found out something."

"Give me a little time?"

"They hurt you."

"Alessandro, please . . . I'll tell you all about it, but for now I just want to be with you. We don't have to tell each other all our problems right away."

He took her hand and led her from the landing pad to the wood-paneled interior of the yacht, and along a stairway with gold fittings down to the main deck. When they were in the open again, Rosa saw that the *Gaia* and the *Colony* were fastened together with cables as thick as a man's arm. They moved from one vessel to the other along a gangplank.

Two men and a woman, all in blue overalls, were standing by the *Colony*'s rail, smoking and looking at them. One of the men, gray-haired and tanned brown by the sun, nodded briefly in Rosa's direction. Professor Stuart Campbell, Englishman and egocentric treasure hunter—he was in charge of the investigations that Alessandro had commissioned the group of marine researchers and archaeologists to carry out.

"Signorina Alcantara," he greeted her.

"Professor Campbell." She didn't like the way he looked at her, as if she were some dumb little blonde who had hooked Alessandro. However, she wasn't interested enough in Campbell for it to infuriate her seriously.

Alessandro let her enter the control room of the *Colony* ahead of him. Half a dozen men and women, also in overalls, were sitting close together in front of a great deal of radar and echo-sounding equipment. The windowless room might as well have been inside the drone that was operated from here by remote control through the trenches and ravines on the seabed. The air was stuffy, and cigarette smoke from outside drifted in through the doorway, which did nothing to improve the atmosphere, but the others didn't seem bothered.

"Here," said Alessandro, pointing to one of the screens. "Take a look at that."

It was a three-dimensional diagram of the seabed, covering three hundred square feet. Alessandro used a touch pad to alter the perspective. As he moved two fingertips apart on the pad, the virtual camera zoomed in on the curving lines of the pattern.

"Those are the exact coordinates from the Dallamanos' documents," he said.

Rosa looked intently at the graphics. They took some getting used to. "Looks empty." Which would explain why when she and Alessandro had tried diving, twice, they had found nothing either time.

"Wrong," said a red-haired woman in her midthirties. Rosa had forgotten her name, but on her last visit the redhead had been the only one on board who would condescend to give her more than a brief greeting. "To call it empty isn't quite accurate."

"But?"

The woman archaeologist moved Alessandro's hand aside and used the touch pad herself. Perspective and size changed rapidly as she zoomed in on an inconspicuous part of the network of lines. A brief tap on the keypad, and at once a second and much finer pattern overlaid the first.

Rosa's brow wrinkled. "Stones."

"That's what we thought ourselves at first," said the woman. "Not statues, anyway—not what we were looking for."

Rosa glanced inquiringly at Alessandro.

Patience, his eyes said.

The researcher dragged a cursor down to the edge of the picture. A column of figures in the corner changed. The framework filled in from the outside; then it looked as if someone had placed a gray cloth over the structure.

Rosa leaned closer to the screen. "*Round* stones?" she asked skeptically.

"Plinths."

"Twelve of them," added Alessandro. "All inside that square."

Rosa ran her fingers through her hair. "Does that mean . . . ?"

"Someone got here ahead of us," said the woman. "Someone snapped up the statues from under our noses."

"But no one knows the coordinates!"

"Are you sure?"

"Dallamano was taking us for a ride," she murmured.

Alessandro shook his head. "Not necessarily."

"You of all people defending him? He almost killed you."

"According to him, your aunt had the documents in her hands, at least for a few hours. And Pantaleone got them from her. We don't know who may have been told about the contents of the documents, by either or both of them."

"Not to mention the fact," the researcher added, "that this area is more than three miles offshore, outside the country's borders, so in theory anyone could have come across them. Maybe by chance, maybe because he knew what he was looking for."

Rosa snorted. "Chance!"

"We don't believe that either," one of the men said behind them. Rosa could smell the cigarette smoke that he brought into the control room even before she turned to him.

Professor Campbell pointed to a monitor on the opposite wall. One of the men at the controls vacated his seat for the professor. Rosa exchanged a glance with Alessandro, who nodded encouragingly at her.

"Let's get to the reason why I asked you to come here, Signore Carnevare. Look at this." The treasure hunter indicated the screen, where the different camera angles of the underwater drone were changing in quick succession. Finally he stopped at one of them. "This one was taken by the starboard camera on *Colony Two*."

One of the floodlights moved over the seabed. Crevices and holes gaped wide in the rock. The Strait of Messina was constantly exposed to underwater earth tremors, and was encrusted with geological scar tissue.

"How deep is it?" asked Rosa.

"Not very deep. A little over a hundred and twenty feet. We're also searching the bed with divers, but that's laborious, and not half as effective as the instruments on board *Colony Two*." Campbell kept the photograph on the monitor and tapped the glass with a ballpoint. "This is what I'm interested in. It's one of our plinths."

Rosa couldn't see much more than a raised round shape, with a few angular chunks of rock in the background.

"It measures roughly three feet in diameter, but it's probably taller than that. We can assume that, like the other eleven, it's sunk deep into the seabed. But we're going to take a closer look at it."

The dim, ghostly illumination from the searchlight and the floating particles visible in the foreground of the picture reminded Rosa of the Dallamano photographs. Those, however, had shown a statue of two animals: a panther upright on his hind legs, with the broad body of a giant snake coiled around him. The reptile's head hung before the eyes of the big cat, and the two of them were looking at each other.

"We've compared the photos you gave us with these." Campbell pressed a combination of keys. The picture of the panther and the snake that they had found at Iole's house moved over the picture on the screen like a film. The perspectives were not exactly the same, but because of the rocky structures in the background there was no possible doubt. It was the same place, but the statue was gone.

"Fuck," whispered Rosa.

The treasure hunter smiled. "My sentiments exactly."

She glanced at Alessandro. The greenish light from the screen intensified the color of his eyes. For a moment she couldn't look away from him. "Did you know about this?" she asked.

"Not until yesterday. I was going to tell you about it today."

"Does it mean that's it? Everything here was all for nothing?"

"Definitely not for nothing," said Campbell drily. "Wait until you see my invoice."

"Wasn't salvaging the statues supposed to be your job?" she asked sharply.

"I'm not through yet." For the first time he spoke as if he took her seriously. "I have some information that will be new to your friend as well."

Alessandro's cheek muscles twitched. "Go on, let's hear it."

Campbell zoomed in closer on the round block of stone. "As I said, the plinths probably go down several feet into the seabed. That assumption is based on values drawn from past experience of the geological nature of this region, tremors, volcanic activity, et cetera, et cetera. . . . But let's look at the surface of the stone, so far as the picture quality allows it. I already have divers down there who will look more closely at our find, put it under a magnifying glass, but it looks like someone cut the statues neatly away from their plinths."

"You mean each plinth and its statue were carved from a single piece of rock?" asked Alessandro.

Campbell nodded. "Do you see that fluted structure? What we have there are either traces left by extremely fine conventional cutters, or a laser cutter manufactured specially for an underwater operation like this one."

"Then someone must have invested a lot of money to get hold of those statues," said Rosa thoughtfully.

"Going down to a hundred and twenty feet isn't a problem for a well-trained amateur diver, and certainly not for experienced deep-sea or military divers. With the right equipment, you can stay at that depth for quite some time. However, we've calculated that to sever a stone block like that cleanly would probably take several hours. Which means that the teams down there either worked with top-quality respiratory technology, probably the kind used by military divers, or worked in several shifts."

Rosa's hand was lying on the back of Campbell's chair. When she felt the touch of Alessandro's fingers, they exchanged a fleeting smile. She couldn't have said just what she had expected of this venture. She had trained intensively as a diver herself, but when she and Alessandro had finally gone down, they had been unable to find anything but rocks and mud. Only after that had they hired a professional salvage team.

"What's more, we're talking about twelve statues," the

treasure hunter went on, "and we can now say for certain that at least seven were removed from their plinths by the same high-precision methods. In the photos you gave us, the statues were all of panthers and snakes. Some of them were in pieces, or badly damaged. But even those remains must have been salvaged to the very last fragment, all but the plinths. Whoever did it was very thorough, and also treated his find with great respect. Those people didn't make it easy for themselves. And we have to assume that they could afford to work without any financial restrictions."

Rosa nodded to Alessandro. She silently formed the word *TABULA* with her lips.

Campbell tapped his keyboard, and the underwater picture disappeared. He half turned and spoke to one of the women at the instruments. "Give me number thirty-four on seven, Ruth, please."

The gray-blue surface of the sea came on-screen, obviously a photo taken at a steep angle from a great height.

"What you see here," Campbell told Rosa and Alessandro, "is secret material that I . . . well, let's say I borrowed it."

"Looks like Google Earth," Rosa commented.

"Almost. And that's why I mention it, so that you won't be surprised, later, about certain items I'll be charging you for." The treasure hunter paused and then went on. "The Mediterranean between North Africa and southern Italy is a part of the world under more surveillance than most. And around Sicily the security network is biggest of all." He added, with an ironic undertone, "There must be a great many people in these parts earning their money through illegal activities."

"With stolen military photographs?" Rosa suggested.

"I'm about to show you an enlargement of our mysterious picture. If the water was as transparent as everyone thinks, we'd be able to see the twelve statues now."

"Or their plinths," said Alessandro.

"No," the professor contradicted him, "because this picture was taken before the statues were salvaged. As you'll see."

"When was that?" asked Rosa.

"On January seventeenth, just under a month ago. Of course there was no nonstop filming of every square sea mile, but photographs were taken at regular intervals. Every yard of the Mediterranean has some satellite camera or other turned on it about every forty-five minutes. All we had to do was get hold of the material we wanted and evaluate it."

"So?"

"Here, forty-seven minutes later." The picture changed, and this time a boat could be clearly seen at its center. "And again three-quarters of an hour later." No change; the vessel was still in the same place. "There they are," said Campbell.

Alessandro narrowed his eyes. "Who?"

"Not the army, that at least is certain. And the boat we're looking at here is obviously smaller than the *Colony*. It has no crane, just a set of cable winches along the rail. Obviously the statues were dragged away underwater, then brought to the surface and unloaded somewhere else."

He zoomed in closer to the vessel, but now the picture was so pixelated that he withdrew again with a grunt. "Ruth, how the hell do I get that filter on-screen?"

The woman behind them at the console told him a sequence of keys. When Campbell entered the code, his face brightened again. This time the picture was much sharper. Once again he tapped his ballpoint on the glass surface. "Here, and here, and here . . . those are the divers they sent down."

The three figures were still not clearly visible, only pale outlines at the rail.

"Looks like they're not wearing diving suits," said Alessandro.

"Strange, isn't it?"

"Do you mean they went down there without any diving equipment?"

Campbell nodded. "No suits. No oxygen flasks. Not even flippers, for God's sake!"

Alessandro shook his head, baffled. "What exactly are we looking at, please?"

Campbell cleared his throat. "Four pictures farther on, they're coming up from the water again." He brought up a new picture on the screen: the boat, the sea—and the three pale outlines, two of them still in the water, the other on a ladder outside the hull. "About three hours later. Not nearly enough time for three of them to cut seven of those statues away from their plinths and collect the leftover fragments."

"Maybe they went down again later," said Rosa.

"We've checked all the pictures from the day when you two were there to the day when we began our investigations. Nothing. The boat was there only on January seventeenth, and for less than four hours. And as far as we can work it out, only those three divers went into the water during that time. Without any equipment apart from a few tools that were probably cutters of some kind."

Campbell paused, to let his words sink in. Rosa and Alessandro said nothing.

"But that's not all," he finally said. "The vessel set off again a little later. It's not in the next photograph. However, we did succeed in tracing its route." He was going to give Ruth instructions over his shoulder, but she was already ahead of him.

"Got it," she called. Rosa heard her fingers tapping the keys.

Several satellite pictures appeared on the screen in quick succession, but this time the coordinates at the edge changed with each photo. "They're on their way south," Campbell explained. "They go south for about an hour. Then they come to this."

Rosa narrowed her eyes as if she could see the picture more clearly that way. Alessandro whistled through his teeth.

The boat looked tiny now. It was lying alongside a much larger ship at least ten times its length. The huge vessel was snow white, with complex superstructures, many decks, and several helicopter landing pads.

The next picture came up. The smaller boat beside the gigantic white vessel had disappeared.

"It doesn't reappear anywhere in this area," said Campbell. "They must have taken it on board. Including what was hanging beneath the surface from the cable winches. It all seems to have happened very fast. I'd say they were pros—except that even professionals would need some kind of breathing apparatus and diving suits. As it is, I can only say I haven't the faintest idea who they were. Not the army. And not any treasure hunters that I've ever heard of. Experts, for sure—but not from the same planet as mine."

Still baffled, Alessandro shook his head. "That's a cruise ship."

Campbell nodded. His fingers moved nimbly over the keyboard, and he zoomed in on the picture.

The view centered on one of the landing pads, indicated on-screen by a letter *H* inside a circle. Rosa held her breath.

Something was inscribed on the deck in big black letters, easily visible to pilots flying that way.

Stabat Mater.

REVENGE

"THANASSIS," SHE EXCLAIMED.

Alessandro and Professor Campbell looked away from the monitor in surprise. "You know the vessel?" asked the treasure hunter.

"Only by name. It belongs to a Greek shipowner called Thanassis."

"I thought he was dead," said Alessandro.

"There were reports in the media a few years back that he was very sick," replied the professor. "But there was never any official announcement of his death, only all kinds of rumors and assumptions. It's a fact that he hasn't been seen in public since."

"And now he's developed a taste for underwater archaeology?" asked Rosa. But she was really thinking of something very different. The Dream Room. Danai Thanassis dancing in her hoop skirt, protected by her bodyguards. Her dreamy, almost ecstatic expression.

Campbell shrugged his shoulders. "All we could find out in a hurry was that the *Stabat Mater* has been sailing between Europe and North America for years. She never seems to stay in any harbor for long, usually just for a few days. Clearly it's impossible to book a passage on board. Either the cruises are reserved for very exclusive customers, or she crosses the Atlantic as good as empty. A kind of ghost ship." He grinned, but Rosa didn't feel like laughing. There was something wraith-like about Danai Thanassis, yes, but she was certainly no ghost.

"Do you think old Thanassis is on board?" asked Alessandro. "And that's why no one sees him these days?"

"Possibly. We got these photos only yesterday evening, so we've hardly had time to research more than the most essential features."

"The shipowner's daughter lives on the *Stabat Mater*," said Rosa. "I think."

Alessandro looked at her in surprise. "How do you know all this?"

She searched her mind for a way to evade the question, but then said, straight out, "From Michele."

He stared at her.

"Let's talk about it later," she suggested.

Campbell looked over his shoulder again. "Ruth, did you find out anything about the route after that?"

The woman in overalls shook her head. "No, nothing. Access is barred, even to our contact."

Alessandro didn't take his eyes off Rosa. "You talked to Michele?"

"Not now." Although everything in her urged her to tell him the truth—and ask what he knew about it himself—she was saving all that until they were alone. She was already annoyed with herself for mentioning Thanassis at all.

Clearly Campbell could sense the tension between them. "Looks like we won't get anything more on the later route of the *Stabat Mater*. We know that she left the Strait of Messina going southwest, but after that her trail is lost in the open Mediterranean. We can't find any more satellite pictures of her. Obviously they were all deleted after my contact got us that first series of photos."

"The Thanassis family has deeper pockets than ours," said Alessandro. There was unconcealed belligerence in his voice. Rosa had always liked that about him, but at the moment it made her furious. Why did he think he could blame her? Because she'd gone against his wishes by getting in touch with the New York Carnevares? She was the one who'd almost been torn to pieces in Central Park. She didn't need him playing the role of her protector in hindsight.

Campbell rose from his swivel chair and looked at the two of them, his eyebrows raised. "How about leaving us to get on with our work now? And there seems to be plenty that you two want to discuss."

Reluctantly, Rosa stopped staring at Alessandro and left the control room.

"Keep me up to date," she heard him say behind her, and then she hurried over the gangplank to the *Gaia* and waited for him to join her on the upper deck.

"You knew!" she cried into the wind. "As soon as I told you about the party in the Village, you knew!"

She was standing by the rail, both hands clutching the cool

iron, staring out at the horizon. Where the sky and the sea met, she could see the blur of a brownish-gray line. Sicily.

The wind tasted salty on her lips and stung her eyes. But she didn't want to turn around. He was standing behind her on the deck, and had listened in silence as she told him everything, but she couldn't bring herself to look at him. She wished she could be somewhere else. Alone with her anger and grief and her unanswered questions.

"I wanted to find out the truth," he said gloomily. "Until you told me on the phone, I had no idea it had happened at that party. You have to believe me. And after that . . . right after that I began asking questions. There are people very close to Michele who owe me. I get information from them." He added, more quietly, "About that, too."

"And when were you planning to tell me the truth? That it was Tano? And Michele."

He said nothing for some time, and she heard him take a step toward her. Maybe he was thinking of touching her, but then he stopped. "Michele will pay for that," he said. "He won't get away this time."

She closed her eyes, blinking the tears away. "I only wanted to *know*. To hear the truth. You should have left the way I went about it up to me." She slowly shook her head, got swirling strands of hair in her mouth, and brushed them back from her face. "All I wanted was for you to be honest with me."

He moved closer; she could feel him now, but she tried to suppress the feverish tingling that he set off when he came near her. Not now.

"I didn't want to keep it secret from you," he defended. "But what did you expect? For me to call you in New York and tell you over the phone that it was Tano, of all people—" His voice was hoarse; he paused, then went on hesitantly. "That it was that bastard and Michele . . . that they were behind it?"

She thought again how exhausted and drained he looked. Maybe discussions until late into the night weren't the only reason for that.

Slowly, she turned to him. "I have to be able to trust you. Trust you entirely and forever. I don't want any secrets between us, or at least no secrets that have to do with *both* of us."

He didn't avoid her eyes, but she could see from looking at him that he would have liked to. "I wondered how to tell you. And when the best time would be. But there's never a good moment to say: By the way, the bastard who raped you was my cousin."

She gently touched his cheek with her hand, ran it over his unruly hair. "So now Michele simply gets away with it."

"Michele is going to be sorry he ever set eyes on you," he told her. "And Tano is dead."

"But not because of *that*," she said. "Only because he wanted to do it again. Because he was a perverted asshole . . ." This would have been the time to rage and scream or do something else dramatic. But she didn't feel like any of that. She still didn't remember anything much of that night, not even pain—those hours might have been deleted from her mind. Now, though, she wondered whether the way she blacked them out was really blindness. Weakness. A failing in her.

"Tano is dead," she said, repeating his words. "So now I can't even wish for him to die. Or suffer. He was dead before he even knew what was happening to him. And maybe you think it's terrible for me to say that I'd have liked it to take a long time and hurt him. Hurt him badly. Because he deserved it. Because even in his fucking grave he still deserves all the pain I can imagine."

He closed his eyes for a moment. "There's something else. I don't know if it makes any difference, but . . ."

She looked questioningly at him as he searched for words.

"Michele was there, but he didn't rape you. Or so my informant says. There were four of them, and Michele certainly told all the others what to do. But Tano was the only one who touched you."

"It makes no difference who just watched and who was—" She stopped when she realized what he was telling her. "Tano is Nathaniel's father," she whispered tonelessly.

Alessandro said nothing. He just looked at her. She was grateful for that. Pity was the last thing she wanted.

Dazed, she shook her head. "It doesn't matter."

"Michele will pay for it—for everything." She was as keenly aware of his eyes as she was of his hands when he took her fingers in them.

"I don't want to lose you as well," she said. "Revenge isn't worth that. Definitely not."

"Are we supposed to act like nothing happened?"

"No." She leaned against the rail and drew him closer to her. "That girl, her name was Jessie . . . he was carrying her in his mouth like a trophy. That's what he cares about. To prove who he is and what he's capable of. That's why he has those hunting parties. And *that's* why he deserves to die."

"He's a bloodthirsty bastard. Tano idolized him."

She felt the rail cold against her back, but everything inside her was numb. "What else did you find out?"

"That business about Michele's brother and the others—that's the truth. Someone is killing the Carnevares closest to Michele, and I'd feel better if I knew who and why."

"He suspects you."

Alessandro smiled grimly. "Me!"

"You know what he did. And he knows about the two of us. If he's even slightly acquainted with you, he must realize that you won't give him any peace."

He bent his head, and she noticed the surprise in his bright, cat-like eyes. "Do *you* believe that? That I've already started taking revenge on him? That I'm in the process of wiping out his family?"

"Not if you tell me it isn't true."

He was silent for a long time. "I have nothing at all to do with it," he said at last.

Then she was the one to smile, and she had never felt so much like an Alcantara.

"That's too bad," she said, and when she kissed him, she sensed his shiver.

FUNDLING'S SLEEP

AN ARSENAL OF LIFE-SUPPORT devices stood beside the sleeping man's bed, but most of them were not in use. Fundling was breathing by himself, but had to be artificially fed through a tube into his stomach. His face was pale and drawn. His thick black hair had grown back since the operation on his skull, but it was not as long yet as it had been when he worked as a chauffeur for the Carnevares. And as an informer for the *capo dei capi*—as well as for Judge Quattrini.

Rosa wondered what else, unknown to her, Fundling had been.

"He looks peaceful," said the nurse who had just put fresh flowers beside his bed.

"He looks dead," said Rosa.

The nurse wrinkled her nose and seemed about to say something, but she must have been deterred by the black look Rosa gave her, because she just turned and left the room.

"Who sent the flowers?" asked Rosa.

"It's all part of the service here," said Alessandro. "A fresh arrangement every day." He was standing by the window of the single room. Outside, a well-tended garden reached to the top of the steep cliff on which the hospital stood. The crests of the waves sparkled like rubies in the evening sunlight.

"What a waste of money," she said, looking at the vase.

"They choose blossoms with a particularly strong scent."

"To drown out the corpse smell?"

"He isn't a corpse."

She sat down on the edge of Fundling's bed and touched his hand. "He got a bullet in his brain, and who knows what harm it did there? He's been in a coma for four months. How is that so different from being dead? Apart from the fact that he's breathing."

"They say that if it becomes necessary, I will have to make the decision. Whether to let him keep going like this, or . . ."

"But you're not even related."

"No one here's interested in that. Officially, he isn't in this hospital at all."

She glanced up at him. "But you had him moved here from a public hospital. So how—"

"His files say something different now."

"You had him declared dead?" It shouldn't have surprised her. In a grotesque way it confirmed what she had just said.

Alessandro turned to look at her. "I've made worse decisions that were easier for me, all the same. But this is about Fundling. He and I grew up together. Reading the word *dead* in his files was almost as bad as seeing him lying here. However, now no one will ask any more questions about what happened at Gibellina. Plus, he's safe only as long as no one knows he's here. Word got around that he was working for the judge, and as you know, that's something the clans would never forgive."

"But he's in a coma!"

"It hasn't been that long here since babies were thrown into vats of acid because their fathers had given evidence against Cosa Nostra to the state prosecutor. Do you think Fundling's condition would stop people bent on that kind of revenge?"

"He can hardly be any quieter than he is."

"Fundling will wake up again one day."

"You think so?" she asked sadly.

He pressed his lips together until all the blood drained out of them. Then he nodded. "Yes."

She turned back to the bed. The nurse had been right. At first sight Fundling did seem peaceful. Only if you looked more closely did it seem as if a silent battle were raging behind that lifeless mask. Rosa wasn't sure what to make of it. In the first few days his eyes had moved beneath their lids, but that had stopped some time ago. His features were still now, and yet she thought she saw movement behind them. As if she could see him thinking—thinking and feeling.

It occurred to her that the flowers hid the picture that Iole had left beside Fundling's hospital bed. The photo of Fundling's dog, Sarcasmo. Rosa stood up, moved the vase aside, and pulled the frame closer to the edge of the bedside table. Maybe it was pointless, but she wanted Fundling to see the photograph if he ever opened his eyes again. He and Sarcasmo had been inseparable, and even after four months she felt every day how much the dog missed him.

Maybe he could hear everything they said. It seemed strange to her to talk to him when there was anyone else present—even Alessandro—and she decided to come by herself next time.

Alessandro followed her eyes to the photo of the dog and

smiled sadly. "Iole says that whatever happens, she's not giving him up."

"She loves Sarcasmo."

"I phoned her while you were gone. She sounded cheerful. The lessons seem to be doing her good."

"She's driving her tutor crazy. Instead of studying, she's been sitting down in the cellar for days on end trying out numerical combinations on a lock."

"She was locked up herself for six years. If anyone knows how to occupy herself on her own, it's Iole."

"But she doesn't need to do that anymore." Another of those maternal remarks—she could have kicked herself.

"How many of *your* old habits have you abandoned since you came to Italy?"

"I'm not stealing now," she said defiantly. "Well, not often."

"You're the head of a Cosa Nostra clan," he said, amused. "You steal nonstop, twenty-four hours a day, without ever lifting a finger yourself."

"It's not the same."

"Tell that to the judge."

His grin infected her, and she leaned forward and gave him a long kiss.

Suddenly it was as if she felt Fundling's eyes on her. But when she reluctantly moved her lips away from Alessandro's and looked at the sleeping man, he still lay there with his lids closed, the same as ever.

Alessandro was smiling so irresistibly that she found it difficult to change the subject. "I'm going to see Trevini tomorrow," she said.

"Better leave him alone, if you ask me."

"I have to rely on him. He's the only one who knows all about the business affairs of the Alcantaras."

"He sent you that video to drive a wedge between us. Maybe even to make you turn to him. So how straightforward do you think his intentions are where your business is concerned?"

"If he really has the profits of the Alcantara companies at heart, as he says, he can't ignore our relationship," she said. "Suppose we took it into our heads to merge the business of both clans?"

He laughed—a bitter laugh. "We wouldn't survive ten minutes. Trevini's not the only one who would—"

"You underestimate him."

"One more reason for you not to go and see him alone. Wheelchair-bound or not, he's dangerous. You don't know what he's planning or what surprises he still has up his sleeve. That video was only bait."

"I can't have him plotting behind my back." She steadily returned his gaze, and at last he seemed to realize that it was pointless to go on arguing.

"You've made up your mind."

"I don't have a choice."

"And you think the video really was shot by this girl Valerie?"

"I was there when she was filming it. The only question is, how did it get into Trevini's hands?" She hopped off the edge of the bed, walked past him, and looked over the gardens at the shimmering sea. Cutters were on the way to their fishing grounds. It was going to be a clear, starlit night, and the moon hung in the sky, bright white in the evening twilight. "You'll look after Iole, won't you, if . . . ?" She watched the window cloud with the moisture of her breath.

"Don't talk like that."

"If something happens to me, either tomorrow or some other day, then I want you to look after her. And Sarcasmo."

"I'm not going to let anything happen to you."

"Promise me." She turned slowly around to face him, and saw that the evening light was bathing the whole room in gold. Fundling, the furnishings, the walls—and Alessandro. Everything seemed to glow. "Iole has no one else in the world."

"I know. And I'm as fond of her as you are."

"Sarcasmo has special diet dog food."

That made him laugh.

"And he loves his Kong."

A sound came from the bed. They both swung around.

A wasp, buzzing, was hovering over Fundling's closed eyes.

Without thinking what she was doing, Rosa lunged forward and opened her mouth—and out shot her long, forked snake's tongue, catching the insect in the air and crushing it in a fraction of a second. Before she realized what had happened, she was standing there, bent double and coughing. She spat the dead wasp out on the floor.

She murmured a curse that even she didn't understand. Her tongue quickly went back to its usual shape, but the horrible taste was left in her mouth.

"I didn't mean to do that," she groaned, shaking with disgust. "It . . . it just happened."

Alessandro put his arms around her. "We can learn how to control it," he said. "How to start the transformation deliberately. Or how to stop it in its tracks."

"And you of all people are going to teach me?" She remembered, only too well, the outbursts of temper that always ended with his transformation into his panther form—at the expense of his jeans and T-shirts.

"It's all just a question of practice."

She raised one eyebrow. "So what do you get up to in secret when I'm not around, *capo* Alessandro?"

He kissed her, but when his lips opened she retreated; she didn't trust her tongue. It probably still tasted of the wasp's poison.

"Well?" she whispered.

"I'll show you how to do it."

"Here and now?"

"No." He was openly grinning now, but with such charm that she felt dizzy. "I know a place where no one will disturb us."

CREATURES OF THE SAME SPECIES

"YOU CAN'T BE SERIOUS."

"I come here often. And I know how we can get in."

"Get into a *zoo*?"

He gently took her face in both hands and smiled. "Trust me."

"Okay."

"Are you sure?"

"Hell, no. At least, not if we stand around here any longer."

At Valcorrente they had left Route 121. In daytime, they could probably have seen the gray volcanic slopes of Etna from here. Now, however, just before midnight, the grounds of the Etnaland water park were a brightly lit island surrounded by deep darkness. Alessandro had parked his Ferrari on a path in the fields, next to a high chain-link fence.

They walked along the fence on foot for about fifty yards and then reached a place where it had been cut neatly apart to waist height. Several small twists of wire held the incision together so that it couldn't be seen at first glance. Alessandro removed them and held one corner back for Rosa to slip through.

"We're *such* a couple of criminals," she whispered.

"I recently donated a hundred thousand euros to the zoo."

Alessandro followed her in, and closed the gap in the wire netting again. "And one of my firms delivers animal feed on special terms."

She made a face. "And let's not forget what kind of animal feed it is."

"That's all in the past. Since the Carnevares got out of the disposal business, everything's above board."

It had taken a good deal of courage—and great difficulty—to give up one of his clan's most profitable ventures overnight, so she merely nodded, and looked through the bushes on the inside of the fence at a path leading farther into the place.

"Aren't there any night watchmen?"

"Yes, two," he replied. "But they're sitting in their lodge at the main entrance playing cards. One of them goes around every three hours. So we still have"—he looked at his watch—"two hours and twenty minutes."

There were only a few lights on, here and there, inside the zoo. Several of the side paths lay in darkness, and the sounds of nocturnal animals came from a couple of the enclosures, but all was quiet in most of them.

They reached a place where two walkways met at a sharp angle. Like an arrow, they pointed to an enormous cage as high as a building. "Cesare financed that," said Alessandro. "Probably the only decent thing he ever did in his life."

The front of it had to be at least thirty yards wide. Rosa couldn't see how far back the cage went on the inside. Two lamps illuminated the paved courtyard, but the light from them did not reach very far into the enclosure. Moving closer, she could tell that the ground sloped downward. Farther inside, there were angular rock formations, but she couldn't see the lowest point.

Alessandro went over to the bars of the cage and breathed in deeply.

She wrinkled her nose. "You smell better."

He had closed his eyes. In the dim light, she saw a black trail of fur rising from his leather jacket and up the back of his neck.

"This is what you call a controlled transformation?"

He opened his eyes again. "Come closer."

She took another step, but stopped at arm's length from the bars, remembering only too well the big cats who had hunted them on Isola Luna.

"These won't hurt you," he assured her.

Her heart was pumping an icy chill into her veins, but she went to stand beside him in front of the iron bars. Suddenly she didn't mind the sharp, animal smell coming from the enclosure anymore.

"Can you see them?" he asked.

Her eyes were getting used to the darkness. Or was her snake's vision taking over? Something down there radiated warmth. The interior of the enclosure was like a crater with graduated rocks, and niches and openings among them. Farther down, a pool of water lay as dark and still as if it were made of glass. On the left bank, the night had come together into a formless, dense heap of something.

"The pride," said Alessandro.

"Won't they pick up your scent?"

"Most of them are asleep. But look over there . . . and there." He pointed to several places in the shadow of the rocks, and she realized that they had been under observation for some time. Big cats, as still as statues, sat on rocky outcrops. The longer Rosa looked, the more clearly she saw their eyes glowing in the light of the lamps on the courtyard.

"They're keeping watch while the others sleep," said Alessandro.

She moved a little closer to him, and he put his arm around her waist. She felt his muscular chest rising and falling faster, and pressing more firmly against hers. He put his hand under her long hair, stroked her neck. Could he sense the chill that was now reaching her lips? Her hands caressed his back, and she knew that panther fur was growing on his backbone under the leather jacket, spreading over his shoulder blades.

Smiling, she bent her head. "What were you thinking of doing?"

"Can't you guess?"

"You lured me here," she said with mock indignation, "in order to—"

"To show you how I've learned to control it." The corners of his mouth turned down. "Only it won't work as well if we do it right here."

She returned his grin and let go of him. "So?"

"So I have to go in there."

She shook her head. "No, you don't."

"Nothing will happen to me. They know me."

Doubtfully, she looked from him to the motionless animals on the rocks. They seemed wild and untamed, even in captivity.

When she looked into Alessandro's eyes again, they were glowing emerald green in the darkness, like the eyes of the big cats.

"You do understand, don't you?" he asked gently.

She shook her head, but perhaps too soon.

Among the older Arcadians, she knew, there was a legend that the souls of their dead slipped into newborn animals of their own species, so that no Arcadian ever really died, but led an eternal life in an animal body, generation after generation. If that was true, there was a good chance that some of the big cats in this enclosure had once been human beings, ancestors of Alessandro and the other Panthera.

She shook her head again, incredulous but also fascinated. "*They* taught you how to do it?"

He nodded, but then added, "I haven't mastered it perfectly yet. It works sometimes, but not always. All the same, we can learn from them."

There was movement in the sleeping pride. One of the animals got up, strolled down to the water, and drank. Then it returned to the others and lay down on the ground again.

"Learn how?" she asked.

"By accepting that we're like them. We have to give ourselves up to them. It's a bit like meditation." He shrugged his shoulders as if he found it embarrassing to discuss. "By becoming one with them."

"May the Force be with you, and all that?"

"Roughly speaking."

He ran his fingers through her hair, and then lightly stroked her arm down to the wrist. His hand reached for hers. "The Hungry Man and the others who miss the old times, all that killing and hunting . . . they make us forget that Arcadia isn't only about barbarism and bloodshed. There's also something else. Something . . . beautiful."

"And I'm supposed to stand around here while you go in?"

"You can come with me if you like."

"I had all the Panthera I needed in New York." She felt his hand, sensed his skin on hers. "Well, more or less."

He kissed her, then let go of her and moved along the side of the cage. "Wait here."

She was about to follow him, but then she stopped and just watched him go. "Whatever you think." She looked for the chill she had just been feeling and was surprised to find that it had worn off.

In the darkness, she heard hinges creak as a door opened in the side of the enclosure. She couldn't see him now, but somewhere keys turned in locks. The entrance was locked again, and she heard his clothes rustling as he took them off.

He appeared a little later, naked, on the top circle. The eyes of the big cats on guard followed him, but they didn't leave their stations. A leopard, sitting closest to him as he passed, purred quietly.

Stepping steadily and surely, Alessandro climbed down the rocks. Rosa bit her lower lip, but realized that she felt no fear.

As he had asked her to do just now, she trusted him entirely.

The light from the courtyard turned his body to bronze. His muscles rippled beneath his skin; only on his back was it covered by the black hair of his panther coat. The fur was not spreading any farther. Alessandro had his transformation under control.

He didn't have to climb now; the rocks were laid out like a wide spiral staircase, and he followed it patiently down. Rosa was watching every step he took, every supple movement of his muscles on his upper arms and thighs, his chest, the sharply defined musculature of his stomach. Once, just once, he looked up and smiled at her. Don't, she thought. Concentrate.

Down by the water, several of the animals raised their heads, picking up his scent. A lion growled softly, but not aggressively, more like he wanted to calm the other members of his pride. She realized, for the first time, that down there all the species of big cats were lying close to one another, tigers next to lions, leopards beside panthers. Why was there no competition among them? No struggle to establish dominance?

She thought of the snakes in the greenhouse of the Palazzo Alcantara. She had been into it only a couple of times, and had never again experienced the place as intensely as on her first visit. But there, too, different species of snakes lived in close quarters. Boa constrictors and pythons, adders and vipers. Venomous cobras and other reptiles side by side.

Alessandro reached the bank of the little lake. The pride

was lying on the other side of it. Without hesitation, he went toward them along the edge of the water.

The big cats got up. Only a few at first, then all the rest in a single shadowy ripple of movement.

He walked into the middle of the pride.

Its leader was waiting for him at the end of an avenue that the others formed for him. Alessandro and the lion stood facing each other as if they were of equal rank. As if the lion did not have the power to tear the boy facing him limb from limb within seconds.

They looked at each other for a long time, while the pride stood around them, motionless. Rosa placed her hands on the ice-cold bars of the cage and then passed her face between them. Spellbound, she looked down into the depths.

Alessandro changed shape. Not explosively, like Mattia in Central Park, but in a fluid, elegant transition from one form to the other. There was nothing unnatural or alarming about his transformation. One body turned into another, and there was a beauty about the shift of shape that brought tears to her eyes.

Alessandro sank to the ground, all panther now. He and the lion crossed the short distance still between them, lowering their heads as if to exchange whispered words.

After a while they moved apart again. Alessandro rose, stood on his hind legs, and shifted back into human form. He turned his face to Rosa, and even in the darkness she saw him smile. He calmly raised one arm, beckoning to her. She was going to shake her head and step back, and then she realized that she was on the other side of the bars already. She had slipped through in her snake form without even noticing the transformation.

The lion roared. A tiger on top of the rocks stood still to let Rosa pass.

Alessandro came to meet her, leaving the main pride of big cats and moving to the foot of the rocks. Patches of fur were passing swiftly over his body like electrical discharges, twitching over his arms, his thighs, covering his hips and moving away again.

Like a torrent of amber, Rosa flowed down the rocks. She reached him, wound her way up him, coiled around his limbs, her scaly skin caressing his muscles, his hair, his entire body. In her embrace he turned back to panther form, and the sensuality of that movement filled her with icy bliss.

THE *AVVOCATO*

THE SUN WAS BLAZING above the sea, its rays sparkling on the rotor blades of the helicopter, which had come to a halt. It was standing on the landing pad below the hotel while its engines cooled off. The pilot sat in the cockpit, leafing through the *Gazzetta dello Sport*.

Rosa stood higher up, on the terrace of the Grand Hotel Jonio, her hands on the wrought-iron balustrade, looking down the steep coast at the gray-blue water. Far below, train tracks ran along a narrow strip of land between the rocks and the breaking waves. A small, red-roofed station building rose from the bleak rock. The old town center of Taormina lay on the plateau to the left of the hotel, six hundred feet above the sea and the railroad.

Rosa was wearing a three-quarter-length leather coat, black boots, and a close-fitting Trussardi dress. She had tied her blond hair back in a ponytail, hoping that it made her look sterner and older. If there was one thing she had learned from Florinda, it was to dress well for business meetings. She wanted Avvocato Trevini to see immediately that she was the head of her clan, not an intimidated girl who had let his video lure her here.

Behind her, she heard the sharp click of stiletto heels on

the marble of the terrace. Rosa waited until the sound stopped directly behind her, then turned around.

"The *avvocato* will be here in a moment," said the young woman who had come out of the hotel to join her. Contessa Cristina di Santis—Trevini's new assistant, confidante, who knew what else?—was descended from the old Sicilian aristocracy, as Rosa's secretary had found out for her. She had studied in Paris, London, and Milan, earning her doctoral and law degrees in record time. There was no di Santis clan in the Mafia these days; it had been almost entirely wiped out in the 1980s by the Corleonese. Its last few members had a good amount of wealth of their own, but no longer kept in active touch with Cosa Nostra.

With one exception. As Trevini's assistant, Cristina di Santis accepted the rules of the Alcantara clan.

Rosa's rules.

"The *avvocato* asks me to say he is very glad that you have come to see us, Signorina Alcantara," said the young attorney formally. "He is extremely sorry that his state of health makes it necessary for him to keep you waiting for a few minutes."

"That doesn't matter," said Rosa untruthfully. The delay was nothing but an attempt at harassment. Trevini had been asking for weeks for an appointment with her, and now that she had come to Taormina, couldn't he turn up on time?

"If I can offer you some refreshment—"

"Thank you." Rosa did not take her eyes off the other young woman, deliberately leaving it to the *contessa* to guess whether she meant yes or no, and watching the way Cristina di Santis dealt with the uncertainty.

The *contessa* was half a head taller than she was, black-haired, slender, but with all the curves that Rosa lacked. Her raised left eyebrow suggested that she was sizing Rosa up. She seemed to be waiting to test Rosa seriously, and then she would show this stupid, full-of-herself American girl how contempt was expressed stylishly here in Europe.

None of this surprised Rosa. In a way, she could totally understand it. What did surprise her was the *contessa*'s reaction when the soft sound of rubber tires on stone announced the attorney's arrival.

An expression of diligent civility appeared on the *contessa*'s face. Like a robot without any personality of its own; as if her emotions had suddenly been extinguished.

Careful not to show any irritation, Rosa turned to the old man in the wheelchair. This was the third time she had met the Alcantaras' attorney, the gray eminence of the clan, and once again she thought that he was like a certain actor, though try as she might she couldn't think of his name. She didn't remember seeing him in any movie; she just had a sense of him staring down at her from a screen, larger than life. Not that there was anything about Trevini to intimidate anyone at first sight. He was an emaciated old man, he had been confined to a wheelchair since childhood, and he was blind in one eye. Threat and intimidation didn't look like that in Mafia circles. Yet there was an aura that followed him, surrounded him, came into a room with him, and lingered in the air out on this terrace.

"Signorina Alcantara." The corners of his mouth moved,

merging with his countless wrinkles. "We meet again at last. I am so glad to see you."

The wind off the sea swept Rosa's ponytail forward over her shoulder, but the *avvocato*'s white hair was untouched by the draft. Maybe he had put gel on its few remaining strands to keep it in place. His lips were narrow and colorless, as if he were parting scar tissue when he smiled.

She went to meet him, with a surreptitious glance at her two bodyguards standing motionless in their black suits at the edge of the terrace. She was already regretting that she had let Alessandro persuade her to take the men with her.

She offered Trevini her hand. *"Avvocato."*

"You received my message," he said.

"You haven't replied to my questions about that."

"Because matters call for discussion face-to-face."

She took this ploy with a good grace. "And that's why I'm here."

"Will you come a little way with me?" He steered the wheelchair along the balustrade of the terrace. The *contessa* was left behind.

Rosa walked beside the wheelchair for some twenty or thirty yards, until they were out of earshot of anyone else. "I haven't seen much of my business managers and the other annoying people who usually harass me whenever they have the chance," she said. "Since I came back from the States, they've left me alone. I assume I have you to thank for that."

"I am sure that you value a little rest after such a strenuous journey."

"What did you tell them? That from now on you would be making the decisions on all economic matters?"

"Is that what you'd prefer?"

She had some difficulty in not letting the milky membrane over his right eye distract her. "What do you think my grandmother would have done, in her time, if you had gone over her head like that?"

He smiled. "I certainly would not be here any longer."

With a sigh, she grasped the balustrade and looked out at the sea. A few isolated yachts were cruising off the coast. Even in February, Taormina was not entirely free of tourists. There was hardly another place in Sicily as popular with foreign visitors as this town high above the water.

"I hate what you're trying to do here, *avvocato*," she said quietly. "I'm sure you think it's stupid of me, but I just don't like it. Not you, or your cheap tricks, or the whole damn thing."

"But you have no objection to all that money, do you?"

Angrily, she spun around, and noticed at the same time that the movement had alerted her bodyguards. With a shake of her head, she let them know that everything was all right.

"Was that really necessary?" asked Trevini, glancing at the two men.

"You tell me."

There was a touch of warmth in his smile. "What makes you think that I don't wish you well?"

"I'm a nuisance to you, Avvocato Trevini. An annoying inheritance from my aunt, and you have to battle it as best you can."

"Do I look to you as if I want to fight anyone?"

"Why did you send me that video?"

"As a warning. And before you misunderstand that, too: a warning not against me, but against the company you keep."

She turned her face to the wind and closed her eyes for two or three seconds. "You know, I'm really sorry to hear that. My family is consumed by fear of the Carnevares. The women managing my companies in Milan, my so-called advisers, they all predict disaster after disaster. And a great many older men make a great many conjectures about my sex life. Maybe I should worry about *that* rather than my relationship with Alessandro Carnevare."

There was a glint of mockery in Trevini's one good eye. "I have never taken the slightest interest in what the Alcantara women do behind closed doors. I am concerned only with the business of the clan: its financial prosperity, profit margins."

"But the responsibility is mine." Big words, but she didn't believe them herself.

"The Carnevares are not to be trusted. You ought never to forget that."

"I'm not sleeping with the Carnevares, *avvocato*. Only with one of them."

"That's not what I've heard."

She stared at him. She thought she was going to have to punch a defenseless old man in the face, here and now. With immense difficulty she controlled herself, understanding that provocation was one of his strongest weapons. The realization didn't make what he had said any less hurtful, but it did lessen its poisonous sting.

"I know exactly what happened on that occasion," he said. "At Eighty-Five Charles Street, wasn't it? Michele and Tano Carnevare, along with a few others. It's no secret, even if you may wish it were, Signorina Alcantara." He slowly shook his head. "I wonder how you can still stay close to a Carnevare, that's all."

"I wasn't raped by Alessandro," she managed to say tonelessly.

"But he's one of them, and he always will be. He was present that evening."

For a moment, doubt entered her mind, and she hated herself for it. She was letting him force her on to the defensive. She couldn't allow that.

"How did you get hold of that video?" There was cold fury in her voice, and a chill was spreading through her.

"You know me a little, Rosa." He used her proper name for the first time, and although she didn't like it, she didn't tell him not to. That would have been admitting that she felt too young for the part she had to play. Let him call her what he wanted.

Cristina di Santis was watching them from the far end of the terrace.

"You know me," Trevini repeated, as if that made it truer. "I would love to tell you about a clever plan that allowed me to acquire that video. But the truth is much more mundane. The cell phone with the video on it was delivered to you at a

Palermo branch of the Alcantara bank. The employees there didn't know quite what to do with it. Simply putting it in an envelope and mailing it to the other end of the island may not have struck them as entirely appropriate." He shrugged his shoulders, which looked odd, because he had difficulty with certain movements. "Or else they felt it their duty to let someone who has been a buffer between the Alcantaras and the harsher side of life for thirty years see it first."

She wondered whether she could manage to haul him out of his wheelchair and throw him over the balustrade. He couldn't weigh much; he was only skin and bone under his elegant gray suit.

"That's how I came by the recording. I saw you on it, Rosa, you and young Carnevare, and I thought it must have some deeper significance, or someone wouldn't have been so anxious to get the video into your hands. So I had a few inquiries made of the New York police. It didn't even take an hour for my capable *contessa* to find all the information." He was beaming. "Ah, I love to call her that—my *contessa* . . . Well, be that as it may, an apparently unimportant snippet of film showing some party or other suddenly became a highly explosive pictorial record."

Rosa glanced at his assistant again. She was standing motionless in her chic skirt suit and elegant high heels. One of the bodyguards was staring at her ass. Rosa decided to fire him.

"The next step was obvious," said Trevini. "I had the person who handed in the cell phone tracked down."

She was fighting against the cold again, and wondered what Alessandro would have done in her place.

"My people found her at a sleazy hotel. She was not in a good state, but she was still able to answer a few questions."

"You talked to Valerie?"

"Of course." Trevini was jubilant. "And so can you. You see, Rosa, Valerie Paige is here with us in Taormina."

THE PRISONER

At the end of a long trek through the basement, some way from the hotel laundry room and wine cellar, Trevini braked his wheelchair in front of an iron door with a bolted and shuttered peephole in it.

"The management was kind enough to outfit this for my purposes," he explained.

Rosa couldn't tear her eyes away from the closed peephole. "Good service."

"I've been living in my suite here for thirty-four years. One can expect a little more than fresh orange juice for breakfast."

She went past him to the door and pushed aside the bolt over the peephole. Before she opened the viewing window itself, she turned to the attorney again. "Was this what you meant by 'further material'?"

"You'll see. I didn't promise more than I could deliver."

With an abrupt movement, she opened the viewing window.

The interior of the cell was decorated with shiny, moisture-repellent paint in the unhealthy green of hospital walls. There was a mattress on a concrete base, with a crumpled quilt and a pillow showing traces of blood.

On the ground in front of it, knees drawn up and empty-eyed, sat a thin figure in torn jeans and a creased T-shirt so dirty that you couldn't make out the logo of the band on it.

Valerie's dark hair was short and untidy; she had probably cut it herself. Her face was emaciated, and the dark rings under her eyes could have been drawn on with finger paint. She had been biting her lips again and again; that was probably where the blood on the pillow had come from.

Without turning to Trevini behind her, Rosa asked, "You haven't been torturing her, have you?"

"She was questioned. But she has no physical injuries to show for it. She was a wreck already."

Valerie's arms were covered with tattoos, all dating from the last sixteen months. She'd had piercings when Rosa knew her before, but now she had several rings in each ear and half a dozen silver pins on her eyebrows, nose, and chin. Whatever she saw at this moment with her bloodshot eyes wasn't anything that was actually in the cell with her.

"Drugs?"

"Sedatives. She's had injections on her arms, between her toes, and under her tongue, but they're not our doing. When my people found her, she'd been pumped full of chemicals. I've no idea what your friend has gone through, but I don't imagine she remembers much of it. Or at least not any of it from the recent past."

Valerie must have been able to hear the voices on the other side of the door, but she showed no reaction.

"Valerie?" Rosa stood on tiptoe so that her face filled the viewing window. "It's me. Rosa."

Not even a twitch.

Rosa took a step back and looked at the lock of the door. "Open that."

"Are you sure?"

"Damn it, will you just open that door?"

The *avvocato* took out a key and handed it to her. "Here you are."

She put it in the lock, but before she turned it, Trevini said, "There's just one thing we ought to be clear about."

"What?"

"Everything else is up to you and you alone. She's your prisoner now, not mine."

Once again she turned to the door, taking a deep breath. The smell of laundry detergent wafted through the hotel basement, and machinery was throbbing in the distance. The pipes under the hall ceiling gurgled.

"Make up your mind," said Trevini. "About what happens to her. Do you want to ask her more questions? Let her go? Dispose of the problem entirely?"

She couldn't look at him. She hated him with all her heart, and even more she hated the fact that he was telling the truth. Now that she had seen the captive in the basement with her own eyes, she couldn't act as if she didn't know about her. Trevini was on her payroll; the Alcantara clan also financed his assistant and the men who had caught Valerie and *questioned* her. Rosa felt bile rising in her.

"You understand what I'm telling you." Trevini found her sore spot and probed it. "If you want to get rid of the girl in there, it will be done. No one will know. She treated you badly. Who could blame you for holding a grudge against her?"

She half turned to Trevini, closed the shutter over the peephole with her other hand, and asked, "What did she tell you?"

"I'm glad to see I've been able to arouse your curiosity after all."

She had come in order to offer him a proposition. Now she was glad that she hadn't mentioned it yet. Seething inside, she realized that it was in her power to dispose of *him* entirely. He knew it, and yet he was playing games with her. Because they depended on each other. Without him and his knowledge of three decades of the Alcantara businesses, she would never survive a tug-of-war for leadership of the clan. And without Rosa, he was just an ordinary attorney whom the rising generation of *capodecini* would be only too happy to replace with a modern legal office in Palermo.

But did she really want to be in a position in which she had to make decisions like this about the life or death of a young drug addict?

"You're sorry for her," Trevini remarked. "You ought not to be. Michele Carnevare told her to take you to that party. And she obeyed him. That's the truth of the matter. She wormed herself into your confidence, Rosa, only to lead you like a lamb to the slaughter."

"Maybe she didn't know what Michele planned to do." She could hardly believe that she, of all people, had suggested such a flimsy reason for Valerie's innocence.

"That's possible." Trevini wheeled his chair a little closer, until the footrests almost touched her shins. "Maybe, as you say, she didn't know. Does that make it any better? Isn't ignorance the oldest and hoariest of excuses?"

Mattia had said that Valerie had flown to Europe to ask Rosa to forgive her. She had promised to pass along his message if she met her, and in return he had saved Rosa's life. Would she really sentence Valerie to death now?

She turned the key and pushed the door open.

Trevini laughed softly. Or was it only the gurgling of the water pipes?

"Valerie." She stopped in the middle of the cell, a few feet from the despondent figure on the floor. Valerie's eyes went straight through her. Rosa resisted the urge to turn around and look behind her.

"Valerie, can you hear me?"

No reaction.

Rosa took another step forward and crouched down. Their faces were level now. She hadn't mourned their friendship over the last year, and she certainly didn't mourn it now. Her mind was full of accusations instead. Anger. How practical it would have been to feel nothing but indifference today. Instead, rage seethed inside her.

Hesitantly, she followed Valerie's gaze and looked over her shoulder.

Only the bare wall.

"It's up to you," she thought she heard Trevini say. Or was that a voice from her memory?

A drop of blood was running down Valerie's chin. She had taken her lower lip between her teeth and bitten it again. But her eyes were as fixed as ever.

Why didn't Rosa feel sorry for her? Was this the inheritance that she had claimed here in Sicily? The cold-blooded nature of her grandmother, and Florinda after her?

She stood up and left the cell, too quickly, too obviously

in flight. Trevini was bound to register that, and when she forced herself to look at him again, his smile was the smile of an understanding schoolmaster.

"I can teach you," he said. "Everything you need to know."

She left the door unlocked and dropped the key in his lap. "Keep her here for now. I spent a year in hell on her account; a few more days won't make any difference to Val."

"And then what, if I may ask? What's to become of her later, after another week or another month?" He weighed the key in his hand as if it were much heavier than before. "You could give her her freedom. You could be gracious and generous. What does your conscience tell you, Rosa Alcantara? And what does your blood tell you?"

She left him behind her and walked quickly down the corridor in the direction of the elevator.

He called after her, "You asked me just now what Costanza would have done."

"I am not my grandmother."

"But you must learn to be like her. You want a life here on the island? You want young Carnevare? Then you must be harder than any of the others, more cruel than your enemies. Costanza knew that. And you will soon understand it as well."

"I'll see you on the terrace," she called back over her shoulder. "We'll discuss it further there." Not down here. Not in the dark.

But the darkness followed her up into the daylight.

A PACT

ROSA BREATHED IN THE fresh air as if she couldn't get enough of it. A cool breeze off the sea was blowing in her face, but she couldn't shake the smell of the hotel basement.

She closed her eyes, but the sun was still burning bright red through her eyelids. Forcing herself not to show any weakness, she looked ahead again, and was irritated to see Contessa di Santis coming toward her on the terrace with a concerned expression.

"Everything all right, Signorina Alcantara?"

"Fine."

"You look pale."

"I have a fair complexion. Always did."

The assistant nodded understandingly. "We can't choose what we're born with, can we?"

Before Rosa could reply, di Santis turned to Trevini, who was guiding his wheelchair out of the hotel lounge and into the open air. Rosa thought this would be a good moment to throttle him from behind.

"Can I bring you anything?" asked the assistant. "Drinks? A little snack from the kitchen?"

Trevini shook his head. "Leave us alone, please."

Di Santis looked back over her shoulder, almost

reproachfully. As she did so, her left eyebrow rose higher and higher, until Rosa began to fear that it might disappear right into her hairline.

"As you wish," said the assistant, stalking away into the lounge. Rosa signaled to the two bodyguards to go into the building as well. Di Santis could not refrain from saying, "Please come with me, gentlemen. Maybe I can do something for you."

Trevini moved his wheelchair past Rosa and over to the balustrade. His good eye wandered over the water in the distance. "We're all inclined to take ourselves too seriously, don't you agree? To think of all that this sea has known in its time! Ancient Greece, Rome, Carthage, the early Mesopotamian tribes. Ur and Babylon, the biblical peoples. And here we are discussing a single life, just one unimportant human being."

"You move me deeply, *avvocato*, you really do. But I didn't come here for a history lesson or to look at the beautiful view."

"Without the sea I couldn't live here," he continued, undeterred. "It's one of the reasons why I never leave this hotel."

"What are the others?"

"I'm too old to take risks." He put his fingertips to his temples. "What I have in here, in my head, is the only capital I have. Did you know that I don't even own a computer? And no cabinets full of files." Of course she knew; it was the first thing she had heard about Trevini. "I keep everything that matters in my mind, as I have for years. No evidence, no trails. I was born with an extraordinary memory, and I imagine it's only right that I pay for it with certain deficiencies in other respects."

She was watching him as he spoke. But he was still staring out over the Mediterranean, into that breathtaking blue space.

"I'm sure you have wondered why I appointed the *contessa* my assistant," he went on. "She has top qualifications and references, she is easy on the eye—but none of that explains why she is really here. The truth of it is that she has the same qualities as me. I have spent a long time looking for someone who can compete with me in that respect. She is young, enormously ambitious, and she is certainly a complex character. I suffer from that more than anyone." The twinkle in his eyes ought to have seemed insinuating, but instead it looked almost friendly. "Above all, however, she has a remarkable ability to absorb facts. She hears something, sees something, and after that it's stored in her head as if it were on a hard disk. I have to resign myself to being less unique than I have always thought. That young lady is perfect."

Rosa sighed. "At least as far as her bra size is concerned, right?"

"I'm sorry," he said in kindly tones. "You don't have to like the *contessa*, Rosa. I'm not even sure that I do. But think of her as your personal security copy of me. Just in case something happens to me one of these days."

"She's been initiated into everything? Every deal? Every transaction?"

"I took the liberty of revealing them to her. We sit together and I tell her the facts. Hour after hour, day after day. The *contessa* stores it all in her mind. I've tested her more than once. She's fantastic. She remembers everything. And with her excellent education, she's in a position to make judgments that surprise even me."

"How nice to know that in the future I won't have only you to deal with, but also"—here she glanced into the lounge and saw di Santis flirting with the bodyguards—"but also the *contessa*."

"Life is a never-ending series of tribulations, my dear."

"If you call me that again, I'll push you over the railing."

He laughed. "Mutual respect is a wonderful thing. But that's not what brought you here. The video interested you, but that wasn't all, am I right?"

The strong breeze off the sea had loosened several strands of hair from the clip she wore, and they were blowing around her face. "I'll make you an offer, *avvocato*. We can beat around the bush for hours, but we both know what the end result will be. We depend on each other. I don't like you at all—well, maybe I like you a little better than I like your *contessa* in there. She's probably unbeatable at sprinting in high heels."

He laughed heartily at that. Ah, so this was the way to get at him. Just tell him the truth.

"You depend on me as much as I depend on you," she said, slightly relieved that now she could fall back on the speech she had prepared in advance. "I don't know anything about the business affairs of the Alcantaras, and I need someone to keep all that at a distance from me. As you've obviously already begun to do. On the other hand, you could never be *capo* of the Alcantaras, because you don't belong to the family. My relatives in Milan and Rome would never accept someone like you as head of the clan. As a lawyer who can spring them from prison, and as a miraculous human calculator and financial genius—no problem there; they love you for that. But you're not an Alcantara, and you never will be."

He was observing her very closely now. "What are you suggesting?"

"I am the head of the clan, and nothing will change that. I'm beginning to feel at home here on the island. I represent what this family stands for, and I am now the public face of the clan, whether the others like it or not."

She had learned it by heart, but she thought it sounded good.

"Why are you doing this to yourself?" he asked. "Why don't you just take a large sum of money and your new boyfriend and go off to live happily ever after somewhere at the other end of the world?"

"Because no one—not you, not those idiots in Palermo and Rome—none of you trust me to do anything. Because everyone's just waiting for me to mess it all up."

"That," he said, smiling again, "that's an unorthodox view of the situation. But I understand what you're getting at."

"I'm accepting my inheritance, *avvocato*. I will lead the Alcantaras."

"And you think you can do it?"

She gave him a sweet smile. "This is where you come in. You do what you've been doing all these decades—you remain the genius in the background. The one who pulls the wires. Lord God Almighty of Taormina. I can butter you up as much as you want. I know how to pay compliments, I promise you I do."

He sighed. "I think I understand you, too. You represent the clan; I do the work."

"That's the plan."

He breathed in and out deeply. "I'm an old man."

"What do you need? Another nurse like your protégée there? With longer legs, bigger breasts?"

"I can be very obstinate. Pigheaded. Difficult to deal with."

"But you have the *contessa*. You can always take it out on her."

He smiled. "You have no right of veto. No say in business affairs."

"Forget it. I do."

"We play the game like that or not at all."

She shook her head. "You obviously don't understand yet, *avvocato. I* make the rules. You throw the dice and see that they always come up sixes."

He blinked, maybe because she was standing in front of the sun. Or because his expression had become a little more forced than ever. "What do you want, Rosa?"

"I'm no Mother Teresa. I know what I'm getting into. But there *will* be rules. No arms deals. No drugs."

He laughed at her, just as she had planned. "Then how are we to earn money? With ringtones?"

"With what's been most profitable to us over the last few years—the subsidies from Rome and Brussels that you fixed.

Money for wind turbines that don't generate any power, for instance."

"It can't be done without the arms deals," he said categorically. "You may have to look around for someone else."

Rosa had seen that coming, and realized that she had to make some concessions. "Where do the arms go?"

"Africa. South America. Southeast Asia. Most of the stuff comes from Russia, but some of it from the USA, Germany, France. Where do you suppose that helicopter of yours was made? It certainly isn't branded 'Made in Italy.'"

"How about the drugs?"

"That trade's not what it once was. Too much competition from Russia and the Balkans. My heart's not set on it. But you can never be one hundred percent sure it's not going on, with some of the *soldati* doing deals of their own."

"If that happens, I should hear about it."

"You won't make friends that way."

"I know." She smiled. "That's why I want you to do it for me."

"You think you're making it easier for yourself, but you'll soon see it's exactly the opposite. It's not the law you want to guard against; it's your own people."

"Then I'd better begin with you, right?"

"I swore to your grandmother, on oath, that my life belongs to this family. And I'm a man of my word."

"You haven't done badly up until now."

"And as we happen to be discussing it, I have one condition. Lampedusa."

"Florinda's favorite project?"

"Some of her signatures still have to be honored. I have, shall we say, a personal interest in the business with the refugees on that island. We can forget about the drugs, we can reduce the arms deals, but Lampedusa must stay as it is. You will not place any obstacles in my way in that respect."

Reluctantly, she nodded.

"We're of the same mind, then?" he asked.

"I don't think we'll ever be of the same mind, *avvocato*. But we have a deal." A pact is more like it, she thought, grinding her teeth.

He offered Rosa his hand, and she shook it without hesitating.

As she left, she gave Contessa di Santis a charming smile, and as they said good-bye to each other, she held the *contessa*'s hand a little too long. On the way back to the helicopter Rosa threw the diamond ring she had been holding in her clenched fist into the sea.

COSTANZA'S LEGACY

ROSA FOUND IOLE IN the greenhouse. The glazed annex was like a long arm reaching out from the north wall of the Palazzo Alcantara. The walls and the vaulted ceiling were made of glass panes that creaked dangerously in high winds. Rust and verdigris covered the iron framework. Like everything else in the palazzo, the place was in urgent need of restoration.

"They like me," said Iole proudly.

She had a snake draped around her neck like a shimmering stole. Iole was caressing its skull. The other end of the reptile was coiled around her waist. More snakes were winding around her feet, darting their tongues in and out and hissing.

Rosa closed the door of the greenhouse behind her and entered the sultry jungle inside. Palm trees, giant ferns, exotic shrubs, and climbing plants had merged into dense thickets over the years. The humid heat that clouded the glass with condensation took her breath away at first. But in a moment her body adjusted to it. In fact it felt like she could breathe freely in the palazzo for the first time in months. Part of her duties, those that had lent a leaden heaviness to the place, had been left behind with Trevini in Taormina. She felt better— but at the same time she was confronting new anxieties.

"Would you like to see it now?" asked Iole, carefully trying to lift the snake off her shoulders. The creatures were remarkably trusting. Iole was not a Lamia, indeed not an Arcadian at all, yet the reptiles accepted her as one of their own.

"Would I like to see what?" Rosa dismissed the image of the captive Valerie that had superimposed itself on Iole's cheerful face.

"The freezer!" Iole made a reproachful pout. "*Hello?* The keypad working the door, remember? Days and days working away down in the dark cellar? Me, the genius with numbers!"

Rosa smiled, and helped her to put the snake down on the floor with the others. The sound of hissing and spitting came from all directions. More and more snakes came winding their way out of the undergrowth and formed a wide circle around Rosa, not as playful as they were with Iole but rather preserving a respectful distance.

Rosa took Iole's hand. "Okay, let's go. Can't wait to see what you found."

Iole beamed. "You really have time?"

"You act as if I never do."

Iole's mouth twisted, and she looked at Rosa as if to say: *Well, think about it.*

Rosa groaned guiltily and led Iole to the door. The snakes swiftly glided aside and formed an avenue for them. Rosa was glad when they had left the greenhouse and the latch clicked behind them. It wasn't that she didn't like to be near the snakes; it was more that she got slightly irritated finding, week after week, how she felt about being near them.

There were several ways into the palazzo cellar. They used

a staircase behind a door in the kitchen, not far from the open range where whole pigs used to be roasted on spits.

The stairway was narrow, and clearly hadn't been used for years. Iole went ahead, warning Rosa of cobwebs and any steps that were shorter than the others, obviously enjoying the role of guide. When she operated an old-fashioned rotary switch on the wall, round lamps in metal frames on the hall ceiling came on.

After the tropical climate of the greenhouse, it was definitely cold down here. A slight draft of air smelled of dank stone and mold.

"There's something I have to ask you," said Rosa as she followed Iole along the brickwork corridors. Iole liked to wear white—perhaps to declare her independence from Rosa's habitual black—and had a strong aversion to anything too close-fitting. In the dim light, there was something fairy-like about the loose material of her dress wafting around her.

"What is it?"

"I don't know if you'll want to talk about it."

Iole didn't look back at her. "What it was like when I was being kept prisoner?"

Rosa sighed softly. "Yes. But something particular about it."

"Ask away."

"How did you feel about the men who were keeping you captive? Did you hate them, or were you angry or afraid of them? A mixture of all that? Or something different?"

Iole shook her head. Rosa could still see her only from

behind. "I didn't feel anything about them."

"Nothing at all?"

"I didn't think about them except when they came to bring me food or clothes. Or when they were taking me to a new hiding place. Otherwise I pretended they didn't exist. Like when you dive into the water with your hands over your ears—you don't hear anything. It works with feelings, too. Everything inside you closes up; it doesn't let anything through. And then it's like you're deaf to feelings. You just don't have them anymore." She stopped and turned around. "Sounds a little crazy, right?"

Rosa hugged her. "It doesn't sound crazy at all."

Raising her head from Rosa's shoulder, Iole looked at her. "Why are you asking?"

"No reason."

"That's not true." Iole tilted her head a little and stared at her, hard. "Are *you* keeping someone prisoner?"

"What makes you think that?"

"There was one of those men who brought me things, and he always seemed a little sad, like he was ashamed of himself. You look just the same."

Rosa took a step back, shook her head, and ran her fingers through her hair. "Let's keep going, okay?"

Iole shrugged. "You have to make sure the prisoner always has something to drink. And something to eat. Not too sweet, not too sour. And a TV set. Otherwise your prisoner goes soft in the head."

Rosa didn't know how well Trevini was looking after

Valerie, but she was pretty sure there was no TV set in her cell. Oddly enough, it was that point that pricked her conscience.

Iole continued walking, and Rosa hurried to catch up with her. She had been down here once before, but none of it seemed familiar. The coarse brown masonry, the cobwebs over the electric bulbs in their metal holders, the cracked concrete underfoot, which had been laid down over even older floors—as if the palazzo were about to show its true face, one that had been hidden behind halfhearted renovations.

"It's cold down here." She folded her arms around her shoulders as she walked.

"It'll be colder in a minute," said Iole.

Soon they reached the space outside the freezer. They had been going for only a few minutes, but it felt to Rosa as if an hour had passed. Below the ceiling, neon tubes came alight, humming. The place was empty except for a metal box beside a heavy iron door.

"And you've been in there already?"

Iole nodded. "Sarcasmo was with me. He got excited when he smelled those things."

"What things?"

"Wait and see."

Iole opened the flap on the little metal box. Her feet crunched on crumbs of dog biscuit. Her fingers danced over an unilluminated keypad. The numbers on the display consisted of large lines in a style that must have been the latest in modern technology two decades ago.

A hydraulic mechanism hissed, as if the iron door were

uttering a reluctant groan. Several locks opened with clicking sounds. It seemed an unusual security system for a freezer that would normally have held provisions and game animals killed in the hunt.

"Give me a hand, will you?" Iole was tugging at the enormous door handle.

Rosa still wasn't sure that she really wanted to see what her grandmother had left here. But the adrenaline junkie in her surfaced. That did her good.

She pulled at the handle with Iole, and retreated, step by step, as the heavy door swung out into the corridor.

Darkness reigned beyond it. The cool air of the cellar retreated before a surge of Arctic cold.

"You do know I'm a vegetarian?" She peered past Iole into the darkness. "If there are ancient pig carcasses or something dangling from the ceiling in there—"

Iole vigorously shook her head. "No, much better than that."

The neon tubes outside shed light into the freezer for only a few feet. To the right and left, it fell on something that looked like rows of cocoons lined up. They hung from the ceiling without touching the ground. An aisle ran between them.

"Wait." Iole pressed a button next to the display on the keypad. More neon tubes lit up on the ceiling, crackling. Their light flickered on in a wave from the entrance to the depths of the freezer. The white light showed a long room, more like a tunnel than anything else. It was wide enough for not just one but three aisles between the hanging shapes.

Rosa went up to the steel doorway. Iole hurried past her, brought a metal doorstop out of the room, and wedged it under the open iron door. "There," she said, pleased with herself.

Vapor rose as Rosa breathed out. "What *are* those things?" Iole went ahead. "Come with me."

Together they approached the nearest dangling forms, which Rosa now saw were fabric bags. Made of linen or cotton, and stuffed very full. Four rails ran under the ceiling, parallel to the side walls. Animal carcasses had probably once been hung in here. The idea turned her stomach.

She looked more closely at one of the bags.

The shapes of arms showed right and left inside the fabric. No legs. No head.

Iole put out one hand and tapped the front fabric bag. The hook fastening it to the rail made a slight grinding sound, and the shapeless thing began swinging back and forth.

"Fine. Right," said Rosa, working hard on sounding matter-of-fact. "Not dead bodies, are they?"

Iole grinned. "Depends how you look at it." She ran both hands over the fabric, found a zipper, and pulled it down with a firm jerk.

Brown fur spilled out of the opening. Iole put one hand inside and stroked the fluffy surface.

"Fur coats," she said. "A hundred and sixteen. I counted them."

Rosa bent her head and tried to look between the rows at the opposite side of the tunnel-like cellar room. But the hanging linen cocoons seemed to be moving closer and closer together at the back, as if to bar her view of the far end of the freezer.

"My grandmother stored her *fur coats* down here?" she whispered.

"They keep better in the cold," said Iole, pride in her voice. "I read that somewhere." She took the fur at the front off the rail, removed it entirely from its bag, and rubbed her cheek against the garment, enjoying its softness.

Once again Rosa realized how cold she was. "Who needs a fur coat in Sicily? And who, for god's sake, needs *a hundred and sixteen* of them?"

However, she could answer that question for herself. Cosa Nostra loved status symbols, from magnificent properties to fast cars to designer fashion. Many a Mafioso collected villas on the Riviera; others surrounded themselves with crowds of beautiful women. Costanza had obviously had a weakness for furs. Florinda had hated her, Rosa knew that much.

She pointed to the rows. "No black leather jackets, I suppose?"

"If you sell all those coats you can buy yourself a thousand leather jackets."

"Then I'll have all the animal-rights activists in Italy after me, not to mention the police."

"I think they're great!" Iole put the coat on. It was much too large for her; its hem fell in folds to the floor around her feet.

Rosa walked slowly past the linen bags. Four rows—that

made it around thirty to each rail. They hung at intervals of a foot and a half. And it seemed that the freezer went on beyond the last fabric bags. She could see the neon lighting at the far end of the room.

"You put one on too," said Iole. "Otherwise you'll catch a chill."

Rosa took one of the coats at random out of its stiff protective covering and slipped it on. The fur was soft and supple, but it wasn't just because she was a vegetarian that she felt there was something unpleasant about the touch of it.

Slowly, she turned once in the middle of the linen bags. Her coat, too, dragged on the floor. "What am I going to do with all this stuff?"

"Bury it?"

"What's beyond the coats at the far end?"

"Containers of some kind," said Iole, shrugging her shoulders.

Rosa frowned and hurried down the narrow aisle between two rows. The broad fur shoulders of her coat brushed against some of the linen bags as she passed them, and set them rocking gently. When she looked back to see whether Iole was following, there was ghostly movement all around her. As if something alive were stirring inside the cocoons and might slip out any moment. Iole was having fun pushing more of them to make them swing, and Rosa had to stop herself from snapping at her. It wasn't Iole's fault that she was on edge.

At last she reached the end of the rows of coats. From a distance it looked as if the long room became narrower and narrower toward the end, but she had been wrong. What she had taken for more linen bags was really a large number of white, circular plastic containers built into a wall. Stacked one above another, they formed a rampart reaching almost from one side of the freezer to the other, right across the aisles. But still she had not reached the far side of the underground room. You could pass to the right and left of the wall of containers.

Iole emerged from the swinging coats behind her. "Containers. Like I said."

"Do you know what's in them?"

"No idea."

"And behind them?"

"A safe on the back wall. That's all."

Rosa went up to the containers and saw, upon glancing through the spaces between them, that there was a second row behind them. She did a rough calculation of their number and counted at least forty containers, each a good two feet high and a foot and a half in diameter.

"Are you going to look inside?" asked Iole eagerly.

"In a minute." Rosa walked on to peer around the corner of the wall. Once again she had been wrong. There were not two but four rows of the round plastic containers. Around eighty, then.

Once again she looked back at Iole, who was already coming to join her. "First the safe. What's in it?"

"It's locked."

"That didn't stop you from opening the door."

"Locked with a *key*."

"Didn't you try to break it open?"

"I tried, but it was no good."

"Let's see."

With a conspiratorial expression, Iole followed her. Nine feet of empty space lay between the last row of containers and the back of the room. In front of the wall stood a gray iron safe, as massive as a church altar.

Rosa investigated the lock. Nothing complicated. Costanza must have relied entirely on the number code at the entrance. She herself had broken into cars on the streets of Crown Heights, and she knew that this mechanism would be child's play. "I need something sharp."

Iole went back around the containers, and Rosa heard her doing something to the rustling linen bags. A little later she came back with a wire coat hanger.

It didn't take Rosa more than a minute before there was a click inside the lock of the safe. "Voilà," she said, stepping back, and she dropped the coat hanger, now bent out of shape, on the floor.

Iole was rocking excitedly from foot to foot.

The two doors of the safe squealed as Rosa pulled them apart.

Countless ampoules containing a yellowish liquid were lined up on five shelves inside the safe. There was no written label on any of them, just row upon row of the little thumb-size glass flasks.

Rosa took one out, and held it up to the light. The honey-colored contents were clear, and as fluid as water.

"What's that supposed to be?" asked Iole.

"I have no idea."

"Drugs of some kind?"

"She wouldn't have kept those here in the palazzo. Far too dangerous. There are secret places to store drugs all over Sicily."

Iole picked up one of the ampoules herself. "Maybe your grandmother used some kind of substance like that herself. Or Florinda."

Rosa could exclude that possibility, at least for her aunt. But as for Costanza . . . she knew too little about her. However, none of this seemed to fit together. The collection of fur coats, these ampoules. The rows of containers.

She put the vial back on its shelf. "Let's see what's in these." She went over to the rampart of containers and tried to lift one of them off the top row.

Iole hurried over. "Wait a minute. I'll help you."

Together they got the container down on the floor. It had a screw lid similar to a mason jar, secured all around with a broad strip of tape.

Rosa's fingernails, painted with black nail polish, were too short to get the tape off. Iole did better. She ripped it off with a tearing sound, got her fingers entangled in it, and then had her work cut out to get the sticky stuff off her hand. Rosa helped her—impatiently, because she was burning with curiosity to open the lid.

Finally, with both hands, she unscrewed the top a quarter of the way to the left. There was a hissing sound like air coming out of a Tupperware container.

"Ugh," said Iole, holding her nose.

Rosa breathed in through her mouth and then took the lid right off. The stench was appalling. She was prepared to see anything.

What she found was a dirty, sticky fur. For a moment she felt sure it was the corpse of an animal. The chill in the freezer and the airtight lid of the container had prevented decomposition inside it, but the smell of old blood rose from the contents.

Iole retched. "Gross."

Reluctantly, Rosa put out a hand and touched the fur. It was a relief that nothing moved underneath it. Hesitantly, she grasped it with her other hand, got hold of the edge of the fur, and pulled it out at arm's length, like an item of laundry.

It was not a corpse, but a sandy brown animal pelt. Dried blood and remnants of skin clung to the underside.

Iole was about to touch it, but withdrew her fingers just before they reached it. "Were they going to make more fur coats out of these?"

"Looks like it."

"There are more in there."

Rosa put the fur down on the floor, then lifted out a second, using only her fingertips, and spread it over the first. She had to bend so far over the container to get out the third that the stench almost made her throw up. There was yet another one at the very bottom, but she left that where it was.

"Four," she said. "Multiplied by eighty."

"That's a lot," said Iole. "How many do you need to make a coat?"

Rosa shrugged her shoulders, and looked at the ampoules full of yellow liquid again. Not necessarily drugs; there was another possibility. She went over to the cupboard, picked up one of the little glass tubes again, and peered at it more closely. Its metal seal had a round rubber center through which a needle could be pushed to draw the liquid up into a syringe. Or a needle for an injection.

"Look," said Iole. "There are little labels on the furs."

Rosa's stomach muscles cramped.

"It says something on them."

Her hands trembling, Rosa began taking off the fur coat she was wearing. It seemed to be sticking to her body as if by suction.

"They're names."

The fur fell around Rosa on the floor. "Iole," she managed to say in a toneless voice. "Take off that coat."

But the girl was crouching over the furs, undeterred, reading out the labels. "Paolo Mancori . . . Barbara Gastaldi . . . Gianni Carnevare."

"Iole. Take the thing off." Rosa's legs felt numb as she took a clumsy step away from the fur coat on the floor.

"Did you know any of them?" asked Iole.

Rosa went around behind her, and had to force herself to touch the fur to lift it off Iole.

"Hey!"

Rosa tugged the heavy coat off her, more energetically this time. "We're getting out of this place." In disgust, she flung the fur aside.

"But—"

Rosa hauled her to her feet, grabbed her by the shoulders, and looked hard into her eyes.

"These furs," she said, "don't come from animals."

"They don't?" asked Iole, her voice husky.

Rosa took her arm and led her around the containers, until they could see the rows of linen bags hanging in front of them, all the coats in their gray coverings.

"All of these," she whispered, "were once Arcadians."

APOLLONIO

"DID YOU KNOW?" SHE spat into the receiver. "Shit, of course you knew!"

At the other end of the line, Trevini sighed. "This is not a subject we ought to discuss over the telephone."

"I want to know the truth. Now!" She had a date to meet Alessandro this evening, but instead of looking forward to it she had to grapple with this filth first.

"You're being unreasonable. You're letting yourself get carried away over something that—"

"That's enough!" She jumped up from her swivel chair, went around the huge desk, and began pacing up and down the study. Her heavy metal-studded shoes hammered on the parquet flooring as if a military commando unit were storming the palazzo.

Far away in Taormina, the attorney let out a breath. "Wait." Something clicked on the line, to be followed by a rushing sound, and then another click. "There, that's better."

"What?"

"I've switched on a distorting signal to keep you from informing on us all. You will never again—*never!*—try talking to me about such matters over the phone without previous warning."

"What are those furs in the cellar? Why did my grand-mother keep them together down there? Where do they come from? And why so *many*?"

"Costanza didn't kill those people, Rosa. If that's what has upset you so much. And if they can be described as people, indeed as human at all."

"Don't you consider me human, Avvocato Trevini?"

He laughed softly. "The fact is, I wish you were *less* human. More like your grandmother."

"She was a monster!"

"A collector with discriminating taste."

"*Taste?* Have you lost your mind? Those furs down there were once men and women! And there are a few hundred of them."

"As I said: She didn't kill them with her own hands. She didn't even contract for their deaths."

"Very reassuring."

"We ought to—"

"Discuss this at your place? Forget it."

"The bugging specialists at the public prosecutor's office never take more than three or four minutes to crack a distortion signal. If they're listening in now, we don't have much time left."

"Then press the button again."

"You're upset because—"

"Because I've found a fucking mass grave in my basement!"

He seemed to be drinking something; she heard a faint clink. She was going to explode with rage any moment now.

He was right about one thing. She had to calm down, control herself.

Reluctantly, she used the brief pause to go back to her chair at the desk. Florinda's spacious study was strange to her. It had once been a living room in the palazzo, with walls paneled in dark wood and a view of the inner courtyard from a wrought-iron balcony. She felt small and out of place here.

There was a crackle and a rushing sound on the line again. Trevini had recoded the signal. Another three minutes.

"Well?" she asked.

"I don't know much about it, believe me. Costanza had a weakness for furs of all kinds. The palazzo was full of them. As hearth rugs, runners, even curtains. She loved furs more than anything. Most of them disappeared after her death. Florinda got rid of them."

"Florinda didn't know about the freezer?"

"Yes, I think she did, but maybe her mind suppressed the truth."

"Who else knows?" Suddenly she had an idea. "Is *that* why all the other clans hate the Alcantaras so much?"

"If the others had the faintest inkling of it, your family would have been wiped out decades ago. And none of this must ever be known, or the palazzo will go up in flames within a few hours—and all of us with it."

She let her head drop back against the leather upholstery of the chair. "That means that you, and I, and Iole are the only people who know it exists?"

"Don't say you told that irresponsible *child* about this!"

"Iole isn't irresponsible. And she was the one who cracked the code to the lock of the freezer. She found the coats."

"Good God in heaven!" His agitation lifted her mood slightly. She liked to shake his composure. "You must silence the girl."

"Iole won't tell anyone. Leave that to me."

His snort was contemptuous. "And there's also someone else."

"Who?"

"A man called Apollonio. He supplied the furs to your grandmother. I didn't know him, had never heard of him before. But soon after Costanza's death he made contact with me and said that she died owing him money. Obviously she hadn't yet paid him for his last delivery."

"What did you do?"

"I transferred the sum to a numbered account for him, to keep his mouth shut. And then I called Davide."

She pricked up her ears. "My father?"

"Of course."

"But by then it had been ages since he'd had anything to do with the clan's business affairs. I always hoped that one of these days he'd come back to take his rightful place as head of the family."

Interesting. Sounded as if Trevini had disliked Florinda so much that he'd rather have discussed the subject with the disinherited Alcantara son than with her. "What did my father say?"

"He was quite upset."

"I can imagine. *I'm* quite upset."

"Davide wanted to know everything about this man Apollonio, and he said for me not to do anything for the time being."

"Did you tell Florinda?"

"He expressly forbade me to do that, too."

"And you were only too happy to do as he said, right?"

"Your aunt wasn't as effective a head of the family as she thought. In addition, she was under the sway of Salvatore Pantaleone. Just as well that he is dead."

Did Trevini know that Rosa was responsible for Pantaleone's death? Impossible, really—but by now she was ready to believe him capable of anything.

"Wait a minute," he said. "The signal . . ." That clicking and rushing on the line again. "Right," he finally continued.

She tried to put her thoughts in order. There were two things that she had to find out more about. "Did my father give you any other instructions?"

"No. He asked me to let the matter rest, saying he would see to everything else personally."

"When exactly was this?"

"Shortly before his death."

The mysterious phone call that her mother had mentioned. Her father's strange reaction to it. And then his hasty decision to leave his wife and his two daughters and go to Europe.

"It was *you*," she whispered.

"I don't understand what you mean."

"You were the reason he left. You called him, and after

that he . . ." She stopped, and turned the swivel chair slowly in a circle.

"I don't know what happened," said Trevini. "But it seems that Apollonio was reason enough for him to become active again himself."

"Tell me all about this man Apollonio. Every last thing."

"As I said before, I don't know much about him. In the first place, an attorney's office in Rome got in touch on his behalf. I finally managed to speak to him myself, but never face-to-face, only by phone. I was aware of Costanza's collection in the cellar—"

Why did he know?

"—and I had always assumed that I was the only person she had taken into her confidence. However, this Apollonio left me in no doubt that he knew all about it."

"Did he try blackmailing you?"

"I had to believe him, like it or not, when he said that he had supplied the furs. And I thought it possible that the last payment hadn't yet been made at the time of Costanza's sudden death. He was threatening to make the whole thing public. That could have meant the end of the Alcantaras."

"A breach of the concordat," she murmured.

"Worse," he told her. "Treachery."

The word seemed to echo down the line for a moment. "TABULA?" she whispered tonelessly.

"Apollonio never mentioned that name. But yes, I do think there is some connection. TABULA carries out experiments on members of the dynasties. How else could he have come by the pelts of so many Arcadians?"

She remembered the video that Cesare Carnevare had shown her. Endless rows of cages, with Arcadians in their animal forms shut up inside them. Obviously the captives had lost the ability to turn back into human beings.

"As far as I know," Trevini went on, "hardly anyone who was abducted and held by TABULA ever appeared again."

"And you think these people are sick enough to skin their victims and sell the pelts? Sell them back to another Arcadian, of all people?" She instinctively thought of Alessandro. Of his silky black panther fur.

"Maybe there are other collectors. Or maybe not. I can't answer that question."

"Right," she said, after a brief pause. "So this Apollonio got the furs from TABULA. He's probably even a member of it himself. And my grandmother did business with him—with TABULA, the archenemy of all the Arcadian dynasties."

"That was the danger I saw looming at the time. And I had to react."

"Did my father know about it?"

"He drew exactly the same conclusions as you did just now."

"You have no idea what he was planning to do?"

"None whatsoever. He expressly told me not to investigate the matter any farther. He was going to see to it all himself."

"And he didn't survive that."

"It's possible that he tracked down Apollonio. And that the meeting didn't turn out well for him." Trevini cleared his throat. "However, all this is pure speculation."

"Do you think Florinda knew about it?"

"If so, she never mentioned the subject."

But how else, if not from Florinda, could Zoe have known? What had the connection been between her father and TABULA—the link that Zoe had been talking about just before she died?

"Is that all?" asked Rosa.

"I respected your father's wish. Apollonio was his business, not mine anymore."

"You expect me to believe that?"

Trevini's voice was icy. "You don't like me. I can understand that. But don't cast doubt on my loyalty. I haven't worked for your family for thirty years only to have you insult me now."

"Do you seriously call it loyalty to have kept something so important from Florinda?"

"What I do is done for the good of the clan. Your father, Rosa, might have been a good *capo*. That's why I was on his side. The way things are now, however, there's only one side in this family, and it's yours. That ought to be enough to persuade you to trust me."

"If I ask you to find out more about this Apollonio—to continue where you left off eleven years ago—will you do it?"

"I can't promise you results, but yes, of course."

"I'd be very grateful." She managed to say it without grinding her teeth.

"We had better end this conversation now," he said. "But one more thing: I hope you're aware that you must not talk to anyone else, anyone at all, about what you found in the cellar."

"By 'anyone' you mean Alessandro Carnevare."

"Whatever you may think of him, whatever you feel for him—don't trust him. This is not just about you, Rosa; it's about the fate of your clan. Everything that Costanza and her predecessors built up."

And it was about him, Trevini, as well. That was what he was saying.

She didn't reply.

"Don't make the mistake of seeing him as only a young man in love," Trevini warned her, with a note in his voice that sent a shiver down her spine. "Alessandro Carnevare is much more than that. He's ambitious. He is angry, and implacable. And he's dangerous. Please keep that in mind, in everything you do." He was silent for a moment, and then he said again, "Don't mention any of this. You have to promise me that."

She didn't have to do any such thing.

"Please," he said forcefully. "Not a word."

Rosa ended the call.

THREE WORDS

"A few *hundred*?" ALESSANDRO exclaimed.

"The entire freezer is full of them."

He slowly shook his head, unable to take it in, and for a moment she was afraid that this could all backfire on her. Suppose he thought she was just like her grandmother? Suppose he began to believe what everyone had been telling him for months? That she was bad news for him, bad news for Cosa Nostra as a whole, and it was a mistake to have anything to do with an Alcantara.

Rosa was sitting beside him on the battlements of Castello Carnevare in the evening twilight, looking out at the plain below the mountain where the castle stood. The land was not as flat as it looked at first sight. The farther you went from the Castello, the hillier the country became. Here in central Sicily the landscape was bleak and inhospitable, a sea of ocher undulations in the ground, with dry riverbeds spanned by ancient stone bridges running across them. The sun had sunk below the horizon in the west. A solitary car was driving along a road a few miles away. Its headlights were two lonely stars in the darkness.

Rosa and Alessandro were nestling close together, enveloped by blankets. Both of them had drawn up their knees and wrapped the thick wool tightly around them. They were sitting on the very edge of the abyss; if anyone were to push them from behind, there would be no stopping their fall. Forty-five feet to the bottom of the castle wall, and nothing in the way to slow their progress along the rocky slope.

But Rosa wasn't even uneasy. Nowhere had she ever felt as safe as she did with him, her shoulder against his, their fingers closely entwined.

"I love you," he said.

Just three words—but it was so sudden that she swallowed. Whatever they had been talking about just now, their emotions were in tune. They both felt equally ready to be there for each other, forever.

She didn't say anything. She still couldn't do it, couldn't bring the words past her own lips, or not so that they sounded genuine. Even as she formed the sentence in her mind—*I love you*—it sounded artificial to her. She had tried to explain that to him, and she could see in his eyes that he understood.

She leaned her head on his shoulder, felt his lips in her hair.

"How do you do it?" she asked, looking into the distance.

"Do what?"

"Be the way you are. Still like me in spite of everything I've just told you."

"That's got nothing to do with us. What your grandmother did—it's so long ago. We can't help what our ancestors did."

She raised her head. The horizon was reflected in the green of his gaze. For a few heartbeats she saw the world through his eyes. Larger, wider, and yet so close that you could put out your hand and grasp it. To him, nothing was beyond his reach.

She had told him everything. About her horrifying discovery in the cellar, and also about her visit to Trevini and the agreement she had made with him. And how Valerie was a captive in his hotel.

"I have to get rid of the whole thing," she said, adding quickly, in case he misunderstood, "I don't mean *her*; I mean the stuff in the basement. But if I have the furs burned, there's a danger that someone could see the names on them."

"We can tear the labels off first."

"Open all those containers? Take out every single fur?" She shook her head. "I'd rather move somewhere else and have the whole palazzo blown sky-high."

"By somewhere else you mean—"

"Not here. That wouldn't be a good idea . . . and not safe," she added a moment later. "It's strange enough that they let us see each other at all."

"Most of them have other things on their minds right now."

"The Hungry Man?"

Alessandro nodded. "Some of them are more worried than ever that he'll return. And others can't wait for it. The mere possibility that he might come back to Sicily from the mainland has them at one another's throats. I've seen them sitting in a conference room in Catania . . . worldly men in expensive suits. If the rest of us hadn't separated them, they'd have torn one another apart. They shifted shape, the idiots. Luckily there were only Arcadians in the room, or else—"

"It's getting out of control, right? The old rules of the dynasties, the laws of the tribunal, all the agreements to keep the peace . . . before long, none of that will mean anything anymore."

He smiled sadly. "I know some who claim that our relationship is already part of it. Nothing's the way it used to be. Alcantaras and Carnevares hand in glove. A package deal."

She plucked at her blanket. "Two of them. Dammit."

He turned to her and put one hand under the soft bedspread. His beautiful, long fingers touched her bare thigh. Moved farther up. She was wearing only a large T-shirt and a pair of his shorts. They had been in the pool down in the castle, and after that in the sauna. Her own black clothes were lying crumpled somewhere down by the edge of the pool.

"Wait," she said, and almost choked.

His hand stopped moving. "Snake alarm?"

"That too. But I have to talk to you. First, I mean. Talk—normally."

His smile widened. A wind from the plain, from the south—maybe from Africa, as he always claimed—blew through his tousled hair. It wasn't its usual nut brown, but almost black. He didn't have his transformation under much better control than she did, no matter what he said the big cats in the zoo had taught him.

"Valerie," she said. "I don't know what to do with her."

He let out a sigh. She felt his fingertips move back like velvet paws. "And you think she's responsible for what happened?"

"Partly, anyway." Why didn't she tell it as it was? Valerie had handed her over to Tano, Michele, and the others. There was no ignoring that.

"Then let her rot away with Trevini." He meant exactly what he said, as she could tell from looking at him.

"I can't," she replied. "I can't give someone orders to kill her. Or simply act as if I don't know about it. It feels like she's next to me all the time. Even when I look at Iole, I see Valerie." A cold breeze blew against the walls and got under the fabric, and she pulled her blanket close. "We both freed Iole because your family was keeping her captive. Am I going to do something like that to Valerie now?"

"Iole was innocent," he said. "Valerie isn't."

"I know that. And yet . . ." She shook his head. "Trevini and the others are right. I'm a disaster as head of a Mafia clan." She laughed out loud. It sounded hysterical, and made her furious with herself. "Even the words are like a bad joke. Head of a Mafia clan!"

"Then ask her questions. Try to find out what really happened back in New York. What Michele wanted with you."

"Tano," she corrected him.

"Both of them." The anger in his voice made her shudder even more than the cool wind from below. But the goose bumps on her arms and legs felt good, perfectly natural, unlike the icy breath of the snake.

"I can't talk to her," she said after a moment's pause. "If I do, I'll go for her throat. It's . . . I'm surprised at myself. When I saw her sitting there, totally helpless, stoned out of her mind—I didn't even feel sorry for her."

"It's what she deserves."

"That sounds so simple. But it's a little more complicated for someone who wasn't brought up knowing the basic rules of the Mafia."

He stroked her cheek, smiling. "Where's the tough Rosa who was on that first flight to Sicily with me?"

"The odd thing is that all this should have toughened me up even more. Made me more realistic about it. But instead just the opposite has happened." She ran her fingers through her hair, and propped her chin on her knees. "I don't understand myself anymore. And that's an awful feeling. I don't want this. Can't everything just go back to how it was before Trevini brought the whole thing up again?"

"He's a calculating man. He knew exactly what he was doing."

"Yes, sure. But now it's too late. I can't just act as if I never watched that video."

He looked out into the dark. "Are you asking me what I'd do in your place?"

She'd known the answer to that for a long time, and it wasn't what she wanted. "No."

Minutes passed, and neither of them said anything. Their hands met again, but he didn't make another attempt to get closer to her. It was probably up to her to take the next step.

All she said was, "And then that ship."

"I have people finding out as much as possible about Thanassis and the *Stabat Mater*. They've come up with nothing but a few newspaper reports. Looks like he's cut himself off from the outside world in every possible way. Erected a kind of firewall around his business affairs and his private life. Not easy to get past that."

"Do you think he's a member of TABULA?"

"How would I know?"

"Exactly. We don't know anything." Alessandro didn't conceal the fact that he was at a loss, and it was good to see him, too, baffled for once. Without any answers. Or suggestions. Or any idea how to get out of this mess.

"There are just too many things I don't understand," she said. "And now my father is part of it as well. Can't anything be simple for once?"

"What did you say to Trevini's proposition?"

"What do you mean?"

"When he asked why you didn't get out of here, taking a large sum of money."

"He can go fuck himself. Figuratively speaking, anyway."

"He's right."

"What?" She stared at him, at the fine profile that looked, against the indigo twilight, as if it had been drawn with a quill. "How can you of all people say that?"

"I've thought of doing it myself," he admitted. "More than once."

"Don't talk nonsense. You're exactly where you wanted to be."

"But you matter to me more."

"I'm not running away from you." She tried a smile. "Hey,

you have a sauna. And a great pool. I wouldn't give that up for the world."

"Maybe we *will* go away, all the same, some time or other."

"Sure." She didn't believe it for a second.

"Can I take a look at them? Those furs?"

"Come tomorrow. Maybe you'll arrive before the villagers march up the mountain with lighted torches to burn the monster on her pyre."

"Your grandmother was a monster. Not you."

She widened her eyes theatrically. "A reptile? Nine feet long? How does that sound to you? There we are, the story of my life. My boyfriend turns into the most beautiful animal in the world, and what do I turn into? Godzilla."

He drew her close to him, and she was thankful for that. He often guessed what would do her good even before she knew it herself. But why did the same never happen to her? Was that why it was so easy for him to say he loved her—and she found it so hard to say she loved him back? How long had she mourned for Zoe? Not long. What did she feel for her mother? Not enough. Couldn't she love like other people? Was that her real problem?

He kissed her, and as the tips of their tongues touched, she thought: Of course I love him, more than anything else in the world.

When his hands felt under her T-shirt, and her fingers touched his arms and went to his chest—all in a tangle of blankets, crumpled shirts, and shorts, rather clumsily and very much her—some things didn't seem to matter, others were more important, and she thought: Don't let the snake control you.

She felt the panther fur at the back of his neck and the scales on her hands. She heard them rubbing together, and the sound thrilled her to the marrow of her bones. It was like a series of gentle electric shocks, a tender vibration that lasted a long time, much longer than usual, before the cold she feared came over her at last, bringing with it the transformation, and the end of something that hadn't even properly begun.

Coiling and purring, they lay together on the battlements, unable to stay in human form. But for the moment it was all right, because it was their nature, what they had in common, and perhaps even their purpose in life, if they only wanted it enough.

CERTAINTY

"WHAT ARE YOU DOING?" Iole was hurrying across the inner courtyard of the palazzo in Rosa's wake. She impatiently brushed the cobwebs that had been clinging to the toolshed door off her face.

Rosa went ahead to the gateway leading to the front of the house. Her footsteps echoed under the vaulted roof, hardly muted by the fluffy patches of mold hanging above her like storm clouds. She had a pickax in her hands, but she quickened her pace in spite of its weight.

"Rosa! I want to be there if you're going to wreck something!" In the tunnel, Iole's voice seemed to come from all sides at once, although she was several yards behind Rosa. She wore loose linen trousers and a white turtleneck, and looked more grown-up than she did in her usual summer dresses. Her short black hair had an almost blue sheen as she ran out of the tunnel into the open.

A glance over her shoulder confirmed Rosa's fears: Iole had Signora Falchi in tow. That was no surprise. Iole had seen Rosa in the courtyard through the schoolroom window, and had stormed out despite her indignant tutor's protests. She had trailed Rosa to the shed, where garden tools and other implements were stored.

"Iole! Signorina Alcantara!" The tutor was flailing her arms excitedly in the air as she followed Iole, some way behind her. "Just for *once*, will you please listen to me!"

Rosa hurried on.

"What are you going to do with that thing?" Iole demanded.

Rosa did not reply. She pressed her lips together firmly. She might change her mind if she said aloud what she was planning to do.

She went around the southeast corner of the palazzo, along the untended path that led to the side of the property facing uphill. Four months ago, when Zoe and Florinda were buried, the weeds and shrubs rambling all over the path had been removed. In the mild winter climate of Sicily, some of them had grown back, though not as wildly as before. At this time of day, the shadow of the chestnut trees on the outskirts of the pinewoods farther up the mountain didn't reach the east facade. At eleven in the morning, the sun was still too high. It shone with a dull glow in the hazy February sky.

As she walked, Rosa turned the pickax around in her hands to avoid grazing her leg on its rusty iron point. The tool looked as if no one had used it for years.

"Signorina!" called the tutor again when she, too, rounded the corner of the wall. She was determined not to be shaken off. "What on earth are you doing?" And, most uncharacteristically, she added a half-swallowed curse.

Rosa stormed toward the entrance of the funeral chapel. The small annex huddled furtively against the facade as if it had occurred to the architects of the palazzo, rather late in the game, that they had nowhere in the house dedicated to prayer and devotion. In fact, Rosa doubted whether anyone in the palazzo had ever prayed. A cast-iron bell hung in a niche above the chapel porch, as black as if pitch had been poured over it.

Just outside the entrance, Rosa stopped. She heard Iole's footsteps behind her and wondered for a moment whether to tell her not to come closer. But she lost patience and pushed both doors inward. All the doors in the palazzo squealed, this one loudest of all. Signora Falchi, still thirty feet away, sighed, "Holy Mother of God!" and slowed down.

Hands firmly clutching the pickax handle, Rosa stepped into the chapel. Inside, it smelled of dank masonry and withered flowers, although the floral arrangements for the last funeral here had been removed long ago. The odor seemed to have sunk deep into the walls and the faded fresco of saints under the ceiling.

The front and side walls were covered with a chessboard pattern of granite slabs, arranged one on top of the other in sets of three. Rosa didn't know when the first of her ancestors had been laid to rest here, but she assumed that the family tree went back centuries.

Costanza's tomb was on the far side of the room, beyond the altar in the front of the chapel. Rosa went up to the panel embedded in the wall and dropped the heavy end of the pickax. The metal crashed on the stone floor, and the sound vibrated through the high interior. The bell on the porch seemed to reply with a deep clang.

Rosa's fingertips touched the lettering carved into the granite surface. COSTANZA ALCANTARA. Black dust had settled inside the characters. Instinctively, she wiped her fingers on her jeans. There were no dates of birth and death, same as all the other tombs. Just names. As if it made no difference when the family members had lived. All that mattered was that they continued the Alcantara line, ensuring the survival of the dynasty.

Iole stumbled through the door, the tutor close on her heels. They both stood speechless. Rosa could feel their eyes on her back.

She placed the palm of her hand on the stone slab, as if feeling whether anything was moving behind it. A little dirt was left under her fingernails. She could see it even through the black nail polish that she had to reapply after every transformation. For a long time she had been making an effort to stop biting her nails. The dirt from the inscription on Costanza's tomb would certainly stop her now.

She withdrew her fingers, grasped the pickax again with both hands, and turned to the interior of the chapel.

Iole watched with bated breath. Signora Falchi's eyes, behind the lenses of her glasses, looked anxious and simultaneously fascinated in a macabre way. *"Signorina,"* she began cautiously.

"Just keep it to yourself," retorted Rosa.

"But—"

"Not now."

Three or four steps, and Rosa was looking at her father's

tomb. Like Costanza's, it was in the middle row of slabs. The one below it bore no inscription; the lettering on the one above it was faded. Curiously enough, no dust had settled there. As if only Costanza attracted all the dirt in this place.

Rosa took a deep breath and swung her arm. With an ear-splitting noise, she drove the tip of the pickax into her father's tombstone.

"Signorina!"

Steps behind her. Clattering heels.

Rosa struck a second time. A crack as wide as her finger ran across the surface like a flash of black lightning.

"Signorina Alcantara, I beg you—"

Spinning around, she let out a hiss that made the tutor flinch. Rosa felt her tongue split behind her teeth, but she took care not to open her mouth as the woman gave her one more dark glance, then turned and ran back to Iole, stationing herself protectively in front of the girl, as if seriously afraid that Rosa might go for her with the pickax.

When Rosa hit the tombstone for the third time, a gray triangle broke off the stone beneath the inscription. She had to strike the slab several more times before it crumbled away completely. The fragments fell to the floor, leaving only a few splinters in the open compartment of the tomb.

She could see the foot of a casket. The last eleven years had left it untouched. A gilded handle shone in the darkness.

Suddenly Iole was beside her. "Here, I'll help you," she said quietly.

Rosa nodded gratefully, propped the pickax against the

wall, and took hold of the broad metal handle on one side of the casket. It was cold as ice. Iole grasped the other handle, and as the tutor stood silently in the background, they gradually pulled the casket forward until the end stuck a foot and a half out of the wall compartment.

"That'll do," said Rosa.

Iole nodded and stepped back.

Out of the corner of her eye, Rosa saw Signora Falchi down on the floor beside the door. For a moment she was afraid that the tutor was going to faint, but she was wrong. Instead the woman frowned, leaned back against the wall as she sat there, and drew up her knees. "Nothing I can do about it," she said, sighing. "I'll just wait here until it's over, if I may."

Sweating now, Rosa raised the pickax. She hit the oak lid of the casket three times, until a hole the size of a human head gaped in the wood, and the pickax stuck in as far as it would go. With a gasp, she pulled the tool out, let it drop, and bent over the hole.

"Let's just hope," remarked Signora Falchi on the other side of the chapel, "that it really is the foot end you have there."

Rosa peered over the splintered edge of the hole. Iole's hand reached for hers and held it tightly.

"Makes no difference," she said a moment later, straightening her back and standing erect as she breathed deeply in and out.

Iole looked at her, and then she too peered inside the casket.

"Oh," she said.

Rosa squeezed her hand once more, then let go. She walked out of the chapel, stopped, and drew fresh air into her lungs. It smelled of the pine trees growing farther up the slope, of grass, and of the salty wind blowing over the hills from the distant sea.

Behind her in the chapel, she heard the sound of the tutor's footsteps as she took her turn glancing inside the casket.

Iole came out onto the porch and stopped a little way behind Rosa.

"Where is he, then?" she asked.

Rosa shrugged her shoulders, and went back into the house in silence.

THE WHITE TELEPHONE

ROSA WAS STANDING ON the balcony of the study with its wrought-iron balustrade, looking out over the inner courtyard and the rooftops to the peak of the mountain, when the telephone rang.

It wasn't the phone on her desk. This one had a ringtone unlike any that she had yet heard in the palazzo.

The muted, almost inaudible sound came from the wall paneling on the west side of the room. It was a *genuine* ring, very old-fashioned, not a trendy modern tone. She'd never heard it except in old movies and as a ringtone to download on a cell phone. But something told her that there was no cell phone concealed in the wall.

After a minute, during which she groped around more and more frantically for hidden mechanisms, the sound stopped. She cursed quietly, but she didn't give up. Finally she tried the obvious and, sure enough, found a panel at chest height that could be slid aside with the palm of her hand. It disappeared behind the panel next to it with a faint sound. A secret door came into view lower down on the wall.

Behind it, the phone began to ring again.

The door wasn't locked. Ducking low, Rosa slipped through it and found herself in a tiny room less than six feet square.

It contained a high-backed armchair and a round table, on which an old-fashioned, snow-white telephone stood. It had a round dial and an enormously heavy receiver. The casing of the phone looked like ivory or mother-of-pearl.

She picked up the receiver. "Hello?"

"Good day."

"Trevini?" She dropped into the chair. "What kind of a phone is this?"

"One so outmoded that Judge Quattrini's people and everyone else who'd like to listen in have forgotten how to bug it. Officially the cable network we're using doesn't exist anymore. But certain persons in, let's say, high places made sure, when the system was modernized a few decades ago, that parts of it were left in place all over Sicily. The authorities know nothing about it. Or if they do, they would be greatly disappointed if they tried tapping into it with their ultramodern digital stuff."

"Why didn't you say anything about this before?"

"To find out how much you know about the secrets of the palazzo." Which told her that there must certainly be others that he wasn't telling her about. Demonstrating his superiority, the bastard.

"What do you want?"

"I want to help you."

"Sure you do."

"No, listen, Rosa. This is something you ought to take seriously."

She shifted in the uncomfortable chair. Traces of dust

were left on her black clothes.

"And I would be glad," he said, "if, when you hear what I'm calling about, you do not hang up."

She could have done it there and then. She had a good idea what this was all about. Or whom.

"In all probability," said Trevini, "it was Alessandro Carnevare who contracted for the murder of his relations in New York."

A startled lizard scurried over the wall of the secret room and disappeared into a tiny hole in the corner.

"I know what you're thinking," he continued. "Can't the old fool keep quiet for once? How often is he going to try to discredit Alessandro?"

"I wouldn't have put it that politely."

"One of the things you pay me for is to tell you unwelcome truths, to your face. And this has nothing to do with my personal dislike of young Carnevare. It's a fact that instructions for the killings came from Italy. Michele Carnevare himself only just escaped an attempt on his life two days ago, and his people succeeded in following the trail back—to someone who was a leading figure in the transatlantic drug trade for many years. A certain Stelvio Guerrini. Not a name you need to remember, and he hasn't played a very active role for some time. Anyway, he sent the killers on behalf of a third party. And Guerrini was a close business partner of Baron Massimo Carnevare—Alessandro's father."

"That proves nothing at all." Her own composure surprised her. Was it because she didn't believe him? Or because she had already guessed it, even though Alessandro had denied it? "Any family in Sicily could have contracted this Guerrini to get rid of Michele."

"Yes, to be sure. Except no one but Alessandro seems to have any reason to wipe out the whole New York branch of the Carnevares. A single contract killing, yes, that would be possible. But attempted assassination of the entire leadership of the American Carnevares? That amounts to an open declaration of war, and there's no one who would risk that, not these days. At the moment most of the families have other anxieties to deal with on their own doorsteps. A clan feud carried out across the Atlantic causes more uproar than most can stomach."

"Do you have any proof of this?"

"Rosa, you and I are not the police. I have no interest in convicting Alessandro Carnevare of a crime. That would be rather foolish, don't you think?"

The receiver shook slightly as she held it to her ear. She clutched it more firmly.

"But the way it looks, he lied to you if he said he had nothing to do with those deaths. Do you understand? What makes you so sure that he hasn't done the same before? Or since?" The attorney's tone of voice was sharper now. "He walks over other people's corpses, and he'll always keep secrets from you. You mustn't trust him. Whatever he says—it could *all* be lies."

"Because you happen to have heard a few rumors?"

"In case of doubt—yes. Those murders are a fact. So is the origin of the orders to have them carried out. It all points the same way. And it's not over yet. First it was Michele's brother Carmine, then several of his cousins. And since the failed assassination attempt on Michele, two more Carnevares have been killed." She heard paper rustling at his end of the line. "Now the targets are openly the younger ones. Thomas Carnevare, who couldn't even speak Italian. He was only twenty. And Mattia Carnevare was—"

"Mattia?"

"You know him?"

"How did he die?"

"The body was burnt. Not much more is known about it. Found in a pile of garbage in Crown Heights. That's a part of—"

"Brooklyn," she whispered.

"Of course. You know your way around there."

"Mattia wasn't murdered by any contract killer," she said. "That was done by Michele himself."

Trevini said nothing for a moment. Maybe he expected an explanation. She wasn't going to give him one. Had Mattia been murdered that night? Had he managed to escape the others at the boathouse, only to be killed later?

"What do you know about it?" asked the attorney.

"Only that Mattia Carnevare's death has nothing to do with Alessandro. It was a punitive operation within the family."

Trevini muttered something angrily to himself. Then he said, "Did you tell Alessandro Carnevare about the furs?"

"No."

"I can only pray that you're telling the truth. That boy is obsessed with revenge—first for his mother's death, then for what Michele Carnevare did to you. Who knows what would happen if he knew that the skins of his family were lined up on coat hangers in your cellar."

Rosa stared at the blank wall. She would have liked to get to her feet and prowl around the room, but the damn Stone Age phone had too short a cord for that.

"Stay out of this," she said, and was horrified to hear the tremor in her voice. "Alessandro is my business. Nothing to do with anyone else."

"I'm afraid you delude yourself. There's more at stake here than the question of who you're necking with."

She wasn't letting him destroy her relationship with Alessandro. No one could do that.

"It's about the family," he said. "The inheritance that you accepted. Your father's legacy. *That* ought to matter to you."

"My father's not in his grave."

"I beg your pardon?"

"I opened his casket. There's nothing but bricks inside."

There was a long silence at the other end of the line.

"No good advice?" she asked after a while.

"I'm considering it. And that you ought to be putting your mind to more important matters than—"

"Than the fact that my father's fucking casket is empty?" she shouted. Whether she liked it or not, she couldn't help going on in the same furious tone. "You can drop the tone of superiority, Trevini! And your warnings and predictions and all that garbage, too. We have a deal. If I need your paternal advice, I'll call and ask for it. Meanwhile, you can stop snooping around about Alessandro."

He stayed calm, which infuriated her even more. Pure calculation, of course. She could sense it even over the phone. "Just as you like, Rosa."

"And I want you to let Valerie go free."

"Have you thought about that carefully?"

"We don't need her anymore."

"Don't forget what she did to you."

"That's my business, okay?"

He seemed to bring his mouth closer to the receiver, because now he was whispering, although his voice was no quieter. "You don't remember that night, I believe?"

"You've seen the police files, haven't you?"

"I know a great deal more than just those files."

"What do you mean?"

He cleared his throat. "Remember the video I sent you?" He paused, as if he actually expected an answer to that. "There's also a second one. When we picked up your friend, she had another cell phone with her. She'd obviously stolen it from Michele Carnevare before setting off for Europe. And there was a video on that phone, too."

For a moment Rosa could hardly breathe.

"I wanted to spare you this," he said. "Believe me, I really did."

"Are you saying that . . . that he filmed it?"

"I'm sorry."

She didn't know which was worse: that a video of her rape existed, or that Trevini had watched it. Cold flowed through her body at breakneck speed.

She managed to speak only by concentrating very hard. It sounded as if someone else were talking for her, like a ventriloquist with a dummy. "Send it here," she said. Getting the words out took half an eternity. "I want to see it."

"Why would you wish to subject yourself to that?"

"To find out what *you* saw."

"This is not about our differences of opinion, Rosa. I don't think it would be good for you to—"

"Send me that cell phone. Actually, send them both."

"If you insist." He seemed to want to give her a chance to change her mind. When she didn't, he said, "And what am I to do with the girl?"

"She can go." Rosa's vocal cords threatened to freeze up, but in a way that she didn't understand, she managed to keep the transformation under control. "I don't want to see Val ever again. Put her in a taxi to the airport. And you'd better book her on a flight to Rome, or New York, or wherever she wants."

"I'll see to it that she disappears."

"No one's to touch a hair on her head. I am *not* giving orders to have her killed."

"I understand perfectly." His own voice sounded mechanical now.

"Give her some money, enough to last her a week or two, and charge it to me."

"I really hope she'll appreciate that."

"Just as long as she's gone."

"And you think that will soothe your conscience?"

"You don't understand. I'm not talking about my conscience."

"No?"

"If I watch that video," she said quietly, "it could change my mind."

"You want to protect her? From yourself, Rosa?" He laughed quietly. "It's your sense of responsibility, then. You don't want to have to make a decision that you'd regret later."

"Maybe I wouldn't regret it at all. Maybe I'd suddenly realize that I *like* making those decisions." The power over life and death. The power wielded by her ancestors.

"Until now, I thought you were only running away from yourself," he said gently. "But in reality you're running away from the ghost of Costanza."

She said nothing until, at long last, he hung up.

LYCAON'S CURSE

"MATTIA IS DEAD," SAID Alessandro that evening, before Rosa could say a word about her conversation with Trevini.

She was holding a steaming double espresso, not her first of the day, and her whole body felt as if creatures of some kind were scrabbling under her skin.

They were standing on the terrace of the Palazzo Alcantara, with its panoramic view over the olive groves and out to the west. The tall palm fronds rising to the sky in front of the stone balustrade rustled in the darkness, and the pump of the swimming pool gurgled quietly, the light of the underwater lamps bathing part of the west facade in wavering brightness. The mild evening air was filled with the song of the cicadas.

"They found his body yesterday," said Alessandro. "Burnt, lying in a Dumpster."

"In Crown Heights."

"You know about it?"

"Trevini called. He told me."

Slowly, he nodded. "And of course he tried to pin the blame on me."

Rosa emptied her cup of coffee in a single gulp, and placed it on the top of the balustrade. "Is he right? Did you have anything to do with it?"

"You've already asked me that question. And I answered you."

"Were you telling the truth?"

"Would you sooner believe Trevini than me?"

"Oh, come on. I can't just leave it hovering in the air between us."

He sighed gently and looked out at the plain again. The countryside was almost immersed in night. Miles away, the lights of a village glinted. Up in the starlit sky, the signal beams of a solitary airplane blinked on and off as it flew silently north.

"When I told you that I had nothing to do with the assassinations, you said—"

"I said it was too bad. I know."

"Did you mean it?"

She nodded without hesitation. "Do you think I've never wished them dead? I've hoped, often enough, that they'd perish miserably."

"It's possible that Mattia was still alive when they set fire to him."

She took his hand, and gently drew him close. "He wasn't there. Mattia wasn't one of them."

"What makes you so sure?"

Could she be sure? What would she see on the second video? Who would she recognize? Only Michele and Tano? At the moment, she wasn't certain if she would ever watch it.

Alessandro's gaze was grave and dark. "Did you ask Mattia? Or did he deny it on his own?"

"Neither."

"Then you don't know that he was innocent."

"He saved my life!"

"And I'm not responsible for his death. Whatever Trevini claims."

Had she really thought that Alessandro was lying to her? She fought down her guilt. "Okay," she said after a while. "Who was it, then?"

His expression told her that he was reluctant to give her the truth. Rosa saw the trouble in his eyes. She stroked his hair and kissed him, just because all of a sudden she felt like it.

"The Hungry Man," he said.

"I thought he was still in prison."

"As if that ever stopped any *capo* from handing out death sentences."

"But why would he do that? What business of his are your American relations?"

"His business is mainly to do with me."

She stared at him. The grief in his eyes, the sorrow in his voice touched her. And slowly, she began to see where all this was going.

"The Hungry Man will soon be out of prison," he went on. "That's not just rumor; it's only a matter of time. Someone in high places—very high places—has seen to it that the inquiry into his appeal was reopened. And everyone can guess the outcome."

The Hungry Man—everyone called him that; no one used his true name—had been the predecessor of Salvatore

Pantaleone, the *capo dei capi* whom Rosa had known. For decades he had ruled the Sicilian Mafia with an iron fist, until he was brought to trial and imprisoned almost thirty years ago. He had been as good as forgotten for a long time, and then, a few years earlier, new rumors began circulating. Ever since, it had been said that the return of the Hungry Man was imminent, that he had influential allies in all the European centers of power, people who ensured that the verdicts condemning him for the worst of his crimes were overturned and sentences for the other charges shortened. Pantaleone was dead; the position of *capo dei capi* was vacant. Who would be the new boss of bosses? Power struggles were going on within Cosa Nostra, but no one had nominated himself for the post. They all seemed to fear the Hungry Man, and no one wanted to risk standing in his way if he really did come back to Sicily to reassert his old claim.

He had given himself the title of the Hungry Man, proclaiming that he was the reincarnation of the ancestor of all the Arcadian dynasties—King Lycaon, the tyrant who, according to legend, had been turned by Zeus, father of the gods, into the first to change between human and animal form. With him, all the other inhabitants of Arcadia had been condemned to the same fate. And so the Panthera were born, the Lamias, the Hundinga, and all the other shape-shifters who had been dispersed around the world after the downfall of Arcadia, but maintained the sunken empire's heritage to the present day.

The Hungry Man, so it was said, wanted to restore the rule of terror of the old Arcadian dynasties. He promised his followers a return to the bloody excesses of antiquity, when the shape-shifters ruled the kingdoms all around the Mediterranean and feasted to their hearts' content on human flesh.

Rosa took Alessandro's hand. "What sort of business does he have with you?"

"He hates my family. For a long time, the Carnevares were closer to him than anyone else, until someone betrayed him, and he blamed us for it."

"And *did* your family betray him?"

He shrugged his shoulders. "I don't know, and I don't think it makes any difference. He swore to take revenge on us more than a quarter of a century ago. And now it's time for him to demonstrate his new strength. He's gradually decimating my family—or what's left of it—beginning with the American Carnevares. With every murder he's coming closer, and someday it will be my turn."

How long had Alessandro known about this? What he and she had between them was still too fragile to withstand so many secrets. When would the moment come when the strain was too much for it?

"You're right at the end of his hit list?" she asked, her voice husky.

He nodded. "At least that's what I assume."

"How many people has he had killed already? Only Michele's brother and cousins, or others as well?"

Maybe he was sorry now that he had told her the truth. But she gave him credit that he hadn't tried soothing her with evasions. Another reason why she was so attracted to him.

"One of my second cousins was shot in Catania the day before yesterday," he said. "And two more in Palermo. Unless there's someone else behind that, his killers have reached Sicily." He rubbed his nose, but it wasn't the knowing gesture with which he sometimes riled her; this time it seemed to be nervousness. "He wants me to panic. Maybe strike out blindly around me, as my father or Cesare would have done. He'd probably like it if I tried to blame other families for the murders and started a clan feud. That would suit him very well. He'd only have to watch us weakening each other, and then he could seize power over all the clans."

"What are you going to do?"

"The obvious thing would be to summon all the Carnevares. But I'd sooner die than ally myself with someone like Michele. Not after everything he did to you."

Maybe she should have asked him not to take her feelings into consideration. But instead she kissed him again, this time harder, and for a while neither of them said a word, not even when their lips parted and they looked at each other.

"It's not my turn yet," he said. "He's probably enjoying the idea of the murders spreading fear and terror among the Carnevares too much for that. He'll take his time before his killers turn their attention to me. But that's not what worries me."

She raised one hand and stroked his cheek and throat. She just wanted to be close to him, very close.

"I'm afraid for you," he said.

"I'm not a Carnevare."

"Word of our relationship has spread. There's a hotbed of

rumor seething, and we haven't gone to any trouble to counter that. I still thought danger loomed from the other clans and our own people. But now . . ." He stopped, kissed the palm of her hand, bent her fingers into a fist, and closed his own hand around it. "Now it's possible that the Hungry Man has you in his sights."

"Me?"

He nodded. "If he wants to get at me, if he's really hell-bent on injuring the *capo* of the Carnevares, then he'll have to take you away from me. He'll try to kill you, Rosa."

"Nonsense," she contradicted him, but even as she spoke, she realized that he was right. There was a long tradition in the Mafia of attacking an enemy by murdering all his loved ones. Obviously she would be on the Hungry Man's hit list herself.

"So now?" she whispered.

"I don't want you going anywhere without bodyguards," he said. "And I don't mean those rustics from Piazza Armerina. You need a security service. Specialists who know what they—"

"Hey, hey, hey," she gently interrupted him, putting a finger to his lips. A smile stole over her face. "I don't want gorillas around me day and night, never mind where they come from."

"But—"

"Where are *your* bodyguards?" she asked. "I don't see any of them around here. You don't like going around with a bunch of apes in black suits any more than I do." She stood on tiptoe and kissed the end of his nose. "We're Arcadians. We'll manage by ourselves."

"Says who?"

"Says me."

"Totally senseless."

"All this is totally senseless. That was obvious from the very first day. Did it stop us?"

His hand was on the back of her neck. He drew her to him again. Her breasts gently brushed his chest, and she felt the nipples harden—as they always did before disappearing and turning to scaly snakeskin. Infuriating.

"I know what we'll do now," she said.

At last his radiant smile came back. "You do?"

"To take our minds off it."

"Oh. Okay."

"The basement," she said. "Those furs."

THE SERUM

WITHOUT SAYING A WORD, Alessandro followed her down the central aisle between the linen-wrapped bundles that dangled from the rails. Now and then he touched one of the bags, then ran his fingers down it as he walked along, but he didn't open any of them. Before they reached the rampart of plastic containers, Rosa took his hand.

At the sight of the containers he stopped walking. "So many," he whispered. In the cold air, the words came out of his mouth as white vapor. "Are there any Panthera among them?"

"Let's just say they're not only mink and sable."

She led him around the stacked containers to the metal safe on the back wall of the freezer. Everything was exactly as she and Iole had left it. The metal doors were open; the two fur coats lay on the floor in front of them.

Rosa went up to the safe. "Did you bring what I asked you—" She stopped herself when she turned to Alessandro.

He was crouching down beside the coat that Iole had been wearing. Only now did Rosa noticed a faint pattern of leopard spots shimmering through the dark brown of the fur. Alessandro had picked up one sleeve from the floor and was stroking it, lost in thought.

She swore quietly. "Panthers are—"

"Black leopards." He didn't look up at her.

She knelt down beside him. "I'm so sorry," she whispered, taking his face in both hands and making him look her in the eye. "If there were any way I could undo it . . ."

"I know."

"Our families have been at odds forever. More people have died than . . ." She paused for a moment. "Than these," she finished.

"That's all right."

"No, nothing's all right." She jerked her head at the metal safe. "There they are. God knows how many vials."

He stood up and went over to the shelves with the little glass flasks lined up on them. The liquid inside shone golden. In the lowest compartment lay plastic syringes in sterile wrappings and bundles of sealed cannulas, along with two syringes like the kind used by diabetics for their insulin.

"Do you have it with you?" she asked.

With a nod, he put his hand in his jeans pocket, brought out a little leather case, and opened it. Inside, there were several vials that looked exactly like those in the cupboard. "This is one of the vials from the Castello. Cesare had his men inject us with the same thing back there. And I had a few with me at boarding school in the States, for emergencies." He had already told her that, months ago, and she had remembered it after Iole led her to the cupboard.

"You said at the time that the prescription was handed down by the first Arcadians. At the time of their downfall."

"That's what Tano always said, anyway."

"And he was given the serum by Cesare?"

"No, the other way around. Tano got hold of it somewhere. I always assumed it came from a dealer. Cesare kept it in a safe in his office, but Tano had a key of his own. I found it among his things."

"Michele injected me with a dose of it that night in Central Park. He said the stuff came from Tano." Rosa took one of the vials out of his hand. "May I?" She placed it beside the others in the metal cupboard. Outwardly there was no visible difference. A yellow fluid in a transparent vial.

"There's a laboratory that used to work for Florinda," she said. "It supplied immunizations for the refugees she trafficked into Europe from Lampedusa. We should be able to find out from that lab if it's the same serum."

"Yes, probably."

"You think so, too?"

He nodded thoughtfully.

She took Alessandro's ampoule off the shelf again, went over to the containers, and looked back at the rows of furs in their linen bags. "If they wanted to take their furs, they had to make sure that they didn't—"

"Change back into human form," he quietly ended her sentence. "They had to see that they stayed in animal shape even after death." He seemed pale, but perhaps it was the chill in here. "The video that Cesare showed us, all the Arcadians in cages and unable to change back again . . . he said that was the doing of TABULA."

"Trevini claims that a man called Apollonio supplied furs

to my grandmother. Does that name mean anything to you?"

"Never heard it before."

"He thinks this Apollonio may have been one of the members of TABULA himself. Or was at least in close contact with them. Could be that TABULA sold the skins of the Arcadians they'd abducted for their experiments to Costanza through Apollonio. Anyway, I guess she also got the serum from him."

"But if it comes from TABULA . . ." Alessandro began. He stopped, then asked, "Do you think Tano got it from them as well?"

"Cesare hated TABULA," she said doubtfully.

Alessandro gave a bitter laugh. "He was terrified of the organization. All the same, I wouldn't put it past Tano to be making deals behind his father's back."

Rosa leaned against the ice-cold plastic containers. "Let's assume that Tano really was secretly in touch with TABULA. Then he could have gotten the serum from them and passed some of it on to Cesare and maybe also to Michele. You said you thought it came from a dealer. But suppose, instead, he was the dealer himself. Suppose Tano sold the serum under the table to Arcadians like Michele, so that they'd be able to stop their own transformations—and other people's."

"It's possible."

"Did he ask you for money? For the serum that you took to the States with you?"

Alessandro shook his head. "I just had to promise not to tell Cesare about them. Or my parents."

"And did you do as he asked?"

"Sure. Tano was the first person to tell me about the transformations. I was actually grateful to him at the time." He obviously wasn't happy with the memory. "I really wish I could . . . wash myself clean of them all. Can you understand that? Tano, Cesare, my father . . . all the lies, all the things they did. I wish there were some way simply to eradicate it all."

"I feel the same way. Florinda lied to me; even Zoe did. You and I have been used for other people's purposes all along. And it never stops."

He put his arms around her again. "If it gets to be too much . . . if we can't take any more of it . . . we can get out of here. And then I won't mind what becomes of all this in Sicily. None of it matters as much as you."

His kiss warmed her, even in the chilly air of the freezer. They held each other close, she smelled his hair, his skin, and at that moment she'd have gone anywhere with him, even to the end of the world. Corny and sentimental, sure, but right now that was what she needed. The biggest, stickiest, sweetest helping of corny sentimentality since the invention of dessert. She wouldn't have minded if it rained rose petals, or if Iole came out from behind the containers playing a violin. Plenty of time for indigestion tomorrow.

Only now did she realize that she was still holding the serum he had brought with him. Slowly, she raised the vial to face level, and as she paused for breath, she glanced at the syringes in the cupboard. His eyes followed hers, and then the corners of his mouth twitched.

She could feel her pulse beating faster in her throat. "Well, it must have its uses, right?"

His hand stroked the back of her head and stopped gently at the nape of her neck. "For a quarter of an hour?"

"Sometimes it lasts twenty minutes."

"Not exactly a long time."

"Better than nothing."

Alessandro's laughter was like a bright flame leaping into the air.

AT SEA

The *GAIA* was cruising the Mediterranean with no other vessel in sight. Evening dusk was falling; the first stars appeared in the clear sky. It was still warm, around sixty degrees, and the water reflected the light from the yacht's portholes.

"What does love mean to you?" asked Rosa.

Alessandro didn't even have to think about it. "Lying awake at night, realizing I'm going to die sometime—but that doesn't bother me, because there'll be someone with me when the time comes." He glanced sideways at her. "How about you?"

"Honeymooning in the Bronx."

"Romantic."

"No, that's the point. People honeymoon in Paris or Vienna or Florence, so they won't have time to fight in those first few weeks. There are so many sights to see, so much else to think about. They're using history to anesthetize the present. But if you really love someone, then you can make do with a couple of weeks in the Bronx. Or Detroit. Or Novosibirsk. That way it's not all about ancient monuments and museums, it's just about the other person and yourself. And that's love."

They had made themselves comfortable in the seating area on the top deck, and were looking into the flames of two dozen little candle lanterns arranged around the table and the deck itself. In the candlelight, the two blue marks on Rosa's upper arm left by the needle of the syringe were clearly visible.

They had felt like junkies, injecting each other with the serum last night. But they had stayed in human form for quite a while, and when the transformations finally seemed about to begin, they had risked a second dose.

Alessandro had given himself the serum before, for sporting events and other occasions at his boarding school, and he swore that he had never noticed any side effects. Rosa had been forcibly injected with it twice, so at first she had been nervous. But she had not for a second regretted taking the serum, and she was actually the one who had insisted on the second dose.

Twenty minutes, twice running. In retrospect it seemed to her much longer, and yet not nearly long enough. Her intention of gaining control over her transformations as quickly as possible was even stronger now. She didn't want to rely on a strange serum, harmless or not. In the old days she had always refused to drink diet soda and energy drinks because of all the toxins they contained. And now here she was injecting herself with some dubious substance, which—if she was right in her assumptions—had been developed by the archenemy of the Arcadians. All the same, she could hardly wait to load up the syringe next time.

Alessandro was barefoot, wearing only washed-out jeans and a pale T-shirt. She liked his feet. The skin over his insteps was the same brown as his chest and his arms. In the candlelight from the lanterns, his body shone like bronze.

Rosa was resting with the back of her head on his lap, letting him push unruly blond strands back from her forehead. He did that often, and very lovingly, but she had only to move and her hair was as untidy as before. Typical, she thought, resigned to it: I can't even control my own hair.

They had taken the yacht out so they wouldn't be disturbed. The sofa where they had been lounging around all day was upholstered in the best white leather, and was as showy as everything else on the vessel. Alessandro's father had fitted the *Gaia* out with the most expensive finishings, from paneling in African woods in the saloon to gilded faucets in the galley. Alessandro was embarrassed by it. More than once, he had mentioned selling the *Gaia*. If he didn't, it was only because of the name of the yacht. His dead mother's name.

Rosa was wearing a black top and a short skirt. She thought her knees were too red and her calves too pale, but it didn't seem to bother him. With Alessandro, she felt for the first time that she wasn't entering some kind of competition. Their families might be rivals, but they weren't.

He kissed her forehead, the end of her nose, her lips. She put her hand on the back of his neck, drew him down to her again, and held him until neither of them could breathe and they moved apart, laughing.

"Do they still hurt?" He pointed to the blue marks where the needle had gone in.

"I'll live."

He made an instinctive sound as she moved away from

him and sat cross-legged on the sofa. She watched him as, once again, he gave her the youthful grin that didn't seem to suit the *capo* of a Mafia clan. A fresh evening breeze blew her hair in front of her face, and she tried to hold it back with both hands.

There was a buzzing sound. Her cell phone was lying on the table in front of the sofa. The vibration from the ringtone made it circle around the glass surface like a drunk bumblebee.

When she looked at the display, she recognized the number. "The lab. Finally." Before they had left the palazzo for the coast, Rosa had sent a driver to Enna with a vial from the cellar and what was left of Alessandro's serum. They must have come up with the results of the tests.

She took the call, as Alessandro expectantly pressed his lips together. A little later she thanked the caller, said the laboratory was to invoice her at the office in Piazza Armerina, and put the cell phone back on the table.

"The same substance," she said. "Probably still effective, even after all the years it's been stored down there."

"Then Tano really was in touch with this Apollonio. Or some other TABULA go-between." She had told Alessandro that her father had forbidden the attorney to pursue his own inquiries, saying that he would follow the trail of Apollonio himself. She suppressed the thought of that empty tomb as best she could, for now.

"Try as I might, I can't remember ever hearing the name before," said Alessandro. "Tano and Cesare talked about many of their business associates, but not an Apollonio . . . or at least not when I was present."

"And the people at the lab said something else. The substance is really an antiserum derived from blood. They tried to isolate its components, but they thought there was something wrong with the original blood."

He looked at her as if trying to estimate just *how* bad the news about to follow was.

"They can't classify it as either human or animal blood," she explained. "Obviously the serum has features of both, different proteins or . . . or whatever. But the serum we sent them is from a single donor, so it's not a mixture of several."

"Sounds impossible," he said.

"That's what they thought, too."

"As long as we're in human form, everything about us is human, including our blood. And after transformation—"

"Yes, our blood is also animal. One hundred percent." She nodded slowly. "However, the raw material for the serum came from someone who's both. Human and animal *at the same time*."

Alessandro linked his hands behind his head and leaned back with a groan. "Hybrids."

Rosa frowned. "Hybrids?"

"Arcadians who stop changing in midtransformation. Half animal, half human."

"Stop changing?"

"It's only a rumor. Don't worry about it."

Her eyes narrowed. "If that means I'm going to be walking

around with a snake's head someday, then I have plenty to worry about."

"I was afraid you'd say that."

"And that's why you never mentioned it before?"

"Sorry."

"What else have you kept from me?"

"I haven't kept anything from you," he snapped.

"How often does that kind of thing happen?"

"I've no idea."

"Once a month? Once a year? Once in a lifetime?"

"You're not going to get hysterical, are you?"

She jumped up, almost sweeping one of the candle lanterns off the table. "As if having to change into an animal wasn't bad enough! And now there's the risk of ending up as a sideshow act on top of it. The amazing reptile woman."

"The risk of dying of a perfectly normal cancer someday is probably a hundred times greater. Or a thousand times. How would I know?"

"So what about the blood in the serum?"

He sighed quietly. "Yes, you have a point there."

"Does TABULA breed these creatures?"

"Why would they do that?"

She went over to the rail and leaned against it. "Why would they capture Arcadians and then skin them? Why would anyone make coats out of the pelts? Damn it, it doesn't matter why all this happens! Just that it *does* happen."

"You think that the experiments carried out by TABULA— and we only know about those from hearsay, right?—led to the creation of hybrids of some kind?"

She took a deep breath and watched him in the light of the flickering candle lanterns. He looked slightly ill. "We don't know anything for sure, do we? But we have to start somewhere."

"Start?" He stood up and came over to her. "Is that the plan? Put a stop to the activities of TABULA? Do away with evil? In the Land of Mordor, where the Shadows lie?"

She shook her head. "I couldn't care less about heroics."

Alessandro smiled. "Because strictly speaking, *we* represent evil, right?"

"What's TABULA, then?"

"Maybe just a specter thought up by men like Cesare to justify what they do. A phantom image of the enemy. Just an excuse to behave even worse than the others."

She held his gaze, felt for his hands. "Is that what you really think?"

"I don't know what to think anymore."

"I want to know what Costanza was up to. And what became of my father. All the things that have to do with me."

With us, said his eyes.

"With us," she whispered.

THE VISITOR

"YOU CAN'T MOVE IN here, Signora Falchi, and that's my final answer."

The tutor was standing on the flight of steps leading up to the entrance of the Palazzo Alcantara. Rosa herself was only just back from the coast when the woman drove her Toyota into the inner courtyard. Now her two bags were sitting on the dusty pavement in front of the steps, with Signora Falchi between them, and Rosa strongly wished that she were anywhere else.

Raffaela Falchi crossed her arms. Her glasses flashed in the sunlight, making her look even readier for a fight. "You wanted a good tutor, right?"

"Yes."

"You wanted the best tutor available for this difficult child."

"Yes."

"And you wanted her for six hours a day."

"Yes!"

"Well, now you're getting her for twenty-four hours a day. At the same price."

"But that's not the point!"

"In this house, I have witnessed toothpaste tubes lying

around with the tops left off. The desecration of graves. Whipped cream sprayed straight from the can into people's mouths. The desecration of graves. Dirty shoes on parquet flooring. Oh, and did I mention the desecration of graves?"

Rosa groaned. "You're always complaining. You're in a bad mood all day. You get irritated with Iole, and you think I'm too young to look after her. So why do you want to come and live here?"

"First: You *are* too young to look after her. Second: You don't want to be responsible for Iole; you can't even cope with being responsible for yourself. And third: I've split up with my boyfriend."

"You had a *boyfriend*?" Rosa had expected almost anything, but not that Raffaela Falchi might be in a relationship. Having sex.

"He's a musician."

"Plays the flute, maybe?"

"Singer. In a rock band."

"*Your* boyfriend?"

"Ex-boyfriend."

Rosa realized that she was standing on the stairway as if defending it with her life against the unwanted intruder. Legs apart, right in the middle of the steps. The pair of them must look ridiculous.

"Why would I want you to live with us?" Rosa asked, sighing.

"I have green thumbs. Ten of them."

"We don't grow plants."

"My cousin in Caltagirone has a florist. She'll give me a discount. And then there's my other cousin—she runs a perfumery. She could get you—"

"Okay. All right." Rosa could hardly understand why, but she went down the steps, picked up one of the bags, and nodded in the direction of the porch over the entrance. "But if I see—or smell—either of your cousins, you're fired."

For the first time, she saw Raffaela Falchi grin, and for a moment, for a fraction of a second, she thought she saw something behind the tutor's usual reproachful expression that might even attract a rock singer.

"Did you go on tour with him?" she asked, as they hauled the baggage up the steps.

"I've had tinnitus ever since."

In the entrance hall, Iole came toward them in one of her white dresses. She stopped dead when she saw her tutor there with Rosa.

"Oh," she said, as her eyes fell on the luggage.

"You'd better put on something else," said Signora Falchi, her tone of voice skeptical. "Whenever you wear that outfit I feel as if I'm seeing the world through white highlighter."

Iole wrinkled her forehead. "Maybe your glasses are clouded up."

Glancing sideways at Rosa, the tutor raised an eyebrow. "*You* didn't buy her those clothes, did you?"

Rosa raised her hands defensively.

"I bought them online," said Iole. "They have such lovely music on that website. You don't get nice music on every site, but you do on that one. I think it makes the dresses even prettier. And if you order three, you get a free packet of sunflower seeds and a CD to help you meditate. Only no flowers came up. I planted them all—well, the seeds, I mean; not the CD. And I watered them. And talked to them."

"I can show you how to grow sunflowers," said Signora Falchi, a little less sternly. "And then we'll order you something new together."

Rosa nodded when Iole looked at her doubtfully. "Signora Falchi is cool," she commented, with a touch of sarcasm. "Her boyfriend is a musician."

"Ex-boyfriend."

Iole glanced at the two bags. "You're going to live with us now?"

Raffaela Falchi looked inquiringly at Rosa.

Rosa nodded again. "For the time being. It's better not to have so many rooms standing empty. To air them. They're damp from the walls." She had expected opposition from Iole, but the girl only rubbed the back of her neck thoughtfully and then shrugged her shoulders.

"Okay," she said.

The tutor beamed.

"Which room is she going to have?" asked Iole.

Rosa gestured in the direction of the ceiling. "We have twenty-three empty bedrooms. Take your pick."

Iole reached for one of the bags and was about to go ahead, but then she stopped and pointed to a small table near the porch. A padded white envelope lay on it. "A courier brought that yesterday. It's for you, Rosa. From Avvocato Trevini.

Feels like two cell phones."

Rosa's heart sank like a stone. She went over to the packet, picked it up, and saw that it had been opened. "*Feels like* two cell phones?"

Iole went red. "I was curious. But I didn't take them out. Word of honor."

Rosa weighed the envelope in both hands, took a deep breath, and then put it back on the table. She would watch the video—later. Probably.

Iole carried the case upstairs to the third floor. Signora Falchi followed her. Halfway up, Iole remembered something else.

"Oh, yes," she said, looking over her shoulder.

Rosa had to force her eyes away from the envelope. "Hmm?"

"Twenty-two." Iole switched the bag over to her other hand. "Rooms, I mean. There are only twenty-two still empty."

"What happened to the twenty-third?"

Somewhere in the house, Sarcasmo barked. Had he been barking the whole time? It sounded a long way off, as if it came from the other wing of the palazzo.

"You have a visitor," explained Iole. "She seemed so tired. I told her she could rest in one of the bedrooms."

"Visitor?" repeated Rosa quietly.

"Very, very tired," said Iole.

Rosa stood before the closed door.

Nothing else seemed to exist. Even Sarcasmo's barking had died out. The dog had left his post outside the room and was now standing at a safe distance, wagging his tail and feeling proud of himself for enticing Rosa this way.

She stood in the dark corridor, on cracked flagstones and in front of faded wallpaper, in the yellowish light of the lamp. Stood there staring at the door of the room where her visitor was waiting for her.

She listened, but couldn't hear anything.

Then she slowly raised her hand to knock. And lowered it again. She took a deep breath. Damn it, this was her house. She didn't have to ask anyone's permission to go into one of the rooms.

Put her in a taxi to the airport, she had told Trevini. *And you'd better book her on a flight to wherever she wants.* She sensed another attempt at manipulation on the attorney's part. If the new video wasn't enough to upset her—seeing *her* would do the trick.

Her fingers touched the doorknob. The metal, clouded with vapor, felt cold in her hand. Sarcasmo growled.

When the handle moved as if of its own accord, she realized that someone had been standing on the other side, hesitating, the whole time.

"Hello, Rosa," said Valerie.

Very tired. Now she knew what Iole had meant. Except that the exhaustion in that face, in those eyes, wasn't ordinary tiredness.

Valerie looked even worse than she had in Trevini's dungeon in the hotel, although she must have showered, because her dark hair was wet. Iole had given her clean clothes. Valerie was wearing Rosa's black *There Are Always Better Liars* T-shirt. On Val, it struck Rosa as very appropriate, although it hung from her bony shoulders as if it were on a coat hanger.

Her eyes lay deep in their sockets; her nose looked long and thin. Triangles of shadow under her cheekbones were emphasized by the ceiling light. When Rosa had first met her, Valerie had just stopped wearing braces; now her teeth were discolored and yellow, and half of one incisor had broken off. It was only with difficulty that she seemed able to stay on her feet. She clearly needed a doctor.

"I know how I look," said Val. "You can leave out the comments."

"Ever thought of giving up smoking?"

"Who wants to get fat?" So there was something still left in there of the old Valerie. Her gallows humor spared Rosa a pang of conscience for feeling no pity.

"What are you doing here?"

Val stepped aside to let her into the room. "I wanted to talk to you."

Rosa stayed out in the hall. "Trevini has my cell phone number."

"Your friend Trevini—"

"He's no friend of mine."

"He's just waiting to stab you in the back."

"Too true. That's why he sent you here."

Valerie shook her head. "No. His people bought me a ticket to New York and dropped me off at the airport. Then I ran away."

"And you can bet they've been doing their best to catch up with you."

Valerie shrugged her thin shoulders. "No idea. Come in. I can't . . . I mean, standing is a bit of a strain for me at the moment."

"Try lying down. On your back. With a couple of guys holding you there."

Sarcasmo came in and pressed against Rosa's leg. He growled at Valerie, who took a step back. "He's been standing outside the door for three hours, yapping," she said.

"Sleep deprivation is one of our specialties here in Sicily. If we don't pump our prisoners full of drugs first."

"Leave the dog and come in. Please."

Rosa gave her a cool stare. "You shouldn't have come here. That ticket was your chance to go back to New York." She looked down at Valerie's emaciated body. "Although I wouldn't be too sure that Michele will welcome you with open arms."

"I'm here because I want to ask you to forgive me."

"Well, then everything's fine again, isn't it?"

"Could we spare ourselves the verbal sparring? I know I have no right to be here. And maybe I really should have disappeared. But I did want to say it to your face, at least once. I'm sorry. For everything. Not only the party, and taking you there. The lies earlier, too. Not telling you anything about Michele. I want to ask you to believe that I'm sorry."

Rosa bent down to Sarcasmo, patted his head, and sent him off with a gentle tap. Then she walked past Valerie into the room, closing the door behind her. Slowly, she went over to the window, pulled back the heavy red velvet curtain—and saw, to her surprise, that there was no glass behind it. The tall window had been bricked up. She remembered noticing it once from outside the house. But she'd had no idea that it was this room.

Then she understood. Iole was so much smarter than anyone expected.

Rosa let her eyes wander around the chamber. There was no other way out, only a door to the bathroom, which had no window. Iole hadn't simply offered Valerie a place to rest. She had shut her in.

"Why is that window bricked up?" Valerie was still standing close to the door, as if afraid that Sarcasmo might be able to press the handle down from outside.

Rosa didn't know the answer to that. But then she noticed the initials embroidered on the canopy of the four-poster bed. And the fact that this room was almost twice the size of most of the others.

Up on the canopy, it said *C. A.*

Costanza Alcantara? Had this been her grandmother's room? The *C* could stand for all kinds of names, yet she felt a strange certainty.

Had Florinda had the window bricked up? Two months ago Rosa had given orders for all rooms in the palazzo to be thoroughly cleaned. All of them without exception, because she wanted to drive the mausoleum atmosphere out of the walls. Had this one been locked until then? A prison for all the memories linking Florinda to the mother she hated?

She said to Valerie instead, "This is what you might call our condemned cell. You wouldn't think it of Iole, but she knows exactly what's up."

The corners of Val's mouth twitched, but she couldn't hide a trace of uneasiness. "If that's it . . . if you're planning to have me killed, go ahead. I've told you the truth. I'm only here to apologize."

"For the rape, too?"

"I didn't know that would happen. That's the truth. I had no idea."

"Michele got you to bring me to that party, and you thought—what?"

"I didn't think anything. I was in love. I was stupid. God, I'd have done anything for him. He's a Carnevare. You know how they—"

"Don't you dare compare Alessandro with Michele!"

"If you say so."

Rosa felt a macabre fascination in watching the play of expressions on Valerie's face. At the same time, it disturbed her to see what a stranger her former friend had become. Only in her tone of voice did the old Val come through now and then: the Suicide Queen who fooled everyone else. Sunsets under the Brooklyn Bridge. Nights in Club Exit. Outwardly, the wreck in front of her had almost nothing left in common with the girl of the old days.

"Were you there?" asked Rosa. "When they did it?"

"No!" Valerie's shoulders sagged even further. "I really

didn't know anything about it. Not that evening. Only the next day—"

"If you felt such a pressing need to apologize, you took your time over it. Almost a year and a half."

"I was ashamed. Not just ashamed. I made myself sick. And I . . . I didn't want you to know that . . . that I'd been obeying Michele when I took you there. I couldn't face you. When you were in the hospital, I wanted to visit you." She shook her head, and avoided Rosa's eyes. "But I just couldn't. It didn't work."

As if the engine of her car had failed to start. Or her subway train had been late. *It didn't work.* You'd have thought someone else entirely was responsible.

"I'll call you a taxi," said Rosa. "Don't try showing up here again. Or anywhere else our paths might cross."

Valerie didn't move from the spot. She shifted her weight uncertainly from one foot to the other, again and again, but she didn't sit down. "It wasn't only Michele," she said.

"I know. Tano Carnevare was there. And a few others."

"Yes. But that's not what I mean. It wasn't Michele pulling the strings. Or Tano."

Rosa didn't want to listen to any more of this. It would be wise to leave the room now. Call the taxi. Forget Valerie and with her all that had happened in the past.

"I eavesdropped on conversations," Valerie went on. "Conversations between Michele and Tano. And for a long time I wasn't sure exactly what I'd overheard. But I had so many months to think about it . . . Tano persuaded Michele to go along with the whole thing. No, I don't mean persuaded. That sounds like I want to defend Michele. Tano *recruited* Michele and his men to help him."

"Help him rape me?"

Once, Valerie had never been at a loss for a smart retort; now she was beating around the bush. Then, hesitantly, she nodded. Her chin was quivering. Exhausted, she let herself drop onto the edge of a chair.

"Tano supplied Michele with drugs for years . . . some kind of stuff, I don't know what it was. I never tried it, but Michele was crazy about it."

Did Valerie know exactly what the Carnevares were? What Rosa was? Had she ever seen Michele in his leopard form? Or did she still think the worst thing she'd tangled with was the Mafia?

"Glass vials?" asked Rosa. "With a yellow fluid inside them?"

Valerie nodded. "Michele always had ten or twenty of them in stock. He kept the stuff in this refrigerator that he could lock, like a safe. Tano got hold of it from somewhere, which was weird. Michele had contacts of his own in Colombia and Southeast Asia." She took an unsteady step toward the four-poster bed and dropped onto the edge of it. For a moment she closed her eyes and breathed deeply. "Tano promised Michele even more of the drug, in return for his . . . his support that night. After that, they fought over the deal. I was listening. Michele wanted more of the stuff than they'd agreed on. Or he wanted to pay less for it—I'm not sure which. Tano was furious. He said they'd had an agreement, and now his supplier wouldn't come up with any more."

"Tano's supplier?"

Valerie's nod looked undecided. "The whole thing wasn't Tano's idea. He talked two or three times about someone who had given him the order to attack you. Michele must have known him. I think he'd met him at least once himself."

Rosa's throat felt clogged with disgust, and aversion, and a sense of panic that she'd thought was all in the past. "And now you're saying it wasn't Tano's own idea? Someone gave him *orders* to do it?"

"I think that was it," said Valerie. "When they were talking, Tano and Michele, it seemed clear enough. Tano had bought Michele's services, and in turn this other man had bought Tano's."

Rosa's voice was hoarse. "If they discussed him, I suppose they mentioned his name."

Valerie nodded. "An Italian. I think."

"What was he called?"

"Apollonio." For a moment Val pressed her lips together, and then she said, "That was the name they used. Mr. Apollonio."

Rosa slowly approached the bed. Valerie looked as if she was about to flinch, but she seemed to summon all her self-control and stayed where she was. Rosa turned and dropped onto the mattress beside her. There they sat, thigh to thigh, staring at the empty room.

"Do you know him?" asked Valerie after a while.

"No."

"But it's not the first time you've heard the name."

"No."

Val hesitated. "Okay," she said quietly.

Rosa still wasn't looking at her. "What are you going to do now?"

"No idea." A shudder ran through Valerie's body. Rosa could feel it in her leg. "Or maybe I do know . . . there's still someone in New York."

"Mattia," Rosa whispered.

Valerie's head swung around. There was surprise in her wide eyes. And a question. But she didn't utter a sound.

"I met him," said Rosa. "When I was in New York. Michele was trying to kill me, and Mattia helped me. He guessed that you'd show up here. He wanted me to tell you something—to say you could go to him anytime, whatever happened."

"He said that?"

"Yes."

"Then he doesn't hate me? Because of Michele? And because I ran away?"

Rosa shook her head.

"He . . . he once told me he liked me." Her voice was vibrating slightly, and it was a second or two before Rosa realized that what had upset Valerie's self-composure was hope. More hope than she had felt for a long time.

"He's dead," said Rosa. "Michele's men murdered him."

Silence.

After a while, a whisper as quiet as a breath passed Valerie's lips. "That's not true. You're just saying it to hurt me."

"They burned him. Maybe he was dead already. Or maybe not."

A high-pitched sob made its way out of Valerie's throat. That was all. Just that one awful sound.

Rosa stood up and went to the door. "I'll call a doctor for you. You can stay until tomorrow morning. Then you're getting out of here."

Val didn't watch as Rosa left. She just sat perfectly still, like someone in a photograph, almost entirely black and white and two-dimensional.

Rosa walked out and closed the door. Sarcasmo ran over to her and sat down outside the room, asking to be praised. She scratched his throat, and then she went away.

Behind her, the dog started barking at the door again.

THE VIDEO

THE LIBRARY PROMISED SECURITY. The shelves along the walls rose fifteen feet high, to the ceiling. Thousands of yellowed books stood there, often in double rows, one behind the other, and even the last spare bit of space was full of volumes stacked horizontally. If you took one out, you often came upon patches of mold. Like all the rooms in the palazzo, this one suffered from the damp masonry.

But Rosa wasn't interested in the books, only in the atmosphere that they created. The room made her feel like she could creep away to hide here, unobserved, undisturbed.

The paper blanked out all sounds. Nothing existed outside your own thoughts.

She sat in a creaking leather armchair with her knees drawn up. Curtains hid the tall windows; the fiery-red evening sky glowed through patches where the fabric had worn thin. An old-fashioned lamp with a fringed shade threw off mustard-colored light.

She crouched there with the cell phones that Trevini had sent her, one in each hand.

She switched on the right-hand phone. Someone had written the password on the edge in waterproof felt pen, in a neat girlish hand. Someone who knew how to crack these things.

Probably Contessa di Santis.

On the display, an atomic mushroom cloud above a desert appeared. Valerie's cell phone, no doubt about it. So Rosa would begin with the video of the party. She knew most of that one already, and breathed a sigh of relief.

Only a single video file had been stored. Trevini and the Contessa had prepared everything meticulously in advance.

So once again she watched the wobbly film of the party, saw herself put a glass down on a table and walk away, saw all the laughing people greeting one another, Alessandro among them. But this time the picture didn't freeze on him. The camera panned around, zoomed at random through the crowd, to the sound of Valerie's intoxicated giggles. Suddenly Rosa came back into the frame, glass in hand. Laughing, she said something to Valerie behind the camera, then drank half the contents of her glass. Put it down. Drank again. Swayed in time to the muted music coming from the overloaded loudspeaker.

The film suddenly stopped.

Rosa's hand was shaking. She hadn't noticed before, because the picture was so unsteady. Once again she considered leaving it at that, throwing away both cell phones, and never giving another thought to the second video.

But then she put the first phone down and took the second in both hands, as if she had to hold it tight to keep it from jumping out of her fingers. Its password, too, was written on the casing in blue felt pen.

Rosa had expected a suggestive background image,

something to suit Michele the club owner, wild nights and every kind of excess. Instead, up came a picture of the cartoon cat Tom, holding Jerry in one hand and a knife in the other.

This phone, too, contained only one file. The thumbnail image in the videos folder was dark and blurred; nothing could be made out on it.

Rosa's thumb hovered over the OK key.

Her hand wasn't trembling anymore. Instead she felt paralyzed. Incapable of completing that last small movement.

She had thought about what she would see. She had imagined pictures of her own, of herself and Tano. His short dark hair. His smiling eyes behind the narrow frames of his glasses.

She remembered her first meeting with him in Sicily, at Baron Massimo Carnevare's funeral. A little later, among lines of silent tombs, Alessandro had given her the tiny volume of *Aesop's Fables*. After that she had met Tano twice more. Once on Isola Luna, the little volcanic island off the north coast of Sicily. And finally, for the last time, when he and his gang of bikers had encircled Rosa in the ruins of an ancient amphitheater and he was planning to tear her to pieces in his animal form as a powerful tiger. She had witnessed his transformation, and then his death. As if in slow motion, she saw the bullet shattering his face in her mind's eye.

Rosa closed her eyelids, felt the key under her thumb. Had to summon all her strength to press down on it slowly, very slowly.

There was a crackle in the speaker of the cell phone. The display went dark, then light again. Reddish.

She was looking at her own face.

Looking into her own eyes, open wide and fully awake.

"I need you," she whispered over the phone. "I want to be with you."

She hated her voice, choked as it was with tears. Even hated herself for calling him.

"I'm going to get into my car," she said quietly, "and come to you."

"No, you're not." Alessandro's voice took on that under-tone with which he could nip any contradiction in the bud. The *capo* tone that he had inherited from his father. "You're not driving anywhere in that state. I'll be right there with you. An hour and a half, maybe I can make it sooner. I'm on my way." She could hear his footsteps in the stone corridors of Castello Carnevare, fast and agitated. His haste gave him away. The calm determination in his voice was only for show.

"I'm sorry," she said. "I . . . I don't want to be alone right now."

Her lips touched the receiver of the phone. It was an old-fashioned one, with a curved receiver on a spiral cord.

"I'm leaving now," she heard Alessandro say, not much later, and the engine of his Ferrari promptly roared.

"That's nice of you."

"I ought to have been there when you looked at the thing."

He must have been burning with questions, but he held them back. She imagined his grim expression. This was going to be difficult for him, too, as she knew. But she wanted him to see it for himself, and then tell her that she wasn't going out of her mind.

"Are you sure it's genuine?" he asked a little later. There was a slight echo to his voice. He had switched on the hands-free headset in the car.

"What else would it be? *Toy Story*?"

"I mean, because Trevini sent it."

"He couldn't have faked this. Not even Trevini."

"He only sent it to hurt you." Alessandro didn't try to conceal his fury with the attorney.

"Could be. But if I hadn't seen it . . ."

"You'd be feeling better right now."

"I can't explain to you over the phone."

The car engine hummed monotonously in the background. In her mind, she saw the Ferrari racing along lonely roads, past bleak, dark hills. "I don't know if I should really look at it," he said. "It's too—"

"Intimate?" she snapped. "What's on that video is about as intimate as a bolt fired into an animal's head in a slaughterhouse."

Once again he didn't reply, probably because he guessed that whatever he said would be the wrong thing. She was sorry, but she wasn't making any headway against her temper. If she weren't so furious, she'd be howling.

She wasn't ashamed to let him see her nakedness. Or her vulnerability, or the sense of being handed over to the mercy of others that she'd seen in her own eyes. Until now, she'd assumed that she had been unconscious through the entire rape. But that wasn't so. She had just forgotten. The drugs in her cocktail had wiped out her memory of it, but she had been awake at the time. She had gone through the whole thing conscious, every damn second of it.

"I'm getting on the expressway now," said Alessandro. "Be with you in less than an hour."

She was still huddled motionless in the armchair, doubled up and hugging her knees to her chest. Her tears ran down her chin and dripped on her black top. "Keep talking, will you?" she asked him softly. "Say something, just so I can hear your voice."

"Trevini's going to be sorry for this. Trevini *and* Michele."

She shook her head, thought for a moment, and then said, "I'm grateful to Trevini."

"He only wanted to hurt you."

"He made sure that I knew the truth."

"But—"

"Tell me what you've been doing today," she interrupted him. "All about your day. Your boring meetings, lunch. What your advisers said. Anything."

He gave in, and his voice merged with the soft, monotonous noise of the car engine. She listened, let his words lull her, and got through the next hour that way.

Alessandro's face might have been turned to stone. His skin looked dull and almost waxen. The flicker of the video was reflected in his eyes as Rosa paced up and down the library, biting her nails.

He didn't say a word all through it. He had wanted to mute the sound, but a shake of Rosa's head had stopped him. She had to hear when the moment she was waiting for came.

Distorted voices in the background merged with the rushing sound of the cell phone's weak microphone. The pictures had etched themselves on Rosa's retina; she had no defense against them. A fire was burning in the hearth of the room where it all took place. Probably the living room of Tano's apartment on Charles Street, one or two floors above the scene of the party. Several people were present, but they were visible only as outlines in the dimly lit background. Michele had been filming with the cell phone; his voice was the most distinct. He had trained the camera on a broad sofa, a kind of divan with a dark cover. Cushions were scattered everywhere. Tano had swept most of them aside.

To take her mind off it, Rosa stopped in front of one of the bookcases, closed her eyes, and ran her hand over the crumbling backs of the tomes. She took out a volume, opened it in the middle, and held it under her nose. The book should have smelled better, of glue and paper, of printer's ink. But she could smell only the dampness that had crept in between the pages.

Suddenly, among all the sounds from the video, she recognized her own voice. Alessandro looked at her and muted the video.

"No one should have to listen to this," he said hoarsely. "Not me, most certainly not you."

"Yes," she protested, putting the book back on its shelf and hurrying over to him. "We're nearly there."

"Where?"

"You'll see for yourself in a minute."

Reluctantly, he looked back at the display. Because she was so insistent, he turned up the sound slightly, but his expression showed how much he disliked it.

His eyes were shining more than ever, she noticed now. She turned away to hide her own tears.

Tano could be heard more clearly now. For a moment nothing else seemed to exist, only his voice—the voice of a dead man—

His tiger face exploded. The bullet from Lilia's pistol blew it apart like a head of cabbage.

A dead man who was still alive and well in this video.

A doorbell rang. Almost at once, it rang again. Someone put the cell phone down in a hurry. It went on filming from a fixed position.

Voices in the background, then Michele's. "Good evening, Mr. Apollonio."

Rosa looked at Alessandro, whose expression was still full of distaste, even revulsion.

"Ah, the gentlemen of the Carnevare clan," said a harsh voice. "A real family party. Have you finished?"

Tano swore.

The newcomer's tone became sharper. "You're not being paid to have a good time."

Alessandro glanced at Rosa, seemed about to say something, but was at a loss for words.

"You have to watch!" Her voice almost broke. "Look at his face!"

He was at the point of flinging the cell phone across the library, but then he looked down.

"No sign of Apollonio," he said, with difficulty. "Michele put the phone down. All you can see is a bit of the sofa."

"Apollonio comes into the frame in a minute."

Now Tano was speaking again. When one of the bystanders made a stupid remark, the visitor lost his temper. "Get out of here! All of you, except you two." By that he must have meant Tano and Michele.

Soon after that, a door slammed.

Rosa walked behind the armchair where Alessandro was sitting and leaned over his shoulder. For the first time since he had started watching the video, she too looked at the display.

"Press Pause," she said. "Wait . . . now!"

Alessandro stopped the film. A blurred red and yellow patch of color, a figure, a face, all extremely indistinct. It could be anyone.

Rosa hurried in front of the chair and sat on its arm, next to Alessandro. "Let me have it."

She took the cell phone from his hand and pressed PAUSE and PLAY three or four times in quick succession. Finally the picture, while still blurred, was clear enough for Apollonio's features to be made out.

She gave the phone back to Alessandro, jumped up, stood in front of him, wrapped her arms around her upper body, and rocked back and forth nervously on the balls of her feet.

He held the display closer to his eyes, then farther away. She could tell that he still had no idea who the man in the video was.

"You don't recognize him," she murmured, disappointed.

"Maybe the picture isn't clear enough."

The photo album that she had looked at and opened before he arrived was lying on a table. Breathlessly, she brought it over and put it on his lap. She pressed her forefinger down hard on a photo stuck into it.

"Is that the same man?"

The anxious lines on Alessandro's forehead deepened. The shadows around his eyes grew darker. "Looks like it."

"Apollonio," she said. Her astonishment and disbelief were back.

"Rosa," asked Alessandro, hesitantly, "who on earth *is* this?"

Her mouth was dry; her tongue stuck to the roof. All the same, she managed to get the words out, quietly, in the faltering voice of a stranger.

"That man," she said, "is my father."

AN EXPERIMENT

MINUTES LATER, THEY STILL hadn't said a word.

Rosa was sitting on Alessandro's lap in the armchair, with her head on his shoulder. In the silence of the library, his heartbeat was the only sound she heard. The artery in his throat throbbed against her cheek. The rhythm seemed to pass through her whole body, filling it from head to toe. As if he were keeping her alive with his own heart, while hers felt dead.

After a while she raised her eyes and looked at him.

"You do see it, don't you?"

"Yes," he said gently. "Of course."

"I mean, really?"

"He looks just like the man in your photo."

She moved apart from him and stood up, walked two or three steps away, and then turned abruptly again. "He doesn't just look like him, Alessandro. That man in the video *is* my father."

He too got to his feet. The next moment he was beside her, intending to hold her. But Rosa raised both hands to ward him off and shook her head without facing him. "The man who gave Tano instructions to rape me was . . ." She broke off, lowered her arms, and stood there helpless for a second. "Oh, shit," she whispered.

He made another attempt to take her in his arms, and this time she let him. She just stood there, and he gave her as much time as she needed.

Suddenly she moved away from him, rubbed her eyes, and straightened up. "There," she said.

"There?"

"That's enough. Collapse over. Good-bye tearful, self-pitying Rosa. The old Rosa is back, all fixed up, house-trained, neuroticized, guaranteed dry-eyed."

He raised one eyebrow. "Neuroticized?"

"If the word doesn't exist yet, then it's mine."

"No one else will want it."

"I do. I like my neuroses. I like them to have their own adjective."

He sighed. "What are you going to do?"

"Step one: Look back at what's happened to date."

Alessandro, anxious, said nothing. He seemed to be waiting for a shock, a fit of hysterics. But she was keeping herself under control. She thought she was the very image of a perfectly poised young woman.

"So my father gets a phone call after my grandmother's death," she began. "A man called Apollonio has come to see Trevini, demanding money—for the fur coats made from the skins of Arcadians that haven't been paid for yet . . . sounds kind of crazy. Like something out of a soap opera."

"Okay."

"Because of that phone call, my father leaves his family and flies to Europe to track down this Apollonio in person. Soon after that, his wife and his two dear little daughters hear that he's died of a heart attack. None of them fly out to his funeral. Big mistake. Because it turns out, later, that his tomb is empty." She wrinkled her nose. "Sound like a credible story?"

"With reservations."

"Since it all seems so run-of-the-mill in these parts, let's introduce a little complication. TV viewers are used to that kind of thing."

To please her, he went along with the game. "Plenty of people have seen *Lost*."

"One of the daughters is raped. Of course she gets pregnant." Cynicism made it easier to talk about it, almost as if it had happened to someone else. "Eighteen months later a video of the rape turns up, and in it there's a man who everyone calls Apollonio. That's weird enough, but there's more: Apollonio is her father! End of season one. Now the scriptwriters have a year to think how to get themselves out of this crazy scenario."

He looked at her hard, as if to make sure that she had not lost her mind and wasn't heading for a nervous breakdown. "What was Apollonio's motive?"

"What does the viewer know about him so far?" asked Rosa. "Not a lot. He probably belongs to a mysterious, super-secret, and of course worldwide organization called TABULA."

"Which has a weakness for fur coats."

"Through which Apollonio earns a nice bit on the side by

selling them to an evil-minded woman who is head of a Mafia clan. He could be doing that on behalf of TABULA, or maybe he's working for himself."

"More likely for TABULA, I'd say."

She nodded. "Apollonio sells the furs to the old Mafia witch on orders from TABULA, then. Maybe to sow discord among the Arcadian dynasties if the deal ever comes to light. He's a faithful supporter of the organization and would never do anything to thwart its aims. Unfortunately for him, soon after that the old woman's son tracks him down and kills him."

Alessandro raised an eyebrow. "How do we know that?"

"We don't. But obviously the son slipped into the role of Apollonio thirteen years later. Now *he* is Apollonio. Same character, new face."

"Objection."

"What?"

"The son can't simply take on a new role. That's not logical. Davide is still Davide—except that now he *acts* as if he were Apollonio. Undercover. Maybe he's some kind of secret agent trying to destroy TABULA from inside."

"But he wouldn't stand by and watch his own daughter being raped by one of the Panthera, just to maintain his own cover. He couldn't do that, unless he *really* didn't care what happened to her."

Alessandro chewed his lower lip.

"So now Davide is Apollonio," she said. "He's turned into a true believer in the aims of TABULA."

"Brainwashing?"

"I'd think it's more likely that they convinced him, won him over. Like the first Apollonio. And now Davide thinks they're right—so much so that he doesn't care about anything else, even his own daughter."

"But is it certain that there were *two* Apollonios? The one with the furs and the one on the video?"

"Good point. If Apollonio and Davide had been the same man from the start, then he wouldn't have sold the furs to Costanza—his own mother—would he? What's more, Trevini would probably have recognized him later."

Alessandro was still skeptical. "You're assuming that Trevini has really told you everything, and has given you the truth."

"That's what I'm going to find out—in step two. For now, however, we're still looking at Apollonio's motives—the motives of TABULA. They made sure that one of the Panthera raped a Lamia. Why?"

"So that she'd get pregnant by him?" suggested Alessandro hesitantly. "You think the whole thing was some kind of experiment?"

"The problem is that we don't know what TABULA is really after. Why are they experimenting on Arcadians? What do they hope to achieve?"

He followed this up with another idea. "You remember the statues of Panthera and Lamias on the seabed? Was it TABULA that salvaged them and removed them from the site?"

"We'll clear up the question of whether Thanassis and the

Stabat Mater are all part of TABULA at the next script conference."

"But all the same, one thing is important," he said. "We've been connecting the statues to ourselves all this time, right? At least I did. As if they were a kind of prophesy, and the two of us were going to make it come true."

"Kind of like that, yes."

"But that had nothing to do with TABULA. We fell in love, but they had no control over that. And they can't have been very happy about it. Agreed?"

Rosa nodded.

Now Alessandro was hitting his stride. "Scientists prefer to carry out experiments in a controlled environment, don't they? In the laboratory, where they can influence everything."

"You think—"

"They knew about the statues. They probably even know what they stand for. And that's why they wanted a Panthera and a Lamia—" He struggled with himself, but he couldn't finish the sentence. "Why it was one of their conditions," was all he added.

"So there's no such thing as artificial insemination where they come from?"

He shrugged his shoulders, unsure.

"The question is," she said in a neutral voice, "did they want a child, or would aborted tissue be enough for them? A fetus?"

Alessandro's cheekbones were working, but he said nothing.

She perched on the edge of the table where she had put down the photo album. Her head felt as if she had unexpectedly run into a glass door.

"I'll go crazy if I play this game to the end. My father has turned into Apollonio, and Apollonio was paying Tano and Michele. Those are the facts. That's all."

"Seems like it." He took a deep breath. "Then it was your father who also supplied Tano with the serum."

Rosa pushed up her sleeve and looked at the blue marks where the needles of the syringes had gone in. "They've probably infected us with their fucking mutant blood."

"But none of this has anything to do with us. With what we did last night."

"No."

"Really?"

She shook her head. "High time for me to get the transformations under control. I can't take that stuff again. It's almost as if my father—"

"Was making sure that *we* slept together, too?"

She looked darkly at him. "I didn't *sleep with* Tano, Alessandro. I can tell the difference."

"Yes . . . sorry. I . . . I don't know why I said that."

She gave him a kiss, first tentatively, then firmly.

"They won't leave us alone," she whispered. "Even if they don't do anything, I mean don't do anything else to *us*, they're there all the same, distorting our thoughts and our feelings and—"

"I know exactly what my feelings are."

She nodded slowly. What she had seen on the video changed everything—and nothing. And if Trevini had thought he could use it to bring her to her knees, he'd been mistaken.

"Thank you," she said softly.

"What for?"

"For understanding me. Even if you don't understand me." She gestured clumsily. "You shouldn't understand me. But somehow you do anyway."

He smiled. "The Rosa version of those three words?"

"Oh, yes."

HUNDINGA

THEY SPENT THE NIGHT on the sofa in the library, sleeping in their clothes, Rosa's head on Alessandro's chest.

But when day began to dawn, that position wasn't nearly as comfortable as it had been a few hours earlier. Rosa moved and felt as if someone had been driving steel nails through her joints. Her back was really stiff.

"Good morning," he said, kissing her on the forehead.

"Morning," she groaned. "Just how good it is I'll find out—if I can stand up without collapsing."

Alessandro moved, shifting his own position, and he, too, let out a groan. "Who the hell builds sofas like this?"

She sat up. "At least it was expensive."

"So we have to put up with the discomfort."

Rosa smiled, but even her facial muscles hurt. She grimaced to relax them, saw her reflection in a glass picture frame on the wall, and cursed. "Well, could have been worse," she finally said. "I could have woken up a hybrid."

"Which isn't—"

Suddenly she leaped to her feet. "Why didn't I change shape?" Her aches and pains were all gone at once. "Because of my father, I mean. I thought it happened on its own with violent outbreaks of feeling?"

"Maybe you have it under control better than you think."

"But I don't want to be able to do something without understanding why! I'm sick and tired of that. Just for once, I'd like to feel like I know *everything* about myself, and not keep seeing a total stranger in the mirror."

"There's no one *I* know as well as you."

"Weird."

"No, great." He smiled with difficulty as he sat up straight. "A person who knows you doesn't have to know anyone else. There are enough facets to your character for twenty people."

"Schizophrenic, you mean."

"You know exactly what I mean."

"At least you're not trying to compliment my eyes."

"Oh, those are only average."

"Idiot."

He stood up, more mobile already. Even as a human he couldn't deny the panther in himself. Rosa, on the other hand, was desperately searching for the supple flexibility of her snake form.

"If you can manage to keep your feelings under control," he said, "then you can also control the transformations."

"But I don't have my feelings under control."

"You did last night. You simply made up your mind to be the old Rosa—and it worked. That was probably how you kept yourself from turning into the snake."

She frowned. "Is that the kind of thing the animals in the zoo tell you at night?"

"More or less."

Rosa shook her head. "I don't even know if I *want* to understand all this."

"It's not about understanding it. All we can do is *feel* the truth. This whole thing, being an Arcadian, the transformations, none of it is logical. The early Arcadians let their instincts and urges guide them. That's why now many of them are so keen for the Hungry Man to come back—it's exactly what he's promising them. No more laws, no reason, just animal instinct and the satisfaction of their desires."

"Then we're no different from them."

"No one said we were. We can't reject our own nature. But giving it free rein, no rules, no consideration—that can't be the solution either."

"Sounds to me about the same as what the Mafia does . . . I mean, what our people out there are doing when they deal in human beings and armaments."

He shrugged his shoulders. "Maybe not. But we can't just press a switch and turn into someone different. I am what I am, Rosa. Same with you."

"I'm not like Costanza."

"And I'm not like my father."

"Too much moralizing first thing in the morning." She breathed into the hollow of her hand. "Time to brush our teeth. Shower. And then—"

"Breakfast?"

She shook her head. "Then step two."

Wild dogs were howling in the hills.

The rotors of a helicopter droned in the distance.

The sun was only just above the peak of the mountain. The silhouettes of trees looked like charred matches against the reddish-gold ball of fire, and the scent of pine needles was wafting down the slope to the palazzo, but it was mingled with the smell of dirty animal enclosures.

"They can't have been lured here by Sarcasmo's barking, can they?" asked Rosa, looking up at the mountain. She and Alessandro were standing in front of the palazzo, close to the gateway leading to the inner courtyard. They had hurried outside when the howling in the woods grew too loud to ignore.

Grimly, Alessandro shook his head. "Hundinga," he said. "Dog men. Slaves of the Hungry Man. The helicopter must have dropped them off up there."

"Slaves?" she repeated incredulously.

"As he sees it, nothing has changed, and classical antiquity never really ended. There are still masters and servants—and slaves. In that respect, he thinks the same as many of the *capi*. I mean, do you think all the Africans trafficked by your family into Europe from Lampedusa were anything but slaves?"

"I tried to stop that trade."

"And of course Trevini wouldn't go along with you, right? The business makes millions."

Rosa pushed the thought aside. "Do you really think it's Arcadians up in the woods? Sicily is teeming with packs of feral dogs."

He nodded again. "Hundinga have always been his most faithful servants. His first, too. The real Lycaon was changed into a wolf by Zeus, remember. Wolves and dogs have always been the Hungry Man's favorites. At the time of the witch hunts, the wolf men were almost wiped out, but there'll always be dogs, and that's also true of the Arcadians among them." He paused for a moment. "Two of my managers were attacked by wild dogs yesterday. One of them was killed in the garden of his villa in Mondello. And there's not much left of the other one."

"You didn't tell me about that."

"I warned you how dangerous the Hungry Man is, and you didn't want to listen." This time he wasn't waiting for her protest. "Look, there are three of my men waiting down at the gate. If you won't hire any bodyguards for yourself, then take mine. They're reliable; they know what to do."

She wrinkled her nose. "Probably the first thing they'd do is shoot Sarcasmo."

"Gianni loves dogs. Real dogs. Not Hundinga."

"Gianni?"

"You've met him. He's in charge of the armed guard at Castello Carnevare. He likes Mozart and reads Proust."

"Nine feet tall, six feet wide? Face like the bark of a tree?"

Alessandro grinned. "I'm not asking you to marry him. If you let him protect you, that'll be enough."

"If I let a troop of Carnevares into the palazzo, word will reach Rome and Milan within the day. And you know just what they'll think there."

He ignored her objection. "If you want to phone Trevini and ask him questions, then go ahead, but please don't leave this house. It would be a good idea to close that portcullis." He pointed to the broad iron teeth protruding from the roof of the gateway above the entrance.

"Doesn't work anymore," she said. "All rusted."

"Will you let Gianni and the others in now?"

The dogs in the woods were howling nonstop.

"Do I have a choice?" she asked.

"Do it for Iole, if you're too proud to do it for yourself." His eyes darkened. "I have to try to speak to the Hungry Man. As long as he's breathing down my neck, we won't have any peace to find out more—"

"About TABULA. I know."

"It won't be easy to get access to him in prison, but maybe I can call on a few of my father's old contacts."

"Are you seriously going to see him?"

"I have to make him understand that we Carnevares weren't responsible for his arrest. We were not the ones who gave him away back then."

"And exactly *where* did you find that out all of a sudden?"

He became evasive, which wasn't like him at all, and once again she had a feeling that he was keeping something from her. "I think I know who it was now. Someone has promised me evidence."

"Someone. And that someone wants money for it, of course."

"No, only a promise. Strictly speaking, two promises. One was that I wouldn't talk to anyone about it. Absolutely anyone."

"Well, you don't have to break your stupid promise on my account."

Smiling, he dropped a kiss on her forehead. "You'll be the first to know when all this is over." He nodded in the direction of the woods. "And until then, keep all the doors locked. Gianni and the others know what they have to do."

There was no point in arguing with him. Even if the howling up in the hills only came from a few wretched strays, he wasn't going to drop the subject. It annoyed her that he hadn't told her either about the attack on his managers or his secret informant. But she consoled herself by thinking that he was soon going to be much angrier with her. Poetic justice. *Surely you can understand it,* she'd say then. *And anyway, you started it.*

Rosa took out her cell phone, called the guards she had down on the driveway, and asked them if there was a car there containing three orangutans in suits. "They can come up," she said.

Alessandro cast an anxious glance at the hills. "If those are really Hundinga, they're going to take their time. They're putting on this show to frighten you. Maybe they'll be satisfied with that for now. It won't be really dangerous until you don't hear them anymore. Then they'll probably be on their way to the palazzo."

He took her hand and went through the gate with her, back to the inner courtyard. His Ferrari was parked at the foot of the double flight of steps up to the porch. "Don't let Sarcasmo out of the house. They'd go for him first."

"He's busy anyway, guarding Valerie in her dungeon."

"You shouldn't have let her stay here."

"I was going to kick her out today, but while those creatures are still roaming the woods it might not be a great idea." She had in fact called the doctor in Piazza Armerina, asking him to come and check up on Valerie; he would be here some time in the next few hours to examine her. Then, and only then, would Rosa throw her out with a clear conscience.

"You actually feel sorry for her." He shook his head, but he couldn't help smiling at the same time.

She leaned against the Ferrari, took Alessandro's hands in hers, and drew him to her. "Promise me you'll be careful."

"If I don't go and see him, there'll never be an end to this. I can't simply stand by and watch him hurt you."

"If he kills you, that will *really* hurt me."

"I only have to convince him to call someone and listen for a few minutes."

"And he'll believe what this person has to say?"

"It's our only chance." He kissed her good-bye and slipped behind the wheel of his car. "If you call Trevini, don't tell him anything about the Hungry Man."

Suspiciously, she cocked her head. "What exactly does Trevini have to do with it?"

For a moment he looked as if he were going to say something, but then he touched her hand through the open window of the car again and started the engine. Moments later the Ferrari was roaring out of the courtyard. Rosa watched it go until it disappeared at the other end of the gate. For a while she listened to it retreating into the distance, on the long way downhill between the olive groves and lemon trees; then she turned around and hurried up the steps to the porch.

Iole came out of the shadow of the open door. "Sarcasmo's scared."

Rosa couldn't see the dog anywhere.

"I think," said Iole, "he's afraid of that howling in the woods."

Even before Rosa could answer, a black Mercedes rolled into the inner courtyard. Three men in dark suits with mirrored shades climbed out. Rosa rolled her eyes.

Gianni, the tallest and broadest of the three, came up the steps. Mozart and Proust—who would have thought? "Signorina Alcantara," he greeted her, nodding. "Signorina Dallamano."

Iole was visibly flattered that he knew her name. "You're a killer, aren't you?"

"No, *signorina*," he said untruthfully.

Iole thought for a moment, then shrugged her shoulders. "That's all right, then."

Rosa discussed what was necessary with Gianni and the two others and let them take up positions inside the palazzo. She had no choice but to trust the three of them. She didn't think they were Arcadians, just highly paid professionals who were well trained in the use of weapons and other ways of inflicting pain. Not the kind of men one liked to have in the house—but better than leaving Iole, Signora Falchi, and even Valerie alone here while Rosa was elsewhere, doing what she had promised herself she would do.

"One more thing," she said to Gianni before the three

disappeared into the palazzo. "There should be a doctor arriving from Piazza Armerina. He's to examine a guest up in one of the bedrooms. I asked him to come, so don't shoot him in the kneecaps on sight, okay?"

Gianni nodded, and then he and the two others entered the house. As they did, they put headsets on.

Iole's cheeks were flushed. "Hey, they're nice!"

"Men from Mars."

"They're here to protect us. And they look like they'd be good at it."

"Yes," said Rosa. "I'm sure they are."

Iole glanced at her. "You're going somewhere, aren't you? And you didn't tell Alessandro."

"How do you know that?"

But Iole simply walked away. "I'll look after Sarcasmo. Take care."

Rosa watched her go. "You, too. And Iole?"

The girl turned back.

"If there's any kind of danger, I don't care what, just hide. There's a secret room in the study behind the—"

"Behind the paneling. The room with the white telephone. I know." Iole waved to her, began humming a tune, and disappeared.

With the soft melody in her ears, Rosa shook her head and set off for the greenhouse.

In the humid, hot, tropical thicket she talked to the snakes.

THE *CONTESSA*

SHE FELT UNEASY AS she went down the driveway, a mile through plantations and light woodland. She had chosen a black BMW cross-country vehicle, not her father's Maserati, so she stepped on the gas harder than usual on the uneven gravel drive. Dust clouds rose behind her, obscuring her view in the mirror. She kept looking out for wild dogs among the trees, but she couldn't see any, and there were certainly no humans in sight. The howling had come from higher up. They might be on the mountain or the nearby hills behind the palazzo.

She'd had the guards down on the road reinforced. Four men were keeping an eye on the surroundings there. A dozen more were patrolling the slopes. Her aunt used to have just as many stationed there; Rosa was relying on the fact that Florinda must have known what was necessary to keep the property secure.

Soon she was racing northward, passing Piazza Armerina and Valguarnera, and at Enna turning onto the A19 toward the east coast. Several times she thought she saw pursuers behind her, but as soon as she had convinced herself that she was being shadowed, the suspicious vehicles disappeared along a side road or turned off into a picnic area.

Two hours later, around noon, she finally drove up the winding road to Taormina. The sky on the cliff tops above the town was overcast. Uniformed police officers at barriers were turning tourists in rental cars away from the historic city center, but Rosa had a special permit obtained by Trevini years ago for the Alcantara family.

She parked the BMW right outside the entrance to the Grand Hotel Jonio. As she got out, she took her bag off the passenger seat. It contained only one item.

She was wearing a black fabric coat, slim pants, and leather boots. Her blond hair fell loose over her shoulders, fluttering in the brisk wind blowing up to the cliffs on the steep coast. In spite of the mild weather, there was a chill to the gusts off the wide expanses of the Ionian Sea.

Two of Trevini's bodyguards, in bespoke suits, were sitting in comfortable armchairs in the hotel lobby. Seeing Rosa, one of them spoke into a microphone in the bracelet on his wrist. Same as during her last visit, there were no other guests around. Maybe Trevini had rented the entire hotel for himself.

She turned to the man at the reception desk. From a distance he looked like any ordinary reception clerk. His expensive jacket bulged under his left armpit, just enough to be noticeable to anyone keeping an eye out for a shoulder holster. Rosa was sure that he had other weapons hidden under the counter in front of him.

The two men in armchairs never took their eyes off her. One of them rose to his feet and strolled between Rosa and the exit.

In a calm voice, she asked to see the attorney, and she watched the reception clerk pick up a receiver and speak quietly into it. She guessed who was at the other end of the line, and was not surprised to be told that at the moment Trevini was in an important meeting. Contessa di Santis would enjoy keeping her waiting.

She leaned as far over the counter as she could, hoping the man on the other side wouldn't notice that she had to stand on tiptoe to do so.

"This place," she said, "is financed by my money. I'll give you one minute to make sure that the *avvocato* sees me at once."

"I know who you are, *signorina*, and I'm very sorry that—"

She wasn't listening to him anymore. Turning around, she went over to an opaque glass double door. Beyond it lay the lounge leading out to the terrace.

"Signorina Alcantara," the man called after her, "I really must ask you to wait until the *avvocato* sends for you."

The bodyguards began to move.

She pushed the lounge doors open with both hands. On the other side, she was expected.

"Contessa di Santis," she said, with an icy smile, as she paused in the entrance.

"Signorina Alcantara." The *avvocato*'s assistant glanced past Rosa at the bodyguards and gestured to them. The two men immediately withdrew. The *contessa* stopped directly in front of Rosa, and lowered her voice. "We should talk."

"I'm not talking to anyone but Trevini himself—"

"Please," replied di Santis, unmoved, "follow me."

With a glance out of the corner of her eye, Rosa made sure that the clasp of her purse was open. She didn't usually have much time for handbags, and until recently hadn't even owned one. But now she was glad to have it with her.

Cristina di Santis went ahead, not out onto the terrace but through a side door and into the former ballroom of the grand hotel. She walked quickly across the room, too, her high heels clicking on the parquet flooring. She was wearing a short, snug dress, dark red like her lipstick, and her hair was just as perfect as it had been the day Rosa had met her for the first time. A signet ring, presumably that of her clan, was her only jewelry. A discreet touch of perfume wafted behind her.

"Are you bringing me to Trevini?" asked Rosa suspiciously, as the *contessa* led her into a narrow stairway.

Di Santis nodded without looking at her. Rosa thought of Valerie's dungeon in the hotel basement, and stopped. She took the *contessa*'s upper arm and made her turn to face her. "What's this all about?"

"Just a moment more. Please be patient."

"What's going on?"

"You'll understand in a minute."

"I didn't come here to—"

"I know why you came here, Signorina Alcantara, and I am doing all I can to help you. I am on your side." With that, she shook Rosa's hand off her arm and led her through another door into a corridor paved with white tiles.

A little later they were entering the hotel swimming pool

area, an impressive, domed chamber with a huge wall of windows looking out over the sea. Tiles the color of turquoise and terra-cotta dominated the room.

Broad flights of steps on all four sides led down to the spacious pool. It was about nine feet deep in the middle. The water must have been drained away long ago; it didn't even smell damp anymore.

Trevini's wheelchair lay, toppled over, in the dry pool. The *avvocato* himself was crouching several feet away from it at the foot of one of the flights of steps. He must have crawled over to it on his belly. Now he was sitting there, exhausted, half propped on the bottom step, his useless legs twisted. His elegant suit was crumpled, his sparse gray hair drenched with sweat.

Rosa's eyes narrowed as she looked at the *contessa* again. "Explain."

Di Santis didn't move a muscle. "It's in your own interests."

Rosa's hand slipped into her bag. Her fingers closed around the handle of the staple gun.

"You came to ask him questions," said di Santis. "This could be your last chance."

At the bottom of the swimming pool, the old man laboriously raised his head. "Rosa . . . this is lunacy . . ."

"What's going on?" she hissed at the *contessa*. "Who are you? And what are you up to?"

The young attorney took a deep breath. "I'd hoped to have more time. I would have liked to learn even more from him."

"He trusted you."

"It was more difficult than I'd expected. He is a stubborn old man, but after a while he warmed to me. The time came when he couldn't wait to pour his heart out to me day after day."

Down in the pool below, Trevini moved. "She knows everything, Rosa. About your family, about Costanza . . . Kill her, before she sells her knowledge to the enemies of the Alcantaras."

"Looks like you did that already, Trevini," Rosa replied coldly.

"Once again," the *contessa* told Rosa, "I am not your enemy."

The handle of the staple gun was slowly warming up in Rosa's hand. "Those men out there in the lobby—"

"Are being well paid for preferring me to their former employer."

"She's out of her mind!" Trevini screamed.

Rosa looked at the *contessa*. "I don't think so."

"Think of it as a kind of job application," said di Santis, in the composed way that Rosa both disliked and admired. "When all this is over, you're going to need a new legal adviser, Signorina Alcantara. Someone in a position to carry on with the *avvocato*'s business in a way that suits you."

"So that's what you're after?" asked Rosa, astonished. "You want to succeed him as legal adviser?"

Di Santis shook her head, amused. "First and foremost it's a case of reparations. Revenge would be a crude way to put it."

"Revenge for what?"

"My family was once a highly respected Cosa Nostra clan. Landed property, factories, all kinds of business firms—the di Santis clan had more than enough of all that. My grandfather was one of the most powerful *capi* in the west of the island. Until he made the mistake of quarreling with the Corleonese bosses."

Rosa knew about that. The capos from the small town of Corleone had waged bloody war in the eighties against anyone who disputed their claim to dominance of the Sicilian Mafia. Massacres and bombs had assassinated whole families. For years no one could do anything against the will of the Corleonese, and it was generally known that the di Santis family had been among those on their hit list. Only the *contessa* and a handful of her relations had survived. Since then, it was said, the remaining members of the clan had retired from the Mafia business.

"For years no one knew for sure who had handed my family over to them." Cristina di Santis walked over to the edge of the top step. For the first time her smooth, serene facial expression changed. The glance she cast at the helpless Trevini was one of deep contempt. "The *avvocato* has worked for your clan for decades, Signorina Alcantara, and very conscientiously, too. That didn't stop him from running his own businesses on the side, and during the course of it, unfortunately, my father and brother got in his way. He started the rumor that my family was secretly scheming against the Corleone Mafia: He forged documents, he bribed two state prosecutors—and from then on it all gathered speed. He had only to lean back and wait until the murderers from Corleone had wiped out a large part of our family at a wedding party. Men, women, almost a dozen children. I was a small child at the time; I'd been left at home with my nursemaid, that's the only reason I survived. My mother was shot—eleven bullets were later found in her body. My elder brother was burned to death when he and several others were herded into the restaurant kitchen, drenched in gasoline, and set on fire. Only a few escaped, including my father, but he was never the same man. For years I had to listen to his whining, hear him justifying his cowardice. When I was finally old enough, I went to northern Italy. But all that time, at university and later, I knew I would go back and find out who was responsible for the extermination of the di Santis family. In the end it wasn't even difficult to find Trevini's name. But it was hard to get him to confide in me. For three years I've been licking his boots, disowning my family, until at last he came out with parts of the truth. I sold myself to him. And now it's finally payback time."

"Why now?" asked Rosa. "Why today in particular?"

"Because otherwise you'd have done it, Signorina Alcantara. Because after all you've seen on that video, I suspect you, too, have a number of questions to ask the *avvocato*. And because there's someone else who will very soon be demanding satisfaction."

"Someone else?" The words were hardly out of Rosa's mouth before she understood. "It was *you*! You promised Alessandro the evidence that the Carnevares were innocent of the Hungry Man's arrest!"

"Unfortunately, events have rather overtaken one another," replied the *contessa*. "I would have liked to take my time about it, be more circumspect. However, Trevini insisted on sending you the video. Then I knew it all had to be done very fast."

Trevini uttered a hoarse crack of laughter. "You talked to Alessandro Carnevare? Cristina, are you out of your mind? There won't be one stone left to stand on here once—"

Narrowing her eyes, Rosa stared at the old man. "You gave the Hungry Man away all those years ago? And pinned the blame on the Carnevares?"

He snorted quietly but didn't answer.

Di Santis nodded slowly. "There aren't many files and documents in this place—his memory really is as phenomenal as he claims. But there is a letter from the state prosecutor's office, now thirty years old. It promises him immunity from prosecution in return for his cooperation in the arrest of the *capo dei capi*. At the time he'd just begun working for your grandmother."

Rosa groaned. "Costanza was involved in this as well?"

Trevini looked up at her again and seemed to be gathering all his powers. "Why do you suppose the Alcantaras were closer than anyone to the new *capo dei capi*? Why did Salvatore Pantaleone think so much of your family, Rosa? I brokered the deal with Pantaleone at the time. He, Costanza, and I made sure that the Hungry Man would disappear—to be succeeded by Pantaleone. If not for that agreement, the Alcantara possessions would long ago have been swallowed up by one of the larger and more determined clans! You owe what you are today to me and no one else, Rosa. And now show your appreciation and put an end to this farce!"

Fury made Rosa's voice hoarse. "The Hungry Man is having the Carnevares hunted down, because he thinks they're the guilty ones!"

"Haven't you learned anything?" roared Trevini angrily. "Are you seriously going to tell me that you mourn for the New York Carnevares? The same men who had a hand in what happened to you? Or doesn't their death secretly fill you with satisfaction? Listen to your heart. How do you feel knowing that Michele might fall victim to an assassination attempt? Damn it, Rosa, don't play the righteous innocent!"

"The Hungry Man has set killers on Alessandro! And now his men are after me as well."

"I told you to keep away from that Carnevare bastard. If you'd listened to me, everything would be fine." Trevini gradually seemed to be retrieving his old self-confidence. "It was all planned, down to the very last detail. Who could have expected you to go throwing yourself at a Carnevare, of all people? You can hardly hold me responsible for the consequences."

The *contessa* said calmly, "He's lost, and he knows it. He'd do anything to—"

Rosa didn't wait for her to finish. With a few bounds she leaped down the tiled steps to the bottom of the drained swimming pool. Trevini raised a protective hand in front of his face as she crouched beside him.

"You're pathetic, Trevini. If the Hungry Man succeeds,

then you'll have not only the di Santis family on your con-science but the Carnevares and Alcantaras as well. What do you hope to achieve by that, aside from not going under alone?"

Trevini slowly lowered his hand. His fingers were shaking. At close range, she saw that he must be in pain. Had the *contessa* pushed him down here in his wheelchair? His left leg was twisted more than it had looked from above. Probably broken.

"Everything I've done for the last thirty years," he got out, breathlessly, "was for the good of the Alcantaras. I acted first in Costanza's name, then in Florinda's, now in yours."

"Florinda knew all this?"

"Your aunt had no idea about anything. But you, Rosa, had it in you to revive some of Costanza's old brilliance. With my help, you could have—"

Rosa placed a finger on his lips, and he fell silent. Then she looked over her shoulder and up at the side of the pool. "Does your job application still stand, *contessa*?"

"Of course."

"I assume you're recording all this."

Di Santis smiled. "Every word."

Rosa sighed. "That's why you brought me here. The docu-ment you've promised Alessandro isn't enough for you. You needed Trevini's confession. Right?"

The young attorney assumed her serene expression again. "I never for a moment doubted that your presence would induce him to talk, Signorina Alcantara."

"Then you have everything you need?"

"Certainly."

"You never intended to kill him, did you? For what he did to your family."

"I don't think that will be necessary now," said the *contessa*, with a small smile.

Rosa turned back to Trevini, whose face had gone even paler. "Good." And without turning again, she said, "As your new employer, I'd like to ask you to leave us for a moment. The *avvocato* and I have something to discuss alone."

"As you wish." Di Santis turned to go.

"Contessa?"

"Signorina Alcantara?"

"I'm relying on you to see that your microphones and cameras are switched off now." She laid a hand under the old man's chin. He was pale as death. "There's no need for anyone else to watch this."

THE THRICE GREAT

ROSA LISTENED TO THE sound of the attorney's high heels moving away from them. In the next moment the door into the swimming pool area latched.

Trevini's lower lip was quivering. "You have so much more of your grandmother in you than I'd assumed," he whispered. "It's you here in front of me, but Costanza looks out of your eyes."

"I'm tired of you, Trevini. Your constant talk, your attempts to influence me—"

"How are you going to manage without me? With the *contessa*'s help? By betraying me, she's betrayed the Alcantaras. And she'll do it again."

"You're responsible for the massacre of the di Santis family, the death of the Carnevares in New York and here in Sicily . . . and *you* are warning me against betrayal?"

"I've done only what your family paid me to do. I've worked out strategies. Tactics. I was loyal. You can't blame me for any of that!"

"The Hungry Man's Hundinga are prowling the hills around the palazzo. He wants to kill me to punish Alessandro. For something that wasn't even done by his ancestors— *you* did it."

"One Carnevare or a hundred, they're no loss. Costanza would not have—"

"My grandmother was a monster, in more ways than one." She gave him a chilly smile. "But I've inherited at least one thing from her." She opened her mouth very slightly, and licked her lips with the snake's split tongue.

Her vision was also changing. In a shadowy corner above the door, a tiny red source of heat that she couldn't have seen with human eyes went out. Di Santis had been as good as her word and switched off the camera.

"Have you ever watched a Lamia shift shape, Trevini?" She slowly leaned closer to his face, to make sure that he could see what was happening to her eyes, to their pupils. "Did you ever see Costanza like this? Was that why you were so fascinated by her?"

He kept his cool, she had to give him that. Still, she felt a sense of triumph. She had control of it. For the first time she could keep herself entirely under control. She didn't exactly understand how she was doing it, only that it went hand in hand with a sense of superiority that she had never experienced before.

"I want answers from you." It sounded almost like a hiss, hardly at all like her own voice. "If I think that you're being honest, for once, I'll let you live."

How easy it was to say the words. She was slightly alarmed to realize that she meant every word of it. It wasn't a bluff. It was in her power to give him his life. Or take it away.

Trevini seemed to lose himself in the gaze of her snake's

eyes. Something in his face told her that, at that moment, his will was broken. All at once his humiliating arrogance had disappeared. She could smell vulnerability on his breath. Could pick up the scent of his fear like vapor from his pores.

Her lips, very narrow now, were only a handbreadth away from his face. He was sweating; his eyes were watering. Yet he didn't blink. He stared at her like a rat driven into a corner.

"Did you know that Apollonio is my father?" she asked.

His lower jaw was shaking slightly, but he said nothing.

Rosa's voice took on a sharper edge. "Did you know?"

"I . . . I don't understand it myself," he got out. "And that's the truth. I saw him on the video, but I don't understand the connection."

"I'll be able to tell if you're lying."

"I've told you that Apollonio was in touch with me after Costanza's death," he said hesitantly. "But I never met him in person. I don't know why Davide is addressed as Apollonio on the video. Do you understand me, Rosa? I simply do not know."

"Still, you didn't warn me. Because you wanted me to come to you in a flood of tears, begging you to help me."

"Di Santis foresaw that it might not turn out that way."

Rosa's tongue licked down to her chin. The split tip touched rough reptilian skin. She had to concentrate to halt the transformation at this stage, although she wasn't sure whether she really wanted to.

"Who's behind TABULA?"

"Don't do it," he said.

She frowned inquiringly, and felt scales trickle down over her nostrils.

"Don't try to take on TABULA," he said. "Your grandmother did the only right thing by allying herself with them."

"Who *is* TABULA?"

He let out his breath heavily. "No one knows . . . *I* don't know."

"But you have an idea, don't you? Costanza must have known. The only question is: Did she find out from you?"

"I have a few scraps, small pieces of the whole truth. No faces, no names. At first I tried to find out more, but then I realized that any answer I got could mean the end for me. TABULA knows its enemies. And TABULA shows no mercy."

"Tell me what you did find out."

He groaned in pain and tried to avoid her gaze.

"It all goes back many centuries," he said helplessly. "*Tabula Smaragdina Hermetis*—I don't suppose that means anything to you, does it?"

"Is it Latin?"

"Yes. And much more than that: words from the language of alchemy."

She hissed quietly, and Trevini's eyes almost imperceptibly widened. "Don't try to fool me," she said.

"You want connections. Very well, listen. This is not about strange hooded figures brewing bubbling potions over open fires. Alchemy is both a philosophy and a science. More of a science than anything else today. And the *Tabula Smaragdina Hermetis* is its beginning, its origin, the coded truth of the thrice great. The legendary emerald tablet of Hermes Trismegistos."

Maybe she really ought to leave him to di Santis and put her mind to something more important.

"Alchemy is the mother of science," he said, apparently mistaking the pool steps for a lecture hall. "When TABULA carries out experiments on Arcadians today, it is with reference to the father of alchemy—Hermes Trismegistos himself. No one knows who he really was. I have read a great deal about him, and his name unexpectedly turns up in the strangest sources. Some say that he occupied the throne of Thebes as its king. Others claim that he was a god of the shepherds of ancient Greece. Or the direct son of Adam. Then again, another opinion is that he never existed at all, and the name is only a pseudonym under which a whole group of scholars wrote their works. It's said that Hermes Trismegistos penned more than thirty-five thousand books."

"TABULA," she whispered sharply. "That's all that interests me."

"You've even inherited your grandmother's impatience." Trevini managed a thin smile, but there was still terror in his eyes. "It seems that the emerald tablet of Hermes was discovered in a cave around the year 300 BC. It isn't mentioned in writing until much later, and the first Latin translation comes from the Middle Ages. No one knows what language it was first written in—maybe Greek or Arabic."

"What does it say?"

"Some say the texts are oracles; others describe them as instructions. There are fifteen verses in all, from the beginning of the universe to the key to eternal life. 'That which is above is as that which is below, and that which is below is as that which is above.' And: 'Thus thou hast the glory of the whole world; therefore let all obscurity flee before thee.' And finally: 'Therefore am I called Hermes the Thrice Great, having the three parts of the philosophy of the whole world.'"

Trevini was now talking like a man in delirium, although he still gave Rosa the impression of being alert, if agitated. But whatever the words might mean, they told her that the attorney had thought much harder about the mysteries of TABULA than he had previously admitted. He knew the words on that damn tablet *by heart*.

"And you think that the organization takes its name from this emerald tablet?" she asked.

"*Tabula Smaragdina Hermetis,*" he said, for the third time.

"But who's behind it? Who are these people?"

"Researchers from all over the world. Biochemists, experts in genetic technology, anthropologists—who knows? They must have unlimited financial means, and they think that they're above the law."

"You know what that sounds like, don't you?"

He let out his breath with a scornful sound. "The Mafia is something quite different. It has never made any secret of its aims. It wanted, and still wants, nothing but power and money. But TABULA? Why are they misusing Arcadians for secret experiments? How do they know about the dynasties at all?" Trevini slowly shook his head. "Anyone who tries following that trail always comes up against a wall. Whether in libraries or on the internet—you never get far."

"No connection with the Arcadian dynasties?"

"A few vague hints, that's all."

She succeeded in keeping her inner cold at bay as long as what he was saying drowned out her feelings. She would have rejected it all as nonsense, stupid stuff that had nothing to do with her or Alessandro. But weren't there other answers lying far back in classical antiquity? What about the ancient statues on the seabed? The myth of the fall of Arcadia? Did the existence of this group go back as far as the history of Arcadia itself? Much of what Alessandro had told her about the origin of the dynasties was just as crazy as what Trevini was saying now. The Arcadian king Lycaon, who was turned into a cross between a man and an animal by angry Zeus, father of the gods. This Hermes Trismegistos sounded as if he came out of the same kind of myth.

"These hints—what do they say?" she asked.

"According to many sources Hermes, as I said, was the god of the Greek shepherds. His legendary magic staff, the caduceus, is an olive branch with two snakes twining around it. The myth says that this caduceus came from the land of Arcadia. Look it up. Try Google. What you find will confirm what I'm saying."

"So?"

"The story goes that the god Hermes was given a staff, and he wandered in the lonely mountains of Arcadia with it. There he came upon two snakes locked in fierce combat. To settle their quarrel, he separated them with his staff, and they were reconciled. Since then the double snake has been the alchemical symbol for peace, new hope, new life. But in the legend of Hermes, the two snakes stand for the making of peace in Arcadia."

"Which even if it were true all those thousands of years ago wouldn't interest anyone today." Rosa was trying not to turn back entirely into human form. If her snake gaze had some kind of hypnotic power that made Trevini talk, she wanted to hold it for as long as possible.

"There's something else." Trevini's chin was trembling. "The staff made into a caduceus by the two snakes had been given to Hermes by another god. By the god of light—by Apollo. Apollonio."

"So someone still knows the legend."

"Because of the myth, snakes always had a special meaning for the ancient Arcadians, long before Zeus cursed Lycaon and his subjects. But did that still hold true after the transformation and death of the king? Costanza, at least, was convinced that far more respect was owed to the snakes than the other Arcadian dynasties pay them today. It seems that even in the lifetime of Lycaon, the Lamias wanted to seize power. It's said that they toppled him from the throne of Arcadia in order to rule the land and the other dynasties themselves."

"Which would explain why the other families hate the Alcantaras so much," she commented. And then she began to see where all this was going. "Is that what Costanza was after? Did she want ancient history to repeat itself?" Rosa was gasping for air, because only now did she realize just *how* crazy her grandmother had been. "Did she stage the Hungry Man's arrest so that she could fix his downfall and restore the old power of the Lamias?"

"At last you're beginning to understand."

"But that's sick!"

"Every time a priest says Mass, he declares that the wine has turned into the blood of Christ. Hundreds of thousands of Muslims go on pilgrimage to Mecca every year. And how about the traditional tales of the Buddha and what he did? Good heavens, even scholars aren't immune to that kind of thing when they speak of an author called Homer, when they can be fairly sure that no one of that name ever lived and wrote. Many people say that even Shakespeare is just an invention! People cling to myths, false and true alike. Why would the Arcadians be any exception? They're all saying that the Hungry Man is about to return, as if he weren't just a leader of Cosa Nostra but really the mythical being he's named himself after."

In pain, Trevini tried moving again. His face was distorted as he went on talking. Perhaps he guessed that this knowledge would die with him if he didn't pass it on.

"Costanza believed in the truth behind the myths, and she was convinced of the Lamias' claim to power. If she had to enter into a pact with a man like Pantaleone to get it, then she would accept that. Nothing could make her give up the idea that she, or one of her female descendants, would rise to power over all the dynasties again. As in the old days of ancient Arcadia."

"What about the serum?" she asked. "Does that come

from TABULA, like the furs?"

"Presumably."

"I've had it analyzed. It was made using blood that has both human and animal characteristics. But we Arcadians are either one or the other, never both at once."

"Hybrid blood," he whispered.

She obviously knew less about that than everyone else. But what had she expected? She had entered the world of the Arcadians only four months ago—she had a lot to catch up on.

"Who are these hybrids?" she asked.

"Mongrels. A cross between humans and animals. Arcadians who didn't complete their last transformation in one direction or the other."

"Do you know any?"

"Me?" Trevini laughed bitterly. "All I know, I know from Costanza. And I worked out a few things for myself. I've told you everything, Rosa. We've reached the end."

"Why did you send Valerie to me? That whole story about how she ran away at the airport—"

"It's the truth. My men"—he corrected himself—"or rather the *contessa*'s men, now . . . they were supposed to put her on a flight to New York. But she got away from them. A clever little thing, your friend. Manipulative, too. Who knows, maybe we could all learn from her."

"She was hardly in any state to stand on her own feet," she objected. "Your interrogations didn't pass over her without a trace, *avvocato*. How could she have run away from men like those bodyguards out there?"

There was genuine surprise in Trevini's face. "She was in good health when she left here. A little weak, maybe, but in perfectly good health."

Rosa's eyes narrowed, and they were no longer the eyes of a snake. She had shifted back without being aware of it, feeling no more than a little tingling and itching. "When Valerie turned up at the palazzo yesterday, she was totally exhausted."

Now that the spell of her snake gaze was broken, the malicious sparkle that made her so furious returned to Trevini's smile. "Then either something happened to her on the way, or she's been acting a part for your benefit."

"How could she have—" But her words died away, because she already knew the answer. "Iole would never have let Valerie in if she hadn't been in such poor condition. But as it was . . ."

"A cunning little thing; I said so. You didn't simply leave her behind in the palazzo, did you? Maybe even without anyone to guard her?"

Rosa rubbed her face. She took her cell phone out of her pocket. It was switched off, and she had to type in the code. Then she called the number of the palazzo.

Trevini bent his head. "No one answering, I suppose?"

"Keep your mouth shut."

"Let's hope nothing has happened . . ."

Impatiently, she put the phone away again and turned to the steps.

"You're not going to kill me?" he asked her retreating back, and he sounded genuinely shocked. No longer afraid. Only surprised.

"No."

"But you can't help yourself, Rosa. Don't you feel that? Lamias are not merciful beings. Lamias never forgive. Costanza knew that."

She went up the stairs, leaving him lying there helpless in the empty pool. "I will also make sure that di Santis doesn't touch you. You're not worth the trouble, *avvocato*."

"Di Santis?" He laughed quietly. "She's only a peon. Yours or mine, what does that matter? Listen to your nature, Rosa. It's in your blood. Why resist it? You are what you are. And so you'll sign my death sentence, if not now then later."

She climbed up over the edge of the pool. "We'll see about that."

Trevini's voice followed her, and now there was something in it that went beyond bitterness. "Your grandmother collected the skins of Arcadians. Your father—well, we've both seen what he's capable of. And what does that say about you, Rosa? *What does that make you?*"

She closed the door behind her, but his words went on echoing in her mind. So she was glad when her cell phone rang once she was in the white-tiled corridor. With shaking fingers, she took it out. "Iole?"

"It's me."

"Alessandro! Thank God."

"Where are you? I've tried calling a thousand times." He sounded harassed. "Bad news. Michele isn't in New York anymore. He flew to Italy yesterday."

She stopped with the cell phone pressed to her ear.

"Michele is here, Rosa—in Sicily."

A DEATHLY SILENCE

AN HOUR AND A half later, Rosa was racing through the twilight in the BMW. She was just turning off the expressway when the cell phone on the passenger seat rang.

"I'm at the driveway now," said Alessandro. The sound of his engine died away in the background.

"Then wait for me there."

"No sign of the guards at the gate."

"Shit."

"I'll take a closer look."

"No!" she said firmly. "Too dangerous."

"What about Iole? She's alone up there."

"Your men are there. They're—"

Alessandro interrupted her. "If Michele's managed to eliminate the guards at the gate, he may well have dealt with Gianni and the other two in the palazzo as well."

She turned up the heating in the car. "Do you think Michele's on his own? Apart from Valerie."

"She makes him much stronger than any bunch of trigger-happy killers. He has someone on the inside. The others in the palazzo weren't expecting that. Nor was I."

She could have kicked herself for failing to lock Valerie in. Suppose Val's fear of dogs was only another ruse?

"I'm such an idiot," she whispered, before she realized what he had just said. But before she could ask any more questions, he admitted, "There's something else."

"Damn it, Alessandro . . ."

"I was *not* lying to you when I said I had nothing to do with the murders of Mattia, Carmine, and the others. I swear that's the truth." He hesitated for a fraction of a second. "But the attempt on Michele's life, the killer that Guerrini sent to New York—"

"So Trevini was right."

"I meant it to fail. I intended for Michele to follow the trail back to me and face me in person, instead of hunting my girl-friend through Central Park. That was a cowardly thing to do."

"You planned it all? For him to turn up here?"

"Not at the palazzo, but in Sicily, yes. That's why I wanted Gianni and the others to be with you. I couldn't know that Valerie was working with Michele. And would still be on his side, even after Mattia's death . . . I should have factored that into the equation. What a mess I've made."

She could have shaken him—but despite all reason she was moved. "You should have told me."

"I didn't want you to have any more to do with it. So that you could put the whole thing behind you. And I *will* kill Michele, one way or another. I'd have liked to do it on my own terms, that's all. The bastard foiled me by planting Valerie on you."

"He isn't as clever as all that," she objected. "I think she really did run away from him, or she wouldn't have stolen his cell phone. But after she got away from Trevini's men at the airport, I guess she didn't know what to do next. She must have called Michele again. And of course he'd have known right away how he could use her."

Alessandro sighed. "I'm sorry, Rosa."

In spite of everything her longing for him, for his touch, was like a physical pain. "Val fooled us both."

"I'm going to put an end to this now. Tonight."

"I'll be with you in half an hour. We'll go up there together."

But his car door was already closing. She heard his footsteps crunch on the gravel.

"Alessandro!"

"There's another car here at the gate," he said. "A green Panda. With one of those cards lying on the dashboard that doctors display so that they can leave their vehicles in no-parking areas."

"It must belong to the doctor I called for Valerie."

There was a metallic click.

"Do you know him?" asked Alessandro.

"Not well. He comes from Piazza Armerina. He's kind of . . . a friend of the family, you might say."

"He's lying in the trunk of his car, shot dead. Michele must have stopped him on the way. Wait a minute . . ."

"What is it?"

"I'm just looking around. There are at least two trails of blood here leading into the bushes beyond the gateway. The gate itself is open . . . the control box has been destroyed. And there are bullet holes."

The dry, hilly landscape was racing past her windows in the dim light. It would be a few miles before she saw more trees. Now and then headlights came toward her, and she was dazzled by another pair in her rearview mirror. Her eyes were reacting more sensitively to bright light than usual.

"Okay," said Alessandro. "I think I know what happened now."

"Are the men dead?"

"Yes. He hauled their bodies behind the bushes. When they realized that the man in the car wasn't a doctor they must have tried to lock the gate again, and someone destroyed the control box."

"The gate wouldn't have kept anyone out! And there isn't even fencing on both sides of it."

"There's a slope, though. And trees. Like it or not, Michele must have had to go a mile up to the palazzo on foot. And I'll have to do the same."

"Wait until I get there, and we'll go together."

"No, this is my fault, and I'm not letting Michele do anything else to you."

"Our chances are much better if there are two of us."

"Rosa, listen to me very carefully. Stay exactly where you are now, and wait until I call you again."

"Oh, sure!" she said. "You bet I will."

"Michele wants to take his revenge on me. That's why he means to kill you first."

"He'd better start a club with the Hungry Man: the Kill Rosa to Punish Alessandro Club." She was making a great effort to hide the unsteadiness in her voice. "There should be twelve of my guards somewhere around the place. What about them?"

"Can't see anyone."

"But Michele can't have eliminated them all on his own."

"The Hundinga have stopped howling."

"Maybe they left."

"Maybe."

Her hands clutched the steering wheel. "But they didn't, did they?"

"No," he said. "They're sure to be roaming around here somewhere. And if they're on their way to the palazzo, or there already, then your people won't—" He let out a low curse.

"What?" she called into her phone, in too much mental confusion to get out a complete sentence. Her fears for him were growing by the minute.

There was a sharp explosion in the background.

"Are those *shots*?" She tasted iron on the tip of her tongue.

"Farther up the slope," he said. "Near the palazzo, I think."

"I'll call the judge. Quattrini can send reinforcements and—"

"The police? How long do you think it will take them to get here? An hour? Two hours? Forget it. And when this is over, you'll be glad there were no police here turning the whole palazzo upside down."

"I don't care whether—"

"Yes, you do. Well, you should. We're *capi*. People like us have no choice but to take charge ourselves."

"If any harm comes to Iole—"

"The police couldn't do anything about that if it would take them forever to get here."

"Men from Piazza Armerina? A couple of calls and I could summon twenty or thirty of them."

"It'd all take far too long. Anyway, I'm already on my way up to the house."

She felt choked by her helplessness and fear. "Stupid idiot," she whispered, but he knew what she meant.

"Love you, too."

"Take care of yourself."

"So will you stop somewhere and wait?" he asked. The climb through the olive groves was beginning to make him sound breathless.

"Okay."

"Really?"

"Of course not!" she said.

"Then I'll have to make sure all this is over before you get here."

"Twenty minutes max. And don't do anything silly."

"Twenty minutes against the rest of our lives. Sounds like a good bargain to me."

"The rest of our lives," she repeated softly, and stared into the gathering night. The outlines of the landscape blurred before her eyes.

"Promise?"

She ended the call and threw her cell phone onto the passenger seat.

"Promise," she swore to the darkness.

CLIMBING UP

ALESSANDRO HAD LEFT HIS Ferrari at the side of the road next to the iron gate. The doctor's Panda stood a few feet away. Its trunk was closed.

Rosa stopped, letting the beam of the BMW's headlights illuminate the undergrowth on both sides of the gate. The gate itself stood ajar, just as Alessandro had said.

She slipped out of her car, while the alarm inside it beeped because she'd left the lights on. Hastily, she closed the door and went over to the Ferrari. She felt a pang at the thought that Alessandro had been here so recently. And now he was gone, was somewhere up there in the dark.

She opened the driver's door and touched the leather of the seat with her fingertips. It was a kind of compulsion. She wanted to feel Alessandro, and this was the best she could do.

Then she slammed the door, much too loud, and wondered whether she owed it to the dead man to look inside the trunk of the Panda. He was dead because she had called him.

Better get used to that kind of thing.

Her headlights had to be easily visible from pretty far away, so she hurried back to the BMW and switched them off. The silence that followed the beeping alarm felt doubly oppressive.

When she stepped through the opening in the gate, she

saw the trails of blood that Alessandro had mentioned. With a lump in her throat, she looked into the undergrowth. The men were lying in a small hollow. Four shapes, twisted and distorted. Yet more corpses.

Pulling herself together, Rosa clambered out of the bushes and back to the driveway, her legs stiff. By now it was almost entirely dark. The full moon cast silvery light on the tops of the trees standing on the hills. She had a moment's shock as a car raced along the road as if out of nowhere, briefly bathing the parked automobiles in bright radiance, and then disappeared again. For once, she wished it had been one of the judge's vehicles keeping her under observation. But today—of all days—there was no sign of any of the people who had been shadowing her.

She guessed that Alessandro must have reached the palazzo by now. Cutting through the olive groves on foot was shorter than walking up the drive. There would probably still be guns lying around here somewhere, but she couldn't bring herself to search the bodies for pistols.

She listened once again for any howling from the Hundinga, but she heard only the sound of nocturnal insects and a single call from an owl. Pressing her lips together, she set off, hurried up the little slope on the other side of the drive, and ducked down among the gnarled olive trees that grew as far as the eye could see. After only a few steps, she found the path along which the olive pickers carried their baskets at harvest time. She had last been this way when she'd stolen out of the palazzo to go to Isola Luna with the Carnevares. Fundling had been waiting for her down on the road, to drive her to the coast.

She had hardly thought of Fundling since her last visit to his sickbed. He made her feel uneasy. The strange young man was still unknowable to her, one of those mysterious *gaps in the crowd* that he had once mentioned. Crazy, confused words.

A shot rang out in the distance, echoing down the slope. Two birds rose nearby and fluttered away.

By this time Rosa was a good third of the way up the drive. She still couldn't see the lights of the palazzo. At that moment heavy clouds moved in front of the moon. The rustling of branches in the evening wind sounded ghostly when the trees were barely visible.

There was something lying on the path in front of her.

Another dead body. But no: As she came closer, the shapeless bundle turned out to be the first of several items of clothing, stripped off and discarded. She knew that sweater. A cell phone was sticking out of one pocket of the crumpled jeans. So Alessandro was stealing through the darkness somewhere up there in his panther form. Maybe he was already at the house. Had the gunshot been for him?

She could have tried her own transformation, and for a few seconds she felt sure that would be the best way to go unnoticed. But she had no experience covering a distance of any length in her snake form, and she wasn't sure how well she would keep up. So she continued walking, sweating profusely and persuading herself that it was only the wind on her damp skin making her shiver.

Points of light emerged ahead of her in the darkness. Only a few of the palazzo windows were lit.

Another shot, then two more in rapid succession.

A dog howled. One of the Hundinga. Or maybe Sarcasmo.

Where the olive groves gave way to lemon trees, she found another bundle on the ground. The man was naked. He couldn't have been dead for long; the gaping wounds in his body gleamed wet with blood. His throat was torn to pieces, his head at a twisted angle. He had been killed with great savagery.

She heard the sound of paws, and panting—it came from the east, where the tall foundation wall of the panoramic terrace rose among a few palm trees. Climbing over an old wooden fence, she pressed close to a tree trunk.

Two more bodies lay not far away. Both were fully clothed. They were two of the guards here on the Alcantara property, and they had obviously been killed when they found something: several bags and backpacks lying at the foot of a palm. The wall of the terrace rose twelve feet high, right behind the tree.

Rosa held her breath and stood perfectly still.

A gigantic Doberman, larger than a wolf, coming from the south, was approaching the dead men and her find. Rosa could see the animal only from its movements, since in the darkness it blended into its surroundings.

There was a crunching, tearing sound as it changed shape in motion. From one bound to the next the creature rose on its hind legs, stretching as the bones shifted and extended. The dog's rough coat merged with human flesh. Muscles showed, moving beneath the skin.

In the faint moonlight, the dog's face changed, the muzzle retreated, the forehead advanced. The man raised his arms— paws became hands—and rubbed his eyes.

A few seconds later, stark naked, he went up to one of the bags and took something out. The display of a cell phone lit up, illuminating the man's face from below. Rosa put his age at about forty, maybe a little older. He had angular, scarred features, and his hair was cut very short.

He spoke into the phone in a whisper. His accent was harsh, maybe from eastern or northern Europe, and he seemed to be reporting back on the situation to someone.

". . . killed two of my men," she heard the Hunding say. ". . . can't wait any longer. The hell with the plan . . . going straight in . . ."

She dared not go any closer. Even breathing was risky, but she couldn't hold her breath any longer.

The man lowered the cell phone and glanced around.

She was in total darkness, yet he was looking straight at her. He uttered one last, angry remark down the phone—". . . for me to decide . . ."—and then switched it off and dropped it into the open bag.

Slowly, he came toward Rosa, a huge outline in front of the gray, moonlit wall. An angry growl issued from his throat.

If she moved her head, however slightly, he would spot her. She could do nothing but keep staring at him, whether she wanted to or not.

Her heart was racing, pumping the snake's icy breath through her limbs with every beat. If she shifted shape now, he would definitely notice her. And she was far from sure whether, in her snake form, she would be agile enough to escape his fangs.

He dropped to all fours and exploded back into dog shape, so quickly that it was like an old-fashioned special effect in a movie. Here was the man—*cut!*—there was the dog. Not even a dissolve.

The creature was still nine feet away from her. His Doberman coat smelled of human sweat.

Once again she heard the howling of the others up at the house. They were besieging the palazzo. Shots rang out from the terrace right above them.

The Hunding froze.

A second Hunding howled in pain in the darkness. A body hit water. The bullet must have knocked one of them into the pool.

The chill in Rosa reached the ends of her hair. Everything about her was tingling, itching, burning. She tried to hold back the transformation, fight it. But she was in deadly danger, and her body reacted uncontrollably.

More gunshots. Howling that lasted longer this time. Another bullet had hit home.

The Doberman let out an angry growl, snapped menacingly at the air, then spun around and stormed along the foundation wall of the terrace to the nearest flight of steps to join the rest of the pack.

Rosa closed her eyes. Behind her lids, the pupils narrowed to slits. Her split tongue touched fangs. She opened her eyes again, but it was still dark. It took her a moment to realize why. Hissing, she glided out from under her heap of black clothes, over dry ground, and on into the moonlight.

THE LEOPARD

SHE WOUND HER WAY up the steps to the terrace, keeping close to the wall. Her reptilian skin shimmered in shades of bronze and gold.

The wide panoramic terrace of the palazzo lay ahead of her, surrounded by a heavy stone balustrade, gray in the pale moonlight. The next front of clouds was already coming up, and soon everything would be in deep shadow again. Someone must have switched off the motion detectors on the outdoor spotlights in the tops of the palm trees.

The first-floor windows were barred, and no light showed in any of them. The living quarters were on the second floor. Here, and on the west side of the palazzo, there were several bedrooms. Signora Falchi was standing at the open window of one of them, aiming a gun down at the terrace.

One dead man lay on the patio; a second was drifting in a cloud of blood in the swimming pool. The bluish glow from the pool flickered over the facade in indistinct reflections. The tutor's face shone in that light as if it were covered with glass.

Rosa saw a movement on the very edge of her field of vision—only a scurrying, but at once a muzzle flash flared at the window. The bullet whipped over the terrace without hitting anyone. The Hunding for whom it had been intended came leaping up the steps, growling, right where Rosa was. He was not the same as the one she had already seen, but a powerful bulldog. With her responsive snake senses, Rosa felt the ground vibrate beneath his paws. At the same time her aggression was roused. In human form she would have run for it, or she might have been frozen with horror at the sight of the monster racing up; as a snake, however, she wanted to accept the challenge.

The Hunding knew that he was facing no ordinary reptile, but a Lamia. He stopped six feet away from her, went into an attack stance, and bared his murderous teeth. Rosa's snake body reared up, and she hissed. He was about to leap onto her, but she was too quick. With a powerful coiling movement she shot toward him and then below him, digging her fangs into the soft skin beneath his ribs. The Hunding yowled in pain and thrust his muzzle downward, but before he could snap at her, she rammed her body against his skull. The yowling turned to a howl, and then she bit a second time, tasted his blood, and felt nothing but triumph.

She made use of the moment of surprise to coil herself around him. He fell heavily on his side, kicked out in panic, and snapped at her again. Quick as a flash, she squeezed her body hard around him, felt his bones breaking, crushed his ribs, his lungs, his internal organs.

More shots rang out, and when she looked up she saw that another Hunding had fallen to a bullet fired by the tutor. He had come out of cover to hurry to the aid of Rosa's opponent. He didn't get far.

Did Signora Falchi know who the snake really was? Was that why she had shot the second Hunding? Or would Rosa be next in her line of fire?

The dead Hunding in Rosa's grip began turning back into human form. She quickly withdrew, glided over the terrace to the outer wall of the house, and followed its course northward. The bars over the windows were too close together for her to put her head through and break the glass with her skull, and the doors had security locks and bolts; her grandmother had made sure that no intruder would find it easy to get in.

She heard panting and growling in the shadows. The farther she went from the pool and its underwater lighting, the darker it was. The Hundinga were watching her. As soon as Rosa moved out of the tutor's line of fire, there would be nothing to hold them back. Presumably most of them knew that she was the only Lamia in the palazzo.

She reached the corner of the building, and with it the end of the terrace. Quickly she slipped out between the stone bars of the balustrade on to the grassy meadow along the north facade. She was looking for a way into the palazzo at ground level, and for that she'd have to cross the open surface.

Behind her, a Hunding leaped the railing and landed on the lawn. Another—the biggest pit bull she had ever seen—raced after him. More shapes were moving among the chestnut trees bordering the meadow.

Rosa wound her way forward as fast as she could, surprising herself by her own agility. Yet she might not be fast enough. The paws of the Hundinga made the ground tremble;

they had to be close behind her. The first was already snapping at her. He missed her reptilian body only by a hairbreadth.

Ahead of Rosa stood the greenhouse. Greenish light shone faintly in the glazed annex. The panes, clouded with condensation, hid the tropical jungle inside.

One glass pane in the bottom row was broken. Rosa made straight for it. The shattered glass had fallen inside; obviously the Hundinga had already tried getting into the palazzo that way. A naked corpse lay among the shards of glass. Someone had halted the charging Hunding; he hadn't gone more than six feet inside the greenhouse.

One of Rosa's pursuers let out a short, sharp bark, and then the ground shook one last time. The Hundinga had stopped. Rosa shot over the broken glass and the dead man, and plunged into the tropical atmosphere of the greenhouse.

Its green twilight sprang to life, hissing. They came from all sides, only a few at first, then more and more. The snakes who lived here, the Alcantaras' totem animals, recognized their mistress and took her protectively into their midst. Some of them turned toward the Hundinga, and Rosa caught the scent of their venom, saw it glittering at the tips of their fangs. She had only recently discovered that a bite from some of these reptiles was fatal. She herself had no venom glands in her snake form, and possibly that was true of all Lamias.

The Hundinga did not follow her through the broken pane. Snarling, they retreated. Locked doors and barred windows wouldn't deter them for long, now that their leader had decided to attack even against the Hungry Man's orders. Rosa assumed that they had guns with them, and probably also explosives. Even if they preferred hunting in packs as Hundinga, ultimately they too were only killers with a job to do.

The snakes crowding around Rosa caressed her, rubbed against her scaly body; every single one of them seemed to want to touch her. She moved with the throng of snakes toward the heavy door leading from the greenhouse to the north wing.

There she closed her eyes, put the menace of the Hundinga out of her mind, concentrated entirely on her human nature, remembered the sensation of having arms and legs. And when she looked, she *did* have arms and legs again. The reptilian scales on her head and neck were dividing into strands, becoming unruly light-blond hair.

The snakes were still winding around her bare feet, but they retreated a little way when Rosa stepped forward to take the key off a hook on the wall. Cautiously, she opened the door and glanced through the crack into a corridor. Imposing frescoes covered the vaulted ceiling: angels, devils, and saints in the midst of cloud-capped mountain ranges and garden landscapes. The hallway itself was empty, but one of the lights that automatically came on after dark gave sparse illumination.

The stone floor was icy under the soles of her feet, but this time she welcomed the cold. She went into the corridor and closed the door after her. Then she crouched down, closed her eyes, and did as she might do if she were an actor calling up emotions in preparation for a scene. She thought of Zoe's death, and her father's betrayal of her; she conjured up the pictures on the video, her own wide, wakeful eyes as she watched what was happening, unable to do anything. Then the reptile stirred inside her. With the strength of an electrical charge, the cold filled her limbs and sent her sinking to the floor in snake form once again.

Immediately she glided forward, down the corridor, and to the staircase up to the floor above. No one came to meet her, and she heard nothing but the dry rustling of her scales moving over the worn stone slabs. She reached the second floor and set off on her way to the west wing in the dim glow of the nocturnal lighting.

Signora Falchi had stopped firing; maybe she had run out of ammunition. The handle of the door of her room was blocked on the outside by an iron rod. Rosa saw three bullet holes in the oaken door, the splinters pointing out into the corridor. It would be impossible for the tutor to open the barricaded door from the inside.

She looked attentively around her and waited until her eyes were used to the darkness. No one in sight. Michele and Valerie must have locked the tutor in her room. She was probably safer there than anywhere.

Rosa glided on to Costanza's old bedroom. The door was open; the lock had been broken. It seemed that after Rosa left Iole had locked Valerie in again after all—but in vain.

Valerie was gone. There was no sign of Sarcasmo either. Rosa was sick with worry about Iole, and the disappearance of the dog made it no better. Had Michele done the girl any harm? Had he shot Sarcasmo? And where was Alessandro?

She quickly moved on to her own room and found it untouched. In the dressing room she returned to human form, slipped into jeans and a T-shirt, feeling dazed, and stole barefoot out into the hallway. There was a cupboard with a lock in the study. Florinda had kept a pistol and ammunition there.

Cautiously, she snuck down the dark corridors, going from niche to niche, immersed in deep shadow. Where two passages met, she stumbled upon the corpse of Gianni. Rosa turned away and ran on.

Her skin was stinging as if she had grazed it, but it showed neither injuries nor reddened patches. Maybe her brain hadn't yet fully registered that she was not a snake anymore. Her joints, too, felt like unfamiliar structures that she would have to accustom herself to using.

She listened for voices, sounds, footsteps. Nothing. But the palazzo walls were thick, and the old tapestries on the walls swallowed up most noises.

What would she do in Michele's place? He wanted revenge, because he thought Alessandro had given orders for the murder of the Carnevares. Part of his retribution was to be Rosa's death. When he had failed to find her at the palazzo, he must have questioned Iole. She had probably told him, truthfully, that Rosa had driven off in her car, and upon hearing that, he had surely begun searching the whole place for her—a hopeless undertaking, considering all its countless rooms and corridors. It made little difference whether Valerie had helped him or had stayed to guard Iole, particularly once the Hundinga began laying siege to the walls. Michele would have had no time to be thorough in his search; the attack must have taken him as much by surprise as it had Iole and Signora Falchi. Presumably he was nervous now. And a nervous man would make mistakes.

The study lay at the end of a long corridor on the third floor and had no door; the only way in was a rounded archway, making it almost impossible to get there unseen. In human form she would stand no chance. Even so, she put off her transformation, because she could sense that shifting shape back and forth so quickly was putting a strain on her strength. She had no idea what she could demand of her body. Biologically, the metamorphoses might be impossible to explain, but that didn't mean that they left no trace behind. Strictly speaking, with every transformation Rosa broke all her bones. In the long run that was bound to have some effect on her physical structure, her circulation, and her metabolism.

To get to the second floor, she used one of the former servants' staircases. The days of valets and lady's maids were long gone, and the narrow steps that they had once used were dusty and covered with cobwebs.

She entered a corridor on the upper floor through a thin door behind a curtain. There was no one in sight, and no lamp on apart from the faint, sulfurous illumination of the nocturnal lighting. For the first time, she thought she heard voices, but when she held her breath and listened hard, there was only silence.

On bare feet, she hurried beyond the curtain and turned

right. The study was in the north wing, looking out over the inner courtyard. Maybe she ought to have gone the long way around through the kitchen, to arm herself with a knife. But she would lose it anyway at her next transformation, if not before.

Concentrating hard, she was approaching a bend in the hallway when she suddenly heard sounds. Soft paws on bare stone.

Alessandro? Michele?

Or one of the Hundinga?

Taking small, silent steps, she ran back behind the curtain and leaned against the closed door to the stairway. The wine-red velvet vibrated in front of her face, not a handsbreadth away.

Through a crack in the curtain, she could see down the corridor. A shadow was coming around the corner.

Rosa fought down her sense of cold. If she shifted to her snake shape now, the sounds of it would give her away.

A big cat was prowling closer. The cat's long tail swished slowly from side to side. Its shoulder blades stood out as the predator kept its head close to the ground, bent and waiting, ready to pounce. Bright eyes glinted silver in the dim lighting. Its whiskers and brows were white; the muscular body was covered with yellowish fur sprinkled with dark brown spots. Each of the animal's four paws was as large as Rosa's face.

The leopard stopped and peered down the hall. Then he began to move again.

Rosa stood pressing as close as possible to the door, intent

360

on making no sound. And on not touching the curtain.

The snake stirred inside her as the leopard came nearer. Soon she would lose sight of him because the heavy velvet would be in the way. But she could hear him, his paws on the flagstones, the scraping of his claws.

Out on the terrace, she had killed a Hunding, a massive, lumbering colossus. One of the Panthera, however, was something else entirely. And Michele might be exceptional even among his own kind. She had seen him hunting, accepted by the others as leader of the pride because he was stronger, faster, more ruthless than the rest.

She felt her skin tense, suddenly turning dry, and tiny scales trickled from her forehead down her cheeks. Her hair formed strands, her knees stiffened, her elbows hurt. A terrible itching ran over her body in waves.

Not now!

Something touched the other side of the curtain, very slightly. Tapped it and withdrew again. The touch was repeated a little farther to the left. The leopard's gently lashing tail. Its tip brushed the velvet as the animal moved past her hiding place.

Her T-shirt was too large for her; she felt as if she were simply passing through it, like the hero in *The Incredible Shrinking Man*. She was the shrinking woman, the snake girl, and in a couple of seconds she would be cat food.

Somewhere in the house, glass broke.

She heard the distant sound of Hundinga howling. The echoes resounded in the corridors and stairwells.

The leopard hissed. Suddenly she heard his paws slapping down on the flagstones several times as he moved into a swift run. Then there was silence.

Rosa's back slid down the door until she was crouching, with her knees pushing the curtain outward. There was nothing she could do about it. Her heart sank, and for a moment she didn't know whether she was in human or snake form. The heavy curtain was pressing in on her, keeping her from breathing. Energetically, she thrust it aside and looked out at the corridor.

The leopard had disappeared. She thought he had run left. The study was in the opposite direction.

She struggled to her feet and went that way.

SUICIDE QUEENS

The hall leading to the study stretched ahead of her like the inside of an accordion, getting longer and longer—an optical illusion. It was all in Rosa's head. In her crazy, bewildered brain.

Pictures in black frames with gold leaf flaking off them hung on the walls. Tables and lamps lined the corridor, along with a suit of armor too small for a man. This palazzo had always been a house full of women, often at odds with one another.

Rosa was sick and tired of hiding. She stepped out into the middle of the corridor and walked toward the open archway leading to the study.

She saw the desk in front of the glazed door to the balcony. Saw the high back of the chair at the desk—it was empty. Saw herself as a faint reflection in the glass of the window, an outline emerging from the gloom of the corridor, the ghost of her belligerent forebears, or just a girl who had come to break with the past.

The whole room opened up before her, big enough to be a ballroom. Thirty feet of polished wooden parquet flooring lay between the archway and the desk. The chandelier was not switched on, but several lamps along the walls gave light.

"Rosa!"

Iole wore only a white nightshirt that came down to her knees. She was sitting on a leather sofa beside the west wall of the study, with her wrists bound. She tried to jump up, but a slender hand grabbed her arm and dragged her back down onto the cushions. Valerie was holding a silver pistol in her hand, pressing the muzzle against Iole's temple.

The corners of Rosa's mouth twitched. It was almost a smile.

"Your hardcore is my mainstream," she said softly—the wording on the T-shirt that Valerie had been wearing when they'd first met in Brooklyn. She didn't know why that popped into her mind just now. Or why she suddenly laughed, a loud laugh intended to wound. The words were in such absurd contrast to the emaciated, drug-addicted girl with the gun that she couldn't help herself. She was laughing at Valerie's betrayal, her sorrow, her naive, obsessive, fatal love for Michele Carnevare. She laughed until it turned to a choking cough, and the look in Iole's wide eyes showed more concern for Rosa than anxiety for her own fate.

"Finished?" inquired Valerie. "Then go over to the desk and pick up what's lying there. Use it."

Rosa's eyes followed her gesture. A syringe ready for injection lay under the lamp on the desktop. The contents shimmered yellow in the sharply outlined circle of light.

Rosa didn't move from the spot. She stood in the middle of the room, the archway behind her, the huge oak desk in front of her, and to her right, fifteen feet away, the sofa with the two girls sitting on it.

"The Hundinga are in the house," she said, not sure whether Valerie knew what that meant.

But Val was in league with Michele now. "They want you," she said. "You and your boyfriend. They're not here on my account, or Michele's."

"Is that what he said? Did he tell you they won't hurt you when they come up here? Or do you think they won't mind at all that there are a few of them lying out by the pool—and not to sunbathe?"

Valerie slowly shook her head. "I'm the Suicide Queen, Rosa. I'm not afraid." The gravity in her voice was shattering. Almost enough to make Rosa feel sorry for her. Almost.

"There's no need to point that thing at Iole," said Rosa. "She hasn't done anything to you."

"I *hadn't done anything* to your friend Trevini, either, but all the same he wasn't particularly nice to me."

"I just got back from seeing Trevini. He won't be hurting anyone again."

"And how long did it take you to decide to let me go? Two days? Three? Why not right away, Rosa?" Valerie's voice was sharper now. "What was so hard about telling him to let me go?"

Rosa held her gaze, but still didn't move. "Because you deserved it, Val. Every damn minute in Trevini's dungeon cell. Because you stabbed me in the back not just once, there in New York, but again here. What do you expect? You think that if you shoot Iole everything will get better? That you'll be better off yourself?"

"I'm just fine. Michele is here. Everything will be all right."

"You're out of your mind."

Valerie's eyes flashed. The pistol stayed where it was against Iole's head. "We know so much about each other, Rosa. All kinds of embarrassing little secrets. Stuff you say in the club at night when you're drunk. Or outside waiting in line to get in. We were good friends once."

"We were never real friends," Rosa contradicted her. "You didn't want a friend; you wanted someone who'd look up to you. Admire you."

"Well—and didn't you admire me?" Valerie laughed a soft, mirthless laugh. "Why do insecure, vulnerable girls like you always need someone to cling to? Someone to keep showing them what they aren't and never will be?"

"Because they still hope to change. To learn how to change. And not go crawling someday to an asshole like Michele Carnevare, begging him to pat them on the head and act as if they meant something to him."

"Michele loves me!" Valerie snapped.

"Nobody loves you, Val. Nobody ever did. That's your problem, right? That was it even with the Suicide Queens. And now you're trying to buy his love by killing Iole? Great plan!"

Iole frowned. "Pretty damn stupid, if you ask me."

Val pushed the gun hard against her skull. "Shut up! This has nothing to do with you!"

"It's *my* head," said Iole.

"Leave her alone," Rosa said again. "This is between you and me. Why are you dragging her into it?"

"And suppose I do let her go? You'll turn into a snake, and I'll be dead before I can fire this gun."

"No one has to die, Val."

But Valerie wasn't buying it. "Take that stuff off the desk and inject it into yourself."

"And then what?"

"Michele will be back any minute. You'll stay in human form if you inject the serum. That's what he wants."

"And what do *you* want?"

"I want you to get on with it and do as I say!"

Rosa knew she'd be dead if Michele got his claws into her in her human form. Her chances as a snake weren't much better, but if she didn't change, Michele would tear her to pieces before Alessandro's eyes.

That was assuming that Alessandro was nearby.

Valerie cursed because Rosa still didn't move. Then she fired the pistol.

The shot echoed deafeningly back from the paneling. It must have been audible all over the palazzo. Somewhere in the endless corridor, Michele would now be making his way straight back to the study.

Valerie had lowered the gun. The bullet hadn't been for Iole's head. For a moment Rosa thought it had shattered Iole's knee.

The girl was white as a sheet, her eyes reddened, but she was still sitting there, rigid with fright. Smoke, or maybe dust as well, was billowing out of a bullet hole in the sofa right next to her leg.

"The syringe!" Valerie demanded again.

Rosa went over to the desk. She resisted the urge to look over her shoulder and through the archway. If she were to see the huge leopard racing toward her out of the dim light in the corridor, it would only paralyze her.

She put out her hand and moved the syringe out of the circle of light cast by the lamp on the desk. The serum shone gold inside it.

"Hurry up," said Valerie.

Rosa reached out her left arm. "You have more experience with this kind of thing than me. Maybe you'd better help me."

"Maybe, because I'm also dumb as a post. You can do it yourself."

Iole let out a cry of pain as Valerie jammed the pistol into her ribs.

Rosa put the syringe to her arm, took a deep breath, and thrust it in. It hurt ten times more than at the doctor's.

"All of it," Valerie ordered. "Down to the very last drop."

The serum was streaming into Rosa's arm. She knew that doctors usually injected directly into a vein. Although she could see her own veins clearly beneath her fair skin, she had deliberately aimed to one side. If she injected the serum under her skin instead of into her bloodstream, it might be longer before it took effect. A swelling was already forming around the place where the needle had gone in because the fluid wasn't dispersing quickly enough.

Still, she emptied the entire contents into her arm, tore it out again and flung it over to Valerie on the sofa. Valerie jumped, then looked at the empty syringe, and nodded. "Okay," she said. "Michele will be here soon."

Rosa put her hand over the swelling and pretended to be massaging the place. Whether she was really managing to delay the effect she didn't know, or how long it would be for. She had to shift shape as quickly as possible.

But the pistol was still aimed at Iole. Valerie seemed capable of anything to prove her love to Michele.

"And what about Mattia?" asked Rosa. "Was that all a show? Don't you care about his death?" She tried to read the meaning of the slight tremor in Valerie's features. "Or that it was Michele who killed him?"

"That's a lie!" cried Val. "Michele never touched him. Mattia is dead because Alessandro had him murdered. Like all the rest of them."

"The moment Michele opens his mouth he tells lies."

A big cat roared somewhere close.

Valerie smiled maliciously. "Tell him that to his face."

Iole was shifting back and forth on the sofa. "My back itches."

The roar came again.

The swelling was going down beneath Rosa's hand. The serum was dispersing faster than she had expected.

Another roar, but it sounded different. As if it didn't come from the same big cat, but from another.

At the same moment, several Hundinga howled. Valerie jumped up, looking anxious, and hauled Iole to her feet.

A muted cracking sound was heard. Wood breaking, very far away. Maybe a door being forced open. At the other end of the house, probably two stories down on the first floor.

"Can you smell that?" Iole's voice was almost drowned out by animal roars, which were louder now. "Something's burning."

For a moment Rosa forgot Valerie and the pistol. "They're trying to smoke us out. They've started a fire."

An expression of satisfaction came over Valerie's face. "Looks like your fairy-tale castle will go up in flames. What a shame."

Rosa could have told her how little she cared about that. How she had toyed with the idea of burning the place down herself. And that she had enough money to buy a new property somewhere else—not to mention all the apartment buildings owned by the Alcantaras.

At the same time, she realized that she did mind what happened to the house. These walls were part of her inheritance. She had grown fond of this cold, dark, damp palazzo, she suddenly realized, and she wondered how that had happened. Had she become more of an Alcantara than she thought?

You have so much of your grandmother in you, Trevini had said. *It's you here in front of me, but Costanza looks out of your eyes.*

"Stay where you are!"

Valerie's voice made her spin around. Without knowing it, Rosa had taken several steps toward the balcony. She had to see exactly where the building was on fire.

"You won't shoot again," she said furiously.

Iole anxiously bowed her head. "Maybe she will, though."

"You bet your life I will," said Valerie.

Rosa's hand still lay on the place where the needle had gone in. She tried to concentrate on shifting. But the serum was in her blood by now. She'd missed her chance.

From her standing position, she ran toward Valerie.

Valerie tore the pistol away from her hostage, aimed in Rosa's direction, and pulled the trigger. Whether on purpose or by accident, the bullet hit the ground right in front of Rosa, tearing up part of the wooden flooring.

"Don't move!" shouted Valerie.

Rosa stopped.

"One more step and you're both dead." There was about fifteen feet between them. Not much. But enough to give Valerie the chance to fire again.

"Michele won't come now," Rosa warned her. "He and Alessandro . . . they're fighting. Damn it, Val, you can hear them, too!"

"Desperation doesn't suit you."

"Are you really that dumb? He's been using you! And now he has what he wanted. He and Alessandro met somewhere in the house. And the Hundinga have set fire to the whole place under our feet. Are you planning to wait until it's too late to get out of here? Do you really hate me so much that you'd rather burn to death with me than stay alive?"

"I'm not going anywhere without Michele."

"Then you'll have to go to him. Even Michele isn't crazy enough to run up to the third floor of a burning building just to . . ." She hesitated. "Just because he promised to."

A vague gleam came into Valerie's eyes.

At that moment Iole dropped to the ground, collapsing as if she had fainted. Except that she was fully conscious. And once again she turned out to be smarter than anyone would have expected.

For a moment Valerie's attention was distracted. She couldn't make up her mind whether to grab hold of Iole again, shoot her, or simply ignore her.

Rosa lunged forward.

The muzzle of the pistol swung in her direction again.

Iole kicked Valerie in the backs of her knees with all her might. Valerie cried out and lost her balance, pulling the trigger of the gun, but the bullet missed Rosa by several feet and hit the ceiling. Stucco exploded in a white cloud.

Furious, and helpless in her rage, Valerie spent a fraction of a second too long wondering whether to fire at Rosa or at Iole.

At the same moment, Rosa was rushing at her. They were both roaring like the big cats and the Hundinga down in the house. Iole rolled over onto her side, was kicked in the stomach, and doubled up in pain. Rosa dropped on top of Valerie, who felt as thin as a pile of twigs below her. Screeching, the weakened Valerie fought back, hitting and kicking and scratching like a madwoman. Rosa had to protect her eyes, but at the same time she rammed one knee into Valerie's lower body; then she rolled aside, taking Valerie with her, and got on top of her again.

By now the pistol had dropped from Valerie's fingers. Rosa didn't know where it had fallen, and she had no time to look around. She had her work cut out for her, avoiding Val's fingers and fists and at the same time trying to get control of her and force her to the floor with her knees and hands.

Once again it looked as if Valerie might get the upper hand. They were rolling on the floor, and for several seconds Rosa was lying under her. Then she braced herself and, with a cry, flung her aside. Val's shoulder and head hit the stone archway. Rosa hauled her around, got her flat on her stomach, and dropped to kneel on top of her. Something cracked under her, maybe ribs. She got a hand into Val's hair at the back of her head, hammered her face down on the flagstones, and realized that her enemy was going limp.

Something touched Rosa's shoulder.

Gasping, she turned her head, prepared for the worst. A leopard's paw about to strike. An animal mouth, wide open, armed with sharp fangs.

With an expression of perfect innocence, Iole was holding out the pistol, with the handle toward Rosa.

"Here," she said. "Shoot her and get it over with."

IN FLAMES

ROSA STARED AT THE pistol, undecided. She crouched on Valerie's back, gasping for breath, eyes wide open, hair tangled. This was her chance to take revenge for all she had gone through in the last eighteen months. The rape. The abortion. All those months of mourning and therapy.

She had Valerie to thank for all that.

And now Val lay there, stunned, on the floor beneath her.

Rosa took the pistol from Iole's hand. The butt felt cool and heavy.

"She deserves it," said Iole, matter-of-factly.

"I know," Rosa whispered.

She set the muzzle against the hollow just above Valerie's neck, in the small indentation between her spine and the back of her head. Her index finger lay on the trigger. The thin piece of metal seemed to throb impatiently against her fingertip, as if it wanted to make the decision for her.

Valerie groaned softly.

Rosa pressed the pistol harder against the nape of Val's neck. It felt right to pull the trigger. It was appropriate to get her back for everything.

The howling of the Hundinga down in the house was wilder now, rage and pain in their voices. In between the howls, the big cats were hissing and spitting. If the idea hadn't been so outlandish, you might have thought the two Panthera were fighting side by side against the Hungry Man's creatures.

Rosa looked down at the back of Valerie's head and the mouth of the pistol again. Out of the corner of her eye, she saw Iole running through the archway and out into the long corridor. She was barefoot, and her legs looked pale and vulnerable under the hem of her nightgown.

"What are you waiting for?" Valerie asked, her voice faltering. If she really had broken any ribs, she must be in considerable pain. She had turned her head aside; her short, dark hair was matted with sweat. A graze on her cheekbone showed where she had hit the stone arch. Her lips were moving, but no more sounds came out.

Rosa concentrated on the gun in her hand, the roughened feel of the butt, its weight, the sense of power it gave her.

But she didn't want power. And the longer she sat there, the less she wanted revenge. It was as if Valerie were already dead—certainly that seemed true of the old Valerie whom she had once liked and, yes, admired, because she was always a little braver, more quick-witted, more grown-up. Had Rosa been wrong about her back then? Had she built up a false image of her, a surface on which to project everything she wanted to be herself?

"Rosa!" Iole had come back out of one of the other rooms off the corridor. "Come and look at this."

Rosa's hand had merged with the pistol. She felt the bullet in the magazine like a part of herself. The Valerie of the old days no longer existed. It wasn't necessary to kill this girl. Whoever it was lying on the floor—blinded by love, drug-addicted, injured—was another person. The Valerie whom she might have wished dead was long gone. Time and Rosa's maturation to adulthood had eradicated her, and whatever the bullet in the pistol might do, it couldn't change what had happened.

She gazed up at Iole through a veil of sweat and tears. For a moment it looked as if the girl were standing on a stage surrounded by dry ice.

Smoke was drifting along the corridor toward them, a thin, gray layer of it above the floor. Iole was stepping from foot to foot.

"They're fighting down in the courtyard," she said excitedly. "Alessandro and the leopard against the big dogs. They've killed a couple of them."

Rosa slipped sideways off Valerie's back and got to her feet. Her knees hurt. "Get up," she told Val.

Valerie moved, still flat on her stomach, as if to crawl away. But the pain was too much and her limbs went slack. A groan came from her throat, turning to words. "Michele is coming for me."

"You really think so?"

"He's here because I asked him to come."

"He's here to get his revenge on Alessandro."

Val laughed, hoarse laughter. "That's what he thinks. But he couldn't help it. He loves me."

Disconcerted, Rosa saw the carpet of smoke moving

toward them. With her free hand, she grabbed Val's arm and tried to pull her up.

Valerie screamed.

Rosa hadn't noticed that Iole had left again, but now she came running back from another of the rooms off the passage. "The first floor is on fire! In several wings, I think."

Something dark moved at the end of the corridor, a hunched, black shape plowing its way through the smoke, coming toward them faster and faster. There was a growl as bared teeth snapped at the wisps of smoke.

Rosa swung the pistol around.

"No!" Iole ran in front of her and snatched her arm up into the air.

Sarcasmo took a huge leap as Iole spun around to him. Then he got up on his hind legs and licked her face in excitement. She was in danger of falling over backward, but she regained her balance and hugged him.

Valerie was coughing pitifully. She tried to brace herself and raise her upper body, but her face was still in the smoke.

"Come on!" Rosa herded Iole and Sarcasmo in the direction of the corridor. "We have to get out of here."

She got an arm under Valerie's armpit and hauled her up, exerting all her strength. This time she was successful. Val howled, and for a moment it seemed as if she were going to pull Rosa down to the floor with her again. But then she got enough of a footing to drag herself through the archway beside her. Iole and Sarcasmo were hurrying on ahead.

"Use the servants' staircase," Rosa called to Iole, "and go

out through the kitchen." She hoped that the Hundinga were concentrating on fighting the Panthera in the inner courtyard.

"How about you two?" called Iole.

"We'll follow you."

"Why don't you just leave her there?"

Valerie laughed. "Because Rosa still thinks she's special. If she leaves me to die, she'll be just like the rest. Someone who couldn't care less about other people."

Rosa let her drop.

Valerie fell to her knees, hitting the floor first with her shoulder, then with her side.

"Spare me the crap," spat Rosa.

Iole whistled and then disappeared with Sarcasmo around the bend in the corridor. Rosa was on the verge of following her. Instead she ran into one of the nearby guest rooms, leaving Valerie behind, and looked down at the inner courtyard through the tall window.

A single lamp above the main steps lit up the scene. The other lights reacted to motion detectors, and the Hundinga had disabled those, like the lights on the outside of the walls.

All the same, her heart beat fast as she recognized a black outline racing through the swirling smoke just at that moment, to attack a gigantic mastiff. Alessandro! Other Hundinga circled around the two of them, but the next moment the ring was broken apart by a leopard, leaving a motionless adversary and charging among them.

Rosa wasn't sure whether the smoke was a help or a hindrance to the two Panthera, and she certainly did not understand why Michele was fighting at Alessandro's side. Probably he had no choice. If he wanted to survive, he had to keep the Hundinga away.

Her heart heavy, she turned and went back to the corridor. Valerie was gone.

Rosa was still holding the pistol. She promised herself she would use it if Val crossed her path again. She couldn't be far.

Half choked by the acrid smoke, Rosa ran down the corridor, around the corner, and over to the curtain where she had hidden a little while ago. It had been pushed aside, and the door behind it was open. She hoped that Iole and Sarcasmo had reached the first floor by now.

There was still something she had to do. Hastily, she ran down the stairs to the second floor, and was alarmed to find how thick the smoke drifting along the passages was here. She held the crook of her elbow in front of her nose and mouth, stumbled through the smoke to the west wing, and with a powerful kick moved aside the iron bar that had been securing the door of Signora Falchi's room.

"Don't shoot!" she shouted, before flinging the door open.

There was no one there. The window was wide open, as before, when the tutor had been firing at the Hundinga on the terrace. The bedclothes lay in a tangled heap on the floor.

"Signora Falchi?" She went into the room and over to the bathroom door. "It's me. Rosa Alcantara."

The bathroom, too, was empty. She ran to the window and looked down. It was over twelve feet to the stone paving of the terrace. The mattress from the bed was lying at the base of the facade.

Signora Falchi was treading water in the middle of the

swimming pool, fending off the drifting body of a naked man with distaste, as if defending herself against his improper advances.

"Signora!" Rosa leaned out of the window. "I'm up here!"

The tutor looked up. "Signorina Alcantara! Where's Iole? Is she safe?"

"Yes," Rosa said, lying. "Tell me about those dogs."

"They were here just now. I thought maybe they were afraid of water. I had a dachshund once that—"

"Did they all run off to the inner courtyard?"

"How would I know?"

"Toward the main entrance?"

"Yes . . . yes, I think so."

How many of them might still be alive? Eight? Ten? Maybe more? Alessandro couldn't last much longer. She had to reach him. She still had the pistol. Maybe—

"Get out of there!" the tutor called up to her. "The whole palazzo is going up in flames!"

Without another word, Rosa turned away from Signora Falchi and ran along the corridor to a guest room overlooking the inner courtyard. She swept the curtain aside, opened the window, and looked out.

She could tell, even through the smoke, that there was fighting down there, but from this vantage point she could make out only two heaps of tangled bodies. She heard the snapping, howling, spitting, and hissing of the opposing sides. And she saw more Hundinga approaching from the gateway, in loose formation.

Without thinking, she raised the pistol and fired. Over the last four months she had practiced using a gun, but she was far from sure of hitting her target.

Her second shot hit a black Doberman—possibly the leader—and flung him to the ground. The next went wide, but the fourth bullet wounded a Hunding in the side. She must have hit his heart, because he was returning to human form even as he fell. The others who had come up from the gate growled at her, but they turned and retreated into the tunnel. They only had to wait. Sooner or later the flames would drive the Panthera and the last humans out of the palazzo and into their arms.

The Panthera also looked up at her. Alessandro's adversary tried to exploit that moment, but Alessandro turned just in time to avoid a savage bite and struck the Hunding a powerful blow with his paw. The Hunding howled, and blood spurted from his throat. Alessandro's fur gleamed, wet with blood. Rosa couldn't tell how much of it came from his own wounds.

She fired again. The Hundinga moved back from the leopard and followed their companions into the tunnel.

A moment later the two Panthera were standing alone in the smoke that was now billowing ever more densely out of all parts of the building and into the inner courtyard. Firelight blazed behind windowpanes, bathing the scene in a flickering red glow.

"Alessandro!" Rosa saw that the leopard was about to pounce on him from behind. "No!" Her voice broke and became a hoarse croak. There was nothing she could do from up here. The risk of hitting Alessandro if she fired the pistol was too great.

The panther was thrown to the ground, dragging the leopard down with him. Both were lost from sight in a thick cloud of smoke. One of the windows near them broke in a cascade of shattered glass.

Briefly, Rosa toyed with the idea of jumping down into the courtyard. The tutor had done it and survived, so why not try it herself? But even a sprained ankle would be a death sentence for her down there. If the Hundinga came back, or Michele attacked her, she would be helpless.

Coughing, with streaming eyes, she ran back into the corridor, then to the servants' staircase, and down to the first floor. She felt the heat of the fire for the first time on the steps. Soon after that she entered the kitchen, to find that the door must have been bolted from the outside. Outside, she heard savage barking. Iole and Sarcasmo must have taken some other way. But which way had they gone?

There might be one possibility. But to try it she needed time, and the cell phone that the Hunding had been using—and that lay below the terrace among the olive trees, at the foot of the palms.

The smoke was taking her breath away and blurring her vision. She hastily wrung a dishcloth out in water under the faucet and tied it over her mouth and nose. Breathing was still difficult, but it was possible to take what little air did get through into her lungs. To be on the safe side, she wrung out two more dishcloths and took them with her as she ran into the corridor, crossed a storeroom, and unbolted a low door to the inner courtyard.

The smoke hung like thick mist between the walls. She heard panting and an occasional growl through its dense gray, probably from the tunnel, where the air would be clearer. The Hundinga kept their distance, lying in wait.

Alessandro and Michele were fighting each other about forty feet away from Rosa: panther and leopard, dark shapes in the middle of the acrid smoke. She heard flames crackling behind the smashed windowpanes of the east wing, and fire danced over the wooden frames. The two big cats were circling each other, coming closer and closer, striking out with their paws, snapping and biting.

Rosa could hardly breathe. Just staying on her feet required all her strength. Half blind, she checked the magazine of the pistol. Three bullets left.

Aiming the gun, she moved out into the open.

"Michele!"

The dishcloth muffled her voice, but the two of them heard it anyway. For a moment they stopped. The leopard hissed at her. His coat was sticky with blood, and terrible wounds gaped open in the middle of dark red patches. The panther, too, had bite marks and deep scratches.

"This is where it ends," she said grimly to Alessandro. "And *I* will pull out this cat's claws."

The muzzle flash of her pistol cut through the smoke, and the pressure wave drove the swathes apart.

The force of the bullet's impact shattered the leopard's

shoulder blade. Michele howled, staggered in the air as he leaped over Alessandro and made for Rosa.

She fired again.

Michele's paws touched the ground once more as he tried to pounce for the last time.

Her third shot hit him in the throat.

He uttered a roar, lurched from side to side, but kept coming toward her, forelegs outstretched. Then he buried Rosa under him.

When they hit the ground, his open muzzle was right above her face.

Pitilessly, his jaws were snapping shut.

THE VOICE OF ARCADIA

A NIGHTMARE IN SEPARATE images.

Movement chopped into a few dozen pictures per second.

The leopard's open jaws filled Rosa's entire field of vision, a black hole surrounded by bloodstained teeth. She seemed to be almost falling into them as his muzzle came down on her. His breath smelled of iron and raw meat. The big cat's weight forced her to the ground, but she hardly felt it.

And as she saw him coming toward her in that endless moment, he changed back into a man. His eyes clouded over. Blood shot out of the wound in the front of his throat where the bullet had gone in, and also the exit wound at the back of his head, where it had shattered the nape of his neck and left his body.

The snapping jaws shrank to human size, the muzzle grew shorter, yellow fur became smooth skin. She saw it all in the extreme, tormenting slow motion of her shock. She heard his cheekbones crack and grow together again, saw his nose and his eye sockets change shape, watched the corners of his mouth move closer together, as the dimples that were so like Alessandro's appeared in his cheeks. And all the time his features continued descending on her. What had begun as a deadly snapping of jaws, a greedy bite full of hate, became a touch, an involuntary kiss, as his lifeless face came down on hers, and slipped off again sideways a second later.

Rosa lay there, buried under Michele's body, and for a moment she was back in the Village on that night. But at the same time she realized that this made it final. Tano had been dead for a long time, and now Michele was dead as well. It was over.

"They're coming back!" someone shouted in hollow tones. "We have to get out of the courtyard." Iole.

Then Rosa heard a familiar barking over by the entrance. There stood Sarcasmo, beside Iole, who was all bundled up and gesticulating wildly in the direction of the tunnel.

Soon none of this will matter anyway, thought Rosa. The smoke will kill us. Maybe it's poisoned us already.

A jolt shook her body as the black panther rammed his head into Michele's side. The body was flung off her, and she was free.

Alessandro, still in animal form, battered and bleeding, nudged her and indicated that she should stand up. Iole ran over and helped her to her feet, supporting her. The slender girl—always underestimated and in no way as helpless as she seemed—led her back into the house, and seconds later the door closed behind them.

Rosa slipped out of Iole's grasp to the floor, felt Sarcasmo's tongue licking her cheek encouragingly, and at the same time saw Alessandro before her. He made no move to change back into human form.

The cold was beginning to spread through her. The serum

had stopped working; scales formed under her transparent skin, grew, and pushed their way out. She tried to stop the transformation, but she was too weak.

With the last of her strength, she explained her plan. Her words tailed off into hissing and spitting. Sarcasmo growled at her and retreated. Iole patted his sooty coat. But Alessandro came closer, bent his panther head over her, and nudged her with his black nose.

He had understood.

He knew what they had to do together.

Iole flung open the door to the grounds.

"Now!" she whispered, holding Sarcasmo with one hand in case he stormed out into the night. He tugged and pulled against his collar, but she wasn't letting him go.

Rosa wound her way over the threshold and outside. With a great leap, Alessandro jumped over her, landed on the gravel path, and took up a fighting stance.

Hundinga were howling in the dark and raced up, panting, digging up earth with their claws. Saliva flew from their chops.

There were three of them, and Rosa hoped that Alessandro could deal with them. She glided over the ground through the darkness, along the facade, keeping close to the space between the wall and the gravel. Behind her she heard snapping and spitting, while up above the heat broke a window. Glass and burning sparks rained down, bouncing off her armored scales.

She reached the terrace, found a Hunding close to the pool,

and at the same time saw the tutor in the water, ducking low under the rim of the basin so that the creature wouldn't see her.

Neither of them noticed Rosa as she coiled around the stone balustrade in a wild slalom course that finally brought her to the stairway. She slid down it, followed the course of the wall, and found the bags that the Hundinga had brought.

One was still open. The cell phone lay in the middle of crumpled camouflage clothing.

This time it all went so fast that she almost cried out as the transformation set in, but only a hiss would come from her snake mouth. Until it turned back into lips, and by then the urge was gone.

She lay naked beside the Hundinga equipment on the ground, breathing hard with effort and the smoke still burning her throat.

Her trembling hand reached for the phone.

There was no list of contacts, only a single number that had been called. Rosa tapped it.

"Yes?" answered a hoarse male voice. Old and unhealthy rather than hungry.

Rosa coughed smoke out of her lungs, gathered all her strength, and said what she had to say.

A little later the noise of powerful rotors could be heard, approaching over the plain.

The helicopter came in without any lights, invisible in the night. The pilot didn't switch on a searchlight until he was right outside the burning palazzo. The light stabbed far through the billowing smoke, passed over the tops of the olive trees, brushed past Rosa, went off and on again three times. A signal.

Howling rose from many throats all around the property—up on the terrace, along the north facade, and at the gateway tunnel to the south of the house.

From the foot of the palms, Rosa watched as the helicopter touched down on the meadow beside the courtyard. Its landing was hidden by bushes and chestnut trees. It was a long, black transport chopper with two antitorque rotors mounted, one above the cockpit and one on the tail. The dark green fuselage showed no visible identification marks. Probably an out-of-service military aircraft.

Rosa heard feet moving quickly on the steps and retreated into the shadow of the wall. Two men picked up the bags and ran toward the helicopter with them. They didn't notice that the cell phone was missing. Rosa was still holding it as she emerged from her hiding place. Her own clothes, left behind here after her first transformation, were lying on the roots of an olive tree. She quickly slipped into her clothing, and hurried up the steps to the terrace again.

The Hundinga were gone, and with them the bodies of their dead. They had even fished the dead man out of the pool. Rosa glimpsed the vague outlines of figures carrying their burdens at the south end of the terrace. Then she saw them one last time against the beam of the searchlight, black marks standing out in front of the bright light behind the trees.

A moment later the chopper took off vertically into the sky. The searchlight was switched off above the treetops. Rosa was dazzled for a few seconds, because she had been looking straight into it. When she could see again, the helicopter had merged with the night sky. The noise of its rotors moved away westward and was soon drowned out by the crackling of the flames.

Signora Falchi had moved over to the edge of the pool, as far as possible from the clouds of blood spreading through the water. She was pale as death herself. Rosa helped her up into the dry air, reassured herself that the tutor was unharmed, and shouted above the noise of the fire that she should run up the steps. "Can you make it?" she asked, gasping.

"Where's Iole?"

"Safe." No time for discussion. "Now get moving!"

"How about you?"

Something crashed inside the palazzo. An eruption of sparks and heat shot out of several windows at the same time.

"I'll be right behind you," yelled Rosa through the noise.

Coughing and dripping with water, the tutor set off.

Rosa ran across the terrace in the opposite direction, to the grassy space along the north wall. She could hardly breathe—the smell of soot was terrible, and so was the heat—but the wind from the plain drove the smoke eastward up the slope and into the pinewoods, saving her from the worst of it.

There was no one in sight outside the kitchen door now. A little farther away, firelight was reflected on the panes of the greenhouse. Smoke billowed out of its broken windows. Rosa hoped the snakes had escaped into the open air.

"Alessandro?" she called hoarsely. "Iole?"

She couldn't see any corpses or anyone injured outside the door. If there had been dead bodies, the Hundinga had taken them away, too.

A dog barked to her left. Among the chestnut trees at the far end of the meadow, Sarcasmo was dancing around Iole, who was leaning against a tree and wearily raised one hand to wave to Rosa.

Where was Alessandro?

She searched her surroundings and saw him in his panther form when he vaulted up and over the stone balustrade of the terrace with a mighty leap. He must have searched for her down by the wall and missed seeing her. Now he was racing across the meadow toward her, and even as he ran he changed back into human form. His skin, stained with blood, gleamed in the firelight as he ran the last few feet, staggering slightly with exhaustion. Rosa hurried to meet him and caught him when he looked like he might fall.

Together, they dragged themselves into the chestnut trees, a good distance from the house, for a chance to catch their breath. They sank to the ground there among the trees. Blood was trickling from Alessandro's wounds, and his strength was leaving him.

Rosa held him close while blazing light licked over the facade, and the rooftop of the palazzo went up in flames.

THE HUNGRY MAN

COPPERY LIGHT FELL THROUGH the hospital windows. The morning sun was still low in the sky over the sea, shining on the paths and lawns of the grounds, edging the top of the cliffs with gold.

"What happened to Valerie?" Alessandro asked.

Rosa shook her head. "No trace of her. Maybe she made it out; maybe she's lying under the ruins of the palazzo." To be honest, she didn't know the answer and didn't care either way.

The doctors had put butterfly bandages over some of the injuries on Alessandro's face, pulling the edges together. It would be some time before the swelling and abrasions disappeared entirely.

He looked at her intently. "You're not going to rebuild the palazzo, are you?"

"I'm not even sure it would be a good idea to have the remains demolished. Maybe it's best this way. Everything lying buried under tons and tons of stone and ash, all those dirty family secrets."

Alessandro was sitting upright in bed, his expression impatient, his hair untidy. He had seemed as if he had been on hot coals ever since being brought here two days ago. The large dressing over his chest looked alarming, but the injuries under it would be healed in a few weeks' time, the doctors said. Whatever they had thought when the heir to the Carnevare fortune was brought into their hospital, covered with bites and scratches, they kept it to themselves. In this place people knew how to keep their mouths shut, because silence was literally golden. The Carnevares were not the only clan to have their members regularly treated for injuries in this hospital.

Fundling was still lying in a coma one room away. Rosa had already been to see him this morning and had spent a long time holding his hand.

Only the day before, the doctors had been tranquilizing Alessandro with painkillers, but now he was fizzing with energy again. It was slightly uncanny to see how fast he recovered. Maybe there was something to the saying that a cat had nine lives, after all.

"What did you tell him when you phoned?" he asked. Rosa herself would rather not have talked about the Hungry Man for now.

"The truth. That it wasn't the Carnevares who gave him away all those years ago."

"And he believed you?"

"Looks like it."

"Come on," he said, "that wasn't all. He called off the Hundinga immediately, no ifs, ands, or buts."

Rosa went over to the window, looked out at the sunrise, and decided not to tell him everything. Not yet. "I told him about the recording di Santis made in the hotel," she said as she turned back to him. "That's the best evidence of Trevini's guilt. I also reminded him of a couple of deals he and my grandmother had made together, decades ago, and how Trevini had turned them into a rope to hang him with. Maybe he wondered why I'd lay the blame on a member of my own family, but anyway, di Santis got the video to him the next day, as well as the copy of a document proving that thirty years ago Trevini was given immunity in return for collaborating with the public prosecutor's office. He was the guilty party, not the Carnevares."

"But your grandmother pulled the strings," he said, concern in his voice. "By the Hungry Man's logic, that would mean the Alcantaras are on his hit list now. Your family handed him over, and you are Costanza's last direct descendant. So why has he left you alive?"

She wanted to avoid his penetrating glance, but she pulled herself together and even managed a smile. "Maybe he's the first to notice that I am *not* the reincarnation of Costanza Alcantara." She leaned over and gave him a kiss.

"There's something you're not telling me, though," he observed.

"We agreed that we didn't have to tell each other everything, right?"

He was about to run his hands nervously through his hair, but he swore and lowered his arms again when the recently stitched injuries under his armpits protested. "Bloody hell."

"Does it hurt badly?"

Sighing, he shook his head. "How's Iole doing?"

"She arrived in Portugal yesterday evening. She's with her uncle."

Alessandro's eyes widened. "With Dallamano? That lunatic?"

"It doesn't necessarily make him a lunatic that he wanted to kill you."

"Thanks a lot."

She kissed him again, a longer kiss this time.

"How did you manage to arrange that?" he asked, impressed. "The witness protection program—"

"Isn't as watertight as it used to be. Dallamano testified against Cesare and your father, so they wanted to get rid of him like the rest of his family. But now that Cesare is dead, the situation isn't quite as critical for Dallamano as it was before. The other clans have too much else on their minds to trouble themselves, in the name of a dead Carnevare, about something that happened years ago. At least, that's how Judge Quattrini sees it. And he himself seems pretty happy that the security measures have been relaxed."

With a groan, Alessandro let his head sink back against the pillow. "Quattrini! You've been talking to her again."

"First thing yesterday morning, once the doctors finished checking me out. Quattrini was pretty curious about what happened at the palazzo. Annoyed, too, because she'd entrusted Iole to my care—and if you ask me, she was right. I'd never have forgiven myself if anything had happened to Iole." She paused, thoughtfully, because the idea weighed more heavily on her mind than she liked to admit. "At least, she thought it wouldn't be such a bad idea to get Iole away from me for a while. And since Dallamano is her only living relative, and he's not in such extreme danger now, Quattrini agreed to send her to stay with him for a week or two."

"Just like that," he remarked skeptically.

"More or less."

"By which you mean . . . ?"

"I mean I . . . well, I had to give her something in return."

"You can't keep on going to the public prosecutor's office every time it suits you and—"

"Lampedusa," she interrupted him. "I gave her the Lampedusa racket on a silver platter. All the files that weren't burned in the palazzo. Lampedusa, more than anything else, was the pet project of Florinda and Trevini. I never wanted anything to do with trafficking human beings."

"But several of your firms and their managers depend on the Lampedusa racket. They'll—"

"*My* managers—exactly," she said coolly. "Which means that I tell them what's what. None of them depend on Lampedusa to pay for their villas and yachts and Swiss boarding schools for their kids. And they got warning three hours before Quattrini's people came knocking at the door. Most of them are probably in the South Seas by now, sipping cocktails."

Alessandro slowly shook his head. "You can't lead a clan that way."

"At least I'm *leading* it now, instead of just sitting around waiting for people to give me stuff to sign. Many of them aren't going to like it. But you of all people can hardly tell me I'm in the wrong."

"I just don't want you to end up like me—*capo* of a clan,

but at the top of your own family's hit list."

"We can't choose what we are—you told me that yourself." She forced a grin. "Now be a good patient, drink your nice peppermint tea, eat your crackers, and watch bad game shows on TV."

"You're leaving already?"

"There's something I still have to take care of."

There was deep uneasiness in his eyes. "Don't do this, Rosa."

She went to the door.

Alessandro leaned forward in the bed, but his injuries would hardly allow him to stand up, let alone stop her. "Don't make any kind of deal with him! Not with the Hungry Man!"

At first she wasn't going to answer him, but at the door she turned around. Came back, kissed him once again, and said, very quietly, "Too late."

The prison gate latched behind her with a steely clunk. Through the barred windows in the corridor, she could see the inner courtyard of the institution. No one appeared in the glare of the searchlights. Up on the walls, spiral coils of barbed wire shimmered against the black sky. It was just before ten in the evening, and official visiting hours had been over ages ago.

The taciturn prison officer who had taken her to the reception desk near the entrance made no secret of his disapproval. God knew what he took her for—maybe a prostitute summoned to the Hungry Man in his cell—but she didn't care at the moment.

A lot depended on how she conducted this visit. Just the same, she was sure the prisoner would see at first glance how edgy she felt. The fact was that she was terrified of him. To most Arcadians, the Hungry Man was so much more than a *capo dei capi* who had been in prison for three decades. They genuinely thought he was the reincarnation of King Lycaon, and would lead them into a new age of glorious barbarism.

She had seen an old photograph of him, black and white, grainy. Even in the photo he hadn't been a young man: He was gray at the temples, with shoulder-length hair and a full beard. The picture had been taken during his internment in Gela. His eyes had been in deep shadow, but from the corners of his mouth Rosa had been able to tell that he was smiling, in spite of the police officers posing beside him. Smiling as if they were the captives, not he.

She knew his real name, but within the dynasties no one used it. They all referred to him merely as the Hungry Man. If you believed his followers, he was both the past and the future of Arcadia. Or alternatively, thought Rosa, a megalomaniac Mafia boss who refused to admit that he, like countless other *capi*, had walked into a trap set by the state prosecutor's office.

Rosa's footsteps echoed back from the security barriers. She was wearing high-heeled boots and was dressed all in black, which made her look taller than she was. She had even put on makeup, for the first time since that night in the Village. She wanted to appear as sophisticated and adult as possible.

The warden stopped at a door, looked right and left, and then opened it. He stepped aside and gestured to Rosa.

"Knock when you're through with the visit."

She walked into a visiting room with a partition dividing it. In the middle of the divider, halfway up, was a window like those at a bank counter. A white plastic chair stood in front of it.

The door was closed behind her, and now she was alone in her half of the room. It was only in this part that a lamp was on; everything was dark on the other side of the partition. The glass was tinted, and hardly any light came through it. Rosa adjusted to the idea that she wouldn't be able to see the man she was visiting, while she herself would be on display to him in bright light.

"Sit down."

It was the voice she had heard on the telephone. So hoarse that after those first words Rosa expected a cough, but it never came. Something was wrong with his larynx. Cancer, maybe. She found that idea encouraging to some extent.

Rosa sat down, crossed her legs, linked her hands in her lap. She didn't want to start fidgeting with something, like the hem of her jacket or her hair.

"I respect courage when I see it," he said. His voice came over a fist-size loudspeaker below the pane between them. Rosa resisted the impulse to squint in an effort to see more through the glass. All she could make out was a vague silhouette. He wasn't sitting but standing there upright, motionless, looking down at her.

"Hiding behind tinted glass isn't particularly courageous," she heard herself saying.

"How old are you, Rosa?"

"Eighteen."

"How old were you when your father died?"

"Is he dead, then?"

He didn't answer that.

"I opened his tomb." Well, really she had smashed a hole in the damn stone slab with a pickax, but it amounted to the same thing. "The casket was empty."

"Why do you tell me that?"

"I don't know anything about my family. Or not nearly enough. I thought I did know a few things, but most of them weren't worth a damn. The fact is that I haven't the faintest idea what my grandmother and my father were doing all those years."

"And you think that clears you of all blame? Because that's what you care about, isn't it?"

"I wasn't even born when Trevini and my grandmother made sure you went to prison. Even my father was still a child at the time."

"And has young Carnevare made you happy?"

"Happiness is relative."

"Nonsense!" he snapped back, but then he calmed down again. "Happiness is the opposite of unhappiness. Good luck versus bad luck. So tell me, Rosa: Has Alessandro Carnevare made you happy?"

"I'm happy when I'm with him."

"Always?"

"Often."

"Much has happened since you two got together. Not all of it good."

She clenched one of the hands lying in her lap into a fist. "For me, it wasn't such bad luck that the palazzo burned down. And I'd say my aunt's death was her own fault."

"How about your sister's death?"

"Zoe lied to me. She spied on me for Florinda."

"A good reason, no doubt, to wish her dead," he commented sarcastically.

He was provoking her, and it infuriated her to be so easily manipulated. "I liked Zoe in spite of her failings. I loved her, even."

"Ah, now we're coming closer to the crux of it."

"Zoe's death wasn't Alessandro's fault."

"But you see a connection. Of course you do. You'd have to be blind not to."

She stood and moved very close to the pane, until the tip of her nose was almost touching the glass. "Could we leave out the psychological games?"

The silhouette in the dark came closer. The distance between them was less than a handbreadth, and yet she still couldn't see his face through the tinted glass. The fact that his voice came over the loudspeaker level with her belly button also irritated her.

"Have you any idea," he asked, "how your grandmother died?"

"In her bed. She was sick, had probably been sick for quite some time."

"Florinda poisoned her."

"So?"

"You have Costanza's eyes."

"And here was I thinking, just now, that we might be friends."

"She looked very like you when she was young. She was a pretty girl, and later a very beautiful woman."

In her heart she was grateful to him for infuriating her like this. It made it easier not to be overimpressed by his aura of superiority. "Why did you want me to come here?" she asked, to end the discussion of Costanza. "On the phone you said it was one of your conditions. So now I'm here. Why?"

"Because I wanted to see who you are. What you are." With a muted sound, he placed the palm of his hand against the glass pane, spread his fingers, and pressed them against it. "How long has it been," he asked, "since you learned about the Arcadian dynasties?"

"A few months." She couldn't help staring at his hand, the deep lines on it, the long, slender fingers.

"Your mother never told you?"

"I'd have thought she was crazy if she had." As Rosa said that, she had to admit to herself that Gemma had been right there. And probably about some other things as well.

"What was it like when you shifted shape for the first time?"

"It felt . . . forbidden. Like a kid staying up late at night for the first time because there's no one else home."

"Isn't it a shame that we have to hide something so

wonderful from the world?"

"I guess it's not so wonderful for the world."

"There have always been hunters and hunted. Some who get what they want because they're strong enough. And others who kneel to them. No civilization, no progress will change that. We didn't make those laws; life itself did. What I stand for isn't a step back. It's the end of our self-denial. The end of a great lie."

She was finding it increasingly difficult to resist his charisma. The labyrinth of lines on his hand, the forcefulness of his voice—it was like standing in front of an ancient temple, a place still awe-inspiring after thousands of years.

"We have lived in the shadows long enough, hiding what we really are from others," he went on. "It's time to be ourselves again. And that has already begun. You, too, are an element in that change, Rosa."

"I am?"

"Lamias have always distinguished themselves from other Arcadians. That's why there aren't many of you left. You rebelled and followed your own aims. Guile and deceit were always your sharpest weapons."

"I prefer more direct methods," said Rosa, thinking of her stapler.

"You are snakes. Your venom works slowly and in secret. I should have guessed that I owed the last thirty years behind bars to Costanza. Instead I believed the faked evidence pointing to the Carnevares. Did you know that they were once my closest allies?"

She nodded.

"Today I have other faithful assistants out there. They're more effective than the Carnevares ever were. I should be grateful to your grandmother. All that time in my cell has opened my eyes to new allies. I'll soon be leaving this place, and I owe that to them."

Rosa watched his fingers curl against the pane. The palm of his hand withdrew a fraction of an inch, looking darker, while his fingertips were a semicircle of pale points against the black background. Rosa couldn't take her eyes off them.

"Is it true," she asked, "that it was the Lamias who toppled Lycaon from the throne of Arcadia?"

The hand abruptly withdrew into the darkness. His whole outline was barely visible now. He must have stepped back. "I had reason enough to wish every one of you dead," he said after a pause, without answering her question. "But I, too, have learned my lesson. I was wrong to let my wish for revenge on the Carnevares consume me. I want a new beginning, not retribution. The dynasties have played the part of gangsters for too long, regarding the business of their Cosa Nostra clans as more important than their origin and their destiny. If all that is to change, there must be new blood. New leaders who don't care about controlling the drug market in Paris or real estate funds in Hong Kong. Join me, Rosa, and all the sins of your ancestors will be forgotten. And if young Carnevare learns that his Arcadian inheritance is more important than his position as *capo* of his clan, then he's welcome to join us as well." He paused for effect again, and then added, "Which is more than you can expect from the other clans. They all despise the pair of you for your relationship. And how long will it be before they find out about your connections with that judge?"

So he knew about Quattrini, too? She should have guessed.

"Sooner or later," he said, "they will kill you and young Carnevare. A number of them would already like to; your own families are making plans to clear you out of their way. I, on the other hand, am offering you the future."

"The Hundinga were trying to kill me," she pointed out. "On your orders."

"They were supposed to be observing you, instilling a spirit of respect in you," he contradicted her. "There are always risks in letting dogs off the leash, and this time they went too far. That wasn't my intention, and they've paid for it. Look at the newspapers. There's been a helicopter crash off the coast."

The longer he talked, the more he sounded like a feudal lord back in the Middle Ages. Without a shadow of doubt he was obsessed with King Lycaon, and whether his idea of Lycaon was a crazed delusion or just something spooky ultimately made no difference. As soon as he got out of here, he would be in command of the others all over again.

"I did what you wanted," said Rosa. "I gave you evidence against Trevini. And I came here because you asked to talk to me. Will you leave Alessandro alone now?"

She had expected a long silence. Dramatic, to show her how small and weak she was compared to him. Instead, he simply said, "Of course."

She pushed back the plastic chair and started for the door.

"Sometime," he said, "I'll be asking you a favor. Maybe a large and significant favor, maybe only a small one. But you will grant it."

She kept her back to him, halfway to the door.

"You will grant me that favor, Rosa Alcantara. That is my condition."

It would have been so easy to say no. She had never had difficulty in doing that before. Just a brief no, that was all. And then the lines would have been drawn. She on the good side, he on the bad one.

Except that it wasn't so easy.

"Agreed," she said.

She took the last few steps and knocked on the door, much too fast and hard, in time with her hammering heartbeat.

"Good-bye, Rosa. And don't forget—"

Over her shoulder, she glanced at the black surface of the glass, in which all she saw now was her own reflection. She was looking into her own eyes.

"—I am not your enemy."

THE ALCHEMISTS

IT WAS A MILD afternoon, and the air smelled of spring. Not unusual here at the end of February, as the taxi driver had explained in broken English as he drove Rosa away from the Lisbon airport. They had been on the road for an hour and a half, the last part of the way up the narrow, winding street leading into Sintra's historic city center.

The colorful palace towering above the town was enthroned on a densely wooded mountain. The Rua Barbosa do Bocage, a little road in the eternal shade of mighty trees, wound its way around the sides. Rosa recognized the wall and the gate of Quinta da Regaleira. She and Alessandro had met Augusto Dallamano here last October, in the villa built by a Freemason and alchemist. Dallamano had taken Rosa ninety feet down into a shaft in the ground along a slippery spiral staircase, and there he had told her more about the statues on the seabed, the stone panthers and snakes that the *Stabat Mater* would later snap up from under their noses.

Today she passed the entrance to the Quinta without stopping. The taxi continued along the narrow street, past dense bushes and walls overgrown with moss, hiding behind them some of the oldest and most magnificent villas of Portugal.

After less than a mile the GPS announced that they had

arrived. The driver stopped in front of a small gap in an ivy-covered wall. A steep path led uphill, turning left after a few steps. Heavy branches hung low above the path up, and weeds grew in the cracks of broken paving stones. The builder of this property might have wanted not to be found too easily, but he hadn't counted on GPS.

The cabbie gesticulated and said something in Portuguese.

"This is it?" she asked.

He nodded and impatiently tapped the price on the meter. Rosa paid him and got out.

She put her bag over her shoulder and began to climb. A few overgrown stone statues stood on plinths to the right and left of the path; you could hardly see them under dense tendrils of climbing plants. In a few months' time they would be entirely hidden under the leaves.

The upward path went around another bend before Rosa saw the three-story villa. She couldn't help comparing it with the fairy-tale palace of Quinta da Regaleira on the other side of the mountain. This house was a cube, with dark yellow plaster facades, in the middle of a garden that had run wild. The tops of trees bent down close to the walls, and dried, brown, twining plants hung like curtains in the branches, keeping the sun away from the tall windows.

The flat roof of the house was dominated by a glazed dome with a stone balustrade around it. With its rusty metal framework and clouded panes, the dome reminded Rosa of the wrecked greenhouse. All at once, the thought of the burned-down palazzo made Rosa more melancholy than ever. For a moment she wondered whether they kept animals up here, too, but she immediately rejected the idea. This was only an old hothouse in the art nouveau style.

The front door of the villa was flung open, and Iole ran out. She was wearing one of the white summer dresses that she liked so much. Rosa had given up trying to break her of the habit. Maybe Signora Falchi would be more successful once Iole was back in Sicily.

They hugged each other, and Rosa was surprised but most of all glad to see how happy Iole looked. She herself had thought Augusto Dallamano a cold, surly man when she'd met him, but Iole seemed to feel at ease in his company.

"Are you okay?" Rosa asked, wrinkling her brow.

Iole nodded. "How's Alessandro?"

"Getting on the nurses' nerves." She leaned forward, with a conspiratorial air. "He's the worst patient in the world. But don't tell him I said that."

"On TV they're the ones who always end up marrying the head nurse."

"The head nurse in that hospital is at least sixty. And they're discharging him tomorrow." Rosa sighed. "Well, strictly speaking he's discharging himself. I guess that once he's gone, they'll all get drunk and have a fireworks display to celebrate."

Iole twirled around in a circle. "I could stay here forever and ever," she cried enthusiastically.

"Signora Falchi would never go along with that. She may have survived the Hundinga, but this place would drive her to quit."

Iole beamed. "It's even nicer inside."

She took Rosa's hand and led her up the steps to the front door.

Late that afternoon, they were sitting with Augusto Dallamano in the villa's conservatory, a rickety glazed annex built onto the back of the house. Outside, the garden came right up to the windows. Two armchairs and a sofa stood among towers of books. Rosa and Dallamano sat opposite each other, leaving the couch to Iole. She had an albino cat on her lap, snow white with red eyes. It was purring with pleasure as she stroked it.

Dallamano had come in only half an hour before. He was obviously doing research of some kind over in the Quinta da Regaleira. Rosa had known that he had started studying sculpture after finding the statues, a discovery that he and Iole's father had made together six and a half years ago. Enough time for him to acquire a certain amount of knowledge. But she was surprised to find him devoting himself so enthusiastically to the mysteries of the Quinta. Dallamano was an academic—an engineer, if she remembered correctly—so he was no stranger to books. For Rosa, who had only just made it through the end of high school, it made more of an impression than she wanted to admit.

He still wore his dark hair shoulder length, and it was still untidy, but he no longer hid behind that bushy beard. Instead, his chin and cheeks were shaded with stubble. Last time she had met him, in the Initiation Well, he had been wearing a pin-striped suit; today he wore khaki cargo pants with a great many pockets, and a brown sweater. Both were covered with dust, and he had brushed off only the worst of it when he'd arrived.

He was leaning back in his armchair, chain-smoking. The ashtray stood on an unsteady pile of books beside the armrest. His dark, intent gaze was turned on Rosa through the clouds of cigarette smoke.

"Iole says she likes living with you," he said, breaking the silence.

Rosa glanced doubtfully at Iole. It was only a few days ago that Val had been holding a pistol to her head.

Iole looked up from the white cat, gave Rosa a silent smile, and devoted herself to the animal again.

"I do my best," said Rosa.

"She told me she has a private tutor. That's good. Iole has a lot to catch up on."

"She was extremely anxious to see you again, Signore Dallamano. You two must be very fond of each other."

He held the cigarette motionless in his hand, and stared into the smoke curling up from the glowing tip. "My brother didn't always leave himself as much time for his daughter as she needed. Someone had to look after her."

Rosa remembered something that Iole had told her. "You taught her how to shoot. How old was she at the time—eight? Maybe nine?"

"I was a different man back then." His mood of regret surprised her. "There are many things I wouldn't do the same way now, and that's only one of them."

Iole cast Rosa a glance that wasn't hard to interpret. It was her ability to handle a gun that had saved both their lives at the Gibellina monument.

"Why are you here?" he asked Rosa. "Iole flew to Portugal on her own. She could have found her way back without you as well."

"Can't you guess why I'm here?"

"More questions? About the statues in the Strait of Messina?" He inhaled smoke, and let it drift out through his lips with relish. "I've already told you and your Carnevare friend all I know."

"The statues are gone," she said. "Someone got to them before us."

He took a deep breath, looking as if he wasn't accustomed to doing so without added nicotine and tar. "Someone?"

"Evangelos Thanassis."

"The shipowner?"

"The statues were taken on board one of his ships. The *Stabat Mater*. Does that name mean anything to you?"

"It's a musical composition."

Rosa nodded. "A medieval poem set to music. The first line runs, '*Stabat mater dolorosa.*' The mother stood in sorrow."

"A few years ago I'd have been impressed," he said. "But these days knowledge has nothing to do with education, only with typing the right questions on a keyboard."

Iole pricked up her ears. "That's what Signora Falchi always says."

"The woman obviously knows what she's talking about."

"The *Stabat Mater* is the flagship of Thanassis's fleet of cruise ships," Rosa went on, undeterred. "At least, she was before he withdrew from public life. Odd name for a pleasure ship, wouldn't you say?"

"To the best of my knowledge, Thanassis is an odd character."

"Did the Dallamanos ever have anything to do with him? I mean, your companies built harbors and so on."

He shook his head. "Thanassis has enough firms of his own to do that for him."

"What about TABULA? Does that mean anything to you?"

"Hermes Trismegistos," he said, without even thinking about it.

Rosa nodded. "The emerald tablet."

"*Tabula Smaragdina Hermetis*. What do the Hermetics have to do with a Greek shipowner?" He abruptly sat up and ground out his cigarette in the ashtray. "So that's why you're here? To ask me about that?"

"You knew so much before about the Quinta, and that crazy Freemason with his stone alphabet. Isn't that what you said the Quinta itself was?"

"A stone alphabet of alchemy."

The white cat yawned luxuriously, and Iole let it infect her with a yawn too. But Rosa wasn't taken in by her show of indifference to the conversation. She knew Iole too well by now for that. The girl had her ears pricked up the whole time, and she usually drew the right conclusions from what she heard, remarkably quickly.

"You seem to be very busy with all these." Rosa indicated the mountains of books in the conservatory.

"Most of them belong to my landlady. There's much more material on the upper floors. She's sublet the first floor here to me."

Rosa's suspicions were stirred. "Is she one of these Hermetics?"

"She's all kinds of things. She doesn't talk about herself much. But you're not here on her account, are you? What exactly do you want to know?"

Rosa caught herself looking through the glazed roof of the conservatory up at the second floor. "There's a group of people . . . an organization . . . They call themselves TABULA, and they probably take the name from the emerald tablet of this Hermes Trismegistos."

"There are many such groups. Most of them consist of muddle-headed persons, esoterics and so forth, and these days they're joined by all the crazy Dan Brown fans—would-be Freemasons making the Templars their hobby. Genuine alchemists are natural loners who hide themselves away in their laboratories. They were like that five hundred years ago, and it's the same now."

"They also hide themselves away behind books?" she asked, glancing at the room.

He lit another cigarette. "Of course."

"I don't think that TABULA really has anything to do with alchemy. The tablet is only some kind of symbol to them. These people are scientists. And they must have some rather prosperous patrons."

"Evangelos Thanassis?"

"Could be. It's only a suspicion so far, that's all."

"But there's something you're not telling me."

Somewhere in the house a telephone rang loudly. The cat jumped off Iole's lap in alarm, leaped up onto a tottering tower of books, and hopped off it again just before the pile collapsed in a cloud of dust.

Dallamano stood up with the cigarette in the corner of his mouth, and bent over the chaos. The next moment he picked up the cat by the nape of its neck and carried it out of the conservatory and into the house. A little later they heard his voice on the phone, indistinctly.

Rosa turned to Iole. "How much does he know?" she whispered.

"About the dynasties? I haven't told him anything."

"You sure?"

"Rosa!"

"Sorry. It's just that—"

Dallamano came back and stopped beside his armchair. "Scientists, then. Top-ranking people, I guess. At least they ought to be, if someone's investing large sums of money in them. In them *and* in secrecy."

"Sounds logical."

"Nobel Prize winners?"

"How would I know?"

"If you have any idea what kind of research this organization is doing, then you'd better start by looking at the list of winners of the Nobel Prize for the last few decades. And it would also be a good idea to find out who was expected to win but didn't. After that you could check who of those has carried out investigations into your subject. It's possible that you might come upon a couple of people who could be involved with TABULA. Depending how much you really know, you might even find a name or two that you've heard before."

"I'll try that," she said. "Thanks."

Dallamano turned to Iole. "The taxi driver called. He's waiting down on the road. If you two want to catch your flight, you'd better leave now."

"If I do find out anything," said Rosa as she got to her feet, "would you mind if we talked about it some more?"

"Of course I'd mind," he snapped at her, then added in milder tones, "but that's not going to stop you, is it? One of these days you'll be at my door again to pester me. Just so long as that young Carnevare doesn't turn up here."

She smiled. "I'll make sure of that."

Outside, in the spacious entrance hall of the villa, Rosa's eyes fell on a figure at the top of the stairs to the second floor.

"*Olá*," she called.

"*Olá*," the woman replied. She was delicately built, and at the most in her midtwenties. Her jeans and close-fitting blouse were black, like the long hair that fell smoothly over her shoulders. Rosa couldn't see much more, but she noticed her strong, dark eyebrows.

The woman stood there at the top of the stairs, with one slender hand on the banister, and Rosa wondered whether she had overheard the conversation in the conservatory.

"Your landlady?" asked Rosa, turning to Dallamano as he picked up Iole's bag to take it out to the taxi.

He nodded, and walked out with his niece. Rosa glanced up at the landing once again. The woman was gone. A door closed up above in the house.

"Coming?" called Iole from outside.

Rosa pulled herself together, hurried down the steps, and followed the two Dallamanos along the enchanted path to the road.

THE ISLAND AND THE
MOON

A GOAT LOOKING FOR tufts of grass among the volcanic rocks
bleated as, a few hundred feet farther down, the waves broke
in cascades of spray on the shores of Isola Luna.

Rosa and Alessandro were on their way uphill along a
rocky slope. They had spent all morning climbing over porous
stones, bizarrely shaped ridges, and lava glaciers frozen solid.
Rosa had grazed her ankles and the palms of her hands, had
lost no opportunity to curse volubly, but it had been a long
time since she'd felt so content and happy.

Now the rim of the crater was directly above them. So close
to their destination, she was almost sorry that the climb was
nearly over. She stopped and looked back at the rooftops of
the higgledy-piggledy house far below, down the mountain.
Aside from the former bunker by the shore, the villa was the
only building on the Carnevares' private island.

The helicopter had brought Rosa and Alessandro there the
evening before, and had then flown back to the Sicilian coast,
thirty miles to the south. Apart from the goats who had taken
up residence after Alessandro demolished Cesare's enclosure
for big cats, they were alone on the island.

Rosa stood with her back to the mountain, enjoying the
sensation of the wind on her face as it came up from the sea.
She briefly closed her eyes, thought of nothing at all, simply

sensed the gentle caress of the breeze on her skin. Then she felt that Alessandro was close, and the next moment his lips were on hers.

"It can stay like this," she said.

"What can?"

"Life. Everything. You and me."

"Not before we've seen the crater," he replied, forcing a smile. It was stupid of him to come on this climbing expedition with his injuries only half healed. But he claimed that he had never been up to the peak and this was the best day for it. He didn't tell her why and she suspected that any other day would also have been the best day for it. Just as long as the two of them were together and no one disturbed them.

"You really never looked into it?"

"Never."

"Not even from the chopper?"

He shook his head.

She looked at the last part of the climb up the mountain. "We still have . . . what, about three hundred feet to go? So this is our last chance to think about what we expect to see."

"A crater?"

"You can be so boring."

He returned her grin. "A base for extraterrestrials."

"The way down to the earth's core."

"A launchpad for nuclear warheads."

"The ruins of Arcadia."

"TABULA's secret control center."

She bowed her head. "Would that be good or bad?"

"How would I know? Let's not talk about TABULA today."

"You started it."

"Only in the heat of the moment."

They set off again. On the way, she said, "I went back to the palazzo yesterday. I've decided to leave the whole place exactly as it is for now. Everything is covered with ash. Even the lemons are gray."

"The rain will wash it off again soon."

"Do you know what I wish I'd done?"

"What?"

"Make a snow angel. In ashes."

"Good idea."

"No, seriously. I almost did it. I've realized that I can do or not do whatever I like. And if I want to lie down in the ashes with my clothes on and leave a snow angel shape there, how can anyone object?"

"Snow angels are only romantic if there are two people making them."

"Then come with me next time."

"I will. I've always wanted to roll about in a bed of ashes with you."

She took his hand, and together they went the last few feet to the rim of the crater. It had been Rosa's idea to come to the island this morning, after they'd heard the radio news reporting the murder of an attorney in Taormina. She badly needed fresh air, and—at least for a while—the feeling of being alone in the world with Alessandro.

"Okay," she said, as they stopped and looked ahead, over the rim of the crater. "Wow! And it's official."

In front of them, a barren rock basin opened up, at least nine hundred feet in diameter and half that depth. Light and dark veins of stone meandered over its sides, meeting at the center in a pattern of countless shades of gray. They saw no hidden extraterrestrial base, no landing strip for flying saucers, only volcanic rock, hostile to all life, where thousands of years ago the lava had solidified into clumps and hillocks. There was a flickering above the bottom of the basin, like the heat of an imminent eruption, but it was only a mirage.

"Look—there's more here than just the end of the world," said Rosa softly, pointing to a solitary dandelion growing from a crevice.

"Or the beginning." He smiled. "No one's been up here for ages. Maybe no one ever. So let's lay official claim to the place as its discoverers."

"We can found a colony. And a mission station for the native population of beetles and spiders."

"And ours are the first footprints here, like on the moon."

"There's only one problem," she said. "The island has belonged to you Carnevares for centuries. Don't tell me there's any kind of remote spot that your family wouldn't have exploited in its business deals."

"Oh," he said, frowning. "You really think so?"

A smile stole over her features. "No, the island was your mother's favorite place. She wouldn't have let that happen."

"She wouldn't have let Cesare murder her, either, given any choice."

She sighed softly. "No." A gust of wind blew through her

hair from behind, sending it fluttering around her face. She had to tame it with her hands so that she could lean over and kiss him.

When she opened her eyes, she saw that he was staring at her.

"Not fair," she complained. "People aren't supposed to look when they're kissing."

"Says who?" His smile was as infectious as ever, and she was glad that he had forgotten his grief again.

"Kissing calls for concentration if you want to do it properly."

"We don't have transformations anymore when we kiss. Did you notice?"

She reacted with pretend surprise. "And I was just wondering what was different from usual."

His grin widened, the dimples were deeper. "Want to go down there?" He pointed into the crater.

Rosa shook her head. "No, I'm sunburned already."

"That'll go away again after the next transformation."

She moved away from him and climbed up a small rise with a flattened surface on top. "Come up here."

In spite of his injuries, he followed her nimbly. They sat down on the rock, held hands, and looked out over the slope of the volcano onto the wide expanse of the Mediterranean.

"It's out there somewhere," she said thoughtfully.

"The *Stabat Mater*?"

"The answer. The ship is only a part of it."

"Probably."

"And Arcadia once lay somewhere there."

They fell silent as their eyes lingered on the horizon, looking for something that might have existed thousands of years ago. They themselves were only an echo of it, the shadow cast by Arcadia into the present.

"We ought to try it again sometime," he said after a while.

"Kissing without turning into monsters?"

"I like you even as a monster."

"But at the end of love stories like that, the monster always falls off the Empire State Building."

"Except that we're both monsters. Or all the others are, depending how you look at it."

This time the kiss lasted much longer. Rosa peeked, but Alessandro's eyes were shut tight. With a warm feeling inside, she closed her own eyelids, searched for the chill of the snake inside herself, and found nothing but a faint breath of icy air that she could easily tamp down. Was it only a question of practice? Of readiness? Of being an adult?

The sun was high in the clear sky, yet the moon was visible, pale in the radiant blue.

"You can only see it from here at this time of the year," he claimed.

She didn't believe a word of it. "Imagine that!"

He hesitated, and then said, suddenly very serious, "I'd like to give you all this, if you'd like to have it."

She stared at him, openmouthed. "The sun? The moon?"

"The island. Well, the moon as well if I could get my hands on it."

"Just like that?"

"You said you liked the villa. My mother loved it, and you once said that you could see why."

"I do like being here. But what about you? I don't want to have an island where you never come to visit me."

"I always liked Isola Luna, and that won't change."

"The weird seventies look of the villa?"

"Throw out what you don't like."

"I like it all. Especially the record collection."

"You're crazy."

"I'm in love."

The sun sank lower, and the moon moved on. The flickering haze in the crater faded.

"It will be dark soon," said Alessandro.

"Not up here."

He stroked her hair and kissed her.

"Not with you," she whispered.

Never with you.

Later, when they were halfway down the mountain, Alessandro's cell phone rang. He answered it, with a guilty expression. Rosa watched him as he listened.

After only a few minutes, he thanked the caller and ended the conversation.

"That was the hospital."

The moon was hovering above the volcano, and the sun had disappeared behind the rocks. Shadows lay on the slope.

"Fundling."